MORDRED'S REVENGE

—Silber banked away from the broaching leviathan, diving desperately out of its path. Kendy looked up just as a pale blue ghost of radiance flickered out from a nacelle atop the Han dreadnought. Silber disappeared like so much dust in a gale. The stern of the airship pulled free of the ocean in a rush of foam and torn netting and Kendy's skiff was drawn into its place. White water rushed over the ruined decks and Kendy felt his grip on the useless tiller being torn away. . . .

Three years after the bloody Peruvian Recurrence the legions of the Han are marching against humanity once again. In their preserving crypts within the earth and hidden in the depths of space the savage Prl'lu await the command to awaken and subjugate mankind once and for always. Marshal Anthony Rogers sees this threat and stands against it—but does mankind stand with him?

THE AMERICAN SCIENCE FICTION
ADVENTURE TRADITION IS REBORN!

ARMAGEDDON 2419 A.D. by Philip Francis Nowlan. . . *the birthplace of the American tradition of Science Fiction Adventure, that inspired the world-famous* Buck Rogers. *A Science Fiction classic!*

MORDRED by John Eric Holmes, from the outline by Larry Niven & Jerry Pournelle. . . *the book that picks up where ARMAGEDDON 2419 A.D. leaves off. Marshal Anthony Rogers faces the twin threats of the resurgent Han and the resurrected Prl'lu, demon warriors from beyond time!*

And now—the saga of humanity's struggles in a universe set against them continues with—

WARRIOR'S BLOOD

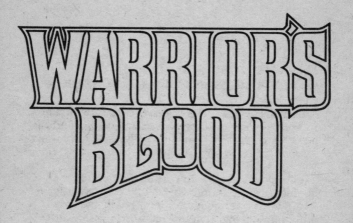

WARRIOR'S BLOOD

Richard S. McEnroe

SF
ace books
A Division of Charter Communications Inc.
A GROSSET & DUNLAP COMPANY
51 Madison Avenue
New York, New York 10010

WARRIOR'S BLOOD is the sequel to ARMAGED-
DON 2419 A.D.
WARRIOR'S BLOOD is written by Richard S. McEnroe
from an outline by Larry Niven and Jerry Pournelle,
based on characters created by Philip Francis Nowlan.
Copyright © 1981 by Charter Communications, Inc.

An ACE Book

First Ace printing: January 1981

Published simultaneously in Canada

2 4 6 8 0 9 7 5 3 1
Manufactured in the United States of America

*To my parents—
who had the good
sense to demand I
get a real job, and
the understanding not
to throw me out and
make it necessary.*

CHAPTER ONE

Bright sunlight cast fleeting silvery highlights off the transparent plastic of the kite framed against the sky.

Jaz Kendy bent to check the thick, braided line for chafe where it passed through the hawsepipe. The wooden ten-meter fishing skiff he captained moved easily through the water at one end of a long line of bobbing seine-floats, tiller lashed, her boomless standing lugsail drawing well in the five-knot breeze. Away to port the small, crewless "draftie", little more than a buoyant platform for a fixed squaresail and angled rudder skeg, plugged steadily along downwind, patiently dragging its end of the net along behind it.

Kendy straightened again, a tall, lean man with close-cropped, graying hair and pale blue eyes forever narrowed and searching the horizon, a seaman's habit picked up sailing those same waters aboard that same boat as deck-boy forty years ago, when a moment's inattention could give a Han marauder previous seconds to spot the skiff before she could find cover. The Han were no threat anymore, not since the government had suppressed their last desperate uprising three years ago, but the sea was still the sea, and Jaz Kendy kept a careful eye upon the waters.

1

He looked again to the sky, where Silber dipped and swerved in the kite, following the school of salmon in its run north along the Washington coast. The contrast might have intrigued someone less used to it: Silber hanging beneath his plastic foil wing, strapped into a harness of gravity-repellent inertron, flying five hundred meters above a wooden fishing boat of a design essentially unchanged in five centuries and more. Kendy never thought about it. It was the way things had always been done, as much a part of life in the Tallpines Gang as the forever-changing mood of the sea or the greed of the downcoast gangs they paid off in smoked fish for the kite riders' inertron belts and the few other supplies Tallpines needed but couldn't produce itself. Things like that didn't change, and Kendy approved of that; a man knew what to expect of his life. People changed, and caused change, even on a scale great enough to cause an entire fishing gang like Tallpines to have to move its port miles inland to flee a melting icecap; but left to themselves, sea and sky remained to the same, to be dealt with in the traditional ways.

Kendy bent to the line again, to take another turn around the forward bollard. He pulled more with his legs and his weight than with his back, the way a man who spent most of his life working in that position quickly learned to do. Kendy had his share of rope-burns and stiff joints, any man who did hard honest work did, but it was a small point of pride with him that his back was still good, and that he could haul fish right along with men twenty years his junior. He set the new bight snug around the bollard and worked the rag chafing collar down the line a bit, so that it still protected the hawser from rubbing against the metal rim of the hawsepipe. They were sailing slowly over the ruins now, over where old Seattle had been in the days before Hammerfall. The wreckage made some of the best fishing grounds on the coast; they were a natural breeding and feeding area; but they were also festooned with miles of netting years old, lost by idiots who didn't watch their depth. A single extra turn around a twelve-inch bollard wasn't going to make any difference, but the effort made Kendy feel better. He tied off the seine-lead again and returned to the cockpit of the skiff. He climbed below and moved to the small stove, picking up the battered pot to pour himself a fresh cup—

—and the skiff heeled violently to starboard, throwing him up against the bulkhead. He had the good sense and reflexes to hurl the pot away from him; scalding coffee washed over the canted deck and over his boots.

The skiff lurched again, her bow angling up toward the sky. Equipment and utensils rained down around Kendy; a flailing piece of tackle caught him a stunning blow with one block as it flew past. Through it all there was a horrible sound of wrenching wood. . . .

Silber flicked the kite into a weak gust and picked up another ten meters' height above the sea. The inertron harness he wore was just barely insufficient to cancel out his weight; wearing it he could fly as long as there was the least wind to head into for lift, a manmade albatross coursing above the ocean.

Silber was a good thirty years younger than Jaz Kendy, and a good ten kilos lighter. That was why Kendy had first taken him on, he knew; they leased their inertron by the negative-kilo, and a ten-kilo saving was a ten-kilo saving. But he had proved himself since then; he knew that Kendy considered him a good fisherman and intended to put him up as Boat Captain when he could no longer go to sea himself.

Silber canted the kite over to one side, dropping slowly towards the sea, the wind whipping at his thin blond hair. God's own distance below, the skiff looked like a child's toy against the clean blue water, its hull a single flat scrap of board, the cabin trunk a shoebox, the loose-footed sail an old handkerchief. Her topsides were unpainted and scarred from years of service, her canvas sunbleached and stained. To Silber she was the most beautiful thing in the world. The first thing he would do when he took her over, he decided, would be to name her. That was something the pragmatic Kendy had never done; to him, the boat was always just "the boat", a tool and nothing more. *Felicity,* Silber would call her, yes, he liked that. . . .

Silber banked off and levelled, swinging over the broad expanse of net towards the little draftie sailing dumbly along its unpiloted course and towing its end of the seine faithfully astern. He was too far up to see the small turnings of the mainsheet-linked tiller as it compensated for the changes of wind-pressure on its small sail, but he could see that it was holding its course steadily as the more nimble skiff curved around towards it, drawing the wide net closed around the trapped salmon—

Silber's grip tightened on the steering bar of the kite. A great dim shape had suddenly appeared beneath the sea, longer and broader even than the silvery mass of the school within the net. The surface began to froth and boil—

Kendy clawed his way above-decks, in time to see the bar-taut seine-lead tear the twelve-inch bollard away from its base. It skidded across the deck and fetched up immovably against the hawsepipe.

Then the skiff was rushing forward as the great gleaming cylinder rose up out of the sea before her. The line

4

parted, and her bow dropped back into the sea, water geysering from a dozen sprung seams. The skiff continued to hurtle forward, caught up in the rush of water flooding into the space now vacated by metal and being driven down by the force of the twin *reps*— repellor beams—lifting the craft. The tiller was loose and unresponsive in Kendy's hands. With a shock that registered even above his fear he recognized the airship: Han.

Silber banked away from the broaching leviathan, diving desperately out of its path. Kendy looked up just as a pale blue ghost of radiance flickered out from a nacelle atop the Han dreadnought. Silber disappeared like so much dust in a gale. The stern of the airship pulled free of the ocean in a rush of foam and torn netting and Kendy's skiff was drawn into its place. White water rushed over the ruined decks and Kendy felt his grip on the useless tiller being torn away. . . .

Rogers decided not to hit him.

"I don't think you understood me," he said to the student seated behind the desk. "I would like to see Doctor Harris." He thought he might make it plainer. "Anthony Rogers would like to see Doctor Ruth Harris. *Marshal* Anthony Rogers would like to see Doctor Ruth Harris, Director of Theoretical Research at Niagra University. That's here, right here in this very building, right through that door that you won't unlock. Now, please let me in."

The student, who wore the granite-gray tunic and high boots of the Altoona Gang, was an engineering major, manning the reception desk only because all students were required to donate time to the administration of the University. It was the sort of economical gesture that helped make the cost of supporting the University more palatable to the government and the Gangs. That

5

didn't change the fact that this particular student was probably much better suited to dealing with the eccentricities of a suspension bridge caught up in terminal wind-induced oscillations than he was to the temper of an unannounced visitor with no appointment. The first was a sensible problem, the latter, much less so.

"Are you quite finished?" he asked Rogers, "Or would you care to recount your ancestry while you're at it?"

A small vein seemed leaped into prominence on Rogers' left temple. He took a long, slow breath, as though tensing himself for some massive exertion. Muscle and tendons moved visibly as he did so, as though his five-foot-eleven frame carried no layer of fat to sheathe their play. Had he not projected such an impression of barely-restrained energy, the student might almost have characterized him as 'gaunt'.

"I am tempted," Rogers said carefully, "to start on yours, my young friend. Now, will you let me in?"

"Dcotor Harris left specific instructions that she was not to be disturbed—"

"Oh, the hell with this," Rogers muttered. He bent forward suddenly and the student skidded backwards in alarm. He made no move to get up. He was not about to challenge an angry Marshal of the armed forces.

Rogers could now see the button fastened to the bottom of the desk in one corner of the legwell. He pushed it. The lock on the office door buzzed and clicked open.

Doctor Ruth Harris looked around from her ultrophone with a flash of anger. "I thought I said I wasn't to be—oh."

"Yeah, oh." Rogers glanced at the phone's screen. Doctor Heric Wolsky, the man who made the study of biological impossibilities such as Anthony Rogers his life's work, looked back out at him, a worried expression on his round, bearded face. "Don't hang up. He's part of this."

"Part of what?" Ruth Harris was a trim, forty-three year old woman with just enough gray in her auburn hair and mature authority in her bearing to qualify her image for her professional status. Three years ago she had been forty years Rogers' junior, as time and old age had returned from their five-century hiatus to finally claim him. It had been a sheer accident that his subsequent 'fatal' heart seizure had caught up with Rogers in the same abandoned mine shaft that housed the enigmatic alien technology that had earlier preserved him for five hundred years before. That same technology, guarded by a stasis field, had still functioned after forty years' exposure to the elements, not just well enough to keep him alive but to return to him the youth and vigor that those intervening forty years had so diligently stolen.

Rogers' rejuvenation had been as much a gift to Ruth Harris as it had been to Rogers. It had given him back his lost youth; it had given her a marvelously difficult scientific challenge—and it had placed within her grasp a childhood idol and adolescent fantasy come true.

"Part of this," Rogers said. He reached into the windflap of his short-sleeved summer tunic and pulled out a phone-stat, which he slapped down on her desk. "Instructions—your instructions, Doctor—to report to the University Clinic for full diagnostics and convalescence. Just what the hell are you playing at, Ruth?"

"I'm *playing* at doing my job, Marshal, as one of the two people in this government with any detailed knowledge of your medical status. Both Doctor Wolsky and I thought those instructions were necessary."

"All right, fine," Rogers said. He started to pace the floor in front of her desk, then wheeled back to face her. "But copies? To my aide, to Dupre and Watson? Why not just broadcast it on an open channel? Dammit, Ruth, I'm trying to put together a new government here. It's hard enough when every boss between two oceans is trying to grab everything he can out of the mess Mordred's handed us; I can't afford to have rumors about my health going around."

"And the country can't afford to have you suffer a breakdown, Tony," Ruth said, quietly, "or cause a scandal."

That stopped him—briefly. Then he resumed his nervous pacing. It was as though movement had become his normal state, and the brief pauses he forced himself to make to listen or speak now consitiued actual effort. Irritably, he rubbed a hand across the back of his neck, messing the thick brown hair—cut a week ago and already looking as though it needed a trim. "What are you talking about?"

Ruth Harris looked at him. He stared back through eyes deeply shadowed by overwork, his lips pressed into a tight, nervous line. In any other man she would immediately have recommended a long vacation and reduced workload. For Anthony Rogers that would have been useless.

"Wol's presented me with a report on your rejuvenation, Tony."

"And?"

"It's hurting you."

"So was being old. Frankly, I prefer the current arrangement. And why did it take you three years to figure this out, anyway?"

Wolsky spoke up from thephone screen. He was willing to let Ruth Harris deal with Rogers' indignation; she

8

was by far better suited for it. But his expertise in his field was being challenged now.

"Because the only samples I had to compare young Rogers with came from an eighty-year-old Rogers. For a long time, it didn't occur to me that it would be unnatural for a man of thirty to be more vigorous than a man of eighty." He scowled out at Rogers. "For some reason, I cannot feel too guilty about that. And there were other questions to demand my attention, such as why the rejuvenation machinery restored your youth and then on an identical setting turned General Gordon into a two hundred pound carcinoma. But the main reason that we—that I—overlooked your condition was that it simply wasn't severe enough to be noticeable until recently. A young, active body can take considerable abuse before it demands attention. In fact, if young Holcomb hadn't come to us, we might still not be aware of it."

"Will Holcomb came to you? What did he tell you?"

"What did you tell the boss of the Wyoming delegation?"

"What he deserved to be told. The idiot proposed a cut in defense appropriation due to the alleviation—his word—of the Han crisis—"

"Still, Marshal," Wolsky said, "Don't you think that there are most likely better ways to persuade him to your position than by suggesting that he, um, take up pederasty with a saguaro cactus? And before the entire Council, at that?"

"Well, I suppose . . . but what bearing does that have on this?" Rogers tapped the stat.

"Merely that it was the latest incident in a record of inexplicable conduct on your part, Marshal. Over the past several months you seem to have become increasingly stressed, impatient and irritable. It was not normal for you; you have always preferred to be active, everyone knows that and appreciates it, Marshal; you might even have bordered on being rash, on occasion—but you have never been manic, never rash to the point of irrationality."

"And you think my—current behavior—as you see it, is due to my rejuvenation?"

"That's my favorite theory."

"You've got to understand, we aren't dealing with a very smart machine, here," Ruth said. "While the device is far beyond anything we've ever seen, to judge by some of the systems we're still finding in the Mount Erebus complex it was a very basic unit by Prl'lu standards and consequently rather 'stupid'. It was designed to heal Prl'lu, nothing else. When Ducall laid you out on the system's couch, that's what it tried to do."

"So my problem is that the machine tried to turn me into a Prl'lu warrior."

"Exactly. Your metabolism is on a permanent cycle of emergency overdrive, more or less. It's trying to function at Prl'lu levels and it can't. That's why you're so greatly agitated, for the most part. Your body is running full out and you're not taking advantage of it. It's also flooding your brain tissues with more oxygen and glucose from broken down body fats than it can use."

"What will this do to me?"

"It certainly won't do you any good," said Wolsky. Even assuming you could eat enough to offset the rate at which you burn energy, it still wouldn't change the fact that you body is producing toxins faster than you can easily dispose of them. Your tissues could soon start to drown in their own garbage. Of course, if that happened, long before that becomes fatal in and of itself, you could expect some significant brain damage. . . ."

"I think I get the picture," Rogers said, dismayed.

"Now for the good news: what's the cure?"

Wolsky was silent. He looked away from his screen.

"We don't have one," Ruth said.

Pause. Silence. Then: "Oh. . . ."

"This doesn't mean we can't *treat* it," Ruth added hastily. "Doctor Wolsky and I have come up with a combination of sedatives that should slow you down, figuratively speaking, as much as the Prl'lu medical system speeded you up. But it's not a permanent cure; you'll have to be extremely careful about maintaining your dosages. And we have no idea how long the treatment will be effective—you could develop a tolerance for the drugs, the Prl'lu treatment could begin to wear off, there may be other effects that we haven't noticed because we didn't know what to look for. . . ."

"Wonderful," Rogers said. "I can either die of old age at twenty-eight or I can go along with your treatments and face life as a happy, well-adjusted hophead. Well, you can forget the pills." He looked from Harris to the screen. "How long will you need me for these tests?"

"The tests I would like to run will take about three days," Wolsky said, "but I should like to keep you convalescent for at least a week for observation—"

"That's impossible," Rogers said. "I can spare you three days; we can cover for my absence that long, but given a week without someone holding the Council together and we'll have to invite the Han back just to get things organized again."

"All right," Ruth said, "then can we send an observer along to keep an eye on you?"

"I'll settle for that. Who?"

"Heric."

"Oh. Nothing personal, Wol," Rogers said to the screen, "but I would have preferred the good doctor here."

"I would rather go with you, myself," Ruth said, "But I've got other responsibilities too, down at Mount Erebus. As you said, if someone isn't there to hold things together. . ."

"No, you're right, I know, Ruth; you belong down there," Rogers said. But he wasn't happy about it.

"It's the biggest Prl'lu installation we've found, Tony—"

"It's the only Prl'lu installation we've found," Rogers corrected her. "It's all right, Ruth."

"—if we're going to find a cure for your condition anywhere, it will be down there—"

"All right, Ruth. Dammit, will you please stop being sensible about this long enough for me to feel good about being so understanding?" Rogers chuckled, but it didn't last. "You're assuming, of course, that there's a cure to be found."

"I'm assuming nothing. There *is*."

"That's not a very scientific perspective."

"Well in this case, Marshal Rogers, sir, you can just put your scientific perspective where the cactus goes."

"I'd rather not," Rogers said, "But I hope to God you're right."

Three years earlier, and a world away:

Earthlight flooded the chamber, faithfully reproduced from the surface monitors a kilometer above.

The figure that stood in the center of the great spherical room, looking out at the blue-white planet suspended in the holographic field that surrounded him, might almost have been taken for human, at a distance. It was only as an observer drew nearer that the differences began to become obvious—and there was no degree of physical proximity that could reveal to the eye the most significant differences of all.

12

Hun't'pir was of the Prl'lu, the Warrior Blood. In human terms, he stood well over two meters tall, better than seven feet, yet he only weighed perhaps one hundred and seventy pounds, less than eighty kilos, the weight of a man a good foot shorter than him. That lighter weight was used more efficiently, as well; Prl'lu muscle tissue was much more coarsely grained than human muscle, the striations and individual fibers fewer but thicker. A Prl'lu might lack the dexterity to paint a sunset—but he could shatter brick with the ease of a karate master. Looking closer, the human observer would further note that each individual muscle cell was more densely packed with mitochondriac elements that its human equivalent: Prl'lu muscle used more energy faster than human. It was a minor advantage for mankind; no human ever born could have stayed with a Prl'lu long enough to tire one out.

Hun't'pir's arms and legs were long in comparison with a human's; the superior leverage this afforded was enhanced by thick, heavy joints able to take the induced strains. A crest of straight black hair arose from the peak of the bony ridge that bisected his face and protected his 'nasal' cavities. In certain lights this ridge could give his face a hawklike, patrician aspect, particularly in association with the wide, lipless mouth that concealed the solid, roughly-serrated ridges of bone that supplanted frailer teeth. In sum, Hun't'pir looked anything but human—and yet, when his most basic difference was considered, simple cosmetic detail faded into irrelevance.

Hun't'pir was Prl'lu, part of the Warrior Blood—but the Warrior Blood was all of Hun't'pir. It was the core of his very existence to fight, and to obey, as much as it was for the Prl'arek to rule or the Prl'an to serve. It was the thing he lived for, that he had been trained for since

13

birth, since *before,* it was the thing engraved in his very genes; it was what he was. It was why Hun't'pir would consent to being ferried across hundreds of light years and placed within a field of stasis buried within an airless, lifeless rock, sleeping sentinel of a world of un-bonded outcasts.

It was why he would feel such distress at the failure of his task.

A door—a sudden rectangle of light piercing the space-black that surrounded him—opened behind Hun't'pir. He heard it, of course; not even a forced sleep of uncounted centuries would dull those senses. He turned.

It was Kors'in-tu, his aide. There was little difference one not familiar with the Prl'lu might find between them; Kors'in-tu's head-crest lacked the shining, oiled highlights that were the mark of age in Prl'lu; Hun't'pir might perhaps move with just slightly less fluid grace than Kors'in-tu. Neither wore any marks of rank or unit upon their plain black tunics. Prl'lu had no need of such devices to know who commanded and who fol-lowed.

"You have completed your studies?" Hun't'pir asked.

"I have, my commander."

"And?"

"The secondary polar base has been activated—and overrun." Kors'in-tu said that last with something that might have been dismayed surprise in a lesser race. Prl'lu were not accustomed to the thought of defeat.

"*Shak'si mir,*" Hun't'pir said quietly, and then: "Show me."

Kors'in-tu did not acknowledge the command. Both knew he had heard it, both knew he would comply. He strode out onto the narrow catwalk that stabbed into the center of the chamber and touched a control on the con-sole at its end.

14

The blue-white globe and its field of blackness disappeared, to be replaced by rolling storm clouds to all sides. Aircraft, of a design unfamiliar to Hun't'pir, suddenly cut through the clouds before him in ragged waves.

"These images were collated from those relayed from the secondary polar base's picket squadron, my commander."

Hun't'pir felt a twinge of annoyance at the sloppy formations the alien ships were holding. Suddenly the air around him was filled with flame and thunder, slashed through with pale lances of energy.

"Analysis shows the attacking force's armament to be a combination of low-grade explosives, primitive fission systems and nonspecific transfer beams, sir. These last seem to be identical in principle with our own diffusers, but working on a peculiarly low frequency. Our ships' armor was able to cope with little difficulty. Only light damage to one craft was reported at this stage of the engagement."

The image changed around them again, to show a ground engagement. The fire and fury of the air battle was visible in the far distance.

"This was transmitted by a light-armor detachment of the base's internal security detail. Apparently this was the second element of a fairly unsophisticated two-prong attack." Small figures, vaguely similar to Prl'lu in form, could be seen dropping away from long cables strung behind two bulky, obviously non-combat aircraft, and hastily fanning out in a defensive arc while the ships dug their way into the soil with their peculiar diffusion beams. The protective detachment was moving into position in long, low leaps; plainly their troops were equipped with counter-gravitic systems. Hun't'pir commented on their peculiar combination of equipment that nearly rivalled Prl'lu sophistication and pathetically primitive weaponry that largely wasted the advantages gained. As if to prove his point, the attacking troops, apparently just noticing the approaching Prl'lu armor, hastily grounded and opened fire with a combination of explosive projectiles and diffusers. That was the only salvo they got off, as the immediate Prl'lu counter-fire of missilery, *karnak* energy weapons and thermal gel devastated their perimeter. The monitor viewpoint swung briefly to show one of the Prl'lu armored personnel carriers rumbling forward, smoke pouring from one nearside drive unit but its forward progress unimpeded. Its *karnak* battery tracked back and forth methodically; fire and missiles continued to blaze forth.

"Again," Kors'in-tu said, standing like some martial silhouette against the fire and explosions, "our forces took only light damage."

"Whoever these creatures are, they can't fight for *mir*," Hun't'pir said. "Those infantry were simply thrown away. I find it hard to believe that this force actually managed to overrun one of our bases."

"It is what happened, sir."

"Show me the rest."

The view shifted back to the air battle. The enemy force had been decimated; only a handful of ships remained, including an unusually large one with an odd double-spherical configuration. The Prl'lu craft swept through on another pass; now only the large enemy ship remained airborne and capable of combat.

Suddenly a new element was added to the battle. The viewpoint monitor shuddered; as it did, a small streak flashed before it. The monitor tracked and magnified: the object proved to be a small sphere that maneuvered with alarming speed and agility.

"*Karnak* proved to be ineffective against these new units," Kos'in-tu explained, "and the initial theory was that they must be unmanned. A large number of them, perhaps several dozen, attacked our squadron simultaneously. They proved highly diffusion-resistant, which leads us to suspect that they are shielded in some fashion, and they maneuvered too well for effective countermissilery. We were able to deflect their first several assaults through use of repulsion beams, but the spheres finally managed to breach our defenses on the left flank." Obligingly, the viewpoint shifted to show a sleek black Prl'lu atmospheric ship curving away toward the ground far below, broken and burning. "After that, they were able to attack our surviving ships from too many directions at once to be driven off. Nevertheless, our ships pressed their attack against the remaining enemy aircraft aloft in that area, driving it down with repulsion beams." The viewpoint monitor twitched again, then spun skyward. "It was at this point that a unit of light enemy aircraft joined the battle." Around them sleek little ships slashed through the Prl'lu formation. Almost immediately, two burst into flame and tumbled from the sky. But to his astonishment, Hun't'pir saw one of the Prl'lu ships, washed over by several of the alien diffusers, begin to crumble and burn.

"What happened there?" he demanded. Even as he spoke, the small craft darted at the Prl'lu squadron again. More of them fell, but another Prl'lu ship exploded behing them.

"We are not sure," Kors'in-tu said, "Either these particular craft were armed with a proper diffusion beam, or perhaps the small spherical craft of the previous attack had managed to breach our ships' armor somehow; perhaps they were a delivery system for some sort of corrosive agent. In any event, our ships proved vulnerable to this attack, and in their turn, these enemy ships were in some way shielded against *Karnak*. We estimate that our forces inflicted some eighty to ninety per cent casualties on these new craft before they were overcome—"

"But they were overcome. Do not speak to me of casualties when they do not grant us victory. Is there more of this?"

"We have complete records of the campaign, sir. But they show substantially the same thing, up to the point where transmission facilities at the base proper were destroyed."

"Prepare them for my study. We are Prl'lu, the Warrior Blood, the Protectors, and we have been defeated. I will know why. I will learn what we face here—and when I have learned that, we shall destroy it."

CHAPTER TWO

The squalor of it all appalled him.

Mordred stalked moodily about his cubicle, glaring at its meager furnishings as though they were personally responsible for the poverty into which his people had sunk.

By non-Han standards, it was all sumptuous enough. The bed was wide and long and possessed of what could only be called a sensible firmness, that yielded to stubborn bone yet offered restful support to tired flesh. There was an abundance of chairs, couches and cushions sufficient for a dozen guests or more, and quiet, efficient machines to tend his wardrobe and provide fine, nourishing food and drink upon demand. A bank of screens allowed him access to and communication with any point in the city or its outlying satellite communities.

But Mordred was Han, in heart and breeding if not wholly in blood. He had been born too late to have seen the great Han cities in America—Bah-Flo, Nu-Yok, magnificent Lo-Tan itself—or even to know save by reputation of the even greater splendor of the original Han metropili of Asia. But even compared to the buried Andean refuge, now three years destroyed at the hands of the Americans—*at the hands of Rogers, genocide and rapist, thief of my true life!*—and Mordred's own ill-fated revival of the Prl'lu warrior-demons, this hiding place for yet another fragment of his fugitive race was a sorry come-down.

It was all so *noticeable*. The valet and cuisine systems were obviously machines set in the walls—sometimes he even thought he could hear them working. In a proper Han residence such units would have been all but invisible, concealed behind ornamental architecture, noticed only when they presented their finished products for their master's use. Beds and furniture would have been not merely shaped, padded frames but art, that added as much to the aesthetic of the room as they did to its function. And screens would not have lined the walls: screens would have *been* walls, to bring the outer world in to him, not just tiny boxes holding representations that reminded him of his confinement as surely as the door that would not open to his command.

But most galling of all was the way these hiding-Han were actually *proud* of their backwards little warren. The household mechanisms were not mounted so obviously out of incompetence but arrogance—to show off the fact that these cowering fugitives still had the sophistication to maintain such devices. That was the thing that most angered Mordred, not the fact of his imprisonment, not the fact of this hidden city's forty years' inactivity against its human oppressors, but the fact that they had accepted the humiliation of their breed, to the point where they actually gloried in their humbled status. That was, to Mordred, quite intolerable, and the fact that he could only press them so hard to change their ways did little to cheer him.

He had done what he could, with the small resources left him after the debacle of his first attack upon mankind: the single Prl'lu scoutship he had used to flee from the human spaceship *Wilma Deering* after his unsuccessful attempt at pirating it. He had not been so rash or trusting as to give over the ship directly into their hands; the ship with its hand-picked, three man crew loyal to him was still in hiding outside the city. As long as the ship remained under his control he was safe, for even with the secrets of *dis*-resistant armor and the karnak weapn that he had given them, the handful of conventional airships this city could put aloft were no match for even his small Prl'lu warcraft. But his safety would last only that long, and not one second longer, for the Han had no use for outbreeds, and failed ones at that. In the meantime they tolerated him for the power and implied threat of the ship he commanded. They would of course show their contempt of him in small and safe ways, such as confining him to his quarters and dealing with him through menials far below his station, but he was used to that. It was normal behavior for Han in a situation where dominance in a relationship had yet to be established. It was galling, of course, but Mordred had endured worse in his time, and he would take his recompense when they realized his value to them.

The door opened and a Han in the scarlet tunic of a soldier entered. Mordred registered every aspect of the insult automatically: the unannounced entry, with its implied superiority of the intruder—*"I control your movements/You lack the power to keep me out"*—and the sending of a soldier—*"You are not a friend/You must be dealt with through a threat of violence"*—but only a common soldier of no rank, and unarmed, at that—*"You present no significant threat to me."*

Mordred looked at the soldier, whose broad, flat face and lidded, vaguely Oriental eyes reflected his freedom from the human taint that marked Mordred's finer, thinner features and slat-gray eyes. He would have to reply to the insult, of course, everything in his very nature demanded it. There was nothing he could do to those who sent the soldier; his only options with them were either to surrender and submit himself to their rule or to order his ship to destroy the city; as an outsider he lacked the connections within their community to make any intermediate responses. But to this soldier, arrogant in his borrowed strength of delegated power, he could react.

Mordred said nothing. The soldier had made his entry; he had made his assertion of power and superiority. But it was wasted if Mordred did not acknowledge it, if he did not respond with the desired futile indignation. So Mordred stood silent, hands clasped behind his back, feet slightly spread, looking down on the soldier from his greater height, his silence and his stance his own declaration—"*You have issued your challenge/Show me why I should answer it.*"

The soldier stood silent in his turn, and Mordred felt a faint glow of triumph. The soldier had picked an indefensible response. Plainly, he had been sent to summon Mordred somewhere for some purpose. Any delay would be held against him. But Mordred had all the time in the world.

The soldier yielded, as Mordred had known he must. "The Scion of the Heaven Born orders your presence," he said. Mordred allowed himself a thin smile and the soldier flushed angrily. Mordred made no reply.

"It is an ill-bred guest who ignores the command of the Prince of a City," the soldier said sharply.

That woke anger in Mordred; it was in one form or another it was a gybe he had lived with all his life, a half-breed among a race of half-breeds who held their brand of bastardry superior to his. But he allowed no flicker of his rage to show—this fool was not worthy of noticing his emotion.

"But how much worse would seem a guest who conducted himself on a level above that of his hosts?" he asked politely. "Where courtesy is not offerred, should he presume to display it?"

The soldier actually tensed visibly, a gross breach of self-control and etiquette even among low Han. "Where courtesy is not merited it should not be sought," he said. In his anger then he did not pause, and force Mordred to take up the burden of continuing the exchange. "And what is there here that merits courtesy? Shall I be polite to a chair for being a chair, or to a bed for allowing itself to be slept in, or—"

"—Or to a member of the Household of the Man-Din San-Lan himself, Last Emperor of the Western Han, Prince of a City whose grandeur even in its destruction was beyond anything you have ever known, trash!" Mordred brought his hands out to his sides, closed into fists, and stepped towards the soldier, enhancing the sharp assertion of his tone with movement. "*That* merits your respect. Or if such splendor be beyond your conception, then consider your manners towards one with the power to restore to this ludicruous little pesthole to the glory it delights in reminding the world it has lost. Consider this, and then lecture me on manners, if you would."

The soldier hesitated, torn between his desire to retain face and his sudden fear of angering one his superiors might wish placated—he hesitated, and yielded.

"Most Worthy Sir, the Prince Ho-Tin, Scion of the Heaven-Born Himself, bids you wait upon him in his chambers."

Mordred noted that the soldier chose the most neutral form of address possible, aware that he could continue the exchange. But the reward was not worth the effort; he held the deference of a soldier from a city that refused to fight of little worth.

"Then we must by all means make haste to serve him," he said politely. "It would reflect ill upon us to waste his most valuable time."

They left the apartment and started down the corridor towards the bank of lifts. Mordred reflected on the victory his hosts had just won over him, in forcing him to spar for prestige with one of such lower status than himself. It told him nothing he didn't already know: that he was vulnerable to their machinations, up to a point, and that they were not as secure about that as they should have been, as Mordred would have been in their position. That cheered him. It showed that between himself and these hiding-Han he was the stronger. He would play his hand to the limit, for he had nothing to lose if he failed, while they would hesitate and persist in using half-measures in the hope of forestalling any resolution of the problem he presented them, for fear of what it might cost them even to win.

A transit disk descended into view through the clear lift tube before them, and Mordred and his escort stepped easily onto it as it floated down past them on its weak supporting *rep*-beam.

They descended through several more residential levels before they broke out into emptiness above the gardens forty stories below them. To Mordred it was another sign of this city's decadence. The gardens below were green and fertile, lit by long strings of criss-crossing lights that served to nourish the plants and mark out the walkways between them, but the roof above their heads was bare stone, unevenly shaped from the hasty *dis*-ray cuts that had originally carved out this sanctuary, and never smoothed. A minor thing, certainly not a necessary thing—but another sign of lack of heart.

The disk stopped at the bottom of the shaft and Mordred stepped out, ignoring the soldier who hurried to follow him. He knew the route from here, and refused to be led into Ho-Tin's presence.

Mordred strode through the gardens, toward the two soldiers, armed this time with *dis* projectors, who stood guard at the tall metal door set in the rock. The door bore the sigil of the House of San-Lan, not in the austere black on silver that it should have been, but in a garish clash of scarlet and gold. Ignoring the guards Mordred walked up to the massive door, which slid into its recess —with just the least, but annoying, whine—to let him enter the presence of the Prince of the City.

The prince Ho-Tin reclined upon a couch at the far end of the low, long room, surrounded by a battery of screens supported on tall, slender pylons. A double line of scarlet-dressed guards marked off path Mordred must take to approach him, each holding a dis-projector at port arms before himself. It was an impressive display of martial spirit and a pathetic attempt at security. Had Mordred been bent on violence the guards would have wiped out at least half their own number in trying to kill him, with an excellent chance of Ho-Tin himself dying from one of a score of wildly flailing *dis*-beams. Mordred had no doubt that Ho-Tin's father, the Emperor San-Lan—*who might have been* my *father, but for Rogers and his bestial lusts*—would have had far more subtle and effective means of protecting himself than surrounding himself with overdestructive weapons in the hands of the unreliable underlings.

Yet for all his cunning, Mordred thought, *my almost-father nevertheless died at the hands of the American savages. And now this fool, his flesh-son, hides in a hole beneath earth and water, and prides himself on his primacy above cowards. He has forgotten what it is to be Han. Now I must teach him.*

Ho-Tin ignored him as he walked down the aisle towards the Prince. He remained deep in conversation with first one and then another of the faces that appeared on the two screens directly before him. As each subordinate was granted audience and then dismissed, a new face would appear on the screens directly behind him, moving gradually around, screen by screen, to the ultimate screens facing Ho-Tin. Although the screens were well above his eye-level, the Prince's own video pickup was set below him, so that the image each subordinate saw of him in their own screens was that of a Prince with his gaze turned skyward in lofty consideration of the matter before him.

At the end of the gauntlet two soldiers stood out from the lines as Mordred approached, barring any further advance. Mordred stopped and assumed the ritual posture of waiting, head bowed and hands clasped before him. But rather than stand quietly with eyes correctly downcast, Mordred fixed his stare on a point at the base and to one side of Ho-Tin's couch, as though something there fascinated him. Ho-Tin was too sophisticated to be taken in by such a simple gambit, but although he never once even came close to losing the thread of his several conversations, Mordred knew that he was aware of the calculated disrespect he was being shown.

The last of the faces finally vanished from the screens, which then replaced them with a series of constantly-changing views of the city and its environs. Ho-Tin ignored Mordred a moment longer, studying the shifting presentations of sterile corridor and murky sea-bottom, then turned to face him.

"Be welcome in our presence, honored guest of this house," Ho-Tin said.

Mordred looked up at him, just slowly enough. "Great Prince, your graciousness, as ever, is overwhelming." Two cats in an alley, facing each other with ears back.

"Our joy at your satisfaction surpasses measure. Truly it is equalled only by our delight at the existence of one who offers our city so much."

"You do this humble visitor too much honor," Mordred said. He didn't miss the faint nod. "For in truth I did come into this city with no greater hope than to be of service to the illustrious Ho-Tin, Prince of the Han, whose cunning and restraint surpass all appreciation." And whose cowardice and incompetence surpass all belief, Mordred thought. Still, he was no worse than the insects Mordred had had to work with in Peru, and through them he had very nearly won back a continent. Ho-Tin could be manipulated. He would serve.

"Such selflessness is to be admired," Ho-Tin said, leaving implied the inevitable Han corollary: *if not to be believed.* "And indeed it has been most amply demonstrated, through your noble contribution of the warrior-demon weaponry that served your cause so effectively in your magnificent campaign against the American barbarians. It is difficult to conceive of a finer effort on behalf of our desperate race, or of a greater sacrifice."

Save perhaps Mordred's placing the Prl'lu warcraft under Ho-Tin's direct control, which would never happen, Mordred thought. He was impressed. In any but such an adversary situation he would have felt nothing but admiration for the many-layered savagery of Ho-Tin's last statement. Without putting the least wrinkle in the sacrosanct Han politeness that flavored their every interaction, Ho-Tin had neatly reminded him that he was a failure, who had brought ruin upon his own kind by the destruction of the Peruvian refuge and his ill-considered unleashing of the Prl'lu.

"The Prince's pleasure at my modest gift is truly a reward beyond the hopes of any ordinary mortal—" *but note, oh Prince, not beyond mine* "—but surely it would have been of little value without his foresight and the skill of his other servants." That was the way: remind him in his turn of his long hesitation at accepting Mordred's offer, and of the subsequent two-year delay while the fools who served him fumbled about trying to find a way to replicate the Prl'lu armaments through the cruder Han technology. Mordred knew little of scientific theory; none in the Man-Din caste did, and he had begun to suspect that even the elite technical cadres of the Han Ki-Ling intelligentsia were little better versed, for all their authoritative publications and pronouncements. Yet it still annoyed him to see the slapdash, haphazard way the Han tried to copy the Prl'lu artifacts a piece at a time, seeking to find a Han-technology analogue for each individual element of the Prl'lu weapons. It had occurred to him that there should have been some way to determine the underlying principles of the weapons, and that once it was known why each weapon worked as it did, the task of duplicating their function should have been that much easier. But he had no idea how to formulate such a method, and even if he had, it would not help him now, here, as he stood before the indifferent Prince of a hostile City. He controlled the Prl'lu warship, and took what power he had from that; such a solid, material threat was the only thing that mattered in that room. For all their knowledge the Han were not wise enough to fear a mere idea.

"Indeed, we are fortunate beyond expression in having such devotion all around us," Ho-Tin said. Mordred felt a slight satisfaction, quickly masked. Ho-Tin's veiled agreement about the ineptitude of his scientists was Mordred's clue that the Prince was ready to listen to an offer.

"Such good fortune is a joy and a blessing," Mordred said, "and should be used to its fullest extent."

"And how might this be done?"

"I am possessed of certain resources, Excellency, as I am sure is known. Nothing would give me greater satisfaction than to employ those resources in your service and that of our people, to free them from their barbarian oppressors."

"That is a most laudable ambition. We would be more than willing to see these formidable resources of yours placed at our disposal."

Mordred snorted in silent indignation at that. He hadn't sparred with these people for three years simply to throw everything away on a semantic point.

"Excellency, nothing on this earth would give me greater pleasure than to see the house of San-Lan possessed of such might, but that would be utter irresponsibility on my humble part. Surely I can be of greater service to my Prince than by merely placing a handful of trivial technological tricks at his feet. Surely such tricks would be of better use to him when managed by someone familiar with their application, and surely it is no more than my duty to spare the Prince of a City the added burden of any further responsibilities."

Ho-Tin smiled. It was not the empty expression of one engaged in the transparent pleasantries of protocol. Mordred felt a warning stir of unease.

"What a rewarding day this has been," Ho-Tin said. "To have twice in one day been approached by noble members of our race bringing valuable contributions to our cause. Can you possibly conceive of such pleasure, gallant visitor?"

"In truth, Excellency, I cannot. Such good fortune

has always been beyond me." *What can he be playing at?*

"Then it would certainly be ungracious of us not to acquaint you with its nature," Ho-Tin said. He raised a hand and the two screens facing away from Mordred spun to face him.

The finned, wasp-waisted shape of the Prl-lu scout ship hung suspended within their frames as it rested in the middle of the city's airship hangar.

In a ripple of switched video channels the tableau on the screens repeated fragments of itself from a dozen different angles and distances in the screens surrounding Ho-Tin. Modred didn't need their added information to define his betrayal.

He was beaten, and he knew it. Without the Prl'lu warship, he was nothing in the eyes of the pure Han of the city. All that was left to him now was to save what little pride he could by his conduct in defeat.

"That is gratifying, is it not?" Ho-Tin asked. "To be the benefactor of three in whom the blood of our kind runs so truly that they abandon all hope of personal advancement in their eagerness to serve?"

"I am sure that is true, Excellency. As I had mentioned, I have never been the recipient of such loyalty. One supposes it is a question of breeding."

"We have ever found it so," Ho-Tin said with a gracious smile.

It stung, of course, to be reminded of Ho-Tin's contempt for his tainted heritage, but it would not be avoided now. So instead Mordred started the exchange, giving Ho-Tin an opportunity he could not refuse. It did nothing to lessen the insult or cool Mordred's anger, but it gave him the minor satisfaction of denying Ho-Tin the chance to initiate the gambit.

"In any event," Ho-Tin said, "We are pleased to accept whatever service you may yet be able to offer. This audience is at an end."

Mordred didn't have to feel the presence of the two soldiers at his back to know that their weapons would be trained on him now as they stepped out and to either side of him. Without speaking he made his obligatory bow, stopping just short of the correct height, and turned and left the chamber.

His soldier was waiting for him outside the door. Mordred said nothing as he passed him and the man fell in behind him.

Damn them, he thought as he stormed through the gardens. Occasional strolling couples stopped and stared at him as he rushed past, and one young woman who had obviously just been dismissed from a relationship and wished to reestablish a liason before her accumulated wealth was depleted approached him, only to turn away at his expression. Let her, Mordred told himself. Any woman who would consider liason with a politically crippled outblood probably wasn't worth the trouble anyway.

He had been a fool to trust the crew he had left to hold the ship in his absence, he realized that now. For all that they had sworn loyalty to him, and in spite of the fact that he had saved their lives, first in the fall of the Peruvian refuge and again when they had fled the *Wilma Deering,* they were pure Han and he was not. He should have known that they would put the call of their own kind and the promise of their old, comfortable way of life ahead of their duty to Mordred and his mission against the humans. Now he was helpless against Ho-Tin. He could expect nothing more than to be kept like some interesting curio for as long as Ho-Tin thought he might have knowledge useful to the city, and after that to be discarded like a used and unfashionable tunic.

He would not let that happen. He was no victim, damn them all, he was no failure, he was Mordred, as much a Prince of the Blood by deed as Ho-Tin was by ancestry, who had commanded forces that made this fugitive city a joke in comparison. He would not serve these petty little Han, and he would not be beaten.

Mordred and his escort stepped from the lift disk onto his level. Mordred dismounted first, leaving the soldier with a six-inch drop to step down as the disk continued to rise. The soldier's foot touched the floor—and in that brief instant of imbalance Mordred spun and slashed the edge of his hand across the soldier's throat. The soldier was still thrashing around on the floor as Mordred stepped aboard a down-bound disk and descended into the depths of the city.

The city of Niagra basked in the summer sunlight.

There was an air of newness about the city, an almost sublimal impression gleaned from the prominence of fresh, unweathered concrete and broad expanses of still-young saplings and shrubberies, the scars of the Han attack of three years ago. It was an impression in great favor with many politicians within the American Alliance—it made a convenient metaphor for "our young nation's ability to rebound from hardship into united prosperity. . ." In spite of that, it was an attractive sight.

Will Holcomb didn't notice. He walked across the broad commons between the Executive Complex's four towers, towards Rogers' office. He walked quickly, in fact he almost marched: in times of stress he had the not uncommon military habit of falling back on the most elementary, basic-training-induced responses, just as no trooper ever stood more rigidly to attention than the hungover AWOL standing before his captain's desk.

Holcomb didn't relish his upcoming meeting with Marshal Rogers, but it did seem to be the logical culmination of his brief career as an administrative ace. Will Holcomb was a flier by training and inclination. He was much more at home in a fast atmospheric rocket than he was in his role as Rogers' aide; he was happier by far taking a lithe and deadly pursuit ship through twenty thousand meters with seven or eight gravities of acceleration pounding a giant's fist into his chest than he was running endless circles through the shifting webs of power and influence that surrounded the reforming government. Piloting a ship, he was in command; as Rogers' aide he felt like little more than a second pair of legs, eyes and ears for his superior. It wasn't a job he was terribly good at. It wasn't a job he was trained for, and it wasn't a job he liked. The only reason he had stayed with it as long as he had without requesting a transfer back to a flying unit where he belonged was the constant assurance he received from all quarters that association with Rogers was sure to help his career. He had come to hate that reasoning during his stay in Niagra. He saw too much of it. At times it seemed as if everybody in the government was involved in it for no other purpose than to better their own fortunes. That wasn't the case, of course, he knew it wasn't; yet even the men and women of the government who could never be accused of abusing their office often could not see beyond the interests of their gang or region or specialty. The people who could see beyond their own small needs to the necessities of an Alliance that served every faction were few and far between.

And now that Will Holcomb had made his own small bid to join their ranks he could feel the axe poised above his neck. Yet what else could he have done? He respected Anthony Rogers as he had respected few men in his young life, but even he could see that Rogers' increasing tension and irritability were interfering with his work—and Rogers' work was nothing less than holding the American Alliance together. He had tried to be discreet about it, going to directly to Doctor Harris, since he knew that she counted too heavily on Rogers' support for her researches to carelessly expose his erratic condition. He knew it had to be done. But it still didn't feel right. It still smacked of betrayal.

The receptionist in Rogers' outer office looked up as Will entered and immediately announced him. He wasn't even going to get a chance to compose his thoughts.

Rogers was standing with his back to him as Will entered. He was looking out through the bay window that took up the outer wall of the office and opened out onto a view of the Falls themselves, once again a raging torrent of foam and distant thunder, though farther upstream than in his native time. That was one thing they could honestly thank the Han for, at least. It would be years before all the water vapor released into the atmosphere by the revived Prl'lu's attempt to melt the Antarctic ice-cap condensed back into the ice fields again, and until it had the long-dead falls would flow with a new vigor.

They might even outlast Will Holcomb.

"Sit down, Captain," Rogers said. He didn't turn around.

"Yes, sir." Holcomb sat. Rogers' tone of voice told him this was no time to argue protocol of rank.

"It may interest you to know that I am currently undergoing medical treatment recommended by Doctors Harris and Wolsky for a condition that I understand you brought to their attention."

"Yes, sir." A null-content answer; it filled the silence as required without comitting Holcomb to an attackable position.

"Yes, sir," Rogers repeated. He sat down behind the black glassite desk, palm flat on the ebony surface, gaze locked on Holcomb's eyes. The strong sidelighting from the window brought out the planes and angles of his face with an unnatural harshness.

"I think you know what I've been trying to do here," Rogers said. "And I think you know what I've been coming up against. Damn near everybody in this government is out to make the best deal that he can for himself and devil take the rest of the country. It's almost impossible to get any cooperation around here, and it's just as hard to get anybody to think in terms of putting the welfare of the country ahead of everything else."

He leaned forward, stabbing a finger at Holcomb, his dark reflection in the tabletop encroaching on Will's blond one. "I've got to put up with all that nonsense just to keep *something* going until the government can get back on its own feet again. And now *you* go running to Ruth Harris behind my back on this. Well, let me tell you something, mister—if you hadn't done exactly the right thing I'd kick your tail right out from under those epaulettes."

Holcomb didn't think his expression could be all *that* funny.

Rogers finally got his laughter under control, and sat back in his chair. "I swear to God, the last three years are almost worth it, just for the look on your face then, Will." And he explained to him about the Prl'lu healing system and the odd changes it had wrought in him. "In any case, I've promised to act like a sane human being for a while." He scowled, slightly. "The problem now is, what am I supposed to do with you, Will?"

"I don't understand."

"You're wasted as my aide, I see that now. I've got too much need for honest, competent men to throw one away carrying my papers and taking my messages. But where can I use you better?"

"As what?"

35

"In a position of some kind of authority, Will, where you can do productive work. The thing is, though, where? There aren't too many places I *can* use you."

"Why not—sir?"

"I mean you don't come from a terribly influential gang, no offense. You're younger than most of the people you'd have to deal with, and that's a point against you as well. And you're a soldier. That cuts a lot of ice in wartime, and it should, but we're at peace now, and most gang bosses will be plenty quick to remind you of it—as if it was all our fault. So the question is, where can I use you that you won't be wasted and you won't have to spend half your time fighting just to be taken seriously?"

"I have no idea," Will said, "I'm sure there are more qualified people in this government for just about any post you'd care to name. Personally, I'd be just as happy to be back flying again."

Rogers grinned. "Bingo. I said the boy was clever."

"How so?"

"You like flying, Will, don't you?"

"Of course I do."

"The higher, the faster, the better, right?"

"Yes . . .?"

"Okay," Rogers said, chuckling, "you're going to get the chance to fly faster and higher than anyone else in history, Major."

"*Major?*"

"Major Holcomb," Rogers said formally, "effective this date you will assume command of the American Alliance space effort, in the form of the Alliance space ship *Wilma Deering* and all subsequent vessels, and all related support, administrative and research facilities."

"Sir, I—thank you, but why me?"

"Because you're competent enough to handle it, I think. Because you're honest enough not to treat it like the patronage plum or political football a certain government committee seems to think it is. And because I have to keep getting poked and prodded by a pack of graverobbers because of you. I couldn't let you off any easier."

Holcomb grinned. "You're going to punish me with power, huh? Sounds like a fate worse than death."

"I don't think you'll find that so funny very soon."

Rogers sat alone in his office. Holcomb had left minutes before, to cut his own orders for transfer to the Badlands Air Base where the *Wilma Deering* was housed.

His phone buzzed.

"Boss Teder is here, sir."

For a moment, he wished he had accepted Harris' pills.

"All right. Send him in."

Cullen Teder was not a young man, and his sixty-three years of age were made more evident by his years of exposure to a harsh Southwestern sun that had cracked and lined his face like shale at the base of some desert butte. His gang hailed from what had been in Rogers' time the state of New Mexico, and had been one of the most aggressive and successful units in the American Army of Liberation. They had been hardened by three centuries of Han persecution and attack. Unlike the more fortunate gangs of the east, they had never been able to take advantage of sheltering terrain to hide their existence from the Han, and in turn their higher visibility had offended the sensibilities of their oppressors more often, so that Teder's people had suffered far more than their share of punitive air raids. In all the war of liberation and the subsequent expeditionary campaigns overseas they had never taken a prisoner.

Cullen Teder shared the harsh strength of his people,

shared their aggressiveness and matched their success in battle with his own success in office. He was a capable legislator, and one who had spoken and voted with intelligence and foresight on many issues where Rogers had sorely needed such support. But beyond that Cullen Teder still shared his people's pathological hatred of the Han, and that drove an immovable wedge between Rogers and him on one matter. One crucial matter.

"You know why I'm here," Teder said, without any preamble.

"It's a new week," Rogers said, "It's your usual time."

"What are you going to do about that Han witch?"

Rogers sighed. "What do you want me to do, Cullen?"

"You of all people shouldn't need telling, Marshal," Teder answered. "You fought in the War of Liberation; you personally ended the last Han threat three years ago. The Han are our enemies, Marshal."

"That's right, they are. They're also defeated. Besides that, this 'Han witch' of yours also saved my life. We owe her—I owe her—something for that, at least."

"She's Han."

"She's alone. We couldn't return her to her own people even if we wanted to. Where would we send her?"

"Toss her out into the woods for one of their refugee packs to find. You know they exist. Let them take care of their own."

"I've heard of these refugee packs," Rogers said. "I've also heard of the bogeyman. I've seen the same hard evidence for both."

"You're going to deny that they exist? That farms have been raided, transport intercepted, men and women killed?"

"We've always had trouble with lone outlaws and crooked gangs. We're more than capable of giving

38

ourselves enough trouble in that area without inventing hordes of Han wild men out for revenge. The Princess Lu-An is a prisoner of war, Cullen. Even if we could find someone to surrender her to, she's too valuable to be released."

"Valuable for what?"

"For her knowledge of the Han, man."

"What do we have to know about something we've beaten?"

"Nothing. Nothing at all; you're absolutely right, Cullen. It doesn't make any difference that they had devices and technology that we still haven't figured out. It doesn't make any difference that we don't even have an accurate idea of how many Han there actually were, or might still be, or where. It doesn't matter that we know practically nothing of them at all. You're right. She's a waste of time. We can't hope to learn anything from a race that held us down for three centuries. We're too smart for that."

Cullen Teder stood silent, and Rogers could see that his argument had made no impression at all. Cullen Teder was alien to him, shaped by strange, hardening forces Rogers had never known, that formed and stiffened his perceptions just as they had distorted and shaped his name to a harsher accent than Rogers was used to.

"You had better do something about her, Rogers," he finally said. "My people don't understand why a damned Han is living as a pampered guest of the American government. They won't stand for it. If you don't do something about it, I'll have to—and believe me, I can."

Kendy went quietly insane.

It had taken him the better part of a day and a night of sailing the awkward little draftie to reach the coast. He remembered almost nothing of the trip, numbed as

he was by the overwhelming fact of a Han attack. He
had abandoned the draftie on the beach, for it would
have been an upwind beat into Tallpines and the little
square-rigger was useless for that. He could make time
faster on foot than he could tacking back and forth
along the shore. And he had to make time. That was
important, that was the only thing that mattered. He
had to warn his gang; he had to save them. . . .

They were already dead.

The fire had swept down from the windward pines,
gutting cottages and shops, and burning away the sails
and rigging on the two boats moored to the charred
dock. The boats themselves were fire-scored but afloat,
and largely intact, as if grimly determined to outlive
their masters. But not a soul was left alive in the village.

They hadn't even tried to flee. All of them, ninety-six
people, lay dead, in the most common and ordinary
places. Old Man Bersig lay sprawled over the gunwale of
one of the boats, a half-woven strand of rigging dangling
from one hand, his tools at his feet. Cooper lay stretched
at foot of his scales, which still held a load of burnt
salmon. Through the window of one of the ruined cottages he could see a family, a woman and three children,
intermixed with the burned remains of a table and the
warped and half-melted tableware of an ordinary meal.
The bodies were burned beyond recognition, but it was
—had been—the Garricks' home. Maj, Bendy, Kate and
Lillen? He didn't know; he would never know, and it no
longer really mattered. It was as if the simple knowledge
of the approaching flames had struck the entire gang
dead where they stood, without even the chance for protest or alarm.

But it wasn't the fire. Jaz Kendy knew that. It was the
Han. They had taken away his boat and his livelihood,
almost in passing, and then they had gone on to claim
his home and his life.

40

For an hour he wandered through the remains of the village. It was too much, it was beyond him. He had no idea where to start, what to do, as if anything he could do now would do the slightest good. Occasionally a low moan would escape his lips, only to be immediately choked off, as if Kendy knew he could never make a sound that could equal this horror.

Then he saw the ship. It glittered with a metallic brilliance as it flew in low over the waves, straight for Tallpines. The sight of it crystallized something in Jaz Kendy, made one thing clear and evident and simple to him.

He ran quickly to the boats tied to the ravaged pier. The one moored to port, the one with Old Man Bersig's body still draped over the side, Garrick's boat. Kendy flung open the hatch and dropped below the decks.

The pistol was still in its drawer, undamaged. It was an old military-surplus rocket gun, kept on board for keeping sharks off the nets. It was the heaviest weapon the gang had possessed, and it was all Kendy would need.

He took the squat, short-barrelled weapon from its resting place, quickly threading on its detachable alloy buttstock. Then he took up a stripper-clip of the stubby explosive cartridges and slid them down into the magazine through the open breech.

Racking the slide forward, he stepped back on deck, kneeling low behind the cockpit coaming, and put the weapon to his shoulder, tracking the incoming ship.

It eased itself down onto the beach in a flurry of blown sand. After a moment a hatch opened and a figure emerged, another, and a third. After a moment, when Kendy was certain that no others would be coming out, he lowered his eye to the sights, aimed, and fired. Fresh fire blossomed on the beach. . . .

CHAPTER THREE

The dead surface of the Moon was marked with the scars of new life.

Hun't'pir stood his familiar post, suspended at the very center of the great monitoring chamber. The perspective he chose allowed him to look 'down' on the lunar landscape and the series of great rings on their pylons marching off to the horizon, aimed like a gun barrel at the blue-white sphere just rising above the distant mountains.

The great assembly drones had finished their work long ago, dragging the massive prefabricated sections of ring and pylon from their stasis-guarded storage and erecting them according to their millienia-old program. The only movement to be seen now was the occasional eruption of sparks where one of the fine-detail drones welded the final connections between the enormous ring-shaped electromagnets and the long-dormant power plants buried in the dead rock beneath the base.

A human commander might have been daunted by the challenge that faced Hun't'pir. The lunar base had never been more than an observation and relay station, intended to monitor the space surrounding the third planet and maintain communication with the outer-system installations. Hun't'pir had only the modest defensive armaments of his installation and a dozen of the

42

Blood with which to wage his battle.

But that human commander would not have been Hun't'pir. A world in his charge had been taken; Prl'lu had been beaten. The Prl'lu commander could not consider inaction under such circumstances.

The rings were his sole offensive weapon. Gigantic electromagnets of enormous power, they had been intended originally to serve as a launching system for shuttles and transports between the Moon and its mother planet. Now they would be the mailed fist of the Prl'lu wrath.

Hun't'pir manipulated the small console before him. "Report the progress made on the projectiles."

There was an instant's discontinuity in a small portion of the landscape filling the chamber, and then Kors'in-tu's face was hovering in the air before him.

"Our fortune is good, my commander," he said, so clearly that he might have been standing there before Hun't'pir rather than in the cramped cabin of a scout car three hundred kirr'eks away. "The vein is very nearly pure ore, so much so that I would venture to suggest that we might consider simply shaping the projectiles in the process of excavation. Such a tactic would greatly reduce the time required to stockpile an adequate supply."

"Indeed it would. Is such a method feasible?"

"It is, sir. I have charted the course of the vein and we may exploit it for virtually its entire length with such a method."

"Then do so. Report to me again when you have determined the time it will require to shape five hundred projectiles."

"Your command, sir." Kors'in-tu bowed curtly and vanished.

Hun't'pir returned to his study of the world before

him. He felt a certain discomfort at his resolution to attack a world under his nominal protection. But he had no option. He would never have been revived if something had not gone drastically wrong. The secondary polar base had fallen to a race of no small sophistication, a sophistication—and a race, for that matter, that had not existed when the bases were established. Worse, studies of the transmissions recorded by Hun't'pir's base monitors while the lunar outpost was still preparing for revival indicated that two races had been involved in the downfall of the base. One of those had proven to be descendants of a Prl'an detachment, support units evidently awakened by their stasis field's independent emergency programming during a limited nuclear engagement involving the native race that had arisen during their suspension. The Prl'an rabble, now pretentiously styling themselves royalty even as they absorbed the mark and mannerisms of the natives they professed to despise, had rapidly been brought into line, according to the polar base's records. But the native race had put up an unexpectedly stiff and persistent resistance. Neither their tactics nor their technology were up to Prl'lu standards, of course, but they had pressed their attacks home bravely and they had shown a disturbing degree of ingenuity, as well. It was obvious from Hun't'pir's study of the fallen base's records that the natives had managed to devise at least a partial defense to the *karnak* weapon after only brief exposure to it, and their technique of weakening Prl'lu vehicle armor with powerful corrosives before attacking with their primitive offensive weapons had proven alarmingly effective, for all its crudity.

These native qualities of aggressiveness and ingenuity, coupled with the unexplained failure of a large portion of the polar base's revival sequence, accounted for the base's fall, even if they didn't excuse it. They also explained Hun't'pir's reluctance to arouse the personnel of the remaining Prl'lu bases on the planet. Even considering the fact that fighting Prl'lu made up only a small percentage of the population still in stasis, Hun't'pir had no doubt that they would be able to defeat any force the natives could throw up against them. But they would be decimated in the process, and without a strong Prl'lu presence to watch over and guide them, Hun't'pir could not be sure that the breeding populations remaining in stasis would thrive. He was charged with the stewardship of this world, not its conquest; he must retake the planet without destroying, reduce the capacity of the natives to resist so that the reviving Prl'lu would be able to subjugate them readily and inexpensively, without reducing the disputed terrain to uninhabitable slag.

Hun't'pir looked down at the long column of rings again, standing stark and gleaming in the unadulterated sunlight. He could do it. . . .

Mordred cursed as he manhandled the heavy cannister onto the conveyor belt.

He was heartily bored, in spite of his constant need for watchfulness. For the past week his world had centered around the short distance between the off-loading ramp of the filtration system and the on-loading ramp of the conveyor, carrying filled cannisters of needed minerals extracted from the surrounding seawater one way, and then lugging emptied cannisters ready for reloading back the other. It was work that could as easily have been performed by a simple extension of each ramp, but then it would not have been available to occupy the time and minds of laborers, such as the man he had killed for his identification.

Mordred had quickly realized that it would not be a

simple matter to escape from the city. He would have been challenged at any of the three main exits, and he could never have bluffed his way past. Single Han did not leave the safety of their city for the dangers of the human-controlled wilderness. And there was no way he could have gained entrance to the hangar levels and his own ship. He could count on Ho-Tin's having had enough sense at least to have taken precautions against that.

So he had gone to ground, killing a common laborer for his identification and assuming his place at his work, until he could plan an escape. It was the perfect disguise for him, since it involved not so much taking on a new role as discarding aspects of his original nature. The search was presumably on for an outblood who assumed the trappings of high rank; the class-bound Han would never think to look for him in the guise of a low-caste worker. They would not see his face behind the severe haircut of a laborer; they would not recognize the wiry man in the gray tunic as the patrician figure clad in prince's scarlet that they sought. Unable to conceive of voluntarily lowering themselves so, they would not believe Mordred capable of it, and so he was as safe as if he walked among them in an entirely different body.

He may as well as have done that very thing, Mordred thought bitterly. The fugitive bastard who posed as a laborer in the hope that he would escape discovery was almost impossible to connect with the outblood prince who had plotted revenge against an entire race and very nearly made it work.

Prince, he thought disgustedly, taking the weight of another cannister in his arms. It wasn't a title he deserved through birth, to be sure. The Emperor San-Lan had already sired a sufficient number of heirs before him to be sure of the competition necessary in Han eyes to ensure a strong successor in his line. Unlike human monarchs down through history, however, he had been able to take precautions to limit the further spread of his royal seed, and had done so. There had been no way for Mordred's mother, Ngo-Lan, to then justify the birth of her grey-eyed child. She had been sent back to the subsistence-level existence that was the best a woman in disgrace could hope for among the Han. Mordred might have looked for no better fate, but for the curiosity of the Ki-Ling academicians of San-Lan's retinue, who had used him as a guinea pig, in hopes of discovering the intellectual limits of such a cross-bred specimen.

They hadn't found them. Mordred had astonished them with his ability to learn and even more importantly to apply the knowledge he absorbed. History, culture, the revived study of military strategy—he had mastered them all. His only lacks were those of his culture—such as his limited knowledge of basic scientific theory—and of temperment. He had little patience with the arts of his people, and their decadent themes of futility of effort and irrelevance of purpose. And he allowed his lifelong ill-treatment at the hands of his contemptuous betters to foster a similar contempt in him for all of them. If he had failed in the years of his slow rise to bitterly be-grudged power it was in his inability to believe that any of *them,* that gray and faceless mass that had held him down and hindered him for so many years, could be quite as competent as he knew himself to be.

The folly of that attitude was being impressed on him now, in the draining, repetitive labor and cold, im-personal workman's life he was forced to lead. He had known that he would have little trouble taking the place of the man he had killed, for workers moved about a great deal, taking quarters close to whatever makework job they were currently assigned to, and being transferred frequently. But the complete lack of relationships between workers had surprised him. Even when several of them roomed together in one of the city-provided rooms, as was common, they shared almost nothing. They conversed little, seemed to form no lasting relationships. Each man would have his own bed and a little storage space for the few personal items he possessed; each man had his own screen, and little more. They would return from whatever job they held at the moment, patiently await their turn at the shared toilet facilities, and spend their remaining few hours in silence watching their respective screens. On the rare occasion when one of the workers would bring a woman back to the apartment—on the rare occasion when one of them could find a woman desperate enough to liase with a common worker—he would simply drop the absurd 'privacy curtain' of his bed into place and carry on from there, without his roomates seeming to pay the slightest attention. Ultimately, Mordred finally decided, it was this very commonality of experience that produced such isolationism. They shared a way of life; they shared the same limited prospects for the future. That was Mordred's greatest protection, that none of them would intrude in his business for fear of risking their own small privacies. So Mordred hid among them, sheltering in their sullen solitude, hoarding the little credit the work earned him and searching for a safe path out of the city. He had yet to discover one, but he would. He had to. Events refused to wait for him. Ho-Tin had already begun the first of a series of guerilla raids to test the full efficacy of the Han-adapted Prl'lu weapons. It was inevitable that the humans soon realize what was happening, and respond. He would not wait passively while the confrontation in the outside world mounted beyond his control.

* * *

Air cracked like lightning-struck oak as the six *Mako*-class pursuit ships flashed over the approach path to Badlands Air Base.

Office personnel crowded to windows. Hangar staff rushed outdoors to gape at the blurred machine-streaks that thundered overhead and dwindled toward the horizon. Only the quiet men of the air defense batteries remained rooted at their seats, staring into their scopes and calmly reporting the progress of the aircraft now banking to overfly the base a second time.

Holcomb pushed gently forward on his stick and the Mako nosed smoothly downward. The Mako had none of the needle-like sleekness of most ships of American design; it was the first aircraft of the Alliance to incorporate features copied from Prl'lu aircraft discovered in the Antarctic stasis base. The alien design element gave the Mako a droop-nosed, predatory look—but there was no denying that it flew like a bandit, and that made it look just fine to Will Holcomb. When he had heard that a flight of the new ships was being assigned to the squadrons guarding Badlands he had jumped at the chance to pull new found rank and bump open a seat in one of their cockpits. Somewhere several hundred kilometers to the east as Will flew tail position to the flight a thoroughly disgruntled lieutenant was sulking in his cramped passenger seat aboard one of the slow, bulky transports flying in the Makos' support element. Will's heart fair bled for him.

There was a hiss of background noise static in Will's headphones. "All right, Major, we're going to put on a little show for the groundhogs." It was Hopper, a slight, quiet man from someplace on the West Coast, captain of the flight. "Now, the word is, you're a real flier, and I hope that's the case, 'cause you're sitting in the place of a good man."

"Well, these darlings aren't exactly the cloth and wire kites we had in the good old days, Captain, but I'll see if I can't keep up."

There was a moment's silence, as the base fell another three miles behind them. "Cloth and . . . Sir, what are you talking about?"

"Never mind, Captain. I've just been keeping some strange company and it rubs off a bit. Now, what's the maneuver?"

"Straight down the runway, on the deck, with rocket assist."

"You must have something against windows." Even as Holcomb spoke Hopper was leading the flight into a wide, smooth turn back toward the base.

"Just like to make a strong first impression, sir."

"Aknol," Holcomb said, and chuckled. "Lead on."

The long runway of the base was a thin, tapering ribbon in the distance. Then it was much larger and suddenly weathered concrete, cracked and baking in the desert sun, rushed by beneath them. Holcomb had flipped open the cover on the rocket-assist arming switch set on his control stick. Now his eyes tracked a constant three-point circuit, from altimeter to the Mako ahead of him to the runway hurtling toward him.

"Ready on boosters," Hopper's voice came quietly. "On command—*now*."

The Makos came thundering back through the base, just meters above the ground. At Hopper's command every pilot thumbed down his rocket-assist switch. Tongues of fire blossomed behind each ship, as rockets designed to push the Makos to supersonic speeds hundreds of thousands of feet above the earth slammed them against and through the thicker air at ground level. The watchers on the ground flinched at the impact as the planes hammered against the barrier of sound-speed.

The shockwaves struck at them like so many fists, like so many precise jabs in the solar plexus, catching them in mid-breath. Windows rattled sharply in their frames, and the sheet-metal roofs of the prefabricated hangars flexed at the impact.

Doctor Jomo Mamboya dashed a clipboard to the floor and shouted something pungent in Swahili as the sonic boom shook the building under the large reflector telescope and its aiming gears slipped several notches. He stormed over to the controls and studied the readouts. Of course they showed no change; the system hadn't been turned on and so would need to be completely recalibrated. A month's work, ruined by a pack of jejune adolescents playing with their noisy toys. Still cursing, he turned and stormed down the stairs that led from the cramped rooftop observatory to the interior of the building.

The journey from the labs to the runway was a formidable exercise for any man of Mamboya's advanced age and considerable bulk, but he took no notice of the sweat that almost instantly began to bead along his brow.

The Makos were edging their way to the line now, gliding ponderously off the runway on fiercely hissing landing jets. Service crew were moving up to the sides of the new ships and pausing hesitantly, uncertain of where to hook up what on the unfamiliar models. The only thing they knew definitely to avoid were the two faint patches of cerulean radiance where the *dis*-fields of the engine's nitrogen intakes shone palely in the sunlight. True, they weren't *supposed* to be set to a level that would affect human flesh—but no one wanted to be the first man or woman to die for want of a tune-up.

Holcomb carefully guided the ship to its landing pad. The big pursuit lost much of its grace and agility once denied its supportive cushion of transsonic air under its delta wings; maneuvering it atop four pegs of expanding gas was almost as challenging as flying the ship proper.

He finally got the ship centered above the concrete stand to the satisfaction of a little man in plastic earmuffs waving a brace of bright orange sticks. He carefully eased the throttles forward, attentuating the *dis* intake fields, and the Mako settled down on its landing gear with a slight creaking of struts.

"Very nice flying, Captain," Holcomb said.

"I have seen worse," Hopper's voice agreed in his helmet.

Holcomb grinned and pulled his helmet jack from its socket. He slid back the canopy, undid his four-way shock harness and the water input for his flight suit's gravity bladders, unplugged his oxygen mask from the ship's internal supply feed and killed the sixteen master switches that governed each individual system that let a Mako pursuit fly and fight. Almost as an afterthought he disconnected the firing lanyard that linked his rocket belt to the ejection seat: it would have been bad form for a new base commander to blow himself three hundred feet into the air the first time he set foot upon his new command.

Mayboya was waiting for him as he climbed down. He was an impressive sight. Where most Americans of the time tended toward medium height and slender though wiry build, Doctor Jomo Mamboya stood a full two meters tall and had to weigh, *had* to, at least three hundred pounds. Yet in spite of the liberal salting of gray in his hair and the deep lines of age in his black face he carried his bulk lightly, not so much as though he was in good condition but rather as if he simply refused to let his girth hinder him.

"Are you people satisfied?" Mamboya thundered.

"Perhaps you'd care to play some more? There's still a building or two standing!"

Will Holcomb looked at him. "Well, they're my buildings," he said mildly.

"And it's *my* work your juvenile exertions have set back weeks, you young—*your* buildings?"

Holcomb advanced on him, hand outstretched. It was a tactic he had quickly learned while serving as Roger's aide: no matter how indignant or self-involved the other party to any argument proved to be, an air of courteous reasonableness, strictly maintained, could be relied on nine times out of ten to embarass them back into civility. Of course, the tenth time the other party was likely to try and tear one's head off one's shoulders, but then nothing is perfect.

"Major Willis Holcomb, Alliance Air Defense Command, new director of the Alliance space effort," Will said. "And you are—?"

Mamboya was brought up short. He was too strictly conditioned to the protocols of international scientific exchange to ignore any introduction, but the formal response it called for jarred against his anger.

"Jomo Mamboya, Doctor of Astronomy, on loan from the Institute of General Sciences, Nairobi."

Holcomb suddenly recognized the man before him.

"You're the man who tracked down the *Wilma Deering* after the Han pirating," he said.

"I have that honor," Mamboya said. Holcomb's delay in recognizing him was understandable. A simple screen presentation of the man could project none of the considerable vigor he radiated. "Of course, that was back in the days when carless pilots didn't shake half my equipment off its mountings."

Holcomb looked at him, concerned. "Did we do any damage?"

53

Mamboya's anger had faded, almost in spite of itself. Nevertheless, he scraped together the last few embers for a last complaint. "All my calibrations have been thrown off. All of them. It will take at least a month to realign everything. This is most unfortunate, Major. What is the point of rushing to complete a spaceship when you have no idea where to take her? There will undoubtedly be complaints voiced at this delay in Council."

"You're probably correct, Doctor," Holcomb said. "That hadn't occurred to me or I probably wouldn't have allowed the men to show off like that." He shrugged. "You do what you can to get things back in line as quickly as possible."

"And when the complaints come in?"

Holcomb shrugged again. "When they come in, I'll tell the Council what went wrong—an error of judgement on my part. They can't blame you for that."

Mamboya looked at him oddly. "Administrator Keegan would not have said that. He had a strong dislike of accountability, at least in regard to his own person."

"Well, that was Administrator Keegan."

"Indeed it was," Mamboya said, as they left the flight line.

"Perhaps the corrections will not take as long as I feared."

The ship hung ten meters above their heads, the negative weight of its inertron counterballasting holding it tight against the heavy cables that tethered it to the floor of the enormous hangar. Fully a hundred feet in diameter, the *Wilma Deering* was designed in the form of a ten-foot thick disc, swelling abruptly to some-etwenty feet through at a secondary disc at the core of the larger one. The ship bristled with pods and blisters, where weapons and maneuvering jets protruded through

54

the hull, and a large, inverted 'sail' extended down from the keel, matching a similar structure rising from the upper deck: weapons pylons, studded all along their inner edge—forward in flight—with missile ports and *dis* projectors.

"In many ways, the Prl'lu did us a favor with their attack upon man," Mamboya was saying. "Before their attack, our greatest concern was in wringing enough inertron out of the Council to completely armor the ship. However, since the Prl'lu struck and Mordred pirated the Deering, our priorities have been reevaluated, shall we say. The ship is now perfectly balanced with regard to the pull of gravity, and completely armored against any conventional assault."

"And against an unconventional assault?"

Mamboya shrugged. "The best defense is as it always has been—don't get hit."

"That's very reassuring."

"It is what is. In any event, what is there to fear? We control the Prl'lu weapons now. There are none less conventional than those."

"We control the ones we know of," Holcomb said. "We have no way of knowing what might exist without our knowledge."

"I will not worry about that. It strains probability enough that this one small world of ours should play host already to human, Han and Prl'lu. I do not consider it likely that there remain further hidden hordes prepared to spring upon us without warning."

"Yet you work to help develop a warship."

"For my own reasons. Assignment here gave me the chance to further my studies of the stars of the northern hemisphere, Major. And this ship is a magnificent effort, in and of itself, whatever its purpose. I would see it continued merely for the doing of it."

"That's very idealistic of you."

Mamboya chuckled. "Oh, I am aware of the pragmatic reasons behind my presence on this project. You people scared the rest of the world rather badly, you know, when you allowed the Han to pirate this craft. They were not at all happy with the idea of some omnipotent dreadnought hanging over their heads, no matter in whose hands. So your Marshal Rogers decided, wisely, I believe, to arrange for several non-American scientific figures of note to be assigned to the *Deering* project. The fact that most of us possess skills and knowledge unavailable within your own Alliance didn't hurt."

"No, I suppose it wouldn't. But you don't really believe that the confederations of Europe, Africa and Asia think that our picking your brains is to be taken as a sign of good faith, do you?"

Mamboya scowled. "The American Alliance's 'picking our brains', as you put it, no. Marshal Rogers' requesting our assistance in a worthwhile endeavor is a different matter. He is a most remarkable man, this Marshal of yours, Major."

"I won't debate that, sir."

"I'm sure you wouldn't. But I do wonder if you fully understand what it is that you admire. Major, did you ever wonder why Marshal Rogers put a military officer in command of what was essentially a civillian project up to this date?"

"Well . . . I'd like to think it was because he thought I could handle it."

"And not because you, as a military officer, are subject to his command?"

Will Holcomb looked sharply at Mamboya and took a half-step back from him, a distancing in space as well as emotion. "I'm subject to my oath to my Alliance first,

Doctor, above and beyond any military chain of command."

"Of course, of course you are, Major; I never meant to suggest anything to the least bit otherwise. But I ask you to consider your appointment from the perspective of my government and indeed most of the governments around the world. You must realize, your American Alliance is something of an exception among them, both in size and organization. Any one of your larger gangs would almost be a complete state elsewhere and there is nothing like your Alliance among them. I speak from experience when I tell you that many leaders in Africa—and I don't doubt in Asia and even among your European elders, as well—find it unsettling to have to deal not with a man but with an entity, an organization, whose decisions and goals are subject to change at every shift of its membership."

"What has that to do with Marshal Rogers?"

"Simply this: that they can understand dealing with him, with one man who can say yes or no and make that decision stand. Your Alliance might not be terribly wise to change that—and I think your Marshal Rogers is not unaware of this."

"If he is, he isn't doing anything about it. No one in Niagra is working harder to reestablish the Council than Rogers."

"I will accept your word on that; I am not privy to such high affairs," Mamboya said. "But I would ask you to consider it in this light: you have, of course, been familiarizing yourself with developments on this project to date, haven't you?"

"Yes."

"And what have you learned?"

Will Holcomb paused, then admitted: "Up until about a year ago, it was a disaster. I've never seen such

57

inefficiency. Decisions that should simply have been *made* took months, decisions that deserved consideration took even longer—and some of the most important ones, from what I've read, were simply never made at all. You've made more progress on this project in the past year than was made in all the time up to the Han Recurrence. This Administrator Keegan of yours must have been an absolute idiot."

"Perhaps. I should not be too hard on Francis Keegan, though, Major. He was a product of his conditioning. Any decision he actually did work up the courage to make was always subject to approval from the Council's Science Advisory Board, which might or might not overrule him, and the Science Advisory Boad was vulnerable to any Councillor who felt like making a speech, whatever his interest or lack of it in science. Tell me, how many times in your experience was the budget or even the continuation of this project used as a pawn, to get some other purpose achieved?"

"Often enough, I suppose."

"Even by your Marshal Rogers. It's no secret that he had little love for the space effort, Major—at least not until Prince Mordred came close to defeating us with it. And now he's placed the project under the control of the military, where it is largely safe within the confines of the defense budget and he can use his full influence as commander of the armed forces to clear away any further obstructions."

"I see nothing objectionable in that."

"Oh, neither do I; I don't believe there *is* anything objectionable in it. But what I am saying is that it is perhaps more significant how this is interpreted outside the Alliance than within it. Most of the world, Major, is run by strong men, individuals, who rule because they can command the resources to feed and defend their peoples. And your Marshal Rogers is something that

58

these men can understand."

"Doctor Mamboya, are you suggesting that Marshal Rogers should be left in command of the government because it would make the rest of the world feel better?"

"Kings have been crowned for less valid reasons."

"Not here. And that isn't Marshal Rogers' style—probably less his than anyone else in the Alliance."

"Of course."

It was a small apartment, and the whole of her world. The Princess Lu-an stood by the single window of the single room they had allowed her. Aside from a phone-screen and the frequent visitors—academics, mostly, and military historians, all out to rummage through her memories as if they were a gaggle of antiquarians digging through a pile of dubious curios—it was her sole contact with the outside world—and it opened out onto the commons of the Four Towers rather than open countryside, so that the power of her captors filled her horizons as completely as it occupied her awareness.

She did not wish for more. She had access to ample literature and electronic entertainments, though they had the peculiar sharp, vigorous flavor of this young culture, and she could exercise some considerable leeway in agreeing to or refusing interviews. She did not miss being allowed one of her quarters for recreation: walking among the humans she could never avoid the feeling that she was nothing more than a prize on display, and for all their conscious civility towards her she was ever aware of the repressed hostility and hatred of many of those she moved among. So she remained within her apartment, and trusted to the exercises all Han girl-children learned to maintain the tone of her body. It was nothing she was not used to; in such poor straits among the Han she could have expected nothing better, and she knew it.

But there was one visitor she never refused, and he came to her that day.

"This is not wise," she said, "I do not need these visits, and they are dangerous for you."

"I don't come here just for your benefit, Lu-An," Rogers said.

"I would understand if you stopped."

"I won't."

"I am glad."

"Cullen Teder was asking about you again."

"His concern touches me."

"You'd better hope it doesn't. I don't think it would be very healthy for you if he could."

"No better for me than it would be for you if Teder ever finds out that we are lovers."

"That's my problem," Rogers said, "and I can handle it."

"I know," Lu-An said. She crossed the room and sat down on the small couch against one wall, drawing her legs up beneath her. The loose tunic and breeches she wore made her seem even slighter than she was, measured against Rogers' greater size. "I could suggest several ways highly recommended among my people."

"Perhaps you could, but don't, please. I need Cullen Teder in the Council, Lu-An. He's a fossil, I know, but he supports me in most things. And I need all the support I can get."

"He would see me dead, Tony," she said quietly. "He remembers the crimes of my people against his. My people are beyond his punishment. I am not."

"Yes, you are." Rogers said. He sat down beside her. "I say you are. And as long as I'm here to say so, you'll stay out of his reach, Lu-An. That's a promise."

Lu-An looked at him for a moment, and then chuckled. "Tony, what you do to my name. Someday I must do something about your pronunciations."

"But not right now, Lu-An."

"No, Tony—not right now."

The sleek needle-shape of the *Mallard*-class personal flyer nosed into the docking-well at the Taos VIP terminal. The heavy flanges slid out from the sides of the well and locked it firmly in place as the jointed metal tongue of the access ramp unfolded towards the passenger hatch.

Cullen Teder strode quickly across the ramp to meet the three men waiting for him. Two he recognized at once: Wood, his executive assistant, a young man with thin brown hair and the look of a Casca about him, lean and hungry; and Helden, the commander of the Southwest's irregular militia and as a man who commanded military not under the direct control of the Council someone to be courted, face dark and sharply planed above his sand-colored jumpsuit. But it was the third man who spoke first, and at the sound of his voice Cullen placed a name to his face.

"Did you speak to Marshal Rogers about my dismissal?" Francis Keegan asked. He had a thin voice, capable of shrillness if not force; there was nothing else thin about him.

"Yes, I did," Cullen said, continuing on past him. Wood and Helden fell in briskly behind him; Keegan made the mistake of trying to trot along side him. The peripheral awareness of the little man scuttling along at his side annoyed Cullen.

"And what happened? What did he say?"

"Make an appointment to see me in my office," Cullen said. "I don't hold meetings on the street."

Wood and Helden neatly slid past Keegan as the cab slid up on its single track. The door was closed and the cab pulling away before he could decide to try to bull his way in after them.

The cab slid smoothly away from the terminal and out into the hot desert sun, fierce even through the smoked canopy.

"Now, what's this about Han?" Cullen Teder asked.

"Sir, there's nothing definite—" Wood started to say.

"A fishing gang's been massacred up on the Northwest Coast," Helden interrupted him. "Tallpines."

"Never heard of them."

"No reason you should have, sir," Wood said promptly, and made a show of consulting a sheaf of notes in his hands. "It used to come under the jurisdiction of the Coastal SubCouncil before the Recurrence. Technically, we've administered it since, but they're way up north, in some godforsaken corner of Old Washington, and they pretty much tend to their own affairs."

"Tended," Helden said.

"So how did we hear of this massacre, then?"

"They did some occasional trading with other gangs farther south, the Friscans and Big Sur, mostly. A Trader from Frisca called there and found their village burned out, before he was attacked by a survivor. He lost two crew before they could subdue him. The Tallpineser claimed his fishing boat was sunk by a Han airship that went on to attack the village. He thought the trader was the Han returning."

"That's all your evidence? A few burned-out buildings and a hysterical fisherman?"

Helden shook his head. "There's enough confirmation besides his word. The fire was supposed to look as if it had swept downwind out of the forest. That's not impossible up there, they do have a fire problem—but forest fires don't start from a series of equidistant blast points. And the people in the village had to be dead before the fire reached them. There was no sign of any attempt to fight the fire or evacuate the people. To judge from the way the bodies were distributed, that entire gang had to have died where they stood, within seconds of one another."

"And the fire was set to conceal the true cause of death?"

"Most probably."

"All right, fine. We'll accept that that gang was wiped out deliberately; but what makes you so sure it was a Han attack?"

"Those people had to have died almost instantly, and they had to have been killed by some weapon whose operation wold be indetectable, to avoid alarming them. The Alliance Armed Forces have such a weapon: they took it from the Prl'lu troops the Han employed during the Recurrence. There's no reason to assume that the Han didn't as well."

Cullen Teder scowled, rubbing one fist.

"Commander Helden, do you realize what you're telling me?"

"I believe I do, sir."

"You're saying that there is still a concentration of Han, right here in North America, with the capacity to mount an organized military effort against us, and that they are currently engaging in open hostilities against humanity."

"Yes, sir," Helden said. "How soon can you report this to Niagra?"

"I'm not going to," Cullen said.

"Sir?" Wood and Helden, together.

"How strong can these Han be, Commander?"

"I wouldn't want to guess, sir; I haven't got the necessary information."

"I'll tell you how strong they are," Cullen said. "They

aren't. If they had any real military capacity, they'd be attacking considerably bigger targets than fishing villages, and they wouldn't be trying to conceal the fact. These are Han, dammit; arrogance comes as naturally to them as breathing. If they had any kind of real power, we'd know about it, believe me."

"What are you getting at?" Helden asked.

"Sir, we *have* to notify Niagra about something like this," Wood said.

"No, I don't think so. I respect Marshal Rogers, Wood; he's done some good work. But he's soft on the Han. I wouldn't care to speculate on his reasons, but the simple fact of the matter is that if there are Han out there, I don't think he's quite strong enough to do what needs doing."

"Sir," Helden said, carefully, "are you suggesting that we usurp the authority of the Alliance Council and take independent action in this matter?"

"Commander, I am *suggesting* that we, and you, do precisely what we, and you, are charged with doing—act to protect and serve the people in our charge. I am not inclined to believe that the Han still have a major military presence on this continent. I am fully confident that the local forces under your command are completely capable of dealing with this threat. That is preferable to running back to Niagra and asking them to wipe our noses for us, in my mind. Now, in your capacity as Commander of the Southwest SubCouncil's irregular forces, what action do you propose to take in this matter?"

"Well, sir. . . ."

The large screen on the wall of Commander Helden's office glowed with a phosphor-dot map of the American West Coast, distorted and driven inland still by the slowly retreating ocean. Small blue dots marked the major gang nexi scattered throughout what had long before been Colorado, New Mexico, Arizona—arbitrary sectionings of land long since replaced in name by identification with the Gangs that now inhabited them, Pueblans, Canyon, Chiricahua and others. Smaller red dots indicated the disposition of major Alliance forces; similar green dots the bases of irregular troops that Helden could draw upon. All of these dots were laced most thickly through the southern and eastern portions of the region, more thinly to the north and west. Beyond the latitude of old Oregon they were reduced to an occasional pinprick of color; by the time one reached dead Tallpines, there were no red dots within three hundred kilometers, south or east.

"Plainly, the center of our operations will have to be the Tallpines site, for now, as it's the only point of contact we've uncovered so far. Our main problem in initiating any action will be in deploying sufficient manpower in the region."

"Why?"

"Our forces are thin up there, very thin. Most of the garrisons that would normally be responsible for the defense of the region were evacuated along with the civilian population ahead of the flooding that resulted from the melting of the Antarctic ice-cap. Since then, they've mostly been incorporated into our own units down here, or dispersed in defense of the relocation settlements. This was never any real threat to our overall defense coverage of the region, since the forces remaining up north were more than adequate to give warning of any attack in time for our air defense units to respond. But now we're talking about mounting an extensive combined forces operation to locate and neutralize this Han strongpoint, and we just don't have the men on the ground to do the job."

"How do you plan on getting around this?"

Helden touched several buttons on the desk before him and a scattering of green dots vanished from their places to reappear clustered at the top of the map. "The only way I can. I'll have to strip the irregulars garrisoning the smaller gang next down south from their posts and send them north, and fill their slots as best I can with relocated troops from the north."

"Why? Why not just send the northern units back to their old ground?"

"Because there's no justifiable reason. The troops we have up there already, are all that can really be accounted for. There's nothing else up there that needs defending. But by sending southern troops north and moving the northern irregulars into the southern garrisons, I can justify it as a training maneuver to familiarize both elements with areas of the region in which they might have to operate one day. Presented like that, the Alliance Command will accept it, and we shouldn't have to worry about interference from Niagra."

"How about air support?"

"We can work that in stages from our bases down here; range isn't a problem and it saves us having to relocate the necessary support units."

"I see." Cullen frowned at the display before him. The thinned cluster of green dots around the gang nexi of the south disturbed him. "I'm not sure I like this, Commander. Those northern units are nothing like the equal of our own troops. This maneuver of yours leaves us pretty thin down here."

"That can't be avoided. If you need men up north, they have to come from somewhere. The only way to fill the gap would be to petition the Alliance Council for regular troops, and you'd never get them without explaining why you want them."

"That's out of the question," Cullen said. "If we explained why we want them, we'd never be allowed to use them to do what's necessary here."

"Then this is how it will have to be, if you insist on restricting this operation to irregular troops. There is a risk involved, but it's a minor one. Our air defenses should not be significantly affected, and in the event of a real emergency the regular garrisons in the area would be sure to take up some of the load. It's workable."

"All right," Cullen said, after a pause. "Let's do it, then."

The hundred and fifty thousand-strong population of the Southwest SubCouncil, the aggregate of one hundred and seventeen gangs, flexed briefly, and contracted, squeezing out some small portion of its number from routine jobs and ordinary lives. Fifteen thousand men and women donned uniforms worn only in training before, and took up weapons they had never fired at an enemy, and prepared to follow Helden at Cullen Teder's command.

A handful among them, perhaps a few hundred, were officers and noncoms of the regular military, training cadre assigned to the irregulars: these were veterans of the Peruvian campaign of three years ago. They found themselves sought out by the uncertain for sage advice on the upcoming effort. The result was not always encouraging.

Klein ducked his head to carry the bulky ration carton through the hatchway into the hold of the personnel carrier. It was his ship; his in the sense that he was one of its jump-belt infantry contingent, one of the ten men and women the carrier would ferry into combat and jettison before rushing off to join the ground-support squadrons. Loading the supplies was heavy work in the blistering afternoon sun: there was entirely too much time spent stumbling back and forth with the crates and far too little time spent in the cramped but cool and dark interior of the inertron-shielded flyer. He had quickly folded back the cushioning hood that was part of his uniform and worn under his battle helmet and rolled up his sleeves, but his feet were swimming in their own sweat in his high, tightly fastened jump-boots. He looked up and saw Morales, his squad leader, standing back and watching—"overseeing", the old bastard would have called it—Klein and his squadmates stuffing the carrier. Morales stood in a letter-perfect at-ease stance, hood up, uniform immaculately creased, zipped and fastened—it didn't hurt that he was standing in the shadow of the piled supply crates—except for his pants' legs, which he wore loose outside his boots. He always wore them that way, him and a couple of the company-level officers, also regular military, in spite of the disapproval of their irregular superiors. But it had never occurred to Klein to question why until then, in the sudden incongruity of seeing him so impeccably dressed in that sweltering heat.

"Hey, sergeant, you dress in a hurry this morning?"

"What's your problem, *compad*?" Morales asked, his accent softened by the abbreviated descendant of Old Spanish that was his native tongue.

"How come you and the regulars always wear your pants loose like that?"

"It lets your feet breathe," Morales said, "And it keeps your ankles from chafing on long jumps. But there's a better reason. Lieutenant Dubrow told it to the Major once, and he didn't like it. That's why you have to wear yours tucked in like that."

"Yeah. What was it?"

"First time somebody takes a shot at you and you let go in your britches, you lose it on the next jump instead of carrying it all over the battlefield."

"There's no way it works," Merrit said.

"I know." Baker stared unhappily at the table of organization and flight schedules scattered over his desk in the Wing Commander's office. The 52nd Pursuit Wing had been presented with an intriguing challenge: they were ordered to organize full air support for the northern region maneuvers due to start in four days, from their base at Barstow *and* without withdrawing from their slots in the air defense envelope covering the southern region. It was a bitch—the *Falcon*-class pursuits the 52nd flew were damned fine aircraft, even if they were no match for the Makos now filtering west as the more prestigious units back East came up to their full strength, but they couldn't be in two places at once.

"There's only one thing I think we could try," Baker said to Merrit. "There's a squadron of *Shrike* advanced trainers stationed outside of Fresno. Maybe we can talk Regional into tying them into the patrol net."

"Shrikes? What's the point? Those flying greenhouses aren't even armed."

"We can retrofit ordnance on schedule. And they'll fill holes. Tying them in will free fifteen Falcons right there for use up north, and I think we can plug a few more holes by having the craft flying support for the maneuvers cover the northern approaches on their way up and back." He looked at his Wing Commander. "It's the only way that might work."

"All right," Merrit finally said. "But I'll talk to Regional. We'll want those toys transferred directly under Pursuit Command for the duration. I won't stand for having to use halfway improvisations *and* having to put up with twice the desk work at the same time."

"How'm I doing, Heric?" Rogers leaned forward and refilled his glass from the half-emptied bottle on the table between the two men, thankful that at least limited relations had finally been reopened between the American Alliance and the Free Republic of Ireland. The locally-produced drink was no worse than anything Rogers had ever bought on the quiet back in the Prohibition days of his first life, but there was no improving on the original.

"Well, that has to be a relative judgment, of course, Tony," Wolsky said. "You haven't attempted to strangle anybody in my presence, you haven't grossly offended any high officials of this or any other government recently, and you haven't declared war on the Federation Canadien all week, so in that sense you're calming down admirably. But—" and he punctuated his exception with a raised index finger, "—you have still been working what I would consider medically excessive hours. Aside from the fact that you're running your staff off their feet, I would remind you that there is such a thing as sleep, and even you need it, Marshal."

"I know, Heric, I know," Rogers said. "But there's just so damned much that needs to be done. In a month the new Council will be officially seated, and there are some things that I have to see begun and established before then."

"Like putting the space project under military control?"

"Yeah, like that. Like the open trade agreement between us and the European Confederacy. Like twenty other things I could name."

"You seem to enjoy playing the power-broker, Tony."

"Shouldn't I? If I can get these things established and rolling before the Council is seated and everything grinds to a halt while they review and debate and legislate, it only makes sense to do it, right?"

"True. I only wonder what you will do to keep busy once you hand over to the Council."

"Don't worry, Heric, I'll think of something." Rogers chuckled. "Believe me, I'd *love* to have that problem. Running this country has been like trying to work out a fringe benefits clause with a Wobbly."

Heric looked at him with a puzzled frown. "A what?"

"International Workers of the World?" Rogers asked. Heric Wolsky shrugged, uncomprehending. "Never mind," Rogers said. "Something like a Han, only not as civic-minded. No fun, no fun at all. No, Wol, between the job itself and the people they're giving me to work with, I'll be happy to let go."

"You're having trouble with your staff? Aren't you satisfied with their work?"

"I wouldn't know," Rogers said, "I haven't seen any of their work to be dissatisfied with. They gave me a new aide to make up for Will Holcomb." Wolsky nodded. "Well, somebody down in Personnel or wherever decided to curry a little favor with me and stuck me with one of my own great-grandsons."

"He isn't working out?"

"I'll give him this much—he doesn't expect to be paid to exist. I think he knows nobody would make him an offer."

"As bad as that?"

"Just about; he's thirty-seven years old and if I didn't rate a captain as my aide he'd never have made it past second lieutenant. If I ever find out who bucked his file up front I'll personally put him in charge of shovelling the sidewalks at the Antarctic complex."

"If he's so inept, why not just get rid of him?"

"I'm afraid to. God only knows what damage he

might do if he wasn't where I could keep an eye on him." Rogers sipped at his drink and sighed wearily. "No, forget it, Wol; I'm exaggerating. He isn't *that* bad —he just isn't as good as Will Holcomb was."

"No, he probably is not," Wolsky said. "But there is more to it than that, Tony."

"Yeah? Like what?"

"Well, don't forget, Tony, that appearances to the contrary, you are a man well into his eighties. A person that age often becomes set in his ways. For all that you admit that Will Holcomb was too competent to be wasted running your errands, you had several years to get used to working through him, and now you resent his absence."

"Good lord. Senility at thirty. What a way to go."

"No, no, Tony, nothing of the kind. Your brain was every bit as thoroughly rejuvenated as the rest of your body. You just have eighty years of habit and idiosyncrasies to deal with."

"Oh, well, that's a real relief, Wol; I'm happy to hear that. I had enough to worry about putting a country back together and dealing with a half-witted staff. I'm glad to know I won't have to listen to my old war stories into the bargain."

"I thought you'd appreciate that."

"I mean, it's not as if I already had enough problems. It isn't as though Mordred was back for another go or anything like that."

Wolsky laughed and held up a warding hand. "Please, Tony, don't even suggest that."

"Why not?" Rogers asked, suddenly serious. "It's going to happen, you know. That's the main reason for all my rushing. We've got to get this country back in one piece before it does."

"I hope you're wrong," Wolsky said.

"I don't think I am."

"But it's been three years."

"It was forty years, the time before that. And there's no evidence that we finished the job then."

"He could be dead."

"No." Rogers even surprised himself with the urgency with which he said that. "The Mordreds of this world don't die by accident. And it's for sure we never got him."

"He may have made another attempt at reviving the Prl'lu, ones we don't know about. They may have turned on him again."

"Not likely." Rogers shook his head. "If he'd revived any more Prl'lu, we'd have known about it by now."

"Why?"

"They'd have taken us." That was part of the reason. There was more, but neither man spoke of. Mordred would never move against the race led by his own father without announcing it to the world.

Rogers scowled into his drink. Mordred hated him, he knew that; he hated him enough to sacrifice thousands of his own people and put an entire world at risk for a chance at revenge. And, Rogers knew, he would do it again and again, for as long as it was in his power to try.

But he could not hate him.

He would resist him. He would oppose Mordred at every turn and if the chance came Rogers believed he would kill him—this strange world and the second life it offered him deserved that much in return for all the good years it had given him since that day in 1927 when the roof of an old mine had collapsed behind him, cutting off the world he had known. But he could find no hatred for this enemy who was his son. Guilt, yes: he could find guilt for the wrong he could not deny having done Mordred's mother, the Han concubine Ngo-Lan.

And Rogers knew a sense of loss, as he had for three years now, that he would never have the chance to know this siring of his, who had the will and the strength to challenge worlds.

Heric Wolsky understood Rogers' silence; he had met this mood before and knew what it signified.

"He could have been lying, you know."

"No." Rogers shook his head. "He wasn't, and I won't, Wol. I did before, to the whole world, because it was convenient and because frankly it was safer. But I won't lie to you and I won't lie to myself. I can't. There are things you can deny and things you can't deny, because they'll come looking for you whether you admit them or not."

The world dropped away beneath him as Klein kicked out away from the carrier's stern drop-hatch, to drift slowly earthward as the ship rushed away from him at five hundred kilometers an hour. There was a brief hurricane blast of wind as he continued to rush forward, then wind resistance had absorbed the forward momentum of his tumbling flight, to leave him drifting gently downward.

He uncurled from his protective tuck and found himself hanging alone in the sky three hundred meters from the ground. He twisted, orienting himself according to the compass on his wrist, so that the jumpers five hundred meters ahead and behind him were now to either side, floating to the ground in line with him. He spared himself a quick glance upward to see his carrier banking and climbing away to join the other carriers of his company, now forming into a ground support element high above the ground troops. Turning back to the ground, he saw tiny shapes coursing along scant feet above the earth and moving into the distance: the company's flying-belt squad, reconnoitering the area of operations ahead of the dropping jump infantry. The earphones of his battle helmet picked up their terse reports to the waiting carriers, clearing section after section for their drops.

Klein touched down and jumped at once, following procedure, not resting at his landing point to offer a target. In a long line to either side of him men and women were doing the same, moving out along their planned courses. Gaps appeared here and there along the line, as long-gun teams and *dis*-squads dropped back and set up their heavy weapons to cover the advance. The holes they left were quickly filled by troops of the second company to drop, while the rest of their unit advanced in a second line, spaced between and behind Klein's company, and their carriers climbed to join the formation overhead.

Moving in low, quick bounds the troops quickly entered thick forest, soon losing sight of each other, reminded of the presence of their comrades only by the occasional gasps of exertion and brief progress reports sounding through their ultrophones. Klein relaxed a bit, out of sight now of the critical eyes of his superiors. It was the third day of the operation. Working outward from the remains of Tallpines, Helden's irregulars were searching in a methodical grid pattern for any sign of the Han redoubt they knew must exist. It was a straightforward strategy: two companies, rotated for rest after each day's activity, would fan out and cross a grid back and forth with a fine-tooth comb, with their own carriers for immediate support and the rest of the force, nearly two full regiments strong, held in reserve for a massive response. Local troops provided intelligence and assisted in reconnaisance. And far above them all the sleek Falcons of the 52nd Pursuit Wing flew top cover, making the two-hour flight up from Barstow and standing four-hour watches before making the two-hour trip back.

Sunlight broke through the thinning trees ahead. Klein glided down from his last jump some fifty meters short of the tree-line and proceeded the rest of the way on foot. He reported his location to Morales and heard the grizzled regular's acknowledgement, cut short by a sharp grunt as he touched down himself.

The settlement didn't look like much, even by Klein's provincial standards—perhaps half a dozen buildings, no more, perhaps just a work station or maybe an expansion settlement of some local gang. Whatever it might have been, there was no movement, no sign of life.

An anonymous voice in his earphones spoke from one of the orbiting carriers and a flying trooper burst from the trees a hundred meters to Klein's right in a blast of cold-rocket noise. Up and down the edge of the forest a handful of other rocket-beltmen broke from the shelter of the forest and hurtled towards the buildings. Voices murmured quietly in the background of Klein's hearing as someone with the carriers spoke coordinates to the long-gun teams to the rear, and they trained their weapons upon the buildings. Other voices told of the *dis* teams picking up and moving to join the infantry where their line-of-sight weapons would be of the most use.

The first of the flying troopers disappeared between the buildings. His mates quickly followed him. There was a silence of long minutes as they scouted the buildings and reported back to the command carrier on their separate frequency. Then the order came to advance, and Klein bounded into the open, weapon at the ready.

Three families had lived there once. It had been a logging village, the family dwellings separated by small toolsheds and a garage for a heavy-duty floater, still tightly lashed to its moorings.

The dead tallied six adults and four children, one an infant found in its crib, unseeing eyes fixed on the ceiling above it. They had been moved from their scattered places about the compound and lined up in the shade of the garage. The flying troopers were using their rain-capes to cover them until body-bags could be provided. They had more than enough capes; one would cover two children easily. Klein got a glimpse of the face of one woman before a trooper laid his cape over her. There was no fear in that expression, no pain, no comprehension. Klein's hand moved almost of its own volition to the cardiogard disc adhering to his own breast, as if seeking the reassurance of its presence.

The dead were still covered by the troopers' capes when the carrier glided in to pick them up. The troopers stood by, waiting patiently until all the bodies had been transferred to the tough foil burial bags before retrieving their capes and rolling them. They had never considered using blankets or sheets from one of the houses; this was something they did for the dead, and it never occurred to them to use something other than their own for the purpose.

Tactics were changed, the search patterns altered to start from known population centers. Three more times they came upon the same mortal tableau; Klein and his company were the first into one of the villages again.

Each location was noted and plotted. Every body was counted and collected. As the grim search continued Morales and the regulars retreated behind a wall of black, silent unapproachability, but they were not unaware of the horror and anger each new atrocity inspired in their inexperienced troops. It would be unfair and not a little callous, to say that they actually approved of the anguish of the men and women they commanded, but each of the regulars silently held the view that it was just as well that their charges finally learn what it was that they had trained to defend against.

They found another village the next day. . . .

"Illustrious Scion of the Heaven-Born, it is my burdensome duty to report a threat to our proud city."

"Then you must share this burden, oh dutiful servant," Ho-Tin said, "else it may prove too overwhelming, and force us to grant you less demanding responsibilities in the future."

"As you wish, Excellency," the face in the screen sketched a brief bow, little more than a nod, all that the dimensions of the screen would allow in the way of protocol. The screen beside him lit up with a map of the surrounding countryside. Six small white dots appeared on the landscape.

"If it would please His Most Excellent Majesty to deign notice my humble presentation, I would ask him to note the markers I have taken the liberty of supplying to denote the sites of our first blows against the barbarian Americans."

"We see them. Where is the threat of which you speak?"

"If you will permit me, Excellency—" Luminous dotted lines appeared overlaid on the map in pale scarlet, in two sets of six. The lines were drawn through each settlement attacked to that date, and angled to intersect at a common point. One cluster of lines intersected at a point well within the territory occupied by the barbarian humans.

The others came together directly atop the City.

"I regret that it is my duty to suggest that His Excellency may have been the recipient of poor advice from those of his officers who suggested that our first targets be chosen in such close proximity to our own home. I believe that I have devised a way to determine the origin point of our attacks simply from the locations of our targets. As I trust is evident, the plotting system I have devised offers two possible origin points. In this case, one point is of no concern to us. But the other—"

"We are aware of what the other signifies," Ho-Tin said. "Why was this threat not noted before? I was told that each attack had been planned with the utmost safety in mind."

"A thousand apologies, Excellency, would be insufficient to rectify such an oversight. I believe that each attack was indeed so planned—but only for the individual mission in question, and not for the campaign as a whole."

"Indeed. What is your name, warrior?"

"Ken-li, Your Magnificence, Sub-Commander in your Chamber of Tactics."

"So. Note, Sub-Commander, that we are indebted to you for this service, and shall make appropriate payment."

"His Excellency is too generous. I had no thought but for my duty to my Prince and my City."

"Truly." Ho-Tin studied the face on his screen. Young. Hungry. Useful? Perhaps that, as well. "We are aware of the problem this presents, Sub-Commander. We trust there is a solution?"

"I believe there is. If His Excellency will grace my presentation with his attention—" The map on the second screen seemed to withdraw from Ho-Tin, drawing more and more of the continent within its confines. As the scale increased the lights surrounding the city dwindled and drew together into a single bright spark. Other sparks began to appear now, marking settlements of the hated humans. "Allow me the presumption to suggest that in great part this difficulty that has arisen is due to the unfortunate proximity of our chosen targets to our beloved city. However, if we were to broaden the area of our attacks—" and here each settlement light pulsed once, brightly"—then the area the barbarians would be forced to search would be correspondingly enlarged, indeed, enlarged far out of proportion to the area of our actual operations. Therefore, I would venture to suggest an immediate extension of our attacks to include the settlements to the extreme south of this coast."

"But would not such a long journey render our ships more vulnerable to detection and tracking? We seem to recall that this was an argument initially advanced in favor of confining our activities to this region."

"Your pardon, Excellency, but I believe that threat may be avoided by routing our fleets out over the sea, here—" and a dotted line curved its way out over the Pacific and back in again "—and thus avoiding the coastal settlements we must otherwise pass over."

"Indeed. We do consider that sensible." Ho-Tin paused, and then said, "We approve of this course of action. See that the necessary steps are taken to carry it out."

"Excellency, the necessary orders are certainly far beyond the authority of a lowly Sub-Commander."

"True. But the High Captain of our fleets should have the necessary power."

Ken-Li made a creditable show of being surprised for one so young. "Pardon, Your Excellency, but surely I am not worthy of such magnaminity."

"Then prove to us that you are, High Captain. We shall issue the necessary proclamations at once."

"As His Excellency wishes. He may be assured of my uttermost devotion to this task."

"That is well. You are dismissed."

His escape was going perfectly—so far.

Mordred had realized that he would probably never find a better opportunity when he discovered the service tunnels. The gigantic plastics-reprocessing system he had been working around that day had siezed, somehow, filling the room with toxic plastic fumes. Desperate to escape, Mordred had thrown himself through an unimpressive door set in the wall along the narrow walkway that ran the length of the machine. Immediately upon his closing the door again, he had found himself in a narrow corridor, well-lit, the air perfectly good. There was a fine patina of dust upon the floor, plainly stating that the corridor saw little use. Moving along it, he discovered that it intersected another tunnel, and that one, yet another still. At that point he had been discovered by a working party of Yun-Yun caste repairmen. It had been a dangerous moment. The Yun-Yun caste were far more aggressive than the sullen workers among whom Mordred had sheltered for so long. Had one of them noticed the inconcealable gray of his eyes, he would have been lost. But Han protocol came to his rescue as it had before. It would be an act of inconceivable temerity for a common Ku-Li laborer to look a Yun-Yun technician directly in the face, as an equal, and so Mordred had stood with eyes correctly downcast and meekly stammered out his explanation of the accident that had driven him by chance into the tunnels. Once his story had been verified, he was safe. A few minutes' abuse, as though the failure of the reprocessor had been his fault, a desultory cuffing about the head and shoulders for his impudence in delaying his betters with his foolishness, and he was taken to an exit and released into the regular streets of the city.

After that he began his methodical exploration of the

tunnels, trying every service entrance he could find and exploring long stretches of them at a time. For safety against the occasional bands of reparimen he carried a bottle of the sort of cheap liquor Ku-Lis favored, and kept a swallow in his mouth at all times. to be hastily gulped down so that he could greet any Yun-Yun who discovered him with a true drunkard's camaraderie, a stumbling embrace and reeking breath. Under those cir- circumstances they never detained him, but he had taken several painful blows and suffered a broken nose that did not promise to set correctly. But he learned his way around the tunnels.

And now he moved through them with a purpose, and a goal. When he had explored he had travelled upward and inland, in search of the dry-land entrances he knew must exist. The arrogant Yun-Yun would never allow their comings and goings to be wholly controlled by their self-styled betters. He was right. They existed. He found them.

Now he followed the long tunnel that took him far out under the land, paralleling the long travelway that linked the central core-city with one of its satellite 'sub- urbs', built to ameliorate population pressure and to serve as an outer defensive bastion. A narrow car-track ran along one wall of the tunnel, but Mordred had not taken one of the available cars, for fear that it would be missed. He walked, keeping as a matter of habit as close to the deep wells of shadow between the widely-spaced light fixtures as possible.

He heard the faint whining before he saw anything. Without hesitating he threw himself into the shadows and under the only cover, the gap between the posts sup- porting the car-track.

There was a sudden glare of headlights and then the car was flashing overhead and gone into the distance ahead of him. Mordred waited until its sound was lost to him, and then rose to his feet with a frown. This was a problem. He would have to watch for the return of the car at the end of its mission, now—or he would have to worry about being discovered somewhere along his path. He shrugged. In either case there was nothing to be done about it then. He continued on his way.

He walked for almost three hours, until the monotonous rotation of lamplight and darkness began to seem all there was of the world. Then, ahead of him, he could see a broader swath of light, and movement. And he heard voices.

He stopped. It was the work party in the car. They were engaged at a terminal that obviously served some mechanism in travelway on the other side of the wall. There was no way past them.

Mordred moved forward cautiously, one patch of shadow, another, until there were only two stretches of dark, covering perhaps sixty feet, between himself and the Yun-Yun party. He knelt slowly and eased his way back under the car-track again.

The light caught him there. One of the repairmen held him inescapably centered in the beam of a hand-torch as the others, with heavy tools or the slender belt-knives common among the Han, spread out to encircle him.

"We were wondering when you would catch up with us," the repairmen with the hand-torch said. A couple of the others—there were five of them in all, he noted—laughed at that.

Mordred stood, and looked at them. There was no point in any further pretense; no Ku-Li could have strayed as far as he had come. He did not act the fool; he did not grope for plausible lies. Instead he faced them, and raised his head so that his pale eyes gleamed in the torchlight. The laughter stopped. One of the repairmen breathed a blasphemous question.

, "It's the outblood fugitive," the repairman with the torch said. He turned to one of the others. "Notify the Man-Dins, and have a party meet us out in the travelway."

"I don't think that's wise," Mordred said calmly. "Hand me over to the Man-Dins and you hand the secret of your illegal exits over to them as well."

The repairman with the torch grinned in the faint back-glow of his light. "No, that would not be wise, bastard. But then we never meant to deliver you alive." He made a curt, imperative gesture with his head. "Kill him."

He stepped back with his torch. One of the repairmen had gone back to the car to relay the torchman's message. That left three men to kill him, advancing with prybar, knife and welding-rods. They advanced easily, unafraid. They saw nothing to fear.

They underestimated Mordred's teachers. The Ki-Ling had not stinted on his education. His tutoring in military theory had been complemented with training in soldier's skills of a far more pragmatic nature.

The repairman with the prybar attacked first, lunging forward and swinging his weapon down overhand like a woodsman's axe. Mordred leaped back and caught the shaft of the bar between his crossed forearms. As the bar struck he pivoted on one foot and drove the other into his attacker's midriff. The repairman staggered backward, losing the prybar as Mordred grabbed it in both hands, gripping it by the ends and swinging it down and across his body to strike away the knife arm of the second repairman as he rushed in. As the man stumbled past him Mordred drew the bar back and stabbed it at the base of the man's skull. The repairman fell and did not move; Mordred rushed upon the man he had wrested the prybar from and dealt him the blow that man had meant for him.

Sparks flew as the repairman with the welding rods struck at him and Mordred barely parried his first attack. The Prince leaped back, arms numbed by the vicious electrical shock the rods had transmitted to him through the bar. The only reason he still lived was that both rods had failed to contact the prybar simultanously; even so it had been near enough for current to arc.

The repairman circled him, the rods held out chest-high before him. The connecting cables were taut from rod-grips to the spring-loaded reels at each hip of the power-harness belt. There was no way Mordred could hook them; they were effectively shielded by the repairman's arms—even if he had he could never have torn one loose before he was electrocuted.

The repairmen's leader circled him with the hand-torch, its glowbobbing and weaving distractingly around him. The other surviving repairman had reached their track-car and was shouting for help into a phone there. And the welder leaped at him with the rods at full extension.

Mordred dodged to the side and parried, against the welder's arm rather than rods. Already off-balance from his lunge, the blow to his arms sent the welder stumbling past Mordred. The rods stuck the wall of the tunnel. Metal slagged and splattered, and spat molten droplets into the welder's unprotected face. He screamed and dropped the rods, clutching at his face. Mordred ended his pain for him.

The leader turned and bolted for the car. Mordred threw himself after him, overtaking him in a desperate sprint and striking at him in passing. He didn't pause to see the effect of his blow, but kept right on running towards the final repairman in the track-car. The repairman dropped the phone and grabbed for the controls of the car. It lurched into motion back towards the city as Mordred reached it. Stretching desperately, he had time for one swing of the prybar as the car rushed past him. Its safety mechanism brought it to a halt ten metres down the tunnel as the driver's lifeless hands slipped from the controls and he slumped forward to rest his crushed head against the dash.

Far down the corridor, Mordred could see the faint spark of a second car's headlights. There would be no fighting these; alerted, they would be armed. He threw aside the prybar and pulled the dead repairman from the driver's seat of the car. Ignoring the foul stains on the seat, he threw the throttles forward and sent the car rushing down the tunnel, away from the city and his pursuers.

It was an agonizingly slow chase. The cars were governed so as not to exceed a speed of more than sixty-five kph. The only thing in Mordred's favor was that his pursuers were capable of no greater speed, and that the narrow, vulnerable tunnel precluded the use of *dis* or explosive rockets. His biggest problem now was whether or not the Yun-Yun would have thought to have a party waiting for him at the end of the travelway.

To his surprise, the small terminal at the tunnel's hidden exit was deserted. He jumped from the car, and still no one accosted him. He rummaged quickly through the chests of tools still in the car, and found a spanner that he could use to wedge the throttles down in their reverse position. The car pulled away, accelerating down the track towards the pursuing headlights in the distance. The car's safety systems would prevent any collision, but they would also stop both cars until Mordred's hunters could clear the throttles and send his car back up the track after him.

Mordred paused briefly to check his supplies. They were meagre enough, all that he could obtain and hoard on his small laborer's credit-stipend. Two changes of clothing, a few packages of dried fruit and subsistence-level protein roll, two light, warm blankets of synthetic fiber and one foil oversheet, a hard-copy map of the surrounding region that he had ordered over a public access screen, and a six-inch belt knife of keen, noncorrosive alloy. The knife rested at his hip, the map folded into a tunic pocket. The rest made a long, flexible bundled rolled into the blankets and oversheet, with a waist-sash fastened into a sling to carry it. It was all he would really need in any case, he thought—he was setting out to survive in the world, not subdue it. Not for now.

He turned and undogged the narrow, heavy door that led to the surface. Shutting it behind himself, he found himself standing in a long, tall shaft, facing a narrow ladder encased in an occasional retaining ring, put there more for the reassurance of any climber than for actual protection. The only illumination came from a pale red light lamp set in one wall.

Mordred started to climb. The bulk of the ladder was shrouded in darkness; the only other illumination in the whole of the tube was a dim red glow similar to the one he was climbing out of, far ahead at the top of the ladder.

He climbed. There was no way to rush in the darkness —for all his awareness of pursuit he had to force himself to search out each rng carefully and establish a firm grip on it before shifting his feet. He held his body tightly in against the ladder, fighting the growing urge to simply sag back against his grip on the rungs. And he climbed. A hundred feet; two hundred; two hundred and fifty. He was more than three hundred feet above the base of the tunnel and a scant thirty feet from the platform at the top of the ladder when the *dis*-beam hit him.

Only the distance saved him. His first awareness of the attack was the faint tingling he felt on the backs of his hands and neck. As he looked closely in the red light he suddenly realized that the fine hairs that should have been there were gone, leaving his skin bare, pocked only with barren follicles. Then, as he watched, he saw small white flakes begin to peel off his very skin, like some savage mutant eczema.

He knew then what was happening. His pursuers had reached the base of the ladder. They were refraining from using sure but noisy projectile weapons on him, but a relatively silent *dis* weapon was another matter. He began to climb for his very life, knowing that he had to get out of their line of fire before the *dis* beam, even attenuated by distance as it was, caused him a crippling injury that would be the same as death that high up—or before they thought to add other *dis*-beams and bring their cumulative effect against him. Panic lent speed to his movements, panic born of the knowledge that every second he remained on that ladder he was slowly *dissolving*, the very stuff of his body rotting away under the erosion of the ray.

There was a sudden snap and his pack started to drop, the delicate material of its sash/strap eaten through. He snapped his head forward and just managed to catch the end of the strap as it whipped over his shoulder. Then he found himself looking down through his legs, at the tiny pinpoint of blue far below him, and instantly shut his eyes before the *dis*-beam could blind him. Sightless now, he groped his way upward.

Suddenly his searching hand found only emptiness above him. He flailed about frantically for a instant before he found the sudden curve in the handrail, where it bent over the lip of the exit platform. In a sudden hysterical rush he threw his bundle up over the edge and clawed his way after it, the abrupt proximity of safety straining the barriers of his control more strongly any threat of *dis* could have.

He lay on the broad platform for several seconds, regaining his breath, aware for the first time of the faint breeze blowing over him as the air in the tube rushed to dispersion in the *dis*-beam behind him. After a moment, the breeze stopped as his pursuers below stopped their useless firing.

He took brief stock of his condition. The backs of his hands and neck had been stripped clean of hair, and the immature skin prematurely exposed by the vanished epidermis had the red, angry look of a moderate case of sunburn. He brushed at the side of his face where it had been exposed to the *dis*-beam during the last part of the climb: bits of eyebrow and flaked skin came off in his palm. He half-whimpered in relief as he realized that his sight, as best he could judge in the dim red light, had not been harmed. His pants' legs had a frayed, worn look about them, like cloth that had been scrubbed and washed too many times. The sash he had used to fasten his bundle was almost useless, mere threads were all that still held it together. Ripping and knotting it, he salvaged enough usable material to allow him to make up a shorter strap for the bundle, that he could still slip over one shoulder if not more securely across his chest, as he would have liked. His pack itself seemed intact, the foil oversheet having proved more resistant to the thinned *dis* than normal fabric.

Rising to his feet, he searched out and worked the controls that operated the smaller of the two doors before him. The door opened onto another chamber, with a—shorter, thankfully—ladder leading up to a circular hatch. Mordred quickly mounted the ladder and spun the dogging-wheel set above him.

The lights went out. He felt a brief stab of alarm, then realized that he should have expected it. The Yun-Yun would not have designed a secret exit that announced its presence by shining out a bright red light every time the door was opened.

He pushed on the hatch and it popped open a crack, momentarily blinding him with a thin bar of daylight. He squinted and blinked in it until his eyes had adjusted; then he pushed the hatch open several inches further and looked out.

He saw a stretch of sweeping, narrow beach, that swung off to his right and then curved back, to end in a rocky point that culminated in a single gnarled, defiant little pine sapling. Waves of indifferent height threw themselves in desultory fashion against the thin strip of sand that seemed to oppose them out of little more than habit. Nothing else moved.

It looked safe enough, and there was nothing else to do, so he threw the hatch fully open and climbed out into the light. He turned and looked behind the hatch, and found that he was standing in a cluster of boulders, that effectively concealed anybody emerging from the hatch from observing eyes further inland.

A subdued hissing at his feet made Mordred look down. The hatch was closing, apparently of its own accord. There was a metallic clamping sound as it touched down and then it was gone, looking like nothing more than another rock in the pile.

For a moment everything that Mordred had planned and intended crumbled inside him under the weight of the single realization that he was committed now, on his own, more utterly and completely than he had been ever before, at any time, in his life. Even during his existence as a despised bastard among the Han, he had never been thrown so completely upon his own resources. There had always been somebody else at least somewhat on his side, if only to the extent of insuring that a valuable experimental animal was not irreparably damaged.

But now he had none of that. He was alone, in a world where no one could be counted upon to help him. All he had was what he was.

Then that would just have to be enough. He started to make his way through the rocks, heading for the trees that backed the beach.

They were waiting for him.

"*Red Leader, this is Sky Five.*"

"*Aknol, Sky Five, Report.*"

"*Reporting zero presence along the coast, grid six-three. Am commencing inland leg—wait a minute. . . . Red Leader, this is Sky Five reporting an unidentified ground party on the beach, grid six-three, exact coordinates three-five-seven by four-four, do you copy?*"

"*Sky Five, three-five-seven by four-four, aknol. Go for hard ID.*"

"*Doing that thing, Red Leader—Red Leader, Red Leader, this is Sky Five. I am taking ground fire from unidentified party, rocket and dis. Evasion effective, one hit, no damage. Please advise.*"

"*Sky Five, Sky Five, this is Red Leader. Local intelligence indicates no indigenous dis armament. Assume party Han and respond accordingly. All air, grid six, join Sky Five, three-five-seven, four-four. All ground, all other air, stand by. Aknol, all units. Happy hunting, Sky Five.*"

"*Aknol that, Red Leader. Have targets on tight scope. This is Red Five going in.*"

Mordred froze where he stood as the first Han rose up out of the beach grass bordering the pines, a *dis* hand-weapon trained on him. In the next second half a dozen more appeared from the grass and behind the trees, all armed, some with *dis,* some with light rocket-guns. Now he understood the absence of a trap in the travelway terminal. The Yun-Yun of the sub-city must have decided not to risk a disturbance on their own ground, and played it safe by laying their ambush where anybody emerging from the secret exit would have to walk into it.

The leader of the party stepped forward. His men moved with him and spread out somewhat to each side, so that Mordred remained in their sight. They were alerted by his victory in the tunnels and plainly taking no chances.

"You are prompt, oh exalted Not-Prince," their leader said. "You have spared us the discomfort of a long wait. We appreciate that. For that, this will be done quickly." He handed his *dis*-beam to the man next to him and drew his knife.

Mordred reached for his own knife. "Surely you do not expect me simply to stand here and let myself be stabbed?"

The Yun-Yun killer paused at the sight of Mordred's blade, and then sheathed his own. "It would have been convenient. Otherwise we are faced with the problem of explaining how an armed party of our people just happened to chance across you."

"Forgive me if your convenience is not my prime concern just now."

The Han shrugged. "No matter. We will manage something." He gestured to one of the *dis* men. "Save the head for identification."

The Yun-Yun killer raised his weapon and aimed. Mordred snarled and started for the leader, his footing poor in the loose sand.

Thunder cracked overhead. Startled, Mordred missed his lunge and fell headlong on the beach. He could hear faint, startled cries above the rumbling. Then he realized that he hadn't died, and rolled over hastily.

His attackers had forgotten him in their alarm. They stood looking after a boxy, winged shape banking back towards them, high over the ocean. Mordred didn't hesitate; he scrambled to his feet and ran desperately for the illusory shelter of the trees.

Behind him the aircraft was swooping down towards the Yun-Yun party again. Had they been possessed of even the most rudimentary training, they would have bolted for the treeline at once. Instead, with their city-thug's experience, they could think of only one response.

They fired on the plane. *Dis* and rockets laced through the air around the diving personnel carrier. A rocket exploded against its flank and it swerved away in alarm.

Mordred was deep under the trees by then, and still running. Reaching the safety of a cluster of boulders, he threw himself into a crevice and looked back.

The Yun-Yun assassins had finally seen the sense of taking cover, but too late. Even as they ran for the concealment of the trees, the personnel carrier was diving on them again, this time to strike a blow of its own. Shields of inertron slammed down over its viewports, leaving the ship to maneuver by means of ultroscopes recessed into the hull, that looked out through periscopic reflectors of mirror-polished inertron. *Dis* beams from the killers' weapons swept over the ship, rockets exploded uselessly against its hull, but the carrier lurched through the turbulence and the detonations, intent on striking a blow of its own. The carrier fired, ignoring its heavy misiles and attacking with the lighter rocket guns and the heavy *dis* beam faired into its hull. The treeline erupted, torn by the stream of rockets and gouged by the shaft of intense blue radiance that blazed ahead of the diving ship. The Yun-Yun party died instantly—but too late Mordred realized that the ship's attack run was not stopping, that the carrier was "walking" its fire deeper into the forest—and directly toward him.

The fraction of a second it took him to realize this used up all the time he had left. Mordred could only throw himself reflexively back into the crevice and cover his head with his arms, screaming in useless denial of the death reaching for him, unaware of its prize.

Fire and thunder broke around him; an impossibly fine dust filled the air—and then it was quiet again, the carrier climbing away, and Mordred unharmed.

He looked cautiously out of his hiding place, and was astonished. The rockets had torn the forest to kindling for ten yards to eitherside of him; the *dis* scar, six feet across and a yard deep, ran directly up to his boulders and continued a full fifty meters beyond it—but the rocks themselves still stood.

There was a jolt through the soil beneath his feet and a sound of powerful engines. Mordred hastily jumped clear as the boulders—or the sheathing disguised as boulders—neatly sectioned themselves and slid aside to make way for the massive *dis* projector rising up out of the earth. Mordred understood then. He was still above the sub-city, whose defenders had been stirred into action by the brief battle above their heads. Within seconds he would be in the middle of a savage battlefield utilising energies no lone man could hope to survive.

He ran then, and kept running, with no thought of rest or hiding, as a thousand lightnings burst into life behind him.

"Red Leader, Red Leader, this is Sky Five taking heavy ground fire from multiple sources. All units heading my location, many heavy weapons these coordinates. Am at-

tempting to disengage—oh, Christ, look—'

"Sky Five, Sky Five, this is Red Leader, do you copy? Sky Five, Sky Five, aknol if possible . . . all units full alert, aknol. Ground units grid six, close and contain coordinates three-five-seven by four-four. Do not engage, repeat, do not engage pending arrival full forces. All units, aknol on tactical channels. This is Red Leader to Blue Leader, Red Leader to Blue Leader, aknol. . . ."

"How could they have discovered us?" Ken-Li stood at the head of the table, facing the dozen nervous branch officers of the city's military. "Where was the lapse?"

"Honorable High Captain, the fault was not ours," Sun-Yin, the Sub-Commander in charge of coordination, said. "All shielding systems have been in perfect order for the past three months. The only recorded sorties beyond the city were the covert raids your unlamented predecessor ordered—and the attack you commanded be launched this morning."

"That cannot have been the cause," Ken-Li said flatly. "If that attack was launched out to sea as I ordered, then the accursed Americans cannot possibly have detected them. And if our shielding was in order as you claim, Sub-Commander, then the American ship should have overflown us without suspecting anything. Plainly, he did not. What then, is your explanation?"

"Exalted Commander, I have none. I can but report what the records available to me show."

"Then perhaps we should have a Sub-Commander in charge of coordination who keeps better records—"

"A thousand apologies for this interruption, High Captain," Ken-Sen, in charge of external security, held up a fax-sheet torn from the copy slot of the screen before him.

"Examination of our most recent perimeter records shows an unidentified party of our people on the surface just prior to the initial assault. There is no record of their authorization to leave the city."

"Are they in uniform?"

"Sir, they are not."

"Then we shall assume they are not of the military. They cannot be of the Man-Din or Ki-Ling. for they would have sent the party out through us. So for now, we shall assume that this is some machination of the damned Yun-Yun, who have brought this attack upon us through their traitorous schemings. This is what we shall tell the Prince, gentlemen." He turned to the screen behind him, illuminated with a map of the area surrounding the besieged sub-city. "As for the attack itself, our established defenses seem to be holding thus far. I shall recommend against dispatching any aid from here or the other sub-cities. Should the complex now under attack fall, it may be that Americans will take it for the whole of our presence and not search further. And bear in mind that our attack upon the settlements to the south has yet to occur. It is possible that it shall do sufficient damage to draw the barbarians back there in defense of their hovels. That concludes our summary for now, Sub-Commanders. Attend to your duties."

Sky Five died quickly. The initial *dis*-beam had missed its target, and the carrier's pilot brought it quickly around to salvo his missiles against the point of attack. But before he could take any further evasive action he was trapped in a latticework of *dis* fired from a score of emplacements. The carrier tumbled wildly downward and into the midst of the first volley of heavy missiles flaming upward. The inertron shielding held, and the strong ultron skeleton beneath it, but the massive concussion ripped electrical connections loose, tore away hydraulic lines, rattled men in their harnesses like rats in the jaws of some savage terrier. Broken and useless, the carrier drifted slowly downward, bearing its dead crew within.

The other nine carriers of Sky Five's company swept in low over the ground, grimly intent on avenging their dead comrade. At their tree-top level only the heavy weapons in their immediate vicinity could be brought to bear on them, but their lower altitude brought them within reach of lighter weapons that until then had remained silent. It seemed as if the entire forest below them peeled away in a solid sheet of flame and *dis*. The lighter beams lacked the destructive strength to leach the air away from beneath the carriers' wings, but now and again they would sweep through the reach of a heavier weapon and stagger in the sudden vacuum. And missiles and rockets struck against them with increasing frequency.

The flight commander wisely decided against leading his small force into that maze of destruction. Any possible damage they might have done was more than counterbalanced by the near-certainty of their own annihilation. They veered off along the fringe of the Han bastion, blasting a constant swath of rocket-and-*dis*-fire ahead of them. The flight commander selected a single heavy *dis* battery that constantly scored the air above them, stubbornly trying to depress its aim quickly enough to catch them. He took his ships in against it in single-file, salvoing their heavy missiles into its position. Fire, smoke and earth erupted into the air before them; rubble rattled off their hulls as they sailed through. As they veered off away from the aroused fortress, that one battery stayed silent. It was hardly missed.

Water was churned into white foam beneath the *rep*-rays of a score of Han ships.

Fleet Commander Ni-Kin sat behind his battery of screens, looking proudly out upon his lethal force. The

.twenty airmen aboard his flagship at the heart of the formation were the only other living creatures in the entire fleet. The five other airships and the fifteen drop-ships that accompanied them were piloted by the eerie robot drones the outblood Mordred had taught the Ki-Ling scientists of the city to copy from the Peruvian design. But for all that they answered to bloodless hands upon their helms, each of those airships was fully as deadly as Ni-Kin's own, armed to their fullest capacity with potent *dis* and missilery and the fearsome *karnak* weapons of the Prl'lu warrior demons; each of those fifteen drop-ships was capable of a lightning dive and savage destructiveness through its single powerful *dis*-beam and its quick-firing rocket battery. Ni-Kin looked upon them all and knew they were equal to their task of striking terror into the heartland of the American savages.

He reached out and pressed a button. A signal was transmitted to the escorting drop-ships and they peeled away from the formation, breaking up into units of three ships each and speeding off towards their pre-selected targets. Each three-ship squadron had been assigned to hit targets deep in the American Southwest, widely scattered for maximum confusion. But it was the six airships under Ni-Kin's command that would strike the most telling blow. He leaned forward again and tapped out a fresh command, repeating it to his own helmsman, and the flotilla leaped ahead with renewed acceleration.

"*. . . Red Leader to Blue Leader, please respond.*"

Jascovic scowled at the urgent voice souding in his headphones as he led his flight of Falcons on their southward leg home. They were already half an hour out of the theater of operations, and dog-tired after the long flight up and the hours on station flying high cover. But that didn't matter.

"Blue Leader to Red Leader, aknol," he said into his microphone. "Go ahead."

"Red Leader to Blue Leader, combat alert." Jascovic stiffened. *"Ground-support air currently engaging strong Han forces, grid six region. Heavy air required. Aknol."*

Jascovic reached for his transmit-button to acknowledge. Before he could speak a new voice came over the channel.

"Blue Leader, this is Ross." It was the voice of the 52nd's 'B' squadron leader. *"You boys have done your shift for today. Take your gang on home and get some rest for the second act."*

"No thanks, Ross. Can't let all you B squadron heroes have all the fun. I guess we'll stick around for the chorus."

"Negative that, Blue Leader. Someone has to cover the north approaches and that someone's you. Go on home, Jasco."

There was no arguing with that, Jascovic knew. That was the way it was laid out. And his butt *was* going numb; his throat was dry and sore from the steady flow of pure oxygen he'd been breathing all day.

"Aknol that, Ross. Have fun."

"Red Leader to Blue Leader, Red Leader to Blue Leader. Blue Leader, this is Helden. Do not, repeat not, return to base. We need that ordnance you're carrying up here. Return to zone of operations fastest. Aknol."

"This is Blue Leader to Red Leader," Jascovic said. "Aknol."

"This is Blue Two to Red Leader," Ross's voice followed. *"Aknol."*

"All right, boys, let's get these crates turned around," Jascovic called to his flight.

The ten Falcons headed south flipped one wing toward the sun and banked sharply, rushing back the way they had come, leaving the sky behind them bright and clear—and empty.

Riding front seat in the tiny Shrike was like flying in a fishbowl. The agile little trainer consisted of little more than a broad canopy between two wings and a brace of seats atop a *dis* engine. Normally it flew with little more than an occasional polite suggestion from the pilot, but today, with the two missiles racked under the wings and the rocket-cannon bolted to the belly pylon, Price was definitely aware that the ship beneath him was butting its way through a resisting medium.

It didn't help that he had company.

"Dammit, Price, can't you keep this thing level?" They may have been on active duty but nobody seemed to have told Captain Anders Dane that. As long as he sat in the back seat he would go on playing flight instructor.

"Sorry, Captain. I've never flown one of these things with an ordnance package before."

"Oh, well, that's all right, Price, don't let it bother you. Just as soon as there's an opening for a permanent post flying an unarmed Shrike we'll bung you right in to it."

"Like flight instructor, sir?"

"Fly the ship, trainee."

The ship bucked slightly in turbulence as Price threaded his way between two towering cumulus spires. Then the pit of his stomach dropped away as if he had flown into the king of all downdrafts.

The enormous cylinders cruised along in golden imperturbability, fifteen hundred meters below them, a hundred meters above the sea. They gave no sign of noticing the tiny American ship far above them, and watching them, Price could think of no reason why they should care.

"Hey, Captain . . .?"

"I see them." The rigid calm tone of Dane's voice was almost more chillding than the sight of the Han airships. "Give me the stick and call in our position."

"Right." The stick wiggled in his hand and Price released it, then opened his mike. "Defcom, Defcom, this is Scouting One-Nine. We have a contact, airshhips, Han, repeat Han, six, repeat, six. Our heading is one-nine-three degrees magnetic, our estimated distance five-six-zero kilometers. Repeating, heading one-nine-three magnetic, range five-six-zero kilometers. Estimated heading hostile airships, nine-five degrees magnetic, estimated speed four-eight zero kilometers. Defcom, Defcom, do you copy?"

"Aknol, Scouting One-Nine. Defcom reads your transmission six Han airships, heading nine-five degrees magnetic, speed four-eight-zero kilometers, range five-six-zero kilometers, do you confirm?"

"Aknol, Defcom, Scouting One-Nine confirms readback." The Shrike banked around after the airships. "Scouting One-Nine turning onto course of hostiles. Please advise."

"Advise, right," Dane said. "We'll take the six of 'em all by ourselves." Price turned to stare at him. "All right, so I don't believe it either."

"Scouting One-Nine, Scouting One-Nine, this is Defcom. Do not, repeat not engage hostiles. Maintain observation same; units being vectored your area. Confirm, Scouting One-Nine."

"This is Scouting One-Nine. Aknol, thank Christ. Will remain on station pending arrival friendly forces."

"Sir, we are discovered," the communications officer said. The small part of his board not given over to monitoring the robot crews of the other airships was devoted to surveillance of the American ultrophone channels. The communication between Scouting One-Nine and Defcom came thinly from one small speaker.

"Have you located the American ship?" Ni-Kin asked.

"Ship Four reports that it is paralleling our course, well above and behind us. There appears to be but the one."

The weapons officer swivelled in his seat to look at Ni-Kin. "Sir, one aircraft presents no threat to us, but this one could guide stronger forces to us. Permission to destroy it?"

"Granted."

A tongue of fire snaked out from the central airship in the formation. Price stared at the missile in horrified fascination as it climbed towards them, curving surely in their direction.

"Defcom, Defcom, Scouting One-Nine taking fire, repeat, Scouting One-Nine under attack—God, break!"

"Not yet," Dane said. The stick didn't twitch and Price fought down the urge to grab for it and heave wildly. The missile arced toward them. "Not yet—now."

The Shrike tumbled wildly away to one side as the missile, moving far too fast to match such a tight manuever, lanced past and above them. Other missiles blazed up from the rushing airships as Dane continued their long, steep dive, pushing the throttles to their stops. The gravity bladders in Price's suit swelled to their limits as Dane threw the Shrike into a wide, skidding turn that slid it out of the way of the rising missiles and brought the plane into a perfect pursuit curve against the rear right quarter of the last airship in line. *Dis* flared from the stern emplacements of the airship, and strings of glowing embers from its short-range defensive rocket batteries; the Shrike in Dane's hands jinked and bobbed and skidded away from each assault, evasion the frail ship's only defense. He closed on his chosen target, into missile range and closer, ever closer, until the top *dis* nacelle couldn't depress far enough to reach them, until the whole world before Price seemed to be filled with a tapering cylinder of golden metal. Then Dane was firing the belly-package gun, and rockets of their own floated out to meet and pass through the fire from the rear starboard battery of the airship. Bright brief fireballs began to burst against the flank of the ship, obscuring the flashes of defensive fire directed against them.

Then the Shrike seemed to leap free of some great burden as Dane triggered their two heavy missiles. The missiles surged ahead of the Shrike, trailing arrow-straight trails of white smoke.

The missiles stuck home. They were of a new type, developed after the harsh lessons of the Recurrence. They were officially defined as SHAPE warheads, for 'soft-head, armor piercing, explosive': warheads of a soft alloy, that would deform and mold themselves to an armored target upon impact, while the explosive charge within drove a keen flechette of inertron through the obstruction to breach the armor. They worked to perfection, but the Han had learned, as well: between the outer and inner skins of their airships they had installed thick layers of alloy mesh matting, that absorbed the penetration of the flechette and cushioned the impact of the explosive charge. The missiles hit cleanly, and did damage, but not as much as they had to.

Dane and Price had no time to realize that. As soon as he saw the missiles clear the ship Dane threw the ship into a climbing wing-over turn that took it skimming over the top of the Han airship—and the tail-end of a streamer of Han rocket-fire burst just behind the canopy and chewed Anders Dane into bloody hamburger.

The wounded Shrike flipped wildly downward before Price could haul and stomp on stick and pedals to bring it out. *Dis* and rocket-fire stitched the sea scant meters beneath the plane; Price had only a trainee's instruments but even those told him that the plane had only seconds to live. The *dis*-regulation circuit in the engine was fluctuating wildly; at any moment his ship might dissolve beneath him.

He didn't think. To his credit or otherwise, Price's last action was an immediate, instinctive response.

Had the robotic crew of the last Han airship in formation been capable of astonishment, they would have felt it then, as the crippled American plane looped back upon them in a mad, final attack. But they could feel no such emotion, they could only react, and so Price's last gesture became to them a simple matter of the speed with which defensive batteries could track pitted against the Shrike's rate of closure.

They lost.

The Shrike tore into the port quarter astern on the airship, directly opposite the scars of its original attack. Armor buckled, frames bent, systems failed. The airship dropped down into the sea and thrashed through the waves on a tangent away from its parent formation before limping back into the air on two good *rep* rays and a third that flickered and stuttered alarmingly. Incapable of acknowledging its grievous injury, the robotic ship staggered after its swifter, whole sisters. The wreckage of the Shrike bobbed on the surface of the Pacific for several minutes, as trapped air slowly leaked out; then it settled quietly into three hundred feet of water.

Klein sat in the tall grass, his raincape about his shoulders, staring at the blue glow on the horizon. He was alone, in the sense that there was no one else within a kilometer of him in any direction, but he was unavoidably aware of the voices of his squadmates muttering in his earphones, over the tactical channels. Klein's squad was grounded in counter-nuclear scatter pattern, just as the squads of his company and the companies of his battalion were similary dispersed, right on up to the full strength of the force. Off in the distance the blue glow of the massive Han *dis* emplacements was beginning to be shot through with rising gouts of dirty black smoke where the missiles of the carriers and the rockets of the heavy long-guns plunged down against earth and armor. A flicker of reflected sunlight off something moving in the distance drew his attention. Klein studied it for a long moment before deciding it was one of the regimental heavy long-gun sleds picking up and moving to evade Han counterbattery fire. A moment later his guess was confirmed as missiles began to burst upon the ground the long-gun team had vacated. He watched the explosions in idle fascination: it was difficult to connect those pretty little bursts of smoke and scarlet flame with something that could kill him.

"Mu'mal, mu'mal," he could hear Morales murmuring, almost as if he didn't know he could be heard. "Oh, this will be bad, very bad."

"Hey, squad," Klein asked softly, speaking into his helmet mike as to a man sitting directly before him, "when do you think they'll send us in?"

"They won't send us into that, my friend. This is too big a game for such as us. Be patient yet."

"Hell, I can wait."

"You're learning."

"Good sweet Christ." Merrit stared at the brief transcript of Scouting One-Nine's contact. "No word since?"

"Not since the attack report. You didn't expect any?"

"Not really. What action have you taken?"

"I've vectored Scouting One-Eight and Two-Zero into Scouting One-Nine's zone, to intercept the Han's last reported course. We're in luck there; they're both Falcons. And I notified you," Baker answered.

"All right. Get on the phone to Ground Defcom. Full alert. Then contact Blue Southbound and get an estimated time of arrival this area. What ships have we got on the ground?"

"Five Falcons from C squadron. That's our whole reserve, plus any armored personnel carriers Ground Defcom can put up."

"Get the Falcons up on the reciprocal of the Han course. Leave the carriers for local cover. Use call sign Falcon Five for C squadron. Then take charge here. I'm going to call Niagra. We're going to need federal air on this."

"Right."

The coastline was a thin ribbon ahead of the Han fleet, thickening steadily as the mountains backing the beaches climbed above the horizon.

"Sir, Ship Six is reporting increasing difficulty in maintaining formation speed," the communications officer said.

Ni-Kin frowned. "Query Six's damage control systems. Determine if the ship is in danger of crashing."

"Yes, sir." The officer bent to his board. "Sir, Ship Six's damage control responses indicate that the ship's airworthiness may be maintained providing a thirty per cent speed loss is immediately authorized. Otherwise my information indicates that fatal control failure will occur in under one hour."

"Damn that American," Ni-Kin said fiercely. "Query Six on remaining offensive capability."

"Sir, Ship Six reports all forward *dis* and rocket batteries operational' *karnak,* operational; two heavy missile systems and all stern defensive batteries incapacitated. Likelihood of repair prior to arrival above our target is minimal."

"Damn." Ni-Kin considered his problem. He could throttle back with the entire formation to protect the vulnerable cripple which could not in its turn fully assist in the defense of the formation, with the implicit risk of being intercepted by stronger forces short of his target, or he could abandon Six to its own resources and make full use of his remaining squadron's speed.

"Authorize the necessary speed reduction," he said. "But instruct Six that it is to proceed to the target at its own pace and press home its attack to the fullest."

"Yes, sir."

The crippled airship dwindled away behind the unheeding squadron. It had quite vanished from sight by the time they crossed the coastline.

"Blue Southbound, Blue Southbound, this is Defcom South, do you copy?"

"Defcom South, this is Blue Southbound, aknol," Jascovic said. The twenty Falcons of his and Ross' combined flights circled on high orbit above the pillar of smoke and *dis* that marked the Han redoubt, awaiting target orders.

"Blue Southbound, this is Defcom South. Major Han attack immiment Defcom South zone. Please give ETA your flight Defcom South."

"Oh, my god. . . ." someone said quietly from the back of the formation.

"Stay off this channel," Jascovic snapped. "Defcom South, this Blue Southbound Leader. Blue Southbound has been recalled for active support of ground forces engaging Han concentration Defcom North. Earliest possible arrival Defcom South one hour-plus, repeat, one hour-plus, please advise."

"God damn it . . ." Hascovic heard somebody mutter.

"Ah, stand by, Blue Southbound, patching in to Defcom

North—what the hell is that call sign? Right, right—Red Leader, Red Leader, this is Defcom South recalling Blue Southbound, do you copy? Red Leader, Red Leader—"

"Defcom South, this is Red Leader. Negative, repeat negative on recall. Am engaging major Han installation. Heavy air needed urgentest."

"Sonofabitch," Jascovic heard someone mutter. After a second he realized that it had been himself. His earphones came back to life.

"Read Leader, Red Leader, this is Defcom South. Han attack by six heavy airships imminent this zone. No, repeat no effective interdiction Defcom South air available. By highest authority, repeat highest, Defcom South ordering recall Blue Southbound, all elements, fastest. Aknol, dammit."

Jascovic wasn't waiting. "Blue Southbound, this is Blue Southbound Leader. Form on me." Ten Falcons peeled away from the formation and went for altitude and speed at full throttle, *dis* intakes flaring brilliantly ahead of them.

"Ah, Defcom South, this is Red Leader. Aknol." That was the last transmission Jascovic heard before he switched off the groundlink channel.

"What?" Rogers said. The hard-copy fax on the Susquannas' balance-of-payments troubles with the Ottowa Gang lay forgotten on his desk.

Captain Brock Rogers, officer by commission and son-of-the-boss by profession, shifted his feet nervously and repeated his statment. He had the infantryman's pack-thickened neck and shoulders; they went poorly with his prominent jawline and the shock of thick black hair that never managed to stay combed.

"Taos reports a major Han attack all along the west coast, sir."

"Good God almighty." Anthony Rogers stood quickly and moved to the rack holding his helmet and flying belt. "Any report on numbers?"

"No, sir."

"Any word on casualties?"

"No, sir."

"Why not?" Rogers stepped through the harness of the flying pack and began to tighten the straps.

"They didn't say."

"Why the hell didn't you ask?" He pulled on his helmet, briefly muffling his words before he popped the visor open. "No, never mind, I don't want to hear it. Now, listen: I'm going to be over in communications. Notify Brigadier Dupre and General Watson that I'm coming over, then contact Doctor Wolsky and Ruth Harris and tell them to meet me there. Once you've done that, call the vehicle pool and have them get my personal field transport ready. Then arrange a tie-in between my PFT and the command communication nets. I'll notify you when I found out which unit we'll be travelling with. Got all that?"

"I think so, sir."

"I hope so." Rogers started for the office patio. 'Thicker than water, hell, thicker than Mississippi mud is what is is. . . ."

Mike Bisaglio squinted into the desert sunlight, taking advantage of what little shade the armor plate of his long-gun offerred.

There were just the seven of them left now, to defend the small well-station that meant survival for the one hundred and thirteen men, women and children of the Butte Gang. All the others had long since heeded the general alarm broadcast from Taos and evacuated, fleeing in every direction across the desert by belt and cargo sled. Looking across the compound, Bisaglio could see the sandbagged bunker—against *dis*, he

thought wryly—where Henneken, Jones, and Old Walk
er sat with their short-rocket pistols, gussied up with
long barrels and scoped sights in a weak gesture at effec
tiveness. Thompson and Young Walker sat in the well
house below him, monitoring the ultrophone and their
single scope. It wasn't exactly an overwhelming host, he
thought to himself. But then again, the Butte Gang well
pump probably wasn't the most important military
target in the world . . .

Young Walker belted up above the edge of the roo
and drifted down next to the gun.

"Hawley's got something on the scope," he said ex
citedly.

"Yeah? Where?" Bisaglio turned in a slow circle, stu
dying the sky around them.

"High. Way up high, he says."

"Oh, yeah, I see 'em. Right up there, ain't they?'
Bisaglio said. "Hell, I wouldn't worry about it. Whoever
they are, they aren't bothering anybody way up there
Probably only ours, anyway—"

"Hey, look, they're turning. Think maybe they saw
something?"

"Could be, I guess."

"Hey! Hey!" Bisaglio looked down and saw Hawley
Thompson standing in the door of the well-house
"Those guys are diving. Comin' down right on top of
us."

Henneken, Jones and Old Walker were standing up in
their bunker now, staring up curiously. The handful of
silvery dots were growing visibly larger as they watched.

"What the hell are they doing?" Young Walker asked

"I dunno." Bisaglio frowned at the plummeting aircraft.

"Let's get this thing loaded," he said suddenly.

He pulled the dust cover off the mechanism of the
long-gun and Young Walker fumbled a gravity-clip of

110

rockets into the breech. Bisaglio butted his shoulders into the rests and swung the weapon around and up, so that he all but hung from the firing grips.

Thompson ran back out of the building.

"They aren't planes! They aren't ours! They're not planes!"

"Call it in," Bisaglio called back, and fired. The descending ships dropped towards them. Young Walker stood and watched; Thompson ran back into the wellhouse; the others could only grip their useless weapons and watch as Bisaglio's rockets burst around and against the diving ships.

The Han drop-ships began to fan out into their characteristic attack-spiral. Bisaglio picked the foremost of the three and held his fire on it, slamming rocket after rocket into its armored hull. *Dis* leaped out ahead of the Han ships, and the others began firing desperately, hopelessly, fully aware that the approaching ships were still beyond any effective attack.

The first *dis*-beam swept through the tiny cluster of buildings. Roofs vanished, unsupported walls collapsed inward under the sudden rush of air moving to fill the vaccum between them. Dust filled the air, particles of random matter cast off by the *dis*-beam and sand stirred up by the disturbed air. Explosions began to rock the settlement as the drop-ships opened fire with their rocket batteries as well.

Bisaglio paid the chaos no mind. All around him was smoke and flame, the other buildings, the other people lost to his view, no sound audible above the concussion of detonating rockets, but he held his sights on the ship he had selected and fired and fired and fired, because there was nothing else to be done.

The lead drop-ship flashed past the settlement. Bisaglio swung the long-gun to track it, still firing, and the last rocket dropped from the clip. He had no time to note his weapon's silence. The roof beneath him heaved; he felt a brushing touch on his arm as though someone had drawn a fine kerchief across it, and then he was sitting on the ground with no idea how he had come to be there.

Young Walker was gone, just gone. The other gunpit was a smoking ruin crossed by a broad *dis* scar. The thing he leaned against was the roof of the well-house, or part of it, the largest part left intact after the impact of rockets and *dis*. But he paid no attention to that. He just sat and stared, at the blood welling steadily from the neatly severed stump of his vanished right forearm . . . .

"Another attack reported, sir." The sixth.

"Where?" Cullen Teder asked quietly. The enormity of the chaos into which his region had been plunged was beyond any rage he might have summoned. He could not afford the energy in any case. At this point no one in the SouthWest SubCouncil could afford the energy for anything except survival.

"A commerce terminal out in Nacogdoches territory, sir." The site was marked by a fresh red dot on the basement screen. "But this time one of the attackers was destroyed; there was a militia unit nearby with heavy rockets and *dis*. They say the wreckage is that of a Han dropship. They report that two other ships got clear, though."

Two others. Cullen studied the other attack sites. The angry red lights were scattered the length and breadth of the SubCouncil. "How the hell many of them are there?"

The communications operator manning the screen took him seriously. "The best estimate to date is between a dozen and twenty, sir, not accounting for reports that haven't come in yet or observer error."

"Of course. Not accounting." The anger broke

through for an instant. "Where the hell are our planes?"

The operator answered, grimly intent on doing his job. "Blue Southbound is reported just entering Defcom South airspace. Falcon Five is flying interdict on the last reported course of the Han airships. All Scouting craft are being recalled and reformed for direct interdiction of zone airspace."

Something nagged at Teder's awareness. "Have there been any other reported contacts with the Han airship squadron since the initial contact?"

That one actually took the operator a couple of seconds. "No, sir. All hostile contacts since have been with drop-ship elements, excluding reports from Defcom North."

The suspicion crystallized in his mind. "I think I know where we can find them. Put me through to Defcom, at once."

"Defcom, Defcom, this is Scouting Two-Zero, do you copy?"

"Aknol, Scouting Two-Zero, go ahead."

"Scouting Two-Zero and Scouting One-Eight reporting hard contact with Han airship, one, damaged, heading nine-five degrees, speed approximately three-zero-zero kilometers, range approximately three-two-zero kilometers, do you copy?"

"Scouting Two-Zero, we read that as Han airship, one, damaged, heading nine-five, speed three-zero-zero, range three-two-zero approximate, aknol."

"Aknol on read-back, Defcom."

"Aknol, Scouting Two-Zero. Please advise on presence of other Han units."

"Negative other units, Defcom. One Han, repeat, One Han solo. Presume damaged by Scouting One-Nine; presume Scouting One-Nine lost, no sign. Scouting Two-Zero and Scouting One-Eight requesting permission to engage hostile."

"Anknol, Scouting Two-Zero. Permission to engage hostile granted. Zero the bastard."

"Aknol that, Defcom."

The robotic crew of the crippled Han airship was fully aware of the two sleek predators hovering above it. But with its rear defenses shattered, and two of its three heavy guided missile batteries down, there was no effective action it could take. Unthinkingly, without fear or rancor, the ship reviewed its options and pressed on toward its target.

The two Falcons broke formation and fell off on opposite wings, plummeting down upon the Han airship. Limping through the air on its weakened *rep*-rays, the airship turned to present its operational defenses to the threat. A missile burst from its launcher and curved around to meet the Falcon swooping in from port; cold blue *dis* flared from the nose of the pursuit ship and the missile vanished. Han *dis* slashed at the air around the second ship, staggering it briefly as the air was torn away from it in three different directions. Then the Falcon triggered its internal rockets and thrust forward out of the net of fire surrounding it.

Disdaining the use of their own missiles and rockets, the Falcons curved in behind the airship more swiftly than it could pivot to track them. *Dis* stabbed around them; rockets burst against the inertron armor of the Falcons; then they were beyond the reach of the airship's bow and midships defensive batteries.

Dis beams stabbed out from the Falcons, seeking the damaged and torn plating of the airship's stern, the scars of Scouting One-Nine's attack. The beams pierced into the unshielded vitals of the airship. Structural members were sliced through like paper; a *rep* generator feed disappeared faster than a bad idea. The weakened frame of the ship, already badly stressed by the uneven pressures of the straining *rep* rays, twisted, buckled—and broke.

The crumpled wreckages of the airship thundered three hundred feet into the ocean and vanished in a cloud of white foam. The waters closed over it almost instantly, broken only by a single blue shaft of *dis* as one battery stubbornly obeyed its robotic commander, until the sea water rushing into the shattered hull ruined unprotesting circuits.

The two Falcons climbed away from the surface, pulling for altitude.

"Defcom, Defcom, this is Scouting Two-Zero, record one Han airship confirmed destroyed, do you copy?"

"Ankol, Scouting Two-Zero, confirming one Han kill. Nice work. Return to base for reassignment interior defense, aknol."

"Ankol, Defcom, Scouting Two-Zero and Scouting One-Eight returning base for reassignment. How's our side doing?"

"They're climbing all over us."

The three robot drop-ships climbed away from their attack run. Behind them the small human settlement was shrouded in flame and smoke. If the unthinking calculator bolted before each ship's controls could have felt satisfaction, it would have had full cause.

The 'commander' of the three-ship squadron registered the execution of this latest step in its programming, and consulted its memory for the next step. Each drop-ship detachment had been programmed to hit a series of human settlements selected at random by their Han programmers; all five units' target listings leaped all over the southwest and interpenetrated each other repeatedly. To maximize the confusion, as it had been instructed, the squadron command-robot accorded each of its remaining target-listings a numerical tag and ran them all through a random-numbers sequencer, the computer-equivalent of picking a slip from a derby. The sequencer returned a number, the tag for a target a good seven hundred miles from the squadron's last victim. Obediently, the three ships turned onto their new course and sped away into the distance . . . .

"What the hell is going on here?" Merrit demanded.

The map in Wing operations was speckled with a dozen angry scarlet blemishes. As Merrit watched, a trooper added yet another, three hundred miles away from the previous attack, and called in fifteen minutes after it.

"If there's a pattern to this, I can't see it," Baker said. "First they hit Ladrone down on the Old Mexican border, then they hit Canyon way the hell back up in Wyoming. But to hit Ladrone they had to pass up a major commercial port at New Dallas. And why hit Canyon instead of the Federal airbase at Badlands? There's no pattern."

"There's a pattern," Merrit said. "They're chewing us up and we aren't touching them. They have to have at least five drop-ship elements operating in our zone, not to mention at least five heavy airships that we haven't got the slightest goddam idea where to look for, and we haven't got enough air cover in the interior to even begin to deal with them. We're in deep trouble, Bake."

"We'll be in worse trouble if we don't find those airships. Any word from Niagra?"

"Yeah. They're putting the regulars on full alert. Badlands and Reno have been instructed to supplement our people to the fullest extent possible without jeopardizing their own defense. I'm still waiting to hear what they're going to send us. And they're mobilizing troops to back up our people up north. But right now we're on our own."

"Damn." Baker studied the map. The scattered ships

of the scouting force were slowly clustering back towards their airfields. Falcon Five was still quartering back and forth across the last known course of the five surviving Han airships. And Blue Southbound was still far from the chaos gripping the heart of the zone. A single gold star marked the point off the coast where the sixth airship had been brought down; another denoted the destruction of the drop-ship brought down outside Nacogdoches. It wasn't much consolation.

"Where the hell are those airships?"

"Believe me," Merrit said, "if I knew, I'd tell you."

The phone on his desk buzzed. Merrit hit the talk switch.

"Defcom Air, Merrit," he said.

The operator on the screen said, "Sir, I have a call from Boss Teder, in Taos."

"Dammit, I haven't got time for this," Merrit said under his breath. "All right. Put it through."

The operator blinked out, to be replaced by the worried, urgent face of Cullen Teder.

"Wing Commander Merrit," Teder said, "has there been any word yet on the current location of those Han airships?"

"No, sir. I'm afraid there hasn't."

Teder's worried expression deepened. "I was afraid you'd tell me that. In that case, I think I know where they're headed."

Teder spoke. Merrit and Baker listened. And believed. Baker was on his phone and giving orders before Merrit could hang up.

"Falcon Five, Falcon Five, this is Defcom, do you copy?"

Major Andreas Saint thumbed the 'speak' button on his control stick. Description would be superfluous; there was little to distinguish him from the other helmeted, flight-suited members of his flight—there was little of him that could even be seen save his eyes: pale gray and nested in clusters of sunborn wrinkles, clouded with tiredness and worry.

"This is Falcon Five Leader, Defcom, aknol."

"Falcon Five, you are ordered to change course and assume interdict station above the city of Taos, do you copy?"

Saint frowned inside his visor. They were a hell of a jump away from Taos. What was happening? "Ah, Defcom, this is Falcon Five Leader. Please confirm my readback Falcon Five to interdict Taos, aknol."

"Aknol that readback, Falcon Five Leader, Interdict Taos."

"Aknol that, Defcom." Saint consulted the chart that flashed on his screen. "Falcon Five, establish course one-two-seven degrees magnetic, aknol." There was a quick string of acknowledgements. Saint banked the nimble Falcon back around onto the correct heading. "Ah, Defcom, Defcom, this is Falcon Five Leader. What about the airships? Do you copy?"

"Defcom aknol, Falcon Five Leader. With any luck you should beat them there."

"Blue Southbound Leader, this is Blue Southbound three, do you copy?"

"Go ahead, Three," Jascovic said. Blue Southbound Flight had penetrated deep into the airspace of Defcom South in the past half-hour, with no sign of any enemy save the periodic and confusing reports of drop-ship attacks taking place to the north of them, to the south, east, wast—anywhere, in short, except where the increasingly frustrated and angry men and women of Blue Southbound Flight could get at them. Orders from Defcom South would send the flight rushing toward one reported attack—and then the tactical channels would crackle with panicked alarms of a fresh attack hundreds of miles away, and Blue Southbound would be called off to await further instructions. Jascovic's patience was long since exhausted; he was just about ready to tell Defcom South where they could put their orders and take his flight off on its own toward the coast to search for the Han airships he had originally been recalled to hunt.

"Blue Southbound Leader, I have bogies at two o'clock level," Three said.

"Aknol that, Three," Jascovic said, "I have them." He could see them then, three silvery dots several miles away, climbing slowly above the Falcons' altitude.

"Defcom, Defcom, this is Blue Southbound Leader," Jascovic called. "I have three unidentified ships my position. Request verification of presence any friendly aircraft my vicinity, do you copy?"

"Blue Southbound Leader, this is Defcom, aknol your request verification. No friendly air reported your location, do you copy?"

"Aknol verification, Defcom. This is Blue Southbound closing for positive ID bogies. Blue Southbound Seven through Ten, break and take station high and forward of bogies. Four through Six, low and astern. Two and Three, we're going straight in. On command, break."

The formation of ten Falcons shattered, elements breaking off for their ordered positions. Jascovic led his element straight for the climbing ships. He activated his targeting scope, dialing for full magnification.

He tensed. There was no mistaking that finned, teardrop shape.

"Drop-ships!" He shouted. "Defcom, Defcom, this is Blue Southbound Leader reporting three Han dropships my position. Am engaging." He shoved his throttles forward and threw his battle-switch. "Blue Southbound, take 'em!"

Intertron shields slid out to seal off his vulnerable canopy as his seat canted back into acceleration mode, locking him away in a tight little world of instruments and targeting scope.

The robot drop-ships detected the approaching Falcons and took the only course open to them. The drop-ship was lethal against anything on the ground or flying beneath one, but it was far from an ideal aerial battle-weapon. Precariously balanced on its single *rep*-ray, it was neither as fast nor as maneuverable as the American ships now closing on them from three directions. Their only advantage was in diving speed, and they used it.

The drop-ships swung back the way they had come and dropped their noses. Blue Southbound Four, Five and Six broke aside as the drop-ships blasted through them in a blaze of *dis* and rocket fire.

"Four through Six, scissors right!" Jascovic shouted. "Seven through Ten, scissors left! Two and Three, form on me!" And he threw his ship down after the plummeting drop-ships.

There was no way any conventional aircraft could keep up with a drop-ship in a dive. Jascovic wasn't trying.

The two units forming the 'scissors' were swinging wide of the diving drop-ships to either side, descending toward the ground far enough apart from the drop-ships to cut them off when they would inevitably have to pull out of their dives. The Han aircraft could neither outfly nor outclimb the Falcons: when they came out of their dives they would be helpless. Jascovic and his element didn't have to catch the drop-ships. All they had to do was follow them down and 'plug the bottle', so that the Han ships could not pull up short without pulling up right into the Americans' sights.

The drop-ships fell earthward. It was all they could

do, and so their dispassionate robot pilots did it, right down to the point, a scant thousand meters above the ground, where it became a matter of pulling out or crashing.

The three drop-ships levelled out and tried to turn into the pursuing Jascovic, which was just what he wanted. Five seconds after they came into firing range, the three drop-ships were tumbling into the ground, the potent SHAPE missiles bursting within their cramped interiors with devastating effect.

Jascovic ordered Blue Southbound Flight to reform on him as he climbed out of his attack run and reported their kills to Defcom. He felt much better.

A brief cheer went up in the operations center of the Badlands Air Base at the report of Blue Southbound's kill. As if in spiteful reply, reports of two more drop-ship attacks came in, to bring the total already on the screen to seventeen.

Will Holcomb sat at his desk at the back of the center, overseeing the screen and the dozen operators there. Mamboya stood behind him, face an expressionless mask.

A face flickered into view on Jolcomb's screen. "Sir, Base Defense reports all posts operational."

Holcomb nodded. "And air?"

"The tower reports D Flight of Baker Squadron taking off now, sir. Able Squadron reports all elements on station. Mako Flight reports all ships operational and standing by."

"Thank you." Holcomb reached out and punched up a readout on the base's status. Out of the forty Falcons that made up the base's complement, thirty-seven were now operational and airborne, surrounding the base with a flying shield that would take a formidable amount of breaching. Beyond that, the base's ground defenses, a dozen guided missile batteries, six heavy *dis* emplacements and the long-guns and carriers of the base's ground troops were all alerted and in position. The *Wilma Deering*, the reason for the base's existence in the first place, reported all posts manned and systems operational.

Holcomb considered his next move. The base was as fully protected as it could be, and the spaceship in his charge was capable of escaping under its own power if it had to. Now he could afford to look to offering assistance to the embattled irregulars on the coast.

He opened his mike. "Orders to Mako Flight and Captain Hopper. Mako flight is ordered to scramble and set a course for the west coast. From this point until the conclusion of immediate hostilities Mako Flight will operate under direct command of Defcom Air South. Aknol."

"This is Mako Flight Leader to Badlands Command. Aknol, sir."

"Do us proud, Captain," Holcomb said.

"We'll see what we can do, Major," Hopper answered. *"This is Mako Flight lifting out."*

"Smash." He switched channels and got the base communication officer. "Lieutenant, notify Defcom Air South that Badlands Air Base is detaching six *Mako*-class pursuits to their command. Then notify Niagra HQ of our action."

Holcomb switched off and sat back, moodily studying the big screen. "I just hope to hell it helps."

Taos was a ghost town.

The city was four-fifths empty already, as the evacuation continued. The machinery of the gangs had been gearing for such a move, of course, ever since the first warning of Han airships; yet it was still a creditable achievement that it was going so well, and so smoothly.

There were—had been—almost thirty thousand people in and around Taos, belonging to more than twenty different Gangs, but they had virtually all been prepared to leave within half an hour. Gang life ensured that sort of flexibility, and Cullen Teder felt a moment's pride that his people could keep so strongly to the old ways.

The hissing passage of a personnel carrier beneath his window brought Teder back to his current reality. Taos was more strongly defended that any of the outlying gang nexi, as befitted the capital of the entire SubCouncil—but even its garrisons had been stripped to send troops north with Helden. Northwestern troops had moved in to fill the vacuum, of course, but even so the city's forces were at barely sixty per cent of their full strength. Helden did not doubt the courage of the men guarding his city, but he was all too aware that there were empty emplacements where long-gun batteries should have been; he was all too aware that the aircraft that should have played such a central part in the city's defense were scattered all over the Southwest, hunting frantically for the elusive Han drop-ship squadrons wreaking havoc among the smaller settlements. The folly of his decision not to call in Federal forces when the Han had first been discovered was being borne in on him more and more strongly the longer this hell continued—

No. He drove the thought savagely from his mind. That was absurd. What was he doing, blaming himself for Han rapacity? The attack upon the Southwest had to have been launched before the Han base to the north had been discovered, otherwise it would never have gotten past Helden's forces. No, this assault would be thrown back, and the destruction those inhuman scum caused would be repaid by Helden and his forces a hundredfold, even if they did have to accept some Federal aid. They would win. They—

Above the mountains to the west, sunlight glinted off golden metal.

"Sir, the target is in sight."

"I see that," Ni-Kin answered calmly. The varied white buildings of the human city gleamed in the sunlight, standing proudly in the middle of the flat plain. Ni-Kin meant to show them the price of such pride.

"We shall attack in the diamond formation," he said, "with the flagship in the center. Give the appropriate orders."

"As you command, Fleet Captain." The communications officer bent over his board. A moment later the five Han airships rearranged themselves, with the robot ships moving to surround their flesh-hearted sister, one ahead, one astern, and to each side. In perfect, unchanging formation, the ships slid down the face of the mountain, an arrowhead aimed at the exposed heart of the city before them.

Cullen Teder was still watching their approach when the aide found him in his office.

"Councillor, we have to get to the basement shelters," the aide said. "This area isn't shielded."

Cullen appeared not to hear him. He remained standing at the window, fists clenched, garing at the ships as though he hoped to force them out of existence with some *dis*-like effort of will. Then he relaxed—then he *forced* himself to relax—and looked at the aide. He saw nothing to match his own rage there, only fear and a desperate resolve not to show it.

"Yes," he said. "Yes, you're right, of course. Let's go."

The four walls of the elevator closed in around him like a fist as it descended into the basement. Deprived of window or screen, Cullen could only imagine the steady approach of the airship squadron, investing their unseen progress with a horror he would never have felt at their reality.

Fire was bursting around the foremost airship as Cullen Teder stepped from the elevator into the basement shelter. The functions of government were repeated here, the dozen-odd offices centered in the building above replicated in this three-level cell framed in ultron and shielded from *dis* and *karnak* with inertron plating and heterodyning electromagnetic fields. Floorspace was at a premium. The severe crowding would normally have had no small effect on the various departments' efficiency—but no one was doing anything anyway. Every head in the shelter was turned toward the large screen set in one wall, that showed the airship squadrons just coming under fire from the city's defenses. Heavy missiles rose on their pillars of smoke to strike at the ships. Some got through; some were caught in sweeping *dis*-beams and vanished. Lighter rockets from the long-gun batteries flew unseen across the screen, to burst against or around the airships. And a handful—too few—of American *dis*-beams played over the hulls of the airships, seeking entrance through missile-torn rents in their armor.

The Han treated these as the most immediate threat. Beams and missiles from the airships darted back along the beam-paths of the defending batteries with inhuman precision. The *dis*-emplacements could not maneuver to outrun the rate of traverse of the Han weapons; they were fixed targets, impossible to miss. They could intercept missiles in flight, destroy them before they reached their targets, but there was no way to counter the *dis*-beams that sought out the American emplacements, no way to armor a firing battery against their effect.

One after another the defending *dis* batteries were destroyed. One after another their beams vanished, until the Han airships hung free in the sky, wreathed in desperate, futile explosions from the frantic missile batteries below them. Then they turned their attention to those.

Teder rushed to a communications console at the back of the room. A young officer sat there, wearing major's tabs and the uniform of an Irregular, frantically communicating with the embattled American defenders above ground. Teder recognized him: Ebben Smith, Helden's second-in-command, sitting in the seat Helden should have occupied, fighting the battle Helden should have been there to fight. "What happened to the *dis* batteries?"

"Zeroed," Smith told him, and went back to muttering orders into his shielded mile. "Now, they're going after the heavy missile batteries," he added.

"What can you do about it?"

"I'm doing it."

A gaggle of smaller ships appeared on the screen, armored personnel carriers, the only air defense the city had. They threw themselves at the airships now coming over the city in a wild swarm, with no attempt at control or organization, just dog-piling onto the airships with everything they carried.

Missiles flew from the carriers, to smash against the armored hulls of the Han ships. Streamers of rocket fire and *dis* blazed out from their fixed weapons.

And the Han returned the fire. The five ships together produced a synergistic effect in their defensive salvoes: the combined fire of all five ships joined in their robotic link provided far more complete coverage than simply five ships firing together. *Dis* traced nets of cold blue destruction around carriers and threw them groundward in pockets of vacuum. Rocket batteries of three and five ships combined to hammer carriers into collections of junk bound in inertron armor. Missiles from one ship parried attacks upon another.

The carriers were being butchered. Once they had expended their two heavy missiles they simply did not have the firepower to act effectively against the massive airships. But they kept on coming. There was nothing else to do.

Finally there was no choice left Smith either. "No good, no good, get them out of there. Order the carriers to break off, now." On the screen the carriers began to scatter, falling back from the advancing airships. In seconds the airships were alone again, riding lordly and great through the hail of groundfire. Now they turned their attention to the city itself.

Dis scored the bases of a dozen buildings at a sweep, undercutting foundations and collapsing walls. Rockets, explosive and incendiary, rained down into the wreckage and fires began to spread. The civilian population remaining in the city either cowered in underground shelters that more than once became rubble-choked tombs or they tried to flee. The sight of escaping humans sparked the Han to new action. *Karnak* weapons came into play. The invisible energies could not be seen on the screen, but needles on a technician's board twitched sharply and he called out a warning of the Han action.

It wasn't needed. Where the *karnak*-fire touched, frantically leaping figures sagged in jump harnesses, sleds and floaters lurched and tumbled out of control. The troops of the city were largely protected by cardiogard discs or hasty injections. But the civilians had no such defense.

Karnak cut down refugees in lifeless swatches. *Dis* and rockets shattered steel and masonry. Even the supporting *rep*-rays of the airships did great damage, crushing their way through frail buildings that blocked the airships' progress. Troops abandoned positions ahead of ravening sweeps of *dis* or fled as ruined buildings thundered down around them.

But they did not break. Men and women pulled overturned long-guns from the rubble and reset them or took their weapons with them as they evaded Han fire. Columns of *dis* swept past, strings of rocket-bursts moved away, and the militia would emerge from their cover and resume fire. Fast jumper and flying belt troops would set up their field *dis* weapons and hose down the airships passing above them, then pick up and run before they could be located for counterfire.

That was the pattern throughout Taos. Smith had given up trying to give orders; his prepared defenses simply didn't exist anymore, and the troops carrying the battle couldn't remain in any one place long enough to establish any kind of coherent pattern. All he could do was sit and watch with Cullen as his people fought and his city died.

"Fleet Captain, we cannot suppress their return fire."

"No matter. We shall destroy their resistance as we destroy their city. Continue the attack." Ni-Kin studied the chaos beneath his ship through his screens. The airships were carving out a solid wedge of destruction through the human city, leaving a trail of *dis*-stripped earth and burning ruin behind them. The board before him showed telltales warning of a dozen small injuries done the ship by the desperate human defenders, but no major damage to any vital systems, and he knew the same was true of his robot fleet. The ships' armor had been breached in a dozen places, but the light portable *dis* weapons left to the Americans lacked the range and power to do him any harm at that altitude.

Ni-Kin sat back, satisfied. He would be able to report a great victory . . . .

A pale blue bar of *dis* swept toward their viewpoint.

An instant later the shelter's master screen went blank and the walls shook as the remains of the building above them cascaded down atop it. There was a blink of lights and instrumentation as the shelter's internal power supply took up the load.

"Get us back visual, Major," Cullen said. Smith spoke into his microphone and the screen lit again, this time looking down on the burning city from a distant slope.

"Got us a phone pickup from one of the mountain shelters," Smith explained.

The airships were a mass of golden metal moving through the heart of the burning city, hurling fire and *dis* ahead of themselves. The groundfire that opposed them seemed thinner now, and appeared to diminish still further as they watched.

"My God, it's a massacre," Cullen said softly.

"No, sir," Smith answered. "It's ammunition. Most of our forces have been driven from their positions. The only supplies they have are what they could carry. That's run out. The fire you still see is coming from the long-gun units on the far side of the city."

"And when that runs out?"

"I order a dispersal and we lose the city."

"That's it?" Cullen turned on him. "That's the best you can do?"

Smith looked up at him. "That's *all* I can do, sir."

"No, you won't, dammit! Those troops stay and fight, do you under—"

There was a shout from somewhere in the shelter. People were standing up at the posts, staring at the screen and cheering.

Falcon Five had come into sight.

"Defcom, Defcom, this is Falcon Five Leader, reporting presence five, repeat five Han airships Taos. Heavy damage evident to city, ground forces still active. Am engaging hostiles."

"Sir, Ship Five reports American aircraft closing from the Northwest."

"I see them," Ni-Kin said. "Instruct the ships to assume full defensive formation and continue the attack."

The commands were transmitted. Immediately, the lead airship edged to the right and upward. The ship to the direct left of Ni-Kin's flagship moved forward and down, while the ships to the right and astern of the flagship repeated the maneuver in reverse. The effect was to open up the formation, stringing it out somewhat —but at the same time it allowed the full firepower of the fleet to be brought to bear on any point around it. Braced now for the American attack, the airship squadron continued across the city at its same steady, lethal pace.

"Falcon Five, this is Falcon Five Leader," Saint called. "We're going in. Our objective will be to turn those ships. We've got to get them out from above the city."

"Then we kill 'em?"

"Oh, yeah," Saint said softly. "Now follow me in, line weave."

The five American planes banked off, following their leader, as he swung around to come in across the bow of the lead ship.

Dis, rockets and missiles clawed at them. But the line weave maneuver brought the Americans ever closer to their targets, bobbing and swerving through the fire directed at them. It was like trying to hit corks bobbing on a choppy sea, the way the Falcons jinked and ducked through and around their line of attack. The robotic gunners fired with mechanical perfection, but *dis* turrets and rocket launchers could traverse, elevate and depress only so quickly. These were not bulky, awkward personnel carriers, pressed into service in a role that did not suit them: these were ships designed to fight and win in the air, and they moved better than anything the robot airships could throw at them.

Saint centered the lead airship in his scope and hit the 'fire' button. A SHAPE missile leaped from beneath his wing and struck the bow of the robot ship. It lurched under the impact, straightening just in time to take a second hit amidships from the next Falcon in line. The third did not expend another SHAPE missile, but streaked past the wounded ship, *dis* flaring from its nose and washing over the airship's scars, seeking the vulnerable systems hidden beneath the damaged armor.

The final two Falcons broke from their line at the last instant, cutting in head-on against the next closest airship.

Ni-Kin gripped the edges of his console as the airship lurched under him and scarlet rippled across the board before his eyes. Panicked cries came from the operators and weaponsmen seated before him; the communications officer swung around in his seat.

"Fleet Captain! The engineer reports penetration of the hull at two points—Sir! They are using *dis* against the opening their missiles have created!"

"Notify the squadron," Ni-Kin said, "to maintain formation on this ship. Pilot: put us about one-hundred-eighty degrees and maintain that course—but keep shifting attitude vertically and horizontally." That should prevent the Americans from getting a long, clear shot at the vulnerable gaps in their armor.

"Falcon Five Leader, this is Five. Hostiles are turning. Sir, they're leaving the city."

"We're not finished with them yet." Saint looked

down on the city, with its enormous dagger's-thrust of ruin cut into its heart. He knew people who lived—had lived—there, remembered their pride in the way their city had grown in just forty years. "As soon as they're clear, we go for the last ship in line. And then the next. It's gonna be a long flight home for those bastards." A touch on the stick, gentle pressure on the pedals. The image on his target scope canted to one side and the instruments surrounding it twitched. "Form up on me."

Ni-Kin watched in his aft screen as the Falcons curved in behind Ship Five. The weaponsmen in his ship bent to their controls and added their fire to the destruction being thrown behind the formation as the airships fled back toward the mountains. Ni-Kin had scored a great victory that day; he felt no need to dispute that fact with these dogged barbarians.

Ship Five staggered as he watched, under the impact of first one missile and then another, and another. The Americans struck with five heavy missiles against the one robot ship, and the last two combined their missiles with *dis* and smaller rockets. Then the five pursuits were flashing past the airships, too fast and too nimble to be trapped by the slashing *dis* beams that sought them, too agile to take more than a few ineffectual hits from the shower of rockets thrown at them.

Ship Five was swinging away out of line. Ni-Kin was stunned to see thick black smoke pouring from its savaged tail.

"Sir!" The communications officer called. "I have lost all contact with Ship Five!"

"I see. Pilot: maintain your course. Weaponsmen look to your arms. *Karnak* system: set your weapon for wide field and short range. If the barbarians dare that maneuver a second time they will pay."

But the Americans did not attack again, not immediately. Ni-Kin watched as the tiny silver mite

132

curved up into the sky and fell upon the diminished Ship Five a second time. A single *dis* beam sought them, and then there was no longer an airship there, just smoke and burning wreckage tumbling to the ground.

Ni-Kin watched the Falcons pull out in straight and level chase behind his squadron. The robots reacted just the way they had been instructed to: heavy missiles flew from their launchers and curved back against the American planes. Not one reached its target. *Dis* and rockets and quick, economical dodges thwarted them. Characteristically, Ni-Kin had yet to feel any real fear of this unexpected enemy; his primary emotion so far was indignation at the temerity of this pack of savages in marring his triumph with expensive casualties.

The Falcons screamed in dead astern of the airships, forgetting tactics, forgetting proper pursuit curves, just using the sheer speed of their ships to haul in the distance between Han and American, ignoring the fire the last ship put out, that the other ships tried to drop on them without hitting their imperiled sister.

Saint held his fire, closing, horsing the ship back into line against the pull of the *dis*-created turbulence around him, countering the lurches of rockets impacting against his fuselage and wings. Then he was in as close as he could get without taxing along the bastard's hull, and let go with a SHAPE that reduced a rocket battery to trash and burrowed on in. Then he stood the Falcon on one wing and went skimming along the flank of the formation. A sudden stinging pain in his chest told him that his cardiogard disc had come to life, pumping current into his heart and keeping it pumping in spite of itself as he flicked through the *karnak* field. Then he was racing out ahead of the Han formation and turning off to the right, climbing out with his flight tight behind him.

Ship Four lasted even more briefly than Ship Five. The steady pounding of SHAPE missiles broke through to the *rep* generators at the heart of the ship and the airship flipped onto its back and drove straight into the desert floor.

Ni-Kin suddenly realized that his flagship was the next airship in line for attack.

"Order ships Two and Three into formation abreast," he said quickly, "and order a retreat at full speed toward the mountains." The view in his screens rotated as the airships turned to flee.

Saint held his forces off above and behind the retreating airships. The five Falcons had eleven SHAPE missiles left between them: enough to definitely eliminate two of the three remaining airships—or, they could spread it a bit thinner. . . .

"Falcon Five, this is Falcon Five Leader. Falcon Two and Three will follow me in against the starboard airship. Falcon Four will take the center and Five the last one. Punch some good holes on this run, boys; we'll finish the job with *dis*."

"*Aknol that, Leader.*" The rest of the flight acknowledged his instructions.

Arcing over high and steep, they fell on the trapped Han.

Fire and smoke burst out in the control room, obscuring Ni-Kin's view of the screaming crewmen before him. In one of his screens, one of the handful still working, he saw the blazing fragments of Ship Three break apart and fall. Then the ship lurched upright and the smoke began to clear as the emergency blowers drew it out of the cabin. Ni-Kin looked around at his command. Everywhere were dead consoles and screens, lightless and scored with the scorch-marks of a dozen violent cross-circuits.

"Pilot, report," he said.

"Fleet Captain, we have approximately fifty percent power remaining on the *rep* generators. Our current altitude is less than three hundred meters but holding.

We are maintaining approximately quarter-speed, sir. We cannot gain sufficient altitude to clear the mountains we must pass and still retain lateral maneuverability. Any attempt to do so will overload at least one *rep* generator and doom us."

"Weaponmaster?"

"*Dis* and rocket batteries still operable, sir, although our store of munitions is badly depleted and the power available for generating *dis* is limited. Still, we have full beam capability on any one *dis* battery at any given moment. All heavy missile launchers inoperative; the *karnak* weapon is gone, for all the good it did us. But we are not helpless, sir." The crew were calming down through execution of their duties, that was good.

"Communications?"

"Sir, Ship Three is destroyed. Ship Two is holding station to port in response to our automatic damage transmission. What readings I can still make indicate that Two can still maneuver but has taken heavy damage to its offensive systems. It can fly, but it cannot flight."

"Whereas our handicap is precisely the opposite. Very well. Pilot: set a course for the mountainside; we shall use it to shield our flank. Communications, order Ship Two to cross to our starboard flank—we shall use its mass to shield us as long as it remains. Then transmit a report of our actions to our Prince and our City."

Everyone understood what that meant: Ni-Kin did not expect to return home alive, to tell his own tales. But he had not yet surrendered hope.

"Communications, what is the present disposition of our drop-ship forces?"

"Fleet Captain, I mark one element operating approximately one hundred kilometers from here."

"Summon them."

"Sir, I must point out that those ships are carrying out

the wishes of our Prince on their present mission, and that they are no match for American fighting craft in any event."

"They are no match for American aircraft prepared for them, Communications Officer. But these shall be otherwise occupied. I will see our work on this city finished, one way or another."

"Yes, Fleet Captain."

Falcon Five circled high above the surviving Han airships, waiting. For several seconds it had seemed as though their work was finished, but now Saint could no longer trick himself into believing that the Han were no longer airworthy.

"All right," he said. "Falcon Five, this is Falcon Five Leader. Those bastards don't know when they're beaten, so we're going in again. We'll go for the outermost ship first, then we'll try to cut that last one away from the mountainside where we can get at him. Copy?" A chorus of assent sounded in his headphones. "Smash. Follow me down."

Ship Two held its course as the American planes dropped on it. The single rocket battery it boasted opened fire, but with its traverse-ring blocked by a strip of torn armor, its shot went hopelessly wide. The gunnery of Ni-Kin's flagship was better. The weaponsmen had given up on trying to track the nimble Falcons; instead, they picked a point the flight had to dive though and saturated it with rockets and *dis*. Saint's Falcon lurched under multiple impacts and a warning light flickered briefly on his board, then he was in the clear again, the rest of the flight swinging wide of the hotspot.

Ni-Kin's ship edged forward of the beleaguered Two to keep the Falcons under fire as they broke from their long, shallow dives, pouring dis and rockets broadside into the dying robot ship. Ironically, the severity of the airship's damage was the very thing that saved it. Much of the American's fire was wasted on further destroying already ruined systems and structures.

But not all. The airship staggered as *dis* and rockets struck home, its stupid, fearless cybernetic pilot doing precisely the things necessary to keep it airborne as system after system was torn into ruin around him.

The airship slowed and stopped, and stood stubbornly braced on four *rep* legs, unable to advance, incapable of surrender, as Falcon Five climbed away for a final attack. Ni-Kin ordered his flagship down, sheltering somewhat under the helpless bulk of the last of his squadron. He waited.

Saint cursed as he swung away above the savaged Ship Two, which hung motionless in the air, swaying slightly as its pilot tried to keep up with the constant fluctuations in the damaged *rep* generators. If the Han had proven this tenacious forty years ago, humans would still be hiding under trees.

"Falcon Five, this is Leader. Let's do it again." He nosed over and dove towards the unmoving airships, the four other planes in his flight tight behind him.

They were halfway to their target when the new voice echoed in his earphones. *"Falcon Five, this is Mako Flight out of Badlands. Start a long break to the right and start it now. You've got three drop-ships coming down on top of you and you can lead them to us."*

Saint popped the top plate of his canopy armor and looked back and up. Three tiny silvery dots were gaining swiftly on the ships following him, growing even as he watched. He buttoned up again and tripped his mike.

"Falcon Five, this is Leader," he called. "Break right, in formation, on me." And he hauled back on the stick and stomped in rudder.

The Falcon slewed out of its dive and into level flight, groaning in protest at the strain of such an abrupt maneuver. But Saint had no time to nurse his ship—Falcon Five was caught in the worst possible position there was for meeting a Han drop-ship. It would be all but impossible to get out from under the Han ships before they came within *dis* range. Their only real chance was to hope that the Han would follow them into Mako Flight's guns.

They did. But not soon enough.

There was a brief cry of alarm as *dis* enveloped the tail ship in the formation, and his control surfaces lost their grip on the air. The pilot immediately went for his cold-rocket assist to break clear, standard operating procedure—but his ship had already begun to tumble and the sudden acceleration drove him right straight into the ground.

"Scatter!" Saint yelled, and the remaining four Falcons broke every which way, each pilot hoping that he would not be the one the drop-ships singled out for the rest of their run. Then his ultroscope screen glowed with a cold blue light and he felt the stick go dead in his hand. His hand started automatically for the red rocket-assist trigger before him, and then checked itself as he saw the nose of the guide on his attitude gauge canting away from the vertical. He was trapped, falling helplessly through a column of *dis*-spawned vacuum toward the ground. He didn't even know how far he had to fall —his altimeter was useless in vacuum—all he could do was pull back in the ineffectual stick and wait for the inevitable impact—

Air suddenly struck at the ship with thick, supporting waves. The altimeter needle threw itself over to register a number shockingly low—and then the nose was coming up, higher and higher as the rate-of-descent slowed, and he was level and safe, ninety meters above the desert.

He swung the Falcon up and around, back toward his

attacker. The drop-ship wasn't there. A long streamer of filthy black smoke culminating in a pile of wreckage marked its passing. A similar pyre marked the desert perhaps a mile past the first, and then he saw the last drop-ship, toylike in the distance, pirhouetting around its single *rep* ray to bring its *dis* beam to bear on some target off his scope. Suddenly the screen went black as, something that shook the Falcon with its passing as an old house would tremble in a gale rushed overhead and at the drop-ship, tongues of fire bursting from beneath its stubbed delta wings and drilling through the thin skin of the drop-ship, to crumple it and strike it from the sky.

Hopper pulled the big Mako fighter around and back into the formation orbiting above the Han airships.

"Mako Leader to Falcon Five Leader," Hc called. "Looks like you've been trying to hog all the business to yourself 'round here."

"Yeah." Saint looked down at the tiny, unreal form of the shattered Falcon pursuit ship lying crushed upon the desert beyond the wreckage of the drop-ships, and past it to the city shrouded in fire and murk. "Well, we had to leave you something, I guess."

"We'll finish things here. You boys head back to Barstow and get some rest," Hopper said.

Suddenly Andreas Saint *was* tired, desperately so. The strain of the long hours in the air and the impact of the high-g maneuvers of the battle with the airships settled on his shoulders in one burdensome mass, as though he had shrugged off some psychic jump-belt and was abruptly forced to bear the weight of his exhaustion unaided. The oxygen his mask fed him scratched and burned his throat when he breathed; his back felt as though it had fused to the material of the seat cushioning. But then he looked down again on the torn and burning city, and the wrecked ship that held his man's corpse.

"Aknol that, Mako Leader," he said, very properly, very clamly. "But I think we'd rather stick around and see the end of it first."

Hopper was smart enough to catch the change in Saint's tone, and smart enough to understand.

"Aknol, Falcon Five Leader, Mako Leader copies." Hopper kept his tone just as level and formal as Saint's. He knew that was all the admission the Falcon pilot would need, and that Saint would not accept a spoken apology for Hopper's flippancy when he did not really believe that the Federal pilot knew what he was apologizing for. "Mako Flight, form on me in two elements, line abreast. Let's finish this fast."

The big pursuit ships ranked themselves into two elements of three ships apiece, lead element lower. Thy flew at far less than their maximum combat speed; there was no need to hurry now. Air-brakes extended from wing-surfaces and fuselages, flaps were trimmed, and the Makos became slow, rock-steady firing platforms capable of putting their ordnance directly where their pilots wanted it. Ponderous and lethal, they cruised toward the waiting airships, their forty-two remaining SHAPE missiles armed and ready.

Ship Two broke up into a thousand burning shards and fell away off Ni-Kin's screen, giving him a perfect view of the six Makos closing on his ship.

The weapons operators didn't even wait for his command, but opened fire on the American ships as fast as their weapons could be brought to bear. Explosions blackened the air around the Makos. They did little else; the pursuits continued to drive toward the airship as through fastened to rails. The Hans' weakened *dis* batteries bathed the Makos in blue disruptive energies that lacked the power at that range to do anything but draw an immediate hail of explosive rocketry in response. The *dis* battery controllers could only sit back and stare at their screens helplessly as their weapons were to chewed to ribbons.

White smoke streamed back from the Makos as they opened fire with their SHAPE missiles. The airship lurched beneath Ni-Kin's seat; fresh smoke began to pour into the cabin. More missiles struck into the airship, and it began to list to one side. As the ship rolled it canted its remaining defense batteries away from their targets. Weaponsmen could only scream with anger and fear as they depressed their launchers as far as they would bear and emptied their magazines in long, futile streams of fire.

The board before Ni-Kin was a solid mass of scarlet cross-hatchings. The smoke was thickening all around him, somewhere within its intangible impenetrability an alarm was shrilling, selfishly demanding attention for its own small problem amidst the anarchy that surrounded it.

The ship lurched again. Ni-Kin reached for his microphone switch, intending to order the ship set down, with some vague idea of fighting it as a ground emplacement and clawing some last small measure of revenge out of the Americans who would come after them. He never reached it. The ship rolled over onto one side as an entire rank of *rep* generators failed under a direct hit, and the cabin fell away from beneath Ni-Kin. Fire and smoke billowed up around him as he hung in free suspension within the falling ship. He never heard his own scream among the shrieks of buckling metal. And he never felt the impact.

The last airship rolled wildly down the mountainside, trailing flame and smoke and wreckage all the way to the desert floor.

Hopper led his ships away from the mountain as he

cleaned his plane up, retracting brakes and flaps, converting her back from airborne weapons system into a sleek flying machine again.

Sunlight poured into the cockpit as the inertron armor slid back off the canopy. Hopper looked back to check the disposition of his flight, and then ahead.

The four Falcon pursuits, missiles spent, smudged and blackened by rocket-burst and wreck-smoke, stood off in perfect formation. Squinting, Hopper could make out within their cockpits the small bright reflections of four helmet visors turned to view the blazing wreckage of the final Han airship. Then, without a word, the four planes wheeled as one and climbed away, toward the coast and home.

Hopper understood. "Mako Flight, this is Mako Leader. Those boys have done their job. We'll stand by here and keep an eye on things until some local air shows up."

"You have to be kidding," Rogers said. His personal field transport, a personnel carrier modified to take the additional electronic and communication gear Rogers required, rested on the pad outside his office tower. He would have preferred a faster ship, better suited to fighting, but he had learned his lesson from the communications difficulties he had encountered during the Peruvian Recurrence. There was no way a commander could keep track of an entire campaign over local tactical cannels without monopolizing them to the detriment of field commanders who needed their communications as badly as he did. A token attempt had been made at making the ship somewhat more combat-worthy by the addition of a traversible two-launcher SHAPE battery atop the hull, but Rogers did not kid himself that this was adequate. He had resigned himself to the fact that others would have to do most of his fighting for him from now on.

Now it looked as though someone might have to do all of it.

"I'm sorry, sir, Brock Rogers said, shifting uncomfortably. "But the Council requests your immediate presence."

"Dammit." Rogers turned and looked overhead as another wave of troop carriers and armored personnel carriers flew past the towers, heading west. "Will Holcomb would have told them I'd already left, Captain." But you're no Will Holcomb, and you didn't, he thought, and now there's no way I can avoid this. "Isn't this something I can handle over the screen?"

"I'm sorry, sir. They insisted on seeing you."

"All right, Captain. Notify the Council that I'm on my way. Then get on to Niagra Air and order a flight of Falcons withheld as escort for my transport."

He was belting for the Council Hall before his aide could answer him.

". . . and so the Federation Canadien had denied our forces permission to cross their territory, Marshal." Council Chairman Dan Gerardi of the Barrens Gang looked down at him from the podium. His round, fleshy face was twisted into an expression of surprised indignation, as though he found it impossible to believe that any country would have the temerity to object to one of his armies tramping over it.

Knowing Gerardi, Rogers thought, he probably did. He sighed. The bosses of today were a different breed from Boss Ciardi and the other leaders he had known in the days of the War of Liberation. Patiently, he set about discovering what they had done wrong.

"Mister Chairman, just how was the Federation notified of our troop movements?"

"Why, we got Boss Loup-Main on screen and notified him that our forces would be passing over Federation airspace en route to Oregon."

143

"And he said?"

"He became extremely agitated and stated that on no account could he allow such an action without consulting with the Bosses of the region affected, and that until such consultations have been completed we were in no wise to attempt to transit Federation borders. Then he disconnected."

Rogers sat motionless facing the Chairman's podium. To an outside observer it might have seemed as if he was merely trying to phrase his next sentence. But in truth Rogers didn't dare move, as the adrenalin rush flooded into his brain; it was all he could do to choose between throwing something then or later.

"Mister Chairman," he said, speaking slowly and carefully, "I believe that we might be facing a problem of semantics here."

"What the hell are you talking about, Marshal?"

Rogers sat back in his chair and gripped its arm. But his tone of voice stayed calm and even and the whitening of his knuckles was invisible from the podium.

"Let me put that another way, Mister Chairman. How would you feel if some boss just got you on screen and *told* you he was moving troops over your territory, without even asking your permission?"

Gerardi puffed up visibly. "That's an entirely different matter."

"Is it?"

"Dammit, Marshal, this isn't some petty gang squabble."

"Then why are you treating it like one?"

"We're talking about Federal troops under Alliance orders here."

"The Federation Canadian isn't part of the Alliance." Rogers' control was fraying rapidly at Gerardi's density. The Barrens boss honestly seemed to consider Loup-Main's rudeness as more important than getting American troops into Washington.

"That's none of our concern," Gerardi said.

"It should be, unless you want to do business with the Han and the Canadians at the same time."

"We didn't call you here for a discussion of diplomatic niceties, Marshal. What we want from you now is advice as to what action this Council should take on this Federation interference in our affairs."

Rogers' temper snapped.

"This Council is not even formally seated, Mister Chairman," he said hotly. "It can and will take no action not authorized by the provisional government of the American Alliance. But if I were to choose to interpret your statement as a *request* for information as to how the provisional government intends to deal with this problem, I would say that I intend to contact Boss Loup-Main personally. Then I would establish the nature of the *misunderstanding* that has occurred, and request his cooperation in dealing with the situation that faces us. That way we can get our troops to where they're needed and not keep them running around in circles because of some stupid display of arrogance on the part of people in no real position to make such a display." Rogers stood. "Now, if the Council will excuse me, I will try and get our forces moving again."

"Marshal Rogers, you are *not* excused." Rogers stopped and looked back at Gerardi. "I would like to remind you, Marshal, that for all your cavalier attitude toward this body, this Council will indeed be seated, shortly. And we will remember this."

"Are you finished, sir?"

"For the moment."

"Good." Rogers turned and strode from the Council Hall.

The screen before Rogers' seat showed the bow where

145

the American forces from the East Coast were being forced to swing south around the spur of Federation territory that spiked down to the Great Lakes. Since the partial melting of the Antarctic ice-cap the Lakes had swollen and overrun their former shores, so that they now resembled more a narrow, twisting sea than a connected series of freshwater bodies.

"Marshall Rogers." Rogers turned as much as he could in the cramped confines of the personnel carrier and looked to where Brock sat at the communications console. Beyond him the two warrant officers in charge of the tactical input systems sat limned in the pale light from their screens, gathering the information that appeared in condensed form on Rogers' panel. In the other direction, facing forward, the pilot and gunner sat in their cockpit, segregated from the men in back by a thick plate of inertron-plated ultron armor. The rest of the carrier's interior, where six other men and women would normally have been packed in, was filled with electronic gear, all the sophisticated necessities for directing a major battle.

"I have your channel to Boss Loup-Main, Sir," Brock said.

"Thank you, Captain," Rogers said. "Put it through on my board, please."

"Yes, sir."

"Sir, I mark several unidentified aircraft on station just the other side of the Federation border," one of the warrant officers said.

"Aknol. Order the flight to orbit this side of the border." Rogers switched channels. "Pilot, hold us here."

"Yes, sir." The four Falcons escorting the carrier broke off and climbed for altitude as the carrier eased to a stop, hovering on fiercely hissing landing jets.

"Boss Loup-Main coming up on your screen now, Marshal."

146

"Right." Rogers turned back to his screen. A picture was forming there, of a stocky, dark-haired man with a sharp-featured face and curly black hair. A silver brooch shaped into a stylized wolf's head fastened shut the collar of his rust-colored tunic. He was frowning.

"*B'jour, Maitre Loup-Main,*" Rogers said, shifting into the French-based patois that most of the Federation on the East Coast favored. He could make himself understood in it; he'd had enough experience with the Canadians of his twentieth century mining days to pick up some of the language.

"*B'jour, Marshal,*" Jean-Jacques Loup-Main said. "*J'ne pense pas que c'est une visite sociale.*"

"No, it isn't," Rogers said. "I wish it was, though. You know we're having some trouble out in Old Washington, of course."

"*Vraiment.* We have been monitoring your people's transmissions. All our forces in the western territories are on their guard."

"I'm glad to hear that. Then you understand our problem."

"*Non.* I understand one of your problems. I realize that the Han have risen again. But your Chairman Gerardi—his problem I do not understand."

"Ah, *ça.* I thought it was something like that."

"Nothing like it at all, Marshal. It *was* that. Does the man expect my cooperation when he arbitrarily informs me that armed forces of a foreign power intend to intrude on the land of my people? Should I not object for them?"

"*Non,* Jean-Jacques. You should have done just as you did. All that I can do is apologize for the insult you have been offerred, and point out that Chairman Gerardi acted without any authority."

"How with no authority?" Loup-Main said angrily. "Every other thing the man said was "by the authority of the Alliance Council this" or "by the authority of the

Alliance Council that". How can you tell me he acted without authority?"

"*Maitre* Loup-Main, the Alliance Council has no power over the provisional government of the Alliance save to demand its dissolution—and they are hardly likely to do that in the midst of a war."

Jean-Jacques Loup-Main looked out at him from the screen in astonishment.

"*Tabernac*," he swore. "Do you tell me that the man has no power at all?"

"Outside of a remarkable power to irritate, none," Rogers said.

"*Sacré!* And these *batardes* hope to run your Alliance? I hope you do not intend to let them, my friend."

"Oh, I won't let them play completely without a nurse-maid." This was no time for a discussion of democratic niceties. "But in the meantime, we have to get our forces west as quickly as possible. Could you authorize our passage over Federation territory?"

"Of course I can. But you will understand if I keep my aircraft on patrol in your vicinity?"

"Certainly." That was only good politics. That way Loup-Main could go to his people and announce that the American overflight was being carried out under strict Federation supervision. "Thank you, *Maitre*."

"*C'rien.* I would never have refused," Loup-Main said. "But you should have asked."

"*D'accord. À bientot.*"

The screen blanked.

"Marshal Rogers," one of the warrant officers said, "the Federation aircraft are veering off."

"Sir," Brock said, "they're giving pemission to enter Federation territory."

"Then let's go," Rogers said. "Notify the units on standby that passage is authorized for Federation territory."

The carrier dropped briefly as thrust was transferred from landing jets to level-flight propulsion, then the ship was picking up speed toward Old Washington as Falcons dropped into place around her.

Klein tensed in his harness as the armored personnel carrier took another hit. He wasn't thrown about very badly; there wasn't room to be. He was wedged in tightly on the narrow bench between Morales and Joanie Custen, the squad's long-gunner, his knees locked between those of the man facing him. He couldn't even get out of the ship before the person in line ahead of him did —that would be like trying to open the middle tooth of a zipper first.

The crowding was the only part of all this that was real to Klein. He could remember the shock and the anger that had run through the militia 'containing' the Han redoubt as the reports of scattered attacks upon their homes in the Southwest began to come in, first in a trickle and then in a flood, until it had been all the regular cadres could do to keep their men from going to their officers in a body and demanding that a relief force be sent back immediately—never mind how it would be organized, never mind what that would mean for the men and women left to face the Han fortress with great gaps in their lines and no reserves, just send us back where we can *do* something, dammit!

The near-mutiny had been defused finally, by the federal troops serving at the squad-and-company-commander levels. The sullen, angry militiamen had gone back to their vigil, watching their artillery and close-support air duelling with the heavy batteries of the Han. Then the word had come down from Regimental that intelligence had decided that the Han had been softened up sufficiently to admit the possibility of an infantry attack. Looking at the pillar of smoke and fire in the distance, stabbed through with blue waves of *dis,* Klein couldn't see that the Han had been significantly weakened. But then he wasn't an officer; he didn't have the military expertise to see the value of sitting out in a field watching airplanes when his home was being burned down behind him. So he joined his squad in the troop compartment of the battered, weapon-scarred personnel carrier that set down at the rallying point, to hear a briefing on their target.

But now, in the crowded semidarkness of the carrier, Klein had no idea of what would happen next. Oh, he knew he was headed into combat, but he had no conception of what that meant. He tried to picture what it would be like to actually go into battle, moving and fighting in the very heart—well, on the edge—of that pillar of smoke and destruction that had become a virtual fixture on the horizon; he couldn't. He could recall the maps he had been briefed from readily enough, and the tricks and tactics of fighting that he had been trained in. And he tried to scale up that dark smudge in the distance, tried to imagine those smokes and fires around himself, those energies directed at him—but his best efforts fell short. There was a solidity, a reality, an *impact* missing that should have been there, and he knew it. . . .

Helden sat in the cramped cabin of the grounded command carrier, watching the crawling blips of light that represented his attack force on the screen. It was not a full attack; the Han fortress was too strong for any attack he could make with the forces he had to succeed. But against that southern spur, where the fortress extended a complex of batteries to provide flanking fire for its main body, a limited assault might bring results.

And Helden needed results, badly. He should never have listened to Cullen Teder; he knew that now. When the first word of Han had come in he should have notified Niagra, brought in the Federals and their stronger forces right at the start. But he hadn't. He had listened to Cullen Teder, with his insane talk of treating *Han* as a 'local' problem, as though they were little more than a border squabble between gangs. He knew why he had listened, too. He had wanted to believe Cullen, and he had stripped away the greater part of the SubCouncil's defenses and brought them north behind him, because a victory over Han would have been the perfect thing to get his career moving upward again. It would have put him right back in line for promotion, after years of being passed over as a regular officer who couldn't handle any job better than nursemaiding a gaggle of irregulars playing Home Guard. Defeating a Han force in Old Washington, right on the doorstep of the Alliance, would have put Helden well up in the rarefied heights reserved for heroes such as Marshal Rogers and the veterans of the Peruvian Recurrence.

Instead, he was now the idiot who had taken his men off to play soldier in the trees while the people he was supposed to be protecting were attacked. The only thing he could do now was hope and pray that the cover story he had given Niagra, about shifting the troops for maneuvers, would hold. But in the meantime, he would make at least this one attack, so that he would have at least one constructive act to his credit before the Federals assumed control of the operation. A victory could be parlayed into considerable good publicity.

If he won one. . . .

The carrier jolted again. Morales stared off into space, listening to a message on the squad-leader's separate channel. Then he reached up and slapped his visor shut.

"Drop in thirty," he said over the squad channel. Klein tucked his chin into his chest and looked down, checking his harness and gear as best he could in the crowded cabin.

The twenty carriers of the attack force snaked in low over the ground towards the Han position, twisting and ducking along the contours of the terrain. *Dis* and missiles sought them out as they came on, rending the earth or evaporating it in great slashes punctuated by the explosive crack of air rushing into vacuum. But heavy batteries designed to deal with fast aircraft at altitude through patterned fire were not ideally suited to the wild, scrambling charge of the personnel carriers striking towards them on the deck.

They didn't always miss. A missile struck one of the armored personnel carriers head-on and stopped it cold, to drop down to the ground as an impervious shell protecting wreckage and bloody flesh. Two more were swept away from the concealment of their low-level flight by massive *dis* beams passing above them, and hammered into junk as they hung suspended in open air. Then the rest were in too close for the heavy batteries to track them.

The drop-ramp in the stern of the personnel carrier cycled open. Through it Klein could see the track of missiles and *dis* clawing at them.

The carrier straightened out into its drop run. Klein couldn't see ahead of the ship, but he knew from his briefing that the carriers were dropping down below the level of a low ridge that lay between them and the Han positions.

"Braking," Morales warned, and then an invisible hand was trying to mash the squad into the forward bulkhead of the compartment as the carrier slowed to a speed that would let them jump without killing themselves on impact.

"Clear harnesses." Klein barely had time to unsnap the two shackles that hooked him to the carrier's harness net before—"Go! Go! Go!"—the squad was shoving its way off the drop-ramp and scattering in ten different directions. All around him, the air was filled with falling bodies.

The carrier was breaking left even as Morales, last man out, cleared the ramp, opening its throttles and slamming the drop-ramp shut as it built up speed for its attack run against the Han.

Morales was barking orders even as Klein touched down and bounced again, putting distance between himself and the next trooper and dressing the line of attack. Off to his left, to the south, he could see Custen and Baker, her ammo carrier, readying their long-gun on its tripod and fixing a gravity-feed magazine of shells to the breech of their weapon. Klein unslung his own rocket-gun and worked a round into the chamber, then reached down to check that his heavy demolition charge was still firmly fastened to his hip. In the distance he could hear the rumble of firing as the heavy weapons to the rear hammered at the rest of the fortress.

New smoke and flame billowed up above the ridge-line, followed by a sullen rumbling. That was the sign of their personnel carriers' attack on their target, and their signal to jump off.

"*Squad, move!*" Morales' voice yelled within his helmet, and Klein kicked off, angling to just clear the ridge—

—and land in hell.

The line cleared the ridge unmolested, and jumped halfway to the Han positions without challenge. Then the field erupted in an earthquake of thunder and fountaining earth as the Han short-range batteries opened fire.

Klein lost sight of the troopers flanking him almost instantly. Then he had no time to look for them. His advance was changed to a frantic series of angled, semi-sidewise broken-field spurts, that carried him forward only because there was no way back through the virtually solid wall of explosions and *dis* that the Han were throwing at them. The interior of his helmet rang with the frantic cries of the troopers in his squad as they wormed their way towards their targets and shouted commands from Morales that nobody could obey because nobody could see what he was talking about. Rockets from the long-gunners began to burst among the Han emplacements in fierce balls of flame and broken earth; Han weapons replied but Klein didn't know it. The roar and shriek of Han weapons firing above him at the long-guns behind was no different from the sound of the weapons trying to kill him directly: it was all blended into one numbing, concussive vibration that admitted no distinction within itself, that admitted no conscious contemplation of anything at all but the maintenance of Klein's constant jinking, swerving advance, a kinetic counterpoint to the chaos of noise surrounding.

A woman screamed; the scream echoed and dopplered into the constant background of noise and was lost. Klein continued forward, swinging the weapon he had fired empty without realizing it. He could see the Hans positions clearly now, unshrouded by American fire. He didn't realize what that meant. A Han solid-slug automatic, an antipersonnel weapon, came into view off to his left. It was tracking back and forth mechanically, firing constantly—rocketfire had knocked out its monitor camera and the gunner was firing blind, just putting out rounds to thicken the curtain of fire that swept the ground before it. Klein dove for the base of the emplacement in one long, flat leap and fetched up beneath the pivoting weapon.

He was astonished at how quiet it had suddenly become. The rocketfire and the whipcrack of *dis* continued, the cries in his earphones went on—though not so loudly, now, not from so many throats—and then he realized that he had stopped screaming, that he had been shrieking as loudly as anyone all the way from the ridge, not from defiance or ferocity but in simple cursing incoherent denial of the death that sought him all around. He suddenly noticed that his weapon was empty, and fumbled a fresh stripper of rockets into the magazine. Then he lay there for a moment, taking comfort in the solid mass at his back, revelling in his comparative safety.

He rolled over on his stomach and looked around. And suddenly realized that he could see no other troopers. Here and there he could see Han emplacements burning, or weapons twisted to some strange angle, broken and useless, but he saw no sign of the men and women who must have done it all. The thought that he might be alone among the works of his enemy drove him closer to panic than anything else that he had been through so far. The fear twisted in him like a strong cord knotted around his vitals as he suddenly realized that his squad channel was silent. Feverishly, he chinned the switch for the general channel and restored the familiar chorus of frantic, half-voiced cries of other troopers. That, and the continuing ranging salvos of Han fire flooding outward, was almost reassuring: he may have been damned but he was not alone.

That didn't mean he intended to stick around any longer than he had to. But he was already within the ring of anti-personnel emplacements that surrounded the heavier batteries, and he still had his demolition charge. He rolled onto his back and noted the position of the next antipersonnel weapon, a light *dis* battery. Turning over, he found what he wanted, a heavy rocket launcher firing out towards the ridgeline. He edged to his knees and paused, thinking carefully, fixing what he intended to do.

Klein sprang to his feet and turned his weapon on the slug-thrower that had sheltered him. A three-shot burst tore it apart. Then he turned and lunged for the rocket launcher. Firing his gun one-handed, he tore the demolition charge from his hip as the launcher trembled under the impact of his rockets. The launcher traversed several degrees and jammed on a damaged section of track. As Klein reached it, it began to descend, being retracted by its operator. Klein lobbed the charge underhand. It struck fair and lodged in the launcher's mounting. Then the launcher was gone and the emplacement's hatch was closing over it. Klein didn't wait. He turned and knelt, bringing his rocket-gun to his shoulder and firing off the last of his magazine into the antipersonnel *dis* battery he had selected. Then he slung his weapon and belted flat out for the gap in the perimeter where the fields-of-fire of the two batteries he had destroyed overlapped.

It wasn't fast enough.

The ground lurched under him. The hatch sealing in the damaged launcher was torn from its mountings by a column of fire that stabbed up from below the earth as his demolition charge triggered the rockets remaining in the launcher. The fireball blossomed outward, hurling dirt and rock and torn metal before it. Something struck Klein a giant's blow in the back and threw him forward through the air, arched cruciform upon the expanding shockwave, to collapse in a heap beyond the Han perimeter.

The pain hit him then, but in a colder and more distant way than he had expected. Absently, he realized that he was going into shock. That became one more interesting fact he would really have to consider sometime soon, he decided, like the fluid warmth flowing down his right side and his overpowering urge to lie down and go to sleep. But for now he knew he had to concentrate on getting away from the Han positions, and so he tried, in a grotesque, lurching stumble that wouldn't have carried him ten yards but for the inertron jump-belt that he wore.

He went away for a little while then, and came back to find himself lying on his back with Joanie Custen bending over him. Her helmet was missing; blood trickled down from under her close-cut brown hair, and she held her left arm oddly, pressed tightly against her side.

"Come on, Klein," she was saying, "you're halfway there already. You can't stay here, dammit, come on!" And she hauled him upright by his jump-belt.

The utter silence finally penetrated the muzzy thickness blanketing his senses. "Nobody shooting," he mumbled.

"No, nobody's shooting," Custen said, pulling him along. "We're not big enough to shoot at."

She dragged him back toward the ridgeline, gasping in pain every time a landing jarred her injured arm. Once she went sprawling forward on her face; it was almost impossible to land easily on ground that had been torn into an earthern tangle by rocket-fire and slashing *dis*. It was several seconds before she could uncurl from her agonized crouch. Klein just lay there, watching her with the same detached interest he felt toward everything else. Finally she managed to get to her feet and grip his belt again, and they resumed their antlike crawling across the torn landscape.

At last they reached the top of the ridge Klein had left such a short time ago. Custen let gravity bring them down the far side, limiting her own efforts to simply keeping them upright as they floated down the slope.

Klein accepted it when Custen rolled him over on his face, leaving him to stare at grass while she examined his wound. He heard her gasp, a thin sound through the pickups of his helmet; idly, he wondered how bad it was.

He looked up at distant sound and saw an armored

personnel carrier flying above them. Then he couldn't see much of anything as Joanie Custen grabbed his helmet and pulled it roughly off his head. She quickly donned it and chinned its phone to the general channel as Klein watched the carrier cruise out of his sight.

Then a great shadow was spreading out around them, and Joanie Custen was shaking him and pulling him upright, so that he could see the carrier settling to the ground nearby, in the shelter of the ridge. The drop ramp slammed down and two troopers were bounding toward them. Klein felt himself being lifted and his head fell back, for an inverted view of the ridgeline, suddenly obscured by the hatchway of the carrier. The ramp began to rise, reducing his view of the world to a progressively-smaller strip of light and landscape. Then the ramp clanged shut, leaving him in darkness, and Klein finally gave in to the sleep that sought him.

Helden watched the scattered dots of the surviving troops pulling back from the Han lines. There were more dots showing the key of the second company in the assault; they had turned back before ever reaching their target. Of the first company, painfully few were left, perhaps one carrier-load out of the initial ten. But Helden didn't care. The 'spur' of Han positions had been blunted drastically, reduced to barely half its length. Its function had not been eliminated. It still provided flanking fire down the face of both the inland and seaward flanks of the Han fortress. But then he had not expected an attack with only two companies to succeed. He had expected it to do what it did—change the shape of his map so that he could go back home and show the people that by God, they were giving those Han bastards a hell of a good fight before the Federals turned up. Even the casualties might possibly be turned to Helden's advantage; they would lend a convincing air of authority to his claim that the expedition up north had not been a mistake—after all, if there were more Han up there, and they were that tough. . . ?

Yes. Yes, this would do him good, Helden decided. Satisfied, he turned to his board and ordered his forces to stand down, to return to their passive containment positions pending the arrival of the Federal troops. . . .

"It would seem, High Captain, that your plan to conceal our city has not succeeded."

Ken-Li was aware of the significance of his personal audience was Prince Ho-Tin. The chances were very good that he would not leave the Throne Room alive. The Prince liked to deliver death sentences in person.

"Excellency, I could not in truth state otherwise."

"So. Several once-distinguished servants of this throne have been disgraced and cast from our favor for earlier mistakes in this venture, and their errors did not even cost us a fleet that we shall be hard-pressed to replace. What then should we do about one who *did* lose us that fleet, and at a time when it could be of great value in the defense of this city?"

"Most Honored Prince, I can conceive of no punishment sufficient for such a crime."

Ho-Tin leaned forward. "Then can you give us one good reason not to order you slain where you stand?"

"Honored Prince, I can give you two—I did not commit such a crime and should I die, this city will die as well."

Ho-Tin stood. The guards in the chamber reacted to this uncommon event by reflexively closing in on Kin-Li, who stood very carefully motionless, never taking his eyes off the Prince.

"We would hear an explanation of this," Ho-Tin said, in that quiet tone of voice that denoted deepest anger.

Kin-Li nodded. "There can be no denying the loss of

the ships, Excellency. Nor can I deny that the main intention of the mission has been a failure. But consider—the Americans to date seem to have discovered the location of but one of our sub-cities. At least, they have not attacked elsewhere, nor are they postioned to threaten either this city itself or any of the remaining satellites. Had we withheld the fleet, we could not send it forth now in our defense without revealing our true location. But, by launching it when we did, Excellency, we have at least done grave damage to the homes and industries of the Americans, even if we have failed in our first aim of concealing our position. Even now, the chances are good that the Americans will be satisfied with the destruction of the sub-city currently under attack, and will look no further. Toward that end, I have ordered the evacuation of valuable personnel and machineries from the sub-city, Excellency. As soon as everything of any important has been transferred, I mean to seal off the transit link that joins us, that the Americans not discover it."

"You are assuming that you will still be in a position to issue such orders."

Ken-Li exulted silently. He had won. For the Prince to have softened from a direct death-threat to mere veiled hints about his demotion was the next best thing to a full apology and commendation for a Han.

"However, you have yet to explain to us your *second* statement. And frankly, we can find no interpretation of it that does not border on the treasonous."

"Honored Prince," Ken-Li said with wounded reproval, "I would never hold it within my heart even to dream of such abomination! I merely meant that should His Excellency choose to exercise his unquestionable prerogative and supplant me in the office to which he most graciously appointed me, my replacement would lose valuable hours familiarizing himself with the situation, hours that this city cannot spare, perhaps. I would not presume to beg His Excellency not to condemn me; but I should advise him that it would be to the best for all concerned if it should please him to forestall such action until the crisis that faces us has passed."

Slowly, Ho-Tin resumed his seat. He looked down at Ken-Li, frowning.

"You say that our fleet has inflicted considerable damage upon the barbarians' homes?"

He was safe. "Honored Prince, to judge by their communications, they are in a state of chaos."

"Very well, then. We are persuaded to trust your judgement, Fleet Captain—at least for a time."

Ken-Li bowed, deeply and fully. "I shall endeavor to my utmost to justify His Excellency's faith in this humble servant."

"Do so. Else we shall not live long enough to resent it."

Hun't'pir stood at the heart of the command chamber, admiring the weapon.

It seemed prosaic enough, in repose: a featureless cylinder of common rock, resting in its cradle within the first of the great magnetic rings marching out across the lunar landscape. The streak of nearly-pure iron ore that those magnets would grip could not be seen, nor could the massive energies building within the rings, energies meant to cast that mass of stone and ore at its target across space. At Hun't'pir's command, the rings would begin to draw the stone/ore cylinder along their length in magnetic suspension, free of the restricting friction of an atmosphere and accelerating constantly, until it burst free of the last ring with a final velocity of better than nine *kirreks* per second, beyond the grasp of the gravity of the small satellite beneath his feet.

The blue-white world that Hun't'pir meant to conquer hung suspended off to one side of the chamber. It annoyed Hun't'pir somewhat, that the target he aimed at should be so far out of line with the muzzle of his weapon, but he consoled himself with the fact that the world would be where it must in time for the weapon to do its job. He felt no doubt about that; Prl'lu did not make mistakes in such things.

Kor-sin-tu approached from his position at the doorend of the walkway. "All is in readiness, my Commander. The weapon is prepared for activation."

"Very well." Hun't'pir reached out to the small console before him and touched the appropriate control. Beyond him in the chamber the great cyclinder suddenly bobbed free of its nonferrous cradle, sole evidence of the sudden outpouring of power from the great machines far beneath him. Numbers appeared in the air before him, glowing scarlet in the harsh angular characters his people used. A human could not have read them, but from the way they suddenly switched from one to another, he might well have deduced that he was observing a countdown.

The final number flashed on the screen, a soft-cornered rctangle, the Prl'lu symbol that represented all-inclusive nothingness in the manner of the human 'zero'. Hun't'pir touched another control.

The cylinder began to move down the line of rings, not all that quickly at first, but always accelerating, faster and faster still, until it was nothing more than a featureless blur even to Hun't'pir's keen sight as it vanished into the distance.

Satisfied, Hun't'pir stood back and contemplated his imminent victory.

CHAPTER FOUR

Rogers was trying to remember what daylight looked like. He had seen it, briefly, when he stepped from his transport to stretch his legs upon arriving at the American positions encircling the Han sub-city. But that had been so long ago, before he found himself effectively chained to his console, trying not only to run a military operation but also obliged to oversee the relief movement to the Southwest SubCouncil.

The last of the Han robot ships had been blown out of the sky the day before, but their job was done. They had been programmed to do nothing but attack population centers—but that in retrospect had proved to be very nearly the perfect battle strategy for crippling the Americans. The Southwestern gangs could have coped with a major attack; they could have diverted the necessary resources from as many small gang nexi as needed to handle the problems of food and water and shelter for the resulting refugees. But a hundred smaller attacks were too much for them. They overloaded the machinery with a cacophony of conflicting demands. All over the Southwest small gangs found themselves without shelter or heavy transport, with foodstocks destroyed and wells gone, and with injured that needed moving and no place to move them to. Taos could offer no assistance. They were still busy digging out from under the ruins of their own Han attack. Cullen Teder and the administration of the SubCouncil were managing to keep track of the situation from their bunker, still buried beneath the wreckage of the administration building above them. That was the only thing that kept matters from going completely to hell in the biggest handbasket available. But knowing what the problem was didn't solve it.

Food and prefabricated shelters and medical supplies were being distributed as quickly as they could be ferried through Badlands and Barstow and Fresno. Will Holcomb had everything that could fly in the air, every cubic inch of cargo space filled. None of the gangs affected had yet objected to moving their injured to one of the undamaged gang nexi remaining, but many were refusing to leave their own territories completely unattended. Gang pride and gang rivalries would not permit it. That complicated matters, as it required shipping small loads to many separate points instead of mass deliveries of supplies to one central location, but Rogers could see no way around it. In any case, he wasn't certain he even wanted the refugees gathered together. The magnitude of the Han attack appalled him, and there was no guaranteeing that more wouldn't follow.

But water was the main problem. All over the desert wells and well-stations had been knocked out, and a water supply system geared to serve almost one hundred and fifty thousand men, women and children, had been reduced to a collection of jury-rigs and overworked backups adequate for barely a fifth of that number. And drilling equipment was not something that could be gathered up in ton lots like boxed food and shipped about as needed.

Well fine, Rogers thought. When in doubt, call somebody smarter than yourself. He activated his phone. "Heric, we've got a problem."

Wolsky looked back out at him from the screen. The untidy shelves of his Niagra office backed him. "So I had understood. Why do you think I'm back here where it's safe?"

"I mean besides the Han."

"Then what?"

"Where am I going to get drinkable water for a hundred thousand people?"

"Hmmm," Wolsky said. "In the Southwestern desert. That is a problem. When do you need it?"

"An hour ago."

"Ah." Wolsky scowled, already sinking into the problem, drifting away from Rogers. "It may not be impossible. I will get back to you on this, Marshal."

"Quickly, Wol, please."

"Of course."

"Then it can be done?" Wolsky asked.

"I don't see why not," Ruth Harris said. She should have been dog-tired and fading after her hasty flight back from the Antarctic Prl'lu base. But Wolsky had presented her with a challenge, and to Doctor Ruth Harris, that was better than benzedrine.

They studied the diagram on the screen before them, a schematic of a common *dis* rocket engine.

"For the distances you're talking about, Wol, it shouldn't matter," Ruth said. "Once you've got the *dis* generator and the receptacle chamber properly synched up, I don't see why it makes any difference whether they're mounted on the same framework or five hundred miles apart. No, as long as you're satisfied with limiting utilization of the effect to the molecular level, you should be fine."

"We'll have to set up a second field, though, perhaps several, to extract the incompatible trace minerals."

"Oh, that shouldn't be any problem, not if the first stage works."

"In that case, I should fly back to the SubCouncil to supervise a test-project. I'll need a couple of your bright young fellows to take care of the minor details like putting the damned thing together."

"No trouble. But what will you be doing?"

"My dear colleague, what should any biologist do when confronted by a problem in advanced physics? I shall wander around looking wise and important."

"Good. I would hate to think you tarnished the name of our profession by failing to appear omniscient."

Alone in a thousand cubic kilometers of emptiness, the rock/ore projectile hung suspended against the stars. For all its great speed it seemed motionless in space, fixed in place above the cold lunar disk that had birthed it. Only the small blue world ahead of it, closer now to the projectile's line of flight than it had been at the moment of the weapon's launching, gave any indication of the progress the great stone missile had made on its journey.

Rogers sat back and looked at his screen unhappily.

The Han redoubt was encircled by a ring of American forces as thickly as a walnut clenched in a strong man's fist. Unfortunately, the analogy went farther than that. Rogers had better than thirty thousand regular troops surrounding the Han perimeter in place of the thinly-stretched irregulars now filtering back south to aid in the reconstruction of their ravaged homes. He had more and heavier artillery, superior logistic support, and a solid umbrella of air power from the reinforcing squadrons rushed west to operate out of Badlands and a dozen temporary fields scattered all over the Pacific Northwest. If push came to shove, he knew he could probably even call on the tough Canadian troops massing on their southwestern border.

But it wasn't enough. He believed he could win—he knew he could win—but he didn't see *how* he could without taking thousands of casualties. One simply didn't order men to rush at *dis* batteries and then expect to get them back alive. Roger had seen too much of that sort of thinking in his first war, nearly six hundred years ago. He wasn't willing to pay that high a price; he wouldn't have been even if he hadn't seen the numbed, broken survivors of Helden's abortive, face-saving assault.

The memory of that crowded ward in the small field hospital awoke fresh anger in him. Rogers hadn't challenged Helden's glib explanation of the irregulars' attack on the Han flanking salient—then—but he hadn't bought a word of it, either. The entire fiasco had smacked of the 'active patrolling' so many officers had been enamored of back in 1917. It hadn't involved a large enough committed force to do anything but get a lot of good men and women killed and ensure that Helden got mentioned in the twenty-fifth century equivalent of dispatches as maintaining the proper tactical posture. It looked good, but Helden had paid for that good impression with the blood of men and women who had a right to expect more responsible treatment from their officers, and that left a bad smell in Rogers' nostrils.

In fact, the entire affair had a bad smell to it. The first notification the government had received of the presence of Han in North America had come with the panicked reports of Han air attacks in the Southwest. Then had come word of the irregulars engaging a Han city—and how had they even known where to look?—and the requests for Federal assistance. And those requests had come not from Helden, but from junior officers suddenly faced with a totally unexpected assault and no resources to pit against it. And wasn't it awfully damned convenient that two regiments of irregulars just happened to go on maneuvers right on top of a hidden Han complex. It almost made up for their being pulled from the cities and nexi they were assigned to defend. But convenience didn't answer any questions. How did Helden hope to justify such a training maneuver that so completely disrupted the defenses of the region he was charged with protecting? The military strength of the Southwest had been *stripped,* there was no other word for it—stripped to add numbers to an unscheduled training exercise. What could justify that?

Rogers thought he knew, and he didn't like the answer. He looked down at the reports on his small desk. They weren't formal documents: they weren't dated, signed, countersigned, annotated, supplemented and/or collated in proper rear echelon fashion—but then Rogers suspected that he would never have seen these particular reports had he waited for them to reach him through channels. The only reason he had these rough faxes that he did was due to his grandson/aide's inefficiency. Instead of requesting a back-action update through the correct channels in the irregulars, Brock had for some ungodly but fortunate reason elected to get reports from each unit at the battalion and company levels, as though hoping to impress Anthony Rogers with quantity of result rather than quality of methods. Whatever his reasons, he had done Rogers a favor.

He now had in his hands reports of half a dozen human gangs found wiped out all over the Pacific Northwest. He had no dates, but it was easy enough to infer from internal evidence roughly when each had occurred—and all of them had occurred before the Han assault on the Southwest.

So Rogers had to face the fact that Helden had chosen to pursue a private little war against the Han without taking the trouble to notify the government in Niagra. Working from that premise, it didn't require an overly paranoid sensibility to assume other lies, earlier lies, about hyperthyroid troop exercises and maybe even about just how much of a surprise the Han surprise attack really should have been.

But that was nothing to be dealt with just then. The immediate problem was that there was a Han stronghold on American soil that had to be dealt with, preferably without massive casualties. To that end—

Rogers swivelled in his chair toward the open drop ramp of the grounded carrier. "Captain—" Brock Rogers quickly entered the cabin. "Get Major Lewis over here, please."

"Yes, sir."

Rogers squeezed past his aide and out into the fresh air and sunlight. It was a welcome break; after all the hours he had spent staring into monitors and phone screens the real world seemed almost to flicker, as though his eyes were trying automatically to track a linescan pattern that was no longer there.

A blast of cold air and a loud rushing sound made Rogers look up just as Major Val Lewis belted in to a perfect landing beside him.

"You sent for me, Marshal?" Lewis asked.

"Yeah, Val. It looks like I'm going to have a job for your people."

"All right, sir, let's have a look."

Back inside Rogers' personal field transport Tony and Lewis bent over the screen Rogers had studied for so long. Lewis' face was impassive in the pale light it cast.

"It looks as if we have them pretty neatly boxed, Marshal," he said.

"I know," Rogers said, "The problem is, though, now that we've got the present wrapped, we can't give it away."

"Why not?"

"Dammit, Val, that place is just one solid weapon. Anybody I try to send in is going to get the living hell shot out of them."

"So soften them up with artillery first. You should have the guns for it."

"Oh, sure. I've got all the guns I need. And the Han have lots of nice deep holes to hide in. No; I don't see anything for it except to send someone down into the holes after them."

"That's no job for regular infantry."

"Hell, that's no job for anybody," Rogers said. "But your people are the only ones with any experience at it."

Lewis shrugged, in that off-hand, dismissive way that most of the Peruvian campaign veterans had. "Then we'll take a try at it. What kind of support can you give us once we're under?"

"Airball, a hundred and fifty units, more or less. Once you secure the surface defenses, everything we can stuff down after you."

"I can see this has been laid out in some real detail," Lewis said.

"We can't plan it any better, Val. All we know for sure about that place is that it's guns on top and whatever else underneath. I can't even tell you what to look for. Peru had almost nothing in common with Lo-Tan, and there's no guarantee that this set-up will look like either."

Again, the casual, uninvolved shrug. "All right. We'll

let you know what we find, after we're done with it."

"Good enough. When can you move?"

Lewis stared at the map. "Five hundred troops and transport, briefing, staging and transit . . . big job."

"Eight hours?"

"Three. And have that belt-snatcher of yours get us a tie-in channel to the airball teams." Brock had the good sense not to notice Lewis's derogation of him and his job, an uncommon display of wisdom on his part.

"You got it. Anything else?"

"No, I don't think so, Marshal. Now if you'll excuse me, I have to go and get you a city."

Ken-Li prayed that the city's shielding was working. The large screen along the far wall of his operations center presented him with a chaos of conflicting imagery as it flickered from pickup to pickup, each bringing in some different aspect of the hidden evacuation of the besieged satellite suburb. Only the rows of consoles between him and the wall, each with its attentive communications officer monitoring one pickup, allowed him to maintain any sort of control, filtering and refining down the great mass of input like blubber from a gutted whale, until the final product reached his own console as information, rendered pure and malleable.

The track-lines between city and suburb were packed with vehicles gliding out from under the surrounding human lines. They were filled to capacity with machinery and Han, the former the sort of heavy equipment that could readily be inserted into the technological ecology of the city, the latter mostly Yun-Yun upperechelon and skilled personnel to run it all. They were the Han Ken-Li most wanted to move to safety, for all his dislike of their caste, because they were the ones he could most readily use. Man-Dins about to be stripped

172

of their hereditary properties by the suburb's fall and Ki-Ling intellectuals too short on achievement or skill at academic infighting to make their mark in the central city to begin with simply didn't carry the same weight in his estimate. The military garrison of the sub-city could not be moved without alerting the Americans to the existence of the main city, and as for the workers and women—well, the city had a surfeit of both already.

But Ken-Li's immediate concern was the steady flow of traffic between the city and its satellite. If the shielding that had concealed them from the American ultroscope teams was still holding, the city was safe; if it had been penetrated then the trackways were nothing more than an enormous arrow pointing directly into the heart of the city, and his strategy of allowing whatever fate was about to befall the sub-city to run its course in the hope that the Americans would be satisfied and leave was a failure.

He looked to his console and considered his other options. He had the combined military power of the city and its remaining suburbs, an aggregate force far more powerful than the American host moving against the Han. He still had the Prl'lu scout ship, with all its armaments and performance, a match for anything the Americans could put into the air. But he couldn't use any of them. The city could not enter the battle without revealing its location; even if they then routed the Americans, crushed them utterly, no weapon, Han or Prl'lu, could outspeed an ultrophone message. The humans would send more forces, in greater and greater strength, pushing the struggle to its conclusion—and Ken-Li was too greatly aware of history to believe that the humans would not rest until he and his city were destroyed. It was a case where he could only win this battle by losing the war, unless the Americans took the sacrifice he of-

fered them and looked no further. It was a bribe he offered them, a bribe of Han lives for Han safety.

He could only hope they would take it.

It was the only way the city could survive.

The thin band of black space separating the projectile
from the rim of the blue-white world had diminished to
an ebony thread . . . .

You learned, Lewis thought. Even through the
anonymity of the inertron-foil combat oversuit, you
could learn to tell the differences between the men and
women you led, keying on subtle shadings of size and
posture and mannerism until the asexual mannequins-
of-war that marched behind (or lay strapped, fastened
and cramped in the tiny drop bay with) you became as
true an aspect of the people who animated them as any
they might choose to present. As true as any, and for
some more true than most. Such as for Val Lewis.

He didn't shy away from that line of thought, the way
he always did when he had the time to follow it too far.
He used it this time, pumping with it, building his anger
to carry him through the upcoming battle. He thought
of crouching beneath the dense forest cover at the base
of a Peruvian mountain, directing troops in the reduction of another Han redoubt. He thought of the sudden
star born atop that mountain, that birthed in its turn the
towering, mushrooming pillar of fire and smoke and the
shockwave, the almost solid wall of air that had been
driven down the mountain to flatten trees like grass,
breaking and scattering men and women all around him.
And he thought of what came next, the invisible, burning poison that had sleeted down all around him in the
haze of dust and rock ash, warped directly back onto the
dazed Americans by some freak of mountain aeolics.

He had survived it, they promised him, repeatedly,

authoritatively. He had been on the fringe of the fallout zone, he had taken nowhere near as great a dose as some of the few American survivors farther in toward the blast center. He understood that. He even agreed with it; he had not been among those who caught the most obvious radiation sicknesses, to die in a protracted agony of sloughed-off skin and bloody bile. Oh, to be sure, the doctors had admitted, there was a definite likelihood of his having some form of cancer problem or another in the next few years, but that just made him one more among many to whom Anthony Rogers had become a walking Lourdes, personification of promised health if and when the scientists ever mastered the complexities of the Prl'lu medic unit. But in the meantime, they told him, because they could tell him nothing else, there was nothing for Lewis to do but live his life and hope for the best. . . .

He had tried, he really had tried. But there was nothing the doctors could do to alter the fact that Val Lewis was a man quite *au courant* with the world around him, anymore than they could alter the fact of the millions of subatomic particles that had torn their blind paths through his tissues. They couldn't alter the fact that Lewis had seen the tapes of the Alliance mission into the Indian subcontinent. They couldn't alter the insane history of that region, where even in the chaotic wake of Hammerfall, Indians and Pakistanis, Chinese and Russians had all seen fit to resolve old enmities in a shower of nuclear warheads. They couldn't alter the fact that Lewis' had seen the results of that madness, still evident more than four hundred years later in the yet-common freak-births and monstrosities that abounded in that region. And they couldn't alter the fact that Val Lewis simply couldn't accept the possibility of his seed producing something like that.

In a way, he had contracted radiation sickness. But it

was fragments of his life that sloughed off, rather than
skin and hair—first the woman to whom he had been
married for twelve years, then his few friends who had
survived the savage Peruvian campaign without injury,
then his transfer from the unit that was filling up too
quickly with strange faces that replaced the ones who
hadn't.

He might have gone on that way, "living" the life of
a retired soldier, the decay of his impotence festering in
his mind more swiftly than any radioactive particle
could ever have worked on his genes. Then Anthony
Rogers had come to him, tracking him down at his own
gang, where Lewis was carried on the roster as being in
charge of local security. It was a nonsense job for a man
of Lewis' qualifications; both Lewis and Rogers knew it.
The difference was that Lewis didn't care.

Rogers cared, though. He cared because he needed
Lewis, or as much of Lewis as he could get. Marshal
Rogers had been shocked by the evident superiority of
the Prl'lu warriors to human fighting men; he had never
deluded himself into believing that it had been anything
but luck that let the Americans contain them during the
Recurrence. And he did not intend to trust to that luck
again, if there should be an again. Rogers had plans for
a unit, a commando, he called it, drawing on the termi-
nology of a war that was dead history even in his own
time. It would be his attempt to create the human
equivalent of a Prl'lu warrior, an elite force: better
armed, better trained, far more aggressive than regular
federal troops. And he was looking for the men and
women to fill this role among the Peruvian veterans—
especially among the veterans such as Lewis.

Rogers didn't lie, didn't try to sugar-coat his premise.
He believed that the best troops for this unit would be
men and women without a future, who would fight per-

haps that much more stubbornly or die perhaps that much more readily for want of anything better to come back to.

It wasn't much, at the time. The Recurrence had been suppressed, and if anyone was worrying about further hidden Han or Prl'lu concentrations three years ago Lewis hadn't known of it. But it was something. If Val Lewis couldn't live as a complete human being then at least he could still do this thing. He may not have been a man but he could still be a soldier. So he had accepted Rogers' offer.

Now he reclined in the swollen belly of a modified Mako pursuit with nine other men and women, riding point ship in the lead wedge of nine similar ships. Mounts and systems for all but four missiles had been stripped from each ship, and the resulting internal space expanded further by extensive modification of the fuselage. The result was a troop carrier with supersonic capability and fighter-class handling, a ship that could get in and deliver its personnel in situations where infantry or armored personnel carriers just weren't fast enough. Nine of these ships bored in toward the Han perimeter now behind a flight of standard pursuit Makos, with the remainder of Lewis' unit following in armored personnel carriers, waiting for the necessary conventional breach of the Han lines.

On the horizon ahead of them, beyond the Han position, the sky began to darken with a swarm of aircraft as the first American rockets and missiles began to burst among the Han emplacements. They were the ships of the regular forces under Rogers' direct command, moving to cover the commando strike. Falcons darted in and out between the massive Han batteries, stabbing with surgical precision at individual strongpoints while the newer Makos swept over the redoubt in tight three-ship formations, their massed salvos of SHAPE missiles gouging enormous scars into the earth where missile batteries and *dis* projectors had been.

Troops tumbled from armored personnel carriers that dropped behind the ridgeline Helden had used in his face-saving attack and then rose again to salvo their missiles into the maelstrom of fire billowing up above the Han bastion. Seconds later those troops added the fire of their long-gun batteries to the missiles of the aircraft and the fire of the heavier mobile guns behind them.

It cost, though. Again and again the tenacious Han gunners locked onto a Mako or Falcon and threw it to the ground in a web of *dis* or pummelled it with rockets and missiles into a lifeless derelict. Missiles sought out the hovering APC's and more than once broke through the defensive *dis* fire to crush the vulnerable machinery and bodies hidden behind inertron armor. *Dis* and rockets scoured the ridgeline, seeking the men and women directing the American fire or clawing through tons of stone and earth in search of the concealed long-gun teams.

But Lewis and his force were hurtling in against the seaward flank of the Han. The diversion was succeeding: only a handful of heavy-weapons positions turned their fire against the small force, not enough to stop them, and in seconds the Makos were below their arc of fire.

SHAPE missiles leaped ahead of the covering Makos now, seeking out the secondary and antipersonnel batteries that could thwart the landing. Even as they fired the troop-Makos broke away and dove for the ground, their own missiles and lighter weapons scouring an area clear of opposition.

Lewis braced as he felt the Mako nose over, knowing what it meant. A handful of seconds later he was slammed forward against his harness as the Mako dropped flaps and airbrakes, jerking itself down to drop-speed. There was an explosive report as the hatch-plate to his side slammed open and his seat was blown out and forward. Immediately as he saw clear air he reached up and unsnapped the shackles connecting his battle-harness and his drop seat. Triggering his rocket-belt he ducked out from under the wing of the descending Mako. It glided slowly down past him, poised on its landing jets, firing steadily. There was no way the massive fighters could ever have accelerated back up from drop-speed before the Han weapons slaughtered them, so instead they continued right on down, to serve as close fire-support for the commandos.

The jolt of landing stung Lewis' ankles. He looked around—his section was already forming up on him. There was a blast of cold air and dust as a nearby Mako pivoted and fired at a Han rocket battery traversing towards them. Lewis threw himself forward, calling out the target for his section, and locking open the bipod of his multiplex assault weapon. The seemingly bulky weapon, carefully balanced with inertron inserts in stock and grip, combined the functions of the three standard infantry weapons; its main element was a standard short-cartridge rocket gun, but slung underneath was a light *dis* projector and it bore four launching tubes for the more powerful long-gun rocket two to a side. With it, one man had the firepower options of a squad. It was the standard weapon of Lewis' unit.

Even as the Mako's rockets walked into the Han weapon ten *dis* beams converged on it. The rocket launcher simply vanished.

The rest of the pathfinder unit was moving out behind the ungainly, hovering Makos, securing a perimeter around the area cleared by the pursuit's weapons. Nothing but Americans moved within that perimeter. Some of the heavier batteries firing inland began to swing towards the commandos, but Lewis ignored them. They had never been designed to fire into their own positions. Secondary and antipersonnel systems were swiftly turning to bear on the Americans but the point-blank return fire from the Makos and the commando's multiplexes made devastating reply to each new volley.

The landing zone was as secure as it was ever going to be. Lewis ducked as a salvo of American rocketry from Rogers' covering force struck down uncomfortably close. He made his decision and keyed in the command channel.

"Bring in the carriers," he ordered.

Seconds later the boxy ships were letting down all around him, disgorging their squads and moving off to join the groundfighting Makos. The ring of American fire spread inexorably across the surface of the Han redoubt, rolling up the perimeter defense in both directions from the point of landing and spreading inward like a potent stain saturating cloth. Casualties were heavy; in twenty minutes Lewis counted twenty per cent of his force dead or wounded—but the advance never stalled. The inertron-sheathed masses of the Makos and the armored personnel carriers provided effective cover against the lighter batteries, and the heavy weapons were already retreating underground in futility. As the commandos moved forward the covering artillery fire rolled back toward the inland perimeter, concentrating its bombardment ahead of their advance.

Lewis moved into the center of the overrun position, rallying several squads around himself. The heavy batteries, those that hadn't been crippled, had escaped to temporary safety below-ground. The lighter weapons had been wiped out, save for a handful of batteries still being cleaned up in a far end of the perimeter. The distant ridgeline had come alive with bounding flea-specks as Rogers ordered the regular infantry forward to consolidate the positions taken. Lewis knew better than to expect the Han to wait for that to happen.

He organized his forces by company, rallying each unit around its own APC's. The Makos he sent climbing out for altitude—they were not designed for what would happen next. His own force he kept in the more-or-less center of the redoubt; the remaining four companies he laid out at four equidistant points around the perimeter. Each unit laagered in, using its carriers for cover and taking full advantage of available concealing rubble. Each unit covered a full three hundred and sixty degree circle around its position—and waited.

A bright slash of *dis* splashed against the hull of the APC to Lewis' right as the first sally port swung open. Lewis didn't wait to see what else would come out; he swung his weapon and discharged two heavy rockets down its gullet. Then the port erupted in a geyser of flame and dis as the men and women around him swung their weapons to bear on it. The destruction was total—but there were other ports opening now. A lot of them; first dozens and then scores and then it seemed as if anyplace the Han hadn't put a weapon emplacement they had put a sally port, each spitting out its platoon or company of Han infantry armed with *dis* and rockets and light solid-slug automatic weapons.

The commandos were firing wildly now, in all directions. It almost didn't seem to matter where you aimed; Han were there to be shot. The carnage was awesome— but so was the blind desperate courage of the Han, if anybody in Lewis' force had been capable of appreciating it. They could win or they could die, and so they attacked, again and again. When the Americans targeted one sally port another would open and Han troops would pour out.

Americans began to die. A woman fell back across

Lewis' legs, gone from the shoulders up. A sally port opened directly in the midst of a company of commandos and the sortie dissolved into a bloody melee at arm's reach. When it had cleared and the Americans had sealed the port with rocket-fire there was less than a squad left standing. On Lewis' orders they collected their wounded and belted towards the nearest American strongpoint, abandoning their dead and the burning carriers.

They never made it. A new port opened and they were cut down in mid-jump. The port faced away from the remaining commandos and their fire tore fruitlessly at the armored hatch as the Han butchered the Americans, fighting and wounded alike.

There was a sudden strong breeze across Lewis' shoulders. He rolled onto his back just in time to see the *dis* beam play across the backs of several of his men. The inertron foil of their combat suits saved them—but for one, who spun directly into the beam and fell back, his head gone behind an evaporated visor.

The first Han lunged up into daylight. Lewis shouted a warning and turned his weapon on them. *Dis* and rockets shattered their first ranks as he scrambled to his feet—and a burst of machine-pistol fire struck him back down again. The tough inertron sheathing of his suit saved his life but the impact took his breath away and a stab of pain in his side spoke of broken ribs. Curled up in a protective ball as the Han troops stampeded over him, he extended his weapon in one hand and emptied his magazine into the port.

A body—a dead Han—fell across him. His helmet speakers rang with sharp cries and faded gunshots. Through the forest of legs around him Lewis could see a personnel carrier backing and weaving on its landing-jets, half a dozen Han hanging off its sides as it fired into the press of Han troops still pouring up from underground. A string of rocket-bursts shook the ground behind him.

Then Han were falling, all around him, and there were new voices ringing in his helmet. The firing around him redoubled and crescendoed briefly—then there was a sharp detonation and suddenly there were no more Han standing as regular infantry flooded into the scene, sweeping the last few survivors ahead of them.

All across the field the sally ports were dropping shut again as Rogers' infantry swept across the surface of the Han complex in long waves to link up with Lewis' commando. Those Han left above ground were butchered in seconds. The battered commando could sit back and take stock—Lewis could still count three hundred and twenty-one effectives and their transport in spite of the Han eruptions within their positions—while infantry officers quickly dispatched covering squads to each revealed sally port while sapper companies began their rounds of the perimeter in search of intact heavy weapons in their concealed pits.

The deep ground-shocks of their detonating charges shook the ground as Lewis watched the orderlies loading his wounded onto the evac carriers. A corpsman edged near him again as he grimaced and pressed his arm tighter against his side, making vague, insistent noises, but Lewis wasn't going anywhere until his troops' situation was secure.

He felt the cold blast of a jump belt and turned sharply, provoking another jolt of pain and another mutter from the corpsman. Rogers took the landing cleanly, with just the right amount of flex in the knees.

"Sir, this area hasn't been declared clear yet," Lewis protested.

"This area won't be clear 'til we reach the bottom

street of the city, Major," Rogers said. "But I'd had enough of sitting on my tail letting you people do my work for me."

"That's what troops are for, sir."

"It doesn't mean I have to like it. What's your situation, Val?"

"Well, sir, we have the surface of the installation, and we've probably done considerable damage to the next level, possibly the next two, with our destruction of the weapons emplacements. There's no way to give you an estimate of the casualties we've inflicted on their infantry—*dis* doesn't leave you much material for a body count—but they put up a good-size force, I'd say at least fifteen hundred to judge by the way they swarmed over us. I don't think any got back under."

"So they probably can't mount another infantry attack?"

"Not right away, sir. I'm sure they have the strength but it will take them time to organize another move—and if they try it again we'll take them out as fast as they climb up."

"I don't doubt it." Rogers slipped his helmet back on briefly, gave instructions. Out beyond the ridgeline troops and machines stirred, and began to move in on the helpless Han sub-city. Doffing his helmet, he turned back to Lewis. "If they'll need time to reorganize, we don't want to give it to them. When my field transport arrives have every commander from company level up assemble there. We're going to have to go down after them."

Ken-li sat expressionless before his screen.

There was an unpleasant silence throughout the ranks of junior officers filtering the tactical information through to him. Most of them had no information to filter any longer. The destruction of the surface defenses of the sub-city had cut off all intelligence from that source; Ken-li no longer could follow the American maneuvers. Another three officers were trying to make sense of the reports filtering back from the failed counter-attack—the commandos practice of firing directly down the sally ports had paid off in wreaking chaos among the command the support units of the Han infantry: the tunnels leading to the surface were a maze of screaming wounded and leaderless survivors.

The only coherent input he was still getting came from the officers supervising the selective evacuation of the sub-city. It was the only good word he received.

"Sir, our communications at the sub-city track head report that the last of the listed heavy machinery is leaving now. But Infantry Commander Lo-Sin is protesting your order to remove medical stores and systems from the sub-city. He claims he will need them for the treatment of his own troops, Excellency."

"Inform Lo-Sin that when the Americans come against him he will have more pressing concerns that nursemaiding his wounded. However, inform him that space is being allocated for the evacuation of his more critically wounded from the counter-attack, provided he is able to distinguish them from his other troops." That would quiet Lo-Sin; the minor concession would be enough to save him face and prevent his being difficult. Ken-Li marvelled at the man's stupidity. Did he really expect to be able to perform a text-book operation, recovering his wounded while American barbarians rampaged through his halls? No, he decided, he could not be that much of a fool. More likely he sought some sign that Ken-Li and the city did not mean to abandon him. Well, he hadn't got one, but he had won something, and Ken-Li counted on Lo-Sin's reluctance to face the hopelessness of his situation to lure him into construing a reassurance in Ken-Li's words that wasn't there.

He keyed in a particular pickup to his screen. The trackway flickered into view, a steady stream of cars proceeding in each direction, laden towards the lens and empty away. Smaller carts could be seen parked between the tracks, loaded with anonymous bulky cargoes that scurrying workers in military work-tunics were busily off-loading beneath the rails.

Ken-Li cancelled the pickup. "I wish to be informed the instant the Americans break into the sub-city."

"As you order, Excellency."

The surface of the beseiged Han sub-city was devoid of all life.

The men and women of Rogers' infantry and Lewis' commando had been withdrawn to the torn fields half a kilometer back toward the ridgeline. Metal stirred among them now, as the heavy sleds carrying the missile batteries and heavy guns of the divisional artillery sections glided ponderously forward. They eased clumsily to the ground and racks and muzzles inclined skyward, nearly to the vertical.

The scene was reduced to manipulable, color-keyed dots on the screen in Rogers' transport. There, it was a simple matter: the American forces held the Han sub-city cupped against the sea, ringing it in unbreakably. Rogers and Lewis crouched over the screen while Brock and the two communications specialists manned their own posts by the hatch, setting up the link between Lewis' commando and the airball teams now moving their units up to the jump-off point.

"Now, we're not going to get any clear ultrophone transmissions until we've got some kind of decent break in the complex's shielding," Rogers said, "So you'll want to make sure your relays are as secure as possible. I'd secure them with at least a squad apiece and make sure each element goes for at least a twofold redundancy on each feeder."

"I think we can manage that."

"You can strip the follow-up units of their short relays, that might help."

"We will. But we want to leave some in the back ranks in case we run into a real mess and lose too many of the forward elements."

"In which case, it won't be *your* problem, will it?"

"Yeah, well, it's the principle of the thing . . . ."

"Okay, do it whatever way you think'll work. But if you can't advance without breaking contact, then don't advance."

"You don't win many battles that way," Lewis said.

"I also don't throw troops into a hole I can't see the bottom of."

"Good point." Lewis straightened. "I can't think of anything else, can you?"

"Not until we get a look at the inside of that place. It's a sloppy way to do business—"

"But it's the only business at hand," Lewis finished. "I'd better join my troops."

"All right. Good luck, Val."

"I'll take it if it's offerred."

The first missile left its rack fifteen minutes later. A solid sheet of missiles and heavy gunfire followed, as the self-propelled artillery of Rogers' forces launched the opening barrage of the assault. The barrage—armor-piercing rockets and heavy SHAPE missiles—climbed over the peak of its ballistic parabola and dropped almost vertically upon the Han redoubt. The massive armor of the Han base was many meters thick, and even the heaviest missiles could only leave shallow pocks—

but Rogers had a great many missiles.

The wreckage-strewn plain disappeared in a sea of flame. The earth and stone above the sub-city vanished, to expose bare metal that flexed and trembled under the American shelling. Rockets and missiles tore at stubborn alloy—or sought out the sockets of ruined weapons emplacements and sally ports and burst through, to wreak havoc among the skeleton force in the upper levels. The survivors fled without thought into the safety of the deeper sections as the first Han infantry moved to their defensive posts within the corridors of their home.

Ken-Li looked up at the officer's cry.

"Excellency! The Americans have begun their assault!"

The large screen at the far end of Ken-Li's command center cut back and forth from scene to scene of the frantic activity within the doomed city. Panicked Han were rushing in every direction, blocking the corridors, obstructing troop movements, forcing their way downward toward the track terminal and an imagined safety.

Ken-Li contemplated the order he had to give. The reality of it was every bit as unpalatable as he had expected it to be—and worse.

"Detonate the tunnel," he said.

A final track-car of wounded Han left the terminal for the long, slow trip to the central city, the last car in a train of dozens. The wounded Han and their attendants never knew it as the demolition charges erupted around them and the collapsing earth pinched off the sub-city's last vital artery.

The screen flickered and blanked out in Ken-Li's command center. Then he reached out and wordlessly keyed in another camera. The screen picked up the sub-city terminal just as the shockwave reached it and struck into the packed masses of fleeing Han. When it passed, the scene returned, cleansed of life and movement.

Ken-Li stood. "Notify me when the Americans force entry to the city," he said, and left the room.

The carafe and glass were waiting on the small table as they did every day. The scarlet-coated young soldier —one of Ken-Li's sons, who had been made to understand quite clearly what would happen to him should the drink ever 'disagree' with Ken-Li—gave a curt nod. Ken-Li raised a hand and the soldier poured him a tall glass of the pale red liquor.

The taste was distant on his tongue. Ken-Li felt no satisfaction with his action, only a growing uncertainty. The Americans had taken the bait he had dangled before them. Ken-Li wished he could be more certain of the safety of the fisherman.

The first small arms fire erupted in the street of the sub-city.

A sally-port, clogged with its own wrecked mechanisms, was cleared in a sibilant burst of *dis*. The Han squad taking cover behind a barricade of wreckage fired as the first commando dropped through. Their *dis* weapons swept across his legs in the approved manner, designed to cut his feet out from under him and drop him into the weapons' path. Instead he struck the floor and bounded forward unharmed, one inertron-protected arm thrown across his vulnerable visor, his own multiplex blazing. A great swath of rubble vanished from their shelter as the Han hastily grabbed for their smaller, secondary projectile weapons.

They never had the chance to use them. There was a hiss of rushing gas and the first airball dropped down through the breach, poised on its cold-gas jet while its operator oriented himself. Then it tilted and rushed forward with the full impetus of its jet behind it.

It struck one Han clean away from the barrier, crushing his upper body with its force of impact. He died instantly. The airball wallowed, and one Han, braver or more desperate than the rest, leaped up and tried to grapple with it. The ball swayed and wobbled precariously on its jets—until the Hans' own small-arms fire cut their man off it. The light machine-pistol rounds glanced harmlessly off the inertron sheathing of the ball. Then the position fell as the first commando and his companions fell upon the distracted Han with *dis* and gun-butts.

The first trooper moved to the lip of the down-ramp the Han had been defending. The landing at its bottom seemed empty and unattended. The commando unhooked the small box of a feeder-relay from his belt and tossed it down the ramp, announcing the action over the airball net. Communication assured, the airball operator sent his weapon down the ramp. *Dis* and gunfire clawed at the sphere from both sides as more airballs and troops followed it down. . . .

The assault had struck down a good three levels and spread out like rainwater puddling against bedrock.

Those three levels had been bad. They consisted of little save the network of sally-port ramps and maintenance walkways for the surface batteries. The Han had not established any strongly-held positions there; instead they had relied on squad-size units, falling back before the Americans and trying to wear down their forward elements or cut them off from behind. They were succeeding all too well. The American rocket-guns were well-suited to their conventional tactics—but those tactics were geared to a fluid, mobile style of fighting on battlefields whose dimensions could be measured in miles rather than feet. An American trooper firing off an explosive rocket in the tight confines of a sub-city corridor risked doing as much damage to himself as to his target. The airballs were of even less use: running a man down with an airball was an inefficient way to kill him, and no one was stupid enough to try detonating one. So the Americans' choice of weapons was reduced to *dis*-ray and bayonet, and the Han, with their light automatic weapons firing solid projectiles, found themselves with a tactical advantage. The commandos leading the American attack were partially protected against conventional gunfire by the same inertron-foil body-armor that shielded them against *dis,* but the thin material could not absorb the entire impact. In three levels Lewis' commando suffered seventy-three further casualties, fifteen of them dead from head and throat wounds. The regular troops that followed suffered heavily as well, when the Yun-Yun technicians began to lead Han troops through their hidden networks of access tunnels. The Americans found themselves under attack on flanks they never knew they had. Units under fire found themselves suddenly cut off from support and reinforcement. Aid stations and stretcher parties abruptly found their relative safety dissolved in a wave of Han seemingly erupting from the walls. The Han infiltrators quickly fell to superior American numbers and the regulars moved swiftly to invest the Yun-Yun tunnels, but the attack had lost its momentum—and two hundred commandos and infantry found themselves cut off a level down and ahead of the main attack.

The fourth level down was the first of the proper residential levels of the sub-city. The maze of tight corridors that typefied the first three levels, where walkways had to be compacted to accomodate the lift bays for the surface weapons, had given way to an enormous plaza off which several much broader avenues opened. The Americans held the down-ramp from the third level and a narrow perimeter along the near wall. The Han defenders faced them from several strongpoints, armored against *dis*, at the mouths of the avenues. The rocket-guns of the Americans regained their lost effectiveness in this comparatively open space, while the Han were limited in their use of *dis* weapons for fear of opening up new channels through which the Americans above could support their beleagured advance guard. But they had seized the advantage by firing first, so that the human troops were unable to reply with massed fire against their positions, pinned down by the fierce rocket-and-gunfire the Han threw against them.

Dorri Burstyn lay prone behind the same ruined statue she had taken cover behind twenty minutes ago, before the world had contracted around her into a choking, confined mixture of noise and explosions. She ducked her head, wrapping a foil-armored arm across the back of her neck as the steadily tracking Han fire swept across her cover again and showered her with fragments of marble and metal. Even with all the guns the Han could bring to bear they couldn't cover the whole of the American perimeter at once. Whenever the stream of fire would sweep past her, Dorri would half-roll out from behind her cover and snap off a shot at the Han a hundred meters away. Once she had the satisfaction of seeing her shot burst against the ceiling directly behind a barricade, and a bloodied Han lurched upright for an instant before dropping back out of sight again. But the rest of the time it had been a matter of firing and then scrambling back under cover as her shots drew the return fire of one or more Han positions, not knowing what damage she might have done.

The reduction of her world to fire and noise didn't worry Dorri Burstyn overmuch, beyond her immediate concern for staying alive; it was all she'd had before she ever entered the sub-city.

Dorri Burstyn was one of Lewis' picked commandos, a veteran of the Peruvian Recurrence. She had been a long-gunner with the first troops sent down there when the Han struck. She had been with the first unit to reach the slopes of the Peruvian redoubt. And she had been one of the first casualties of the Han nuclear deadfall.

She had reenlisted in the regulars after less than two years back with her own gang following the campaign. It had been as good a place as any, she had thought at the time; certainly she could find as much of a sense of community in the military as she could have in her gang—more, because in the end the community of squad and company would make no demands upon her that she couldn't meet. And that was for damn certain something the gang—and the husband she had taken on her return from Peru—couldn't claim. America was still in many ways recovering from its centuries-old domination by the Han, and one aspect of that recovery was an unvoiced assumption that whatever else she might contribute to the community, a woman would be expected to bear children and increase a gang's numbers. They couldn't expect that of Dorri Burstyn, not after her first child, as much a product of hard radiation as any seed of her husband or herself. Truthfully, her gang—and the husband—had been happy to authorize the divorce and let her return to the service.

Dorri Burstyn had thought the change would solve—or at least mute—her problems. She had been wrong. She had returned to her old position with a squad long-gun team—and another woman, then a second, and a third. None of them bore the unseen stigma of nuclear contamination; to all of them their service in the regulars was something to be finished and put behind them, so they could get on with their own lives. Dorri Burstyn didn't have that option—and a cripple should never sit on a crowded street watching the traffic go by unless she wants to be reminded all the more strongly of her own handicap. So when Val Lewis made his request for volunteers for a unit to be drawn from the Peru veterans, Dorri Burstyn had known what he meant—and her CO hadn't objected.

Fresh fire clawed at the pile of rubble she hid behind, driving her back down again. Then she rolled out and fired back, doing the only thing she could do in the only place she could be . . . .

Lewis raged at the unresponsive communicator.

He had kept up a steady stream of commands and instructions for the past hour, sending feints and sorties against the Han cutting off his forces from the trapped Americans. Nothing was working. They had managed to wipe out the infiltrating parties that had cut into their rear. They had managed to secure the Yun-Yun tunnels behind their own front. But they could not break through. Whenever an American attack pierced the Han lines it found itself outflanked and threatened with entrapment by Han boiling out of some other portion of the tunnels, and the humans would then have to pull back.

Lewis was in a bind and he knew it. He knew he could break through to the two hundred encircled troops, through sheer weight of numbers—but only by losing two or three times as many troops as he was trying to save. That was what the Han wanted, of course—a Han commander would never have hesitated at sacrificing his own trapped forces under the same conditions, but they knew the Americans, lacking the justifying armor of caste and anonymity, would not.

So Lewis attacked again and again, all along the Han line, losing men, losing time, and gaining nothing. The cramped cabin of the personal field transport left no room for pacing back and forth, but Lewis could not repress his growing frustration as tactic after tactic failed. He was fidgeting, twisting in his seat, slamming his fist into the console-top, and every motion only served to aggravate the pains in his side.

Rogers watched over his shoulders as the polite little simulations of the screen showed their version of a platoon-strength probe being driven back in blood and noise and fire.

"It isn't working, Val," he said.

"I know that, dammit."

"Then let's try something that might."

Lewis spun in the seat, grimacing as the torque caught up with his ribs. "Like what—sir?"

"Look, Val, what's always been our one advantage against these people?"

"Why don't you tell me?"

"Our mobility, right? We've always been able to move around the Han, left and right and over, haven't we?"

"But we can't do that, now, Tony, that's the god-damned problem!"

"Then let's create a situation where we can!" he leaned past Lewis to the console mike, stabbed a button.

"Get me an all-units channel," he said.

Ten minutes ago, the exhausted American troops would have sworn that nothing in the world could have surprised them anymore. The six tired survivors of the squad had been pulled back out of the line for a brief rest, but even in the relative safety of the American back-corridors they couldn't relax, not completely: even slumped against the wall of the corridor, helmets beside them and weapons laid half-forgotten across their knees, not talking, not thinking if they could avoid it, their eyes still automatically tracked back and forth across their surroundings, as though waiting for the walls to burst open and spill Han into their midst. But that didn't happen, and as far as they were concerned, there wasn't a damn thing else that mattered.

Or so they would have thought.

There was a sound of footsteps and the corridor began to fill with troops. Fresh troops, helmeted and harnessed, with clean, unfired weapons and bulging magazine pouches. In seconds, the corridor was full of troops, and the battered squad found itself looking up through a forest of legs at the airballs hovering near the ceiling.

There was a stirring in the packed ranks of soldiers. One of them looked up and said something over his helmet phone that the bare-headed squad couldn't hear and the new troops edged back to leave an unpopulated gap in the corridor. The lone squad-member left sitting in the evacuated space looked around uncomprehendingly for a moment. Then he noticed that even the inertron-armored airballs overhead were moving away and he decided to join the crowd.

The standing troops were slipping the slings from their shoulders and chambering rounds in their weapons. The ignored squad watched as they oriented themselves towards the vacated space and braced as though to leap on some unseen opponent.

There was a sussurant inrushing of air as the four *dis* beams sliced downward through the ceiling of the corridor and into the floor. The rubble between them fell inward, dissolving as it fell into the beams' path.

The beams flickered out and the massed troops leaped forward, following the airballs as they plunged down through the new opening. The stood-down squad stared at the column of infantry pouring down out of sight, and got to their feet.

But they took the long way back to their unit.

Dorri stared as the Han positions across the plaza erupted in a shower of explosions. A second later the blasts were echoed down the rampway behind her as American troops dropped down through the *dis*ed ceiling atop the unprepared Han. There was a confusion of battlesound to either side of the surrounded Americans, and then a solid column of fresh troops was leaping down the ramp to join the troops standing now in view above the Han positions across the plaza. Many of the trapped Americans, the ones who still had officers and noncoms to rally them, got up and followed them. Many didn't. They couldn't. Some were dead, some wounded, but most, without officers to rally them, simply did not get up, but lay where they were and watched the new troops rush forward . . . .

The Han defense of the fourth level collapsed. They controlled lateral mobility throughout the level but the Americans commanded the vertical, striking down through the floor of third level to enfilade and overrun every Han position as soon as it had been discovered. Rogers had brought forward every *dis* beam that could fit the Han downramps and opened up hundreds of drop shafts deep below the Han battle line. Now the Han caught a taste of the chaos they had attempted to wreak on the Americans, and they didn't enjoy it. No Han soldier surrendered on the fourth level, though many positioned near lift-tubes and downramps were able to retreat. The ones who couldn't fought savagely, but even in the confines of the walled avenues the Americans' skill with jump-belt, bayonet and knife proved superior.

In twenty minutes the fourth level belonged to the invading Americans. They had taken no prisoners. Troops moved past the drop-holes already burned into the floor by the initial *dis* volley and began setting up projectors to drill new ones, knowing that any Han reserves would already have the earlier ones targeted. As the women of the *dis* teams canted their weapons toward the floor, the first airballs glided into position over their heads . . . .

"We're down to level eight, Marshal," one of the communications techs announced. "Advance units reporting noncombatant casualties."

Rogers looked at the tech, reduced to graceless androgyny by battle gear and comm helmet. "What kind of noncombatant casualties?"

"Han civilians, sir."

"Dammit," Rogers swore.

"We've broken them," Lewis said. "They can't have any kind of organized defense left if they haven't even evacuated their civilians from the combat zones."

"It isn't that," Rogers said. "What kind of civilians are the troops meeting?"

"They didn't say, sir."

"Find out!"

"Yes, sir." The tech repeated Rogers' demand into a microphone. There was a pause. It grew. Uncomfortably.

"Well?" Rogers demanded.

"I'm not getting any acknowledgement, Marshal."

"God damn it!" Rogers switched his own ultrophone to the tactical channel and opened his mike. "This is Marshal Rogers! I want any troops eighth level or lower to acknowledge and give me a description of the Han civilians being encountered."

There was a brief hiss of carrier wave. Then:

"Sir, this is Lieutenant Cord of the Adirondack Regulars. I can't speak for anyone else but the civilians I've been encountering have been males, plainly dressed, wearing their hair loose. I have also encountered women, in comparable numbers, dressed in several styles." There was a pause. "Sir, what the hell am I supposed to do with these bastards?"

"Hold your position, Cord," Rogers said. "We'll get back to you as fast as we can." He closed his mike. "Val, those sound like common workers and unattached women. We shouldn't be meeting them in any numbers this close to the surface."

"And they sure as hell wouldn't be coming to meet us," Lewis said. "So they must be being driven our way."

"To slow us down," Rogers agreed. "While we're getting all tangled up in them, the Han are probably digging in on the lower levels."

"Well, we sure as hell aren't going to let that work."

"How do we stop it, Val?"

"I can think of one way."

"I know you can. But I can't allow it."

"Damn it, Marshal, these are Han!"

"And we're humans. I know, Val. That's why we can't butcher them."

"You think they'd hesitate?"

"I know they wouldn't, Major. I lived among them."

"I remember that now, *sir.*"

Rogers was out of the chair before he knew he'd decided to move. Lewis didn't flinch. With an effort, Rogers halted the fist he'd been prepared to drive into the commando's face.

"Now listen to me," he said. Keeping his voice level was the hardest thing he'd ever done. "We—are not—Han. We don't butcher unarmed civilians."

"We 'butchered' them in the War of Liberation."

"That was the War of Liberation. This is today. I'm in command here, Major, and I'm ordering you to sit down at the phone and order all Han civilians sent up to the surface. You will then detail a battalion to mount guard above them. That is a direct order, Major."

"And if I refuse it?"

Rogers was amazed at how steady his hand was as he drew the pistol and levelled it at Lewis. "Then I will find you guilty of dereliction of duty in the face of the enemy, Major, and I will shoot you dead, right here. Now give that order."

Lewis stared at him an eternal second longer. Then he edged around Rogers and sat down at the command console. He swivelled in the chair to look back at Rogers one last time. "I'm going on the record as protesting this, Marshal. It's a mistake. This isn't one of your old-time gentleman's wars. You're letting yourself in for problems you can't even imagine."

"Give the god-damned order!"

Lewis turned away from him and began to speak. As quickly as the rage had come upon Rogers, it was gone, and he wasn't sure he felt anything there to take its place. Holstering his pistol, he turned to see the two comm techs pointedly staring into their screens—and Brock Rogers with his own holster flap cleared and his hand on the butt of his weapon. Rogers didn't know whether to feel hurt or gratified. He settled on indifference; it was the easiest course.

"Who were you going to shoot?" he asked wearily. "Him or me?"

"I'm . . . not sure, sir."

"Well, hell. At least you're honest."

Cord was almost more afraid than he had been during the fighting. At least in combat he had had his unit around him; at least in combat he had had that much control over the situation.

But now he stood alone in a mass of terrified Han civilians, driving them to the rear and the ramps to the surface with angry shouts and gun-butt proddings. They spoke no English, he spoke no Han. It didn't matter. He had a weapon, and he had purpose, and the civilians didn't. They moved past him in a steady flow, not understanding what he wanted but knowing that if they moved away from him they wouldn't have to endure the screaming and the blows. They had been moving that way from the front of Cord's area, not knowing where they were going but moving away from the Americans and their own troops who had driven them from their apartments at gunpoint. They had no destination, they only hoped that if they kept moving they might finally reach a place where nobody would make them go someplace else.

Cord shoved and cursed at the swarming people around him, praying that their numbed compliance would continue. His nearest trooper was twenty meters up the corridor at the next branching, keeping the people moving toward Cord. It was his hope to get some kind of steady movement going and keep it going until more American troops showed up; there was no way he could even think of moving forward until someone came along to take the refugees off his hands. If he tried to advance and left them unsupervised behind his company they would be cut off as completely as if he had brought the ceiling down behind them.

The voices of his troops were a single exasperated roar over his helmet phone. The squad-leader channel was no improvement. The fewer voices there only offered a sharper distraction with each new outburst.

The screams almost didn't penetrate the confused garble.

"Jesus God, Han! Han!"

That was a hell of a thing to yell here, Cord thought —then the sound of gunfire reached his helmet pickups above the panicked screaming of the civilians around him. A moment later the Han ahead of them were throwing themselves to the floor as another mass of Han came around the bend, in civilian clothes and with weapons in their hands, firing. The irritated complaints of his men up and down the corridors shifted in mid-voice to cries of alarm and pain, and Cord knew that the same thing must have been happening all through his area, that the Han had secreted troops in mufti throughout the civilians, and that each of his isolated men was under mass attack.

Then he had no time to think. Something struck him in the side and his leg suddenly didn't work anymore. He fell back against the wall as the pain swept over every other sensation. More Han gunfire ripped into the wall around him as he brought his gun up and pulled the trigger, not looking, not aiming, just sweeping the corridor before him with explosives—

"Marshal, the Adirondacks are reporting heavy fighting all along their forward area. It seems that the Han have been using the civilians to cover their moving in guerillas."

"Oh, God." Rogers didn't turn; he knew Lewis was there; he knew what his expression would be. "How many casualties?"

"No telling, sir," the tech said. "The reports are too confusing."

Rogers sat there, suspended on the realization of the enormity of his error. Had Lewis been right? Had he tried to impose obsolescent ethical niceties on a situation where they had no place?

No. No, Lewis had to be wrong; it couldn't have been a mistake to refuse to sanction slaughter.

But men were dying for his moral rectitude . . . .

"Get me a tactical channel," Rogers said. "I'm going down there."

The American perimeter had been driven back almost to the fourth level plaza by the time Rogers reached the scene. He called and a haggard captain belted over to stand unsteadily before him.

"What's the situation?" Rogers asked.

"Past this point, sir, I have no idea. We hold the plaza and forward positions in the various corridors, about three hundred meters back from our original line. Beyond that we have scattered individual troops holed up in rooms all along the corridors, in phone contact but cut off by Han forces. The airball teams are operating between our forward positions and the downramps to the fifth level, spotting and attacking armed Han parties where they find them. That's as detailed as I have, sir."

"It's more than I hoped for. What kind of casualties have we taken?"

"We're in voice contact with maybe twenty-five per cent of the forces originally occupying the forward line. Some of those are wounded, there may be others alive but out of communication. That's all I know."

"All right. What's the Han situation here?"

"We've got about two hundred in custody here, sir. Parties have been coming in since the attack. Most of them seem to have been unarmed, but a lot of the men aren't waiting to see."

"I can't tell them they should, Captain." Rogers felt a moment's dismay, suppressed it savagely. "All right, here's what we'll do. How many men have you got in fighting shape?"

"Maybe two hundred, a few less."

"Right. I've got two battalions of Delawares on their way down here. We'll divide up the Han corridors when they arrive; you'll take your people down the central corridor, preceded by airball; we'll put a company of Delawares on each of your flanks and two companies on theirs, all down the line. Then we'll advance along the entire front, each unit matching its advance to the others, until this level is completely secure. Any questions?"

"One, sir. The Han noncombatants. How do we treat them?"

Rogers took a deep, slow breath. Then he said what he knew he'd have to say.

"Captain, our objective is to secure this level, and all subsequent levels until Han resistance ceases. To that end you will concentrate on attacking the enemy with whatever force is necessary to reduce that resistance. There are to be no overriding considerations, none. Any Han noncombatants still in an area after that point are then and only then to be sent to the surface, provided such transferral can be managed without threat to your own troops. If that is not feasible they are to be left where they are found, providing you are certain of their noncombatant status. Otherwise—take whatever action you deem necessary for the safety of your men."

Something down in Rogers' gut was still protesting, still voicing its twentieth-century refusal to grant these men the license he had just given them. Rogers hated that something, wished it would just go away—and knew that if it ever did there would then be no difference at all between himself and Cullen Teder—or even Val Lewis.

"Yes, sir."

"Very good, then. See to your men."

Submachine gun fire broke uselessly against the inertron flanks of the airball as it rounded the corner before the improvised Han barricade, a flimsy pile of furniture scavenged from surrounding apartments. The ball's operator sent the weapon rushing at the barricade high along the ceiling as the Han civilians in the way screamed and tried to cram into the already-full apartments. The Han troops ducked as the ball rushed overhead, then doubled back to crush a man screaming against the barricade.

Their attention diverted by the airball, the Han didn't see the American trooper who swung his weapon around the bend in the corridor and fired. The futile barricade vanished in the detonation of the first rocket; many of the civilians, some of them already wounded by ricocheting bullets, were struck by shrapnel and furniture fragments. The Americans ignored the terrified noncombatants as they belted down the corridor—all but one, who knelt in the corridor and held his weapon trained on the crowd as his mates leaped over them. Some of the Americans halted long enough to strip the dead soldiers of their machine pistols and spare magazines, having learned that these were more practical weapons for this cramped battleground.

A second unit of Americans came around the corner just as the last man of the first group disappeared from view. These paid careful attention to each of the civilian-crammed apartments, searching them at gunpoint for any weapons.

In another corridor a similar unit was making its search when their mates forward came under fire from a new position. These wasted no time on searches, but simply put a round of explosive rocket through each door in their stretch of corridor and then belted onward to reinforce their comrades, never pausing to observe the carnage they wrought.

Rogers glided down the corridor, pistol at the ready,

flanked by two troopers with captured Han machine pistols. He knew that the corridor they were advancing down had already been scouted by airball. He knew that there were other columns of troops to either side of him in the adjacent corridors, and he knew that airball groups were parallelling them all down the network of Yun-Yun tunnels that separated them. It took none of the adrenalin edge off his alertness.

This was the easy part, he thought, although he would never have dared say that to these men that followed him, this was the part where it was all simple and clearcut and reduced to the most readily understandable terms—there were people you tried to kill and people who helped you kill them. Unless, of course, some idiot too noble for his own good started setting down impossible conditions that were liable to get you killed yourself. How much of that was the adrenalin and how much of it was a simple refusal to think Rogers didn't know—but none of it lasted past his first sight of the bodies.

A single American trooper lay sprawled against the wall, his gun on the floor before him, slide locked open on an empty magazine. His tunic front and legs were black with dried blood. Between him and Rogers several Han lay sprawled where the gunfire of their own infiltrating troops had reached past the trooper to cut them down. Past the trooper there were more bodies, and parts of bodies, not sprawled in the wreckage, nothing so tidy and organized, but rather intermixed a limb and organ at a time with the rubble and twisted structures torn apart by the trooper's rockets.

"Cord," one of the troopers with him said, identifying the dead American. Rogers realized that Cord was probably the only corpse in the corridor that the man had even noticed: dead Han were not distinguished from other broken furniture.

Rogers looked at the bodies as they moved past them. They weren't any different from the bodies he'd seen in Lo-Tan, sixty-odd years ago; they were just as dead, dismembered just as gruesomely; but these were dead at the hands of men under his command and now he had given the order to kill more of them in the same way. That was something new to him. He had always managed to rationalize away, more or less, the slaughter of the Han civilian populations during the War of Liberation. He had not been in command during that war, and even if he had, there was no way the resurgent Americans of 2419 could ever have been prevented from taking revenge on their oppressors of three centuries. He had rationalized it away because if he hadn't, he would have been forced to admit that it was his gift of twentieth-century military skills that had let humanity take that revenge. And he had rationalized it away because that was the only way he could avoid admitting that the woman who had been his wife and companion for sixty years had been as vengeful and murderous as any of them.

He still could not condone the blood he had seen spilled in those sanguine conquests—but now he understood the urges that could produce such slaughter. These had been his people. These Americans they passed lying dead in the corridors, Cord and all the others. They had been there because he had sent them there, and they had died because of his stupidity in trying to half-fight a war. It was a mistake the Han had not made, and it was one he would not make again.

He only wondered if he would be able to stop not making it when the war was over.

Lo-Sin watched the Ki-Ling specialists making the modifications he had ordered to the sub-city's power plant. He was mildly surprised at how little rage he felt.

If any Han had ever betrayed him as thoroughly as Kin-Li had before, Lo-Sin's every waking moment would have been devoted to seeking such a complete and total revenge that the offender would have been driven to the lowest levels of the city for all time. But such ambitions were futile now, and Lo-Sin knew it. He would never have the chance to revenge himself on Kin-Li; even the one last blow he could strike against the damned Americans would be posthumous: when he threw the switch that would for an instant fuse together the two magnetic bottles that held apart the enormous pools of separated protons and electrons that gave the sub-city its power. He would have a moment's satisfaction, as the particles rushed with the impetus of substomic forces down the mile-long corridor that separated the two facilities to their violent joining, and then the Americans would die. But Lo-Sin would die first.

Every soldier in the city who could carry a weapon had been sent to the levels above. Lo-Sin meant to put up the most intense defense he could, right up to the moment when he ordered the shielding dropped. That way he could be certain of luring the strongest American force possible into the city—and of inflicting the heaviest casualties. Even the Yun-Yun had finally acknowledged publicly the weapons caches everyone in the city had known they possessed, and sent armed parties into the levels and tunnels above to strengthen the defense. They didn't know, of course, that Lo-Sin was planning to destroy the city: managing the sub-city's technical affairs was the province of the Yun-Yun but the separate-particle power systems were well out of their bailiwick. Separate-particle generation was an area where practice and theory shaded into one another, and the Ki-Ling guarded their theoretical knowledge zealously, considering it no affair of uneducated machine operators.

That was why they were carrying out Lo-Sin's orders now, and why he trusted them to continue carrying them out. Status assumed could be even more inflexible than the status one was born to; Lo-Sin knew that the Ki-ling's affected superiority precluded any thought of their surrendering to the upstart humans they had hounded into the forests for so many years. Rather than surrender the sub-city to the Americans they would destroy it, and that was all Lo-Sin asked of them, whatever their motivation.

A wall communicator chimed and Lo-Sin moved to answer it. "Yes?"

"Commander, the humans have moved through the last of the delaying positions and are advancing through the uncontested levels now. They will be moving against our final lines shortly."

"Have we prepared against their new *dis* tactics?"

"As best we might, commander. As you ordered, we have concentrated our heaviest forces around the armored corridors of the upper power complex. In addition we have established small strongpoints of *dis* resistant alloy in certain vital intersections to provide a covering fire for our main positions. It is impossible to predict how long these will last—but as long as they last they will kill Americans."

"It has been done as well as I may have expected," Lo-Sin confessed. "The important thing is time. Each position must be held as long as is possible."

"It shall be done, Commander. Our lines shall last as long as is needed to reopen contact with the city."

If that were true, Lo-Sin thought, *then I would need fear nothing, for the lines would hold forever.* But that was impossible, just as reopening the tunnels to the central city was impossible. The originals had been cut and reinforced with the greatest Han cunning; all attempts to burn them open again with *dis* had simply brought more rubble crashing down in its place. In the end, Lo-Sin had realized what he was doing and had stopped. To have opened the tunnels again would only have led the Americans directly to the central city and, for all Lo-Sin knew, all of the Han that remained on Earth. He could not allow that, and he knew that Ken-Li must have come to the same conclusion. It ameliorated none of his rage and betrayal. But he knew what he had been sold for, and it was a flattering enough price.

The communicator chimed again. "Commander, the forward outposts are reporting contact with the Americans."

"Understood." Lo-Sin turned to the Ki-Ling supervising the disconnection of the power plant's governing system. "Do your operations progress? Haste is of the essence."

"All shall be ready shortly, Commander," the Ki-Ling said, "Our every effort is bent to this; nothing is more important than striking this blow against the barbarians."

"Oh, that is hardly the case," Lo-Sin said, "We must maintain our perspective. It is merely the most important thing we are still capable of; that is hardly a universal standard to judge by."

"Of course, Commander."

Amazing, Lo-Sin thought as the scientist withdrew, how we continue to play at our games and pretendings. Still, it was most likely for the best: if one could not aspire to longevity than perhaps such constancy was the next best goal.

The mass of hurtling stone intersected the forward edge of the blue globe before it . . . .

The tactical scope operator moved up and down the corridor before Rogers, intent on his portable screen. He would move several feet, stop and fiddle with his unit, and then move again. Once he knelt and chalked a mark on the floor. Moving across the intersection before them under the cover of Delaware guns, he moved down the far corridor for several yards before he knelt and chalked another mark. He did it a third time, following the corridor that branched off to their left, and a fourth, to the right. Then he belted briskly back to the waiting Rogers.

"It's an armored installation of some kind, Marshal," he said. "But it shouldn't be there. Every other corridor we've come through has run vertically parallel with the one above and below it. But this one doesn't. There's an armored structure where hall should be."

"Aknol," Rogers said absently. He was studying the crude map laid out before him, a rough sketching of the Han floor plan they had become familiar with. Darkly shaded areas indicated other shielded anomalies beneath the Americans, blocking off several corridor intersections ranged around a larger shaded area in the middle of them.

"There's no reason to assume this next level has to be the same as the ones we've just come through," he finally said. "We're deep enough that we can start looking to hit the industrial and technical levels sometime soon. This could be the first. If it is, then the layout will be a lot different from any residential level we've come through. What the layout could be then, I don't know." He looked up at the silent Delaware officers crouched over him. "But I do know that we aren't going to that central position first."

"Why not, Marshal?" Rogers looked up. The man who had spoken wore a noncom's tabs, probably a junior sergeant bucked up to company level by casualties. Rogers relaxed. If an officer had asked such an obvious question Rogers would have relieved him on the spot. But then no officer who would have asked such a question could have survived this deep into a Han citadel.

"Look at the way these outer positions are laid out, sergeant," Rogers said. "A lot of them can't cover the others because the central position is set directly in their line of fire. So the outer positions have to be set up to cover the areas between the themselves and the central position—and that means it's probably a lot more vulnerable without them. So we take the outer positions first. Excuse me." He keyed in a command channel. "This is Rogers. I want heavy launchers with SHAPE capability down here, one unit each to my last reported position and the company posts for each of the Seventh Delawares." He switched back to the company level channel. "If we do this right, I think it can be finished in an hour."

It was nothing that humans would have called atmosphere, but faint flashes of ghost fire traced themselves across the great stone bullet, as delicate wisps of gas, handsful of light atoms clutched in gravity's fist, intersected its path high above Earth. The blue world was visibly turning beneath it now . . . .

The cargo sled drifted to a halt with a faint keening of turbines as a Delaware trooper waved it to a stop. Rogers pushed through the tightly-packed infantry as two men stepped down from the sled and started towards him. Then one of the two noted the sigil on his companion's helmet and dropped back. Rogers looked to the remaining man and scowled.

"What are you doing here, Major?"

"I've moved down here to take command of the final attack, sir."

"Not with those ribs, you're not, Major."

"Not with your rank, you're not, Marshal."

"I don't think that's your decision to make," Rogers said.

"And it's a bad decision for you to make. You're the commanding officer of this expedition, Marshal. You're responsible for every man and woman in this force."

"That's why I'm here—"

"That's what you're running away from. We both know why you came down here, Marshal. But playing infantryman isn't going to change anything. It isn't going to make your mistakes go away, and it's only going to make it easier to make more. Look at this." He gestured at the crude map Rogers held half-wrapped in one hand. "Did you actually expect to direct troops with this in the middle of a fight? How the hell did you hope to keep track of a whole battle by scribbling marks on paper without getting shot in the meantime? And what would I have done with the command if you and your map were lost?"

"Dammit, Val . . ." Rogers felt awkward, to say the least, addressing the man by his first name scarcely four hours after threatening to kill him. But after those four hours, it was the only way he could say what he meant to say. "Did you come down here through the eighth level?"

"I had to."

"Did you see them, those men up there—never mind the Han, Val, I'm talking about our people, now, the Ohios and the Adirondacks and the Delawares we lost taking those levels back? I killed them, Val. I made a mistake and they died for it."

"So now you're going to take a chance on getting

213

killed, as though maybe it'll make up for it if you are. Well, it wouldn't have, Marshal, because there isn't any debt there to be paid."

"The hell there isn't."

"The hell there is—or if there is, you aren't ever going to be able to die enough to repay it. If you want to make up little responsibility fantasies then play with this one: you don't owe for a few lives, you owe for thousands, because you're responsible for every man and every woman who ever died carrying out one of your orders. You think Anthony Rogers dying here would ever make up for that?"

"God damn you—"

"No way it would, and you know it. There's only one thing you can give that can pay those people back—win here. Be the commander you can be. Keep a few people alive who might not stay alive if you go running off playing guilt-ridden hero. You can't do that with a gun. You can do it with your head."

"You bastard." But even as he said it, Rogers knew Lewis had won. So did the commando.

"Your belt-snatcher and a tech are back with the launcher sled. They've brought a screen, patched into your transport."

"Right." Rogers sighed, looked to where the stolid Brock was watching the launcher team manhandle their weapon off the sled.

"Let's get you filled in," he said.

"This is a most unseemly exertion for one of my intellectual bent," Wolsky said. He lifted the screwdriver and fastened another screw into the emissions bell of the *dis* engine bolted incongruously into the desert floor. A second unit was set catty-corner to the first, mounted much more lightly. Two of Ruth Harris' physics students were holding the bulky bell in place; Wolsky's complaint met with little sympathy.

"Sir?"

"Yes?"

"Well, sir, I realize that it might be bad form to criticize one's elders, especially when they're operating outside their field, but why do we need the second unit?"

"Lazy, aren't we?"

"Whenever possible."

"Well, we need the second unit because people cannot drink salt water. I am a scientist, young man; I know about such things, you know."

"Oh, I'm sure, sir—*unf*," the young man sagged to get his shoulder back under the bell as it tried to pivot around the loose screw, "—but why not just set the transmitting unit to only pass pure water?"

"Because it wouldn't pass any for very long."

"Oh?"

"Yes, 'oh.' What makes salt water salty?"

"Watch it," the other student said. "That sounds like a trick question."

Wolsky's opponent was game enough. "Salt?"

"Good enough. Now where does the salt in the salt water go when the *dis* intake takes the water away?"

". . . all over the intake?"

"Very good. And when you have enough salt on top of the intake?"

"The water can't reach it."

"I really must compliment Doctor Harris on the caliber of her students. Proficient in physics, receptive to basic chemistry, and even capable of a certain rudimentary logic—"

"Fat old biologists get sarcastic."

"I noticed."

"Hold the bell," Wolsky said.

He torqued the last screw into place and they stood back. The flaring muzzle of the main *dis* engine stared past its mate into the deep pit cut into the desert bed before it.

"Well, assuming we remembered to attach this thing to a power source, it should be all set. Shall we see?"

They moved away from the unit to the small control box resting in the cab of the cargo sled. Heric leaned in and threw three switches. The first activated the filtering *dis* beam, and the faint blue glow of its field lightly silhouetted the heavier unit. The second switch activated the main unit, and the third sent an ultrophonic signal to its intake element resting in three hundred feet of water off the coast of one of the Eastern Baja islands ninety-three miles to the south.

A line-straight bar of seawater thundered out of the heavily-braced receiver and into the waiting pit, cleansed and desalinated by the filtering *dis* field it passed through en route. Trace minerals and reduced organic matter drifted away in a fine cloud to windward, borne on the mild desert breeze.

"It's working," one of the students said. But Wolsky didn't answer him. He was looking to the sky.

The light grew as they watched it: first a finger, then a spark, then a ribbon of fire stretching across the sky to the west curving away and down beyond the horizon . . . .

"Clear!" the loader shouted. Those troopers even vaguely in the launcher's line of backblast pressed back tighter still against the wall.

"Fire!"

The gunner pressed his stud. Fire blossomed from the back of the launcher, biting into the back wall of the improvised bunker. That wall was blackened and scorched already from half-a-dozen previous rounds;

the billowing fumes obscured all vision in the cramped bunker for a second, then cleared, wafted away through the ruined wall that had too briefly shielded its Han defenders.

"Call it," the gunner ordered.

The fire-team's carrier, doubling now as spotter, leaned cautiously around the lip of a firing port. "Clean hit, low and left of the last. Puncture. Adjust right one, up one."

"Aknol."

"Hold your fire, trooper coming in!" The loader deftly fielded the SHAPE round he had been fitting to the breech of the launcher and turned as Lewis and an escort of two troopers crowded into the bunker.

"This won't work, sir," the loader said, indicating the two troopers. "Someone'll get cooked for sure."

"You're right," Lewis said. He dismissed his escort. "And stay clear of that doorway." He turned back to the gunner. "What does it look like?"

"Like whoever laid this out was on our side, sir," the man said. "Look out there." A trooper moved aside to let Lewis edge up to firing-port.

"The Han hold that big bunker in the center of the area, sir—" Lewis studied the battered structure in the middle of the vast chamber, a good seventy-five meters distant. "—we hold these little bunkers and they ring that thing right in. They can't move out of it without our knowing it, and—look, pick up the tactical channel and you'll see, sir."

Lewis chinned the tactical frequency.

"—elawares, you've got a party of ten hostiles moving on your leftside position as I see it."

"Aknol that, Adirondacks; can you take them off us?"

"Can do. Keep your heads down, fire going out."

"Aknol."

There was a brief pause and then Lewis heard the

sibilant rush of rocket-fire crossing the chamber before him. An unseen corner of the chamber shook with the subsequent detonations.

"That seems to have done it, Delawares."

"Aknol that, Adirondacks, thank you."

"Anytime."

Lewis chinned off-channel and looked back to the loader.

"That's all there is to it, sir. We shoot up that bunker and they die; they try to counterattack and they die; they keep coming up and we keep killing them."

"I'm sure that's very gratifying, but it isn't getting us anywhere. Can't we cut down past them?"

"I don't think we can, sir." The loader patted the floor. "The scope teams say that beyond this level the whole floor/ceiling structure is armored."

"Well, in that case, carry on."

"Yes, sir."

The loader turned to fit the missile to its launcher again. He had just locked it into the breech when the first rumblings reached them . . . .

Mordread cast his pack ahead of him to the crest of the low ridge.

He had little clear memory of the time that had passed since he left the sub-city. The succeeding days had blended into a jagged montage of flight and hiding as Mordred made his way through the loose American lines inland. Sleep had become a rarity—for all his field training Mordred could not avoid the differences in accomodation between a proper Han apartment and sleeping on the ground under an open sky. Beyond that, what little sleep he had been able to catch was constantly interrupted; he had learned to ignore the high-flying Falcons and Makos but the sound of an armored personnel carrier, no matter how distant, would bring him awake—and once he had roused to an unfamiliar sound and found himself in the middle of an American battalion using the cover of darkness to move its positions forward. For the rest of the night he had lain in the precarious cover of a clump of brush as weapons carriers glided overhead and jump-belt infantry bounded past him on all sides.

Mordred sought for a last handhold and pulled himself over the ridgeline. He still could not risk constructing any sort of shelter that might be detected from the air, but the ridge promised ample places of concealment along its slopes, and the chance of a stream at its base.

He stood up, careful to use the brush along the ridgetop to conceal his silhouette. In the far distance to his left he could see the snowcapped peak of the high mountain that was his primary landmark; to the right, to the south, he was forced to rely on his memorization of the contours of the horizon. And of course behind him, to the west, lay the beleaguered city—

The first projectile struck home as he turned. There was a streak of incandescent brilliance, painful to look at even at that distance, as the ore missile struck the ocean above the Han city. The air trembled visibly, sending out delicate traceries of shockwaves as the molecules of gas were driven against each other in the speed of its passing. The initial impact against the sea was less spectacular: from Mordred's point of view he could not see the way the incompressible seawater was driven back as though held by invisible walls clear to the sea-bottom. From where he stood, all that was visible was a low ridge of water that rose around the point of impact and then collapsed inward. Scarcely ten seconds later the sound reached him, and although it would be the better part of an hour before the full shockwave reached him, the ground was trembling beneath his feet, transmitting as much of that thundering report as the air around him.

Then the pillar of steam and seawater erupted above the Han city and the realization struck Mordred. The kinetic energy of the impact had to go somewhere; some tiny portion of it went into throwing that geyser of seawater thousands of feet into the air.

The rest of it struck into the last stronghold of the Han on Earth.

Mordred's scream was lost in the thunder . . . .

The uppermost levels of the Han city ceased to exist. Even before the first level had a chance to collapse the levels beneath it were buckling; the structural supports simply disintegrated at the first overwhelming impact.

Further down the city withstood the assault, briefly. The total force of a hundred tons of ore dropped from lunar orbit translated into at best a couple of kilotons, a shock that could be in the main absorbed by the upper levels of the city, although the impact shattered walls and structural members to the deepest heart of the complex.

Then the ocean returned, to reclaim the ground the projectile had taken. A wall of water three hundred feet tall fell inward atop the ruined city. The mass of rubble and crushed flesh that had been the upper levels of the Han city were driven downward. Stressed ceilings and walls disintegrated before the assault, and added their mass to the lethal plug being driven down the core of the city.

There was no place to run. As though in an act of grim mercy, the flood gave most of the trapped Han little chance to realize what was killing them—but some, deep enough down, knew.

Ho-Tin had time only for an inarticulate realization

that something was wrong as the initial concussion shook his audience chamber and pitched him into darkness, killing lights and screens. Then his city killed him, the collapsing ceiling driving the curved poles of his audience screens down upon him like so many sectioning knives.

The ornate gardens outside his chambers were flattened in the rush of compressed air driven ahead of the descending battering ram of water and wrack, ruined before the sea ever reached them.

Ken-Li perhaps realized what had happened: his screen gave him a brief kaleidoscopic view of disaster as every monitor in the city tried to broadcast its alarm in its instant of destruction. Then he died as quickly as every other Han when the sea drove the ceiling in upon him, with time for nothing but a stab of outrage at this unexpected attack that made a mockery of all his plans.

The questing flood broke through to the lowest levels of the city, and the entranceway to the abandoned, sealed trackway. The sealing charges had been planted a full mile down the tunnel, for maximum effect—but that just gave the ocean a running start against it. The tons of stone blocking the tunnel became merely another weapon as the invading ocean drove the rock ahead of it down the tunnel.

"Clear!"

"Fire!" Another missile cleared the launcher to burst against the Han position. When the smoke cleared there was a fresh wound in the armor of the Han position, and the bunker's return fire faltered briefly as dead were removed and fresh Han troops brought up. The rocket fumes hung in the air of the American bunker for an instant, and then were whisked away—too quickly, Lewis thought. He had been uneasy, worried about something he could not identify, since that deep, brief rumbling that had shaken the floor beneath them minutes ago. He keyed in the command channel.

"Marshal, are you holding up those reinforcements?"

"Stopped them at the fourth level, Major," Rogers voice came back to him. "Now can you tell me why I should have?"

"Not yet. There's something happening down here that I don't understand. Wait a minute—" The trembling was back, and this time it did not diminish. "That vibration is starting up again. I still can't see any reason for it. Nothing else is happening—" He broke off in an instinctive flinch as the rocket team fired again. Then he straightened quickly, looking around the bunker.

The fumes were gone, as quickly as they had billowed up from the launcher.

"Wait a minute, Marshal. There's something happening down here." Lewis hesitated, then opened his visor. He felt it immediately. "Wind. We're getting wind down here, Marshal."

"Wind?"

"Or a strong draft. It's just started."

"Major." Roger's voice was suddenly calm, in a way Lewis had never heard before. "I'm pulling our forces back up to the higher levels. Get your people moving now. Don't get fancy; just get them moving. Get any noncombatants you see moving too, but don't lose any time on it."

"Sir, what the hell's going on?"

"Take it from an old mining man, Val. Sudden drafts underground are a good reason to get out. Now move it."

"Yes, sir." Lewis switched back to the tactical channel. "This is Major Lewis to all units. We're pulling out. Airball teams leave your weapons in place to cover our withdrawal. Everyone else, just get upstairs. Aknol, all units." There was a chorus of assents. Lewis looked down to the fire team stripping their weapon. "Leave that. Just get moving."

If anything, the Americans could ascend through the sub-city even faster than they had come down. Every *dis*-bored dropshaft erupted with Americans leaping upward from level to level.

"Commander, the Americans are withdrawing."

Lo-Sin cursed the unresponsive communicator. It wasn't fair. He had *decided,* he had accepted the fact that he was going to have to die and that he would at least have the satisfaction of taking the Americans with him. But now they were withdrawing.

He could still kill many of them, he knew. They could never outrun the radiation from the destructing power plants—but if they were retreating, if for some reason they were actually leaving the city and all he would do would be to wipe out the very people and property he was charged to defend, then he would have been wasted; Lo-Sin would not waste himself.

"Keep me informed," he ordered.

"Yes, Excellency." There was the pop of a broken connection, followed almost instantly by the chime of a new call. A different voice came from the speaker.

"Excellency, the tremors have begun again."

Lo-Sin looked around. He felt nothing, but then the power plant complex had been strongly buttressed against seismic disturbance. "Are the Americans still retreating?"

"They appear to be, Commander . . . ."

Lo-Sin swore again. Could this be another trick of the humans? He would not put it past them—but what power did they control that could shake the very earth to such a depth? A faint rumbling came over the speaker. Lo-Sin felt the first stirrings of a new alarm. If he could hear an earth tremor over a communicator, what might it feel like?

It felt like the trembling that he could feel beneath his feet now, filtering up through the reinforced floor of the complex. Behind him the Ki-Ling scientists were running from console to console, frantically trying to maintain their machines' equanamity until the moment they were ordered to disrupt it violently.

The shaking increased. Lo-Sin heard cries of alarm and things falling over the speaker. Then it went dead. He turned and stalked out into the center of the control center.

"Ready yourselves!" he shouted, inwardly pleased that it had come out so strongly. "We will detonate the complex—"

A geyser of stone and wreckage erupted under him, throwing him upward to be crushed instantly against the ceiling. The doctored failsafes of the complex failed even as their controllers died—failed to no end, as the massed, separated particles found their path to each other blocked by thousands of tons of stone that shut the tunnel like a pleat in cloth.

The entire complex lurched at the impact. Rogers belted up through another level, and made a new decision.

"All units, fourth level and higher, get to the surface, now, we're pulling out. All surface units move back inland from the Han perimeter. Don't waste time reforming, don't wait for a buddy or a squad-mate, just get going. Move!"

He cleared the next *dis* hole and suddenly realized he wasn't stopping; he continued to glide as though pushed on by an unseen hand. He knew what that hand was: air, compressed and driven ahead of a rising flood-wave. He had felt it before, in an Altoona coal mine five hundred years ago, when some sorry bastards had blasted a vein into an underground river that had flooded almost a quarter mile of tunnel.

The Han civilians were fleeing now, too—they didn't know what that distant thunder might be or where the wind that gusted through their corridors was coming from, but the Americans were fleeing before it, and the Han had fled before the Americans.

The corridors became a chaotic tangle of people. The American troops seemed to be erupting vertically from the mass of screaming Han, shooting from dropshaft to dropshaft; more than one Han reversed the feat, jostled by the crowd and dropping into the gaping pits cut in the corridors. What had been minor jams before where dropshafts were offset became serious obstacles now, as American troops tried to force their way through the packed corridors. Some took to leaping from back to back above the crowd, but that had risks; a missed step, a foot slipping from a Han shoulder and the trooper would fall beneath the crowd, to be lost. Nothing that fell in that crowd could get up again. Some of the more ruthless or more frightened troopers took a more direct route, clearing a path to the next dropshaft with *dis* or simply burning a new shaft into the ceiling above their heads, regardless of who or how many might be standing there.

The sea drove freely into the sub-city now, its rate of passage limited only by the mass of rubble it drove before it and the resistance of the air being compressed into the upper levels. Wreckage and water overtook fleeing Han by the hundreds—any screams they might have screamed were lost in the thunder of their destruction; it was not a place where announcements of human pain mattered.

The American army fled in a host of leaping motes away from the torn ground above the Han subcity. Behind them came the slower mass of fleeing Han civilians. The units that had remained above ground fled in better order, perhaps, by unit and with most of their equipment—but they fled just as quickly, and with just as much encouragement:

The waves towered over the shore, building as they rushed at the beach. Behind them the pillar of sea and steam billowing up from the Prl'lu attack dwarfed the waves—but even overwhelmed by their mighty parent as they were, those waves could sweep the beaches clean of life to the Han sub-city, and beyond.

Rogers watched the waves coming on as he drifted slowly across the plain, urging his troops past him. Carriers were circling across the fields, dropping down to pick up the scrambling American troops, dipping and rising as the soldiers jumped to meet them without breaking stride. Soldiers clawed their way through drop hatches and clung to tow cables or to the harnesses of troopers already made fast there. More than once a carrier swooped down in front of Rogers only to be waved off as he directed them to troops nearer to the city than he was.

Rogers turned to see the wavetops bubbling into foam as they began to topple off their own height down upon the waiting shore. Han were still pouring up out of the sub-city, fleeing the ocean rising up behind them. Rogers could only watch—

There was the hissing report of a flying belt behind him as Lewis dropped out of the sky.

"Marshal, you can't stay here."

"They're going to die, Val—"

"Yes, sir, they are. Now let's get out of here."

There was nothing else Rogers could do, he knew. But

he should do *something*. Instead he grabbed onto Lewis' harness as the commando officer cut in his belt rocket and rose above the plain.

From his new vantage point a hundred and fifty feet up, Rogers could see the main body of the Americans bounding over the ridgeline that had been the main human line against the sub-city. That was some consolation . . . .

Then he looked back.

The first wave struck, a wall of foam topping a swirling green base, and toppled, collapsing down upon itself and spreading inland in a sheet of lethal froth.

The wave overtook the mass of Han still rising from the sub-city and absorbed them without a sign. It swept on, engulfing the altitude-dwarfed figures as it passed. Then the turbulence of the wave's passage over the opened city cut its onrush short as the bulk of the wave poured down into the city to meet the seawater rising up from below. As the wave withdrew the land beneath came back into view, stripped of life; the mass of fleeing Han had been reduced to a thin crescent of figures abandoned on the plain.

"Oh, my God," Rogers said softly.

"There was nothing you could do, Marshal," Lewis said. He worked the thrust-increment control of his rocket belt carefully, to ease the strains of momentum of his bad rib. Rogers didn't answer him, so he continued, bluntly: "Anyway, their troubles are over, now."

Rogers looked back up at him, then down to the scattered Han survivors again.

"They may be, Val," he said.

"But ours are just beginning."

CHAPTER FIVE

The small blue-white planet had taken more abuse in this least part of its history than it had in all the long epochs since the spasms in its heart had cast up continents and mountain ranges. It had been cleansed of the choking, corrosive works of humanity by the purging scourge of Hammerfall, but whole other species of her children had perished beneath that cosmic fist, archipelagoes and coastlines had been ground away and lost forever. Yet the planet had survived that and those wounds had healed over, made right again by wind and water and the hardy, peristent life that had struggled through the famines and plagues and climatic shifts. It was even recovering from the great Prl'lu engines that melted billions of tons of Antarctic ice cap to drive the seas inland.

But now Earth bore a fresh scar, and Hun't'pir was pleased with it.

The great observation chamber was working at full magnification. Earth filled the entire hemisphere before him, and the spreading cloud of the projectile-strike covered an area the size of his palm.

Kors'in-tu approached him along the slender walkway.

"Commander, the weapon has functioned more effectively than we had hoped. There is no indication of life within the city of the Prl'an deviants. All transmissions have ceased; what readings we can still obtain through the impact cloud indicate no controlled energy use within the structure."

"Excellent," Hun't'pir said. "Report on the progress in construction of the remaining missiles."

"Discounting the projectile expended on the deviants, Commander, we now have some three hundred and nine ore missiles in inventory. The remainder shall have been completed and transported to the launching site within another sunward cycle."

"Very well. In the meantime, initiate targeting procedures for the native urban concentrations."

"As you order," Kors'in-tu left.

Hun't'pir studied the steam cloud expanding above the ruined Han city. This was not truly combat to his liking. It lacked immediacy; it did not allow for the satisfaction of facing an enemy directly. It did not allow him the pleasure of using his strength and skills to their utmost—it did not *feel* as though he were actually doing battle with an enemy. All he was doing was standing there and ordering the destruction of a foe that could mount no effective resistance. It seemed almost beneath his talent.

But it was his duty, and he would fulfill it. The reality of engaging in combat again had whetted his appetite for more, that was all. That appetite was still a pale shadow of his inbred desire to fulfill his charge. It would be fulfilled when his responsibility had been discharged. And that was all any Prl'lu could ask . . . .

"They're going to try and turn this around on you, Tony," Ruth said.

"They've already started," Rogers answered. "How

229

the hell did they manage to shove that hearing motion through?"

"They had blood on their side," Wolsky told him. "It's all very well to want to look into the SubCouncil's possible mishandling of the Han crisis—but the Han killed their friends, Tony, and murdered their families. They aren't interested in justice or responsibility; they want revenge."

"But the blood they want revenge for is Helden's fault," Rogers protested, then added, "and Teder's."

"You can't prove that," Ruth Harris said.

"I don't have to, dammit."

"If you bring that up on the Council floor, you'd better. Or Cullen Teder will hang you with it."

"He'll try."

"He will. You haven't got much support in this Tony," Ruth told him. "You're talking about Han, and that's just too frightening. Even the eastern gangs aren't going to back you on this—I couldn't even get the Wyomings to do better than abstain. They want a decision on the Han prisoners, first—then maybe you can talk about what the west did wrong during the campaign."

Rogers sighed and looked out the window of his office. The sight of the government towers no longer raised any proprietary satisfaction in him. The machinery those buildings housed was slipping from his control as the Council stirred, and began to assert the power he knew he could not deny.

"So what do you suggest I do about this hearing?" he asked.

"Let the Council have it," Wolsky said. "It isn't entirely outside their jurisdiction—and if they decide you're rebuffing them they could use it as an excuse to bring down the provisional government."

"No, they won't. If they had the guts to do that,

they'd have done it long ago. They've had enough chances."

"I'm sorry, Tony, but you're wrong. Before, they had every reason to leave you and the provisional government in charge. Even the densest Council member could see that some very unpopular decisions were going to have to be made while the Alliance was recovering from the Recurrence, and they were perfectly happy not to have to make them. They may have complained, but they did so as much for show as for any real reason; it looked good to the gangs back home. But this isn't some point of rationing allotments or economic allocation. This is different. This is—"

"—this is Han, yeah, I know. All right, so we let Teder have his hearing—"

"—and we let him win it," Ruth said.

"Why?"

"Because he's going to want to take action against the Han, Tony, and the gangs want action taken."

"That's right, he will." Rogers felt cold. "And you know what kind of action he'll want."

"It isn't hard to guess."

"I can't let that happen, Ruth."

"You'll have to."

"I can't!"

"You must. Teder has to win this, Tony, it's the only way he can avoid the scandal of an investigation into the mishandling of the Southwest SubCouncil's defense."

"He'll butcher the Han to cover his own tail!"

"And you have to let him. You *have* to. Either you let him destroy the Han or he'll try to use your defense of them to destroy the provisional government and you. And right now, I think he could do it . . . ."

It was the waiting that put him so on edge.

There was nothing Rogers would have liked better than to leap to his feet at any of a dozen points during Cullen Teder's speech; he wanted nothing more than to jump up and curse Cullen Teder away from the podium and out of his life. But he didn't. He couldn't; an outburst like that against a Council member would have wasted any slim chance he might have had of swaying them. So he simply sat at his table at the front of the Hall, and listened.

Teder didn't put a foot wrong.

He ran his presentation like a fine show. He made extensive use of the scope records of the airship attack on Taos and the records of the irregulars' early operations in the Northwest. He played the recordings of the 'phone conversation that led up to the deaths of Price and Dane in Scouting One-Nine. Then he read out loud, slowly and clearly, the names and casualties of every gang in the Southwest that had suffered in the Han attack.

As he read, the images of burning American cities and dead American civilians continued to cross the screen behind him. Rogers could feel the rage mounting around him in the chamber, higher and higher, but deprived of an object, incapable of resolution within the Council auditorium. Teder meant to give it one, though . . . .

The undercurrent of anger surrounding Rogers grew until it nearly matched his own impotent fury. He knew what Cullen Teder was going to call for. He almost approved. The montage of destruction behind Teder moved him as strongly as it did anyone else who witnessed it, even though he understood Teder's motives. There could be no forgiving such savagery, no tolerance, no forgetting. There could be only one payment for such atrocity—but the only Han face he could see above the bell of the *dis* weapon was Lu-An's.

Suddenly the anger was gone, replaced by an icy purpose. Rogers knew what he had to do.

Teder ended his recitation. The small prompter screen receded back into the podium and he looked up at his scowling, restless—utterly captive—audience.

"We've suffered," he said calmly. "The Southwest gangs have lost their homes, their families, everything they've worked to build for fifty years and more. Every gang from the East that sent to troops to our aid has lost husbands, wives, brothers, sisters." He paused. Then:

"And it's our own fault," he said.

"Sixty years ago we came out of the hills and the forests and we broke the backs of the Han. We pulled down their cities on this continent; we crossed the seas and drove them out of Europe, and Asia, and Africa.

"And then we stopped.

"We levelled their cities and we drove them into the wilderness—and it never occurred to us that they might survive as we survived. We never considered that the Han might be so nearly human as to want revenge.

"So we went about our lives, as though the Han didn't exist because we couldn't see them anymore. We turned away from our responsibility to make the world safe for mankind again, and wasted our energies on personal profit and petty rivalries.

"What happened then? The Han rose again in Peru and we nearly lost our world to them a second time. But did we learn from that?

"We did *not*. We crushed *one city* and went back to our own affairs—and the Southwest lies in ruins because of it.

"We cannot let that happen again. It *will not* happen again. And I demand in the name of the living and the dead that this Council order the one action that ensure that." He looked up to Gerardi seated in the President's chair. "Mister President, sir; the Southwest yields the floor."

Rogers let the uproar burn itself out as each delegate tried to be heard at once. Then he stood, and waited as they slowly realized that shouting was futile.

"Mister President . . . . a point of information."

"The chair recognizes Marshal Rogers."

"Boss Teder, I admire your eloquence. Now perhaps you would care to share with us your notion of this one necessary action you demand."

"Very well, Marshal. I believe that mankind will not be safe as long as Han exist."

"What do you propose to *do* about it?" Rogers' question hung flat in the air between the two men.

"Marshal, your forces are holding approximately two thousand Han—"

"Eighteen hundred and sixty-three, men and women."

"Not Eighteen hundred and sixty-four?"

"Government troops are holding eighteen hundred and sixty three Han in the temporary compounds erected at the Badlands Air Base."

"Ah. Well, that is sufficient to make the point of my comment, Marshal; the government is holding—and maintaining—Han. The exact number—and their disposition—are not of immediate concern. But how long does the government propose to maintain this policy?" His expression hardened. "To put it most simply: how long does the government propose to keep these Han alive?"

"The government doesn't know what else to do with them," Rogers said.

"I can think of another choice, Marshal—for one prepared to face it."

"Why should we kill them?" That was the end of the sparring.

"No. The question is, why should we keep them alive?"

"There are less than two thousand Han left alive, Teder. What kind of threat do they pose?"

"I know what kind of threat they were, Marshal—my people died because of them. I know what kind of threat they might become: half the gangs in this Council numbered less than two thousand at the time of the Liberation. Can you guarantee us that these two thousand Han will never become as dangerous to us as we were to them? We've made that mistake twice now, Marshal, and look what it's cost us!"

"Eighteen hundred Han are no threat!"

"But they won't be eighteen hundred Han in twenty years! They'll be thousands! And I will not see them thrive when humans have died at their hands!"

"And I will not be a party to murder, sir," Rogers said.

"But you will be, Marshal, every second longer that you defend these Han. They *have* murdered; we only demand that they be paid in their own coin!"

"When did you become a plurality?"

"I feel safe in anticipating the vote of this body."

"Be my guest," Rogers turned and looked up at the tiers of delegates ranked above him. "But let me say this: this body is free to vote on anything it wishes. But the provisional government will not accede to any demands for genocide while it exists and I head it."

"That will change, Marshal," Teder said.

Rogers turned back to him.

"You're welcome to try."

"God damn it, Tony, you're throwing away everything you've ever worked for, and you're throwing it away for nothing!" Ruth stormed back and forth across his office, in an ironic, unconscious parody of Rogers'

235

impatience with her just weeks before. But it was Rogers' posture, as he sat slouched and sullen behind his desk, that portrayed the greater anger.

"I don't think I am," he said.

"You don't think so? Then you aren't thinking, Tony. You aren't thinking at all. Teder's already introduced a motion on the floor to dissolve the provisional government."

"No he hasn't. He's introduced it into committee, the way he has to. It still has to get out."

"You think it won't?"

"It might."

"Might?" Ruth stared at him. "Tony, can you think of one thing any Council member will want to vote through faster than this?"

"I'm hoping for several."

"What do you mean?"

"I mean that if the Council is willing to dissolve the government rather than let it handle the Han situation, then the government won't handle anything else. I've already suspended negotiations on trade with the European Confederacy, and the talks on the Canadian border dispute, and everything else the government should be taking care of—and I've made it clear to every Council member involved that those functions will not resume until they decide just what government is going to handle them."

"You did what?" Ruth was horrified. "Why didn't you just disband the government on the spot? Why didn't you set fire to the Four damn Towers? You've set the Alliance back years, Tony, years!"

"I've done nothing of the sort," Rogers said. "I said the talks were suspended, not stopped. I've made it perfectly clear to the foreign delegations that this suspension is purely an internal affair. Amazing how well

236

they took it—seems to be a rather Continental way of handling these things."

"And what about the country's internal affairs? Are you just going to put the whole Alliance in suspension until this thing is settled?"

"The Council seems willing to. It's their choice. If they want to dictate policy they can be responsible for carrying it out."

Ruth Harris sat on the short couch facing Rogers' desk. "Tony, you're going to put the reconstruction back months, years—God only knows how long. All the work you've done, all your effort—"

"I didn't do it for butchers."

"Who are you doing this for, Tony?" Ruth asked quietly. There was a pause.

"What do you mean?" Rogers asked.

"I mean I know you, Tony. I've listened to you when you've talked about how you felt about the retaliations against the Han after the Liberation and why you didn't oppose them—but this time it's at least as serious; you certainly stand to lose more." Ruth hesitated. "Is she worth this, Tony?"

Rogers exhaled slowly. "You're skating on *very* thin ice, Ruth."

"You don't have to deny anything to me, Tony. Did you really think I wouldn't know?"

"I would very much like to know how you found out. I thought I'd left orders that surveillance was to be cancelled during my visits."

"That was a clue right there, Tony. Also, for all your visits, how much data did you contribute to our studies?"

"Another clue, I see." He grinned. "They could have been just courtesy calls . . . ."

"Don't make a joke of this, Tony," she said.

"I'm sorry," Rogers apologized. She accepted it with a shrug. "But you're taking this very calmly."

Ruth looked at him levelly. "How should I take it, Tony? I don't own you; I can't dictate to you. You've never tried to run my life. And I know you, Tony. I know you're aware of the dangers involved in this. I don't think you'd sleep with a Han just for sex."

"So that's all Lu-An is, as far as you're concerned? 'A Han'?"

"Don't push, Tony. I'm smart enough not to fight a fight I couldn't win for losing—but you can't ask me to approve."

"I don't," Rogers said. "Ruth—I'm grateful you're taking this the way you are. I never wanted to hurt you; if this was something I had any control over—"

"Well, it's something you'll have to make a decision about, Tony. Not just for me—I don't make any demands in this. This is a place where demands cause resentment and resentment . . . finishes things. But Lu-An colors your judgement about the Han and about what defending them could do to you and to the Alliance. She can break you, Tony—and whether I can have you to myself or not, I don't want to see you broken."

"Thank you," Rogers said. "I understand what you're telling me, Ruth. I'll think about it. Hell, I've been thinking about nothing else for the past month. If there's an answer, if you can help me reach it—"

"I could give you an answer," Ruth said. "But I won't. It isn't an answer you'd want to hear and I said I won't force it on you." She stood and walked to the door. "For what it's worth, Tony, I'll keep the Deerings behind you. I'll be behind you."

"Thank you," Rogers said.

Ruth Harris turned to leave. Rogers' voice drew her back.

"Ruth. I've been playing a lot of games for these last

three years. I've been playing games to take power and games to use it the way I think it should be used. But there are some things I wouldn't want to lose to those games." He looked up at her. "I hope I haven't."

She smiled. "Tony, there are some things that just won't let themselves be lost."

"That's good to know. Thank you."

The door closed behind her.

Out in the corridor, Ruth leaned back against the doorjamb for a long moment, fighting the rush of emotion that sought to claim her. Then she straightened again, calmer. Certain.

Anthony Rogers wasn't the only person in the Alliance who could have a purpose.

"Hello, Lu-An."

"Doctor Harris." Lu-An looked at the other woman uneasily. Ruth Harris had been one of the most frequent visitors to Lu-An's apartments in search of information about the Han. Many others had come once and not again, when they realized that Mordred's sister was unschooled in the technical aspects of Han life. But Ruth Harris had never made that mistake, often gleaning much fresh knowledge of captured Han technology simply from paying close attention to Lu-An's descriptions of witnessed use. But it was night now, late, past any reasonable time for such an interview. Yet Ruth Harris stood in her doorway.

"We have to talk," Ruth said.

Lu-An did not so much admit her as give ground before the human woman as she entered the apartment.

"This is an uncommon hour for a history lesson."

"I don't want to discuss history, Lu-An; I'm hoping to prevent it."

"What do you mean?" Lu-An asked. These attempts at subtlety were out of character in Harris—or in any

American. Their presence alarmed her. "What history do you propose to 'prevent'?"

"The collapse of the American Alliance," Ruth said levelly. "The extinction of the Han. And the destruction of Anthony Rogers."

She waited for a reaction. With an effort, Lu-An held her face calm.

"You know what's happening," Ruth said.

"I have a screen, Doctor," Lu-An said.

"Then you know that your—that Han have attacked the American Southwest, and that a Han city has been destroyed."

"I know."

"You take it well."

"I never knew them. Everyone I knew has been dead for three years; anyone I cared for has been dead for more than twenty. I was the daughter of a woman who produced an outblood son; no other Han has ever given me reason to mourn them, Doctor."

"Then you don't care that the Alliance holds almost two thousand Han captive."

"They are alive. There was never a time when I could be grateful for much more. Let them live so."

"Lu-An." Ruth's voice turned Lu-An back to face her; the Han woman had put as much distance between them as the small room would allow. "You have to know that Cullen Teder wants those Han dead. And you have to know that Tony's opposing them."

"He can't win."

"I think even he realizes that. But he's going to make a fight of it anyway—and we both know why."

Lu-An nodded. "Me."

"Teder wants the Han dead, all of them. He won't make an exception in your case, especially if he wins on the larger issue of the Han prisoners. Your execution would make his victory over the government complete.

240

The government only stands because Tony makes it stand; if he's beaten it will collapse, and if Teder can break the government—"

"—then he will be the strongest figure in the Alliance," Lu-An finished for her. "You have surprised me, Doctor. I never doubted Cullen Teder's hatred of me but I would never have thought him capable of such cunning."

"All the more reason to fear him if he comes into control. A dangerous man is bad enough. A stupidly dangerous man is worse."

"I have reason enough to fear him already, Doctor. He wants my life. And he will break Tony if he must to take it."

"You understand the problem."

"Perfectly. Too well, perhaps. Tony must sacrifice his power or me, and if he is driven from power then I shall die in any event. He must realize this."

"He does. He's fighting anyway."

"Yes. That is like him. That is his weakness, you know. Anthony Rogers is too easily haunted by his actions. He is more suceptible to guilt than a man in his position should be. Otherwise he would see his only real choice. He must remove Cullen Teder."

"Or you, Lu-An."

"Or me. But he is not capable of that. Not Anthony Rogers."

"But a Deering would be."

Lu-An looked at her in surprise. "A Deering—yes, a Deering would be capable of that. We remember her."

"She was my aunt," Ruth Harris said.

"So." Lu-An was startled by the calm that settled on her. "And that is why you are here."

"Tony won't give up on the Han question as long as his defeat threatens you."

"So I must be eliminated. Very good, Doctor—a Han

241

solution to a Han problem. Your aunt was much like us in this way. But you are wrong to think that my death would allow Anthony Rogers to yield in this—what he began out of desire he would finish for vengeance. And he would be destroyed just the same."

"That's right. If Tony is broken defending you, you will die. If you die, Tony will be broken. But if you *escape*, he'll have to yield. He'll have no one to defend and no reason to seek revenge."

"I had considered that," Lu-An said. "And if there were a place I could escape to, I would attempt it, for all our sakes. But there isn't."

"Then I'll make you one."

Will Holcomb rushed through the door into the Badlands op center. The first thing he saw was Hopper, shrugging into his G-suit.

"Hopper, what the hell's going on?"

The squadron commander jerked his chin at the big screen on the far wall. "That."

The screen was alive with light. Wave after wave of brilliant little pinpoints sweeping down on Badlands out of the west.

"Oh, my god." Automatically, he checked the scale of the image. Five hundred kilometers, and the ultronic blizzard was already well within that border. "Any ID?"

"We've called; they don't answer."

"Did we get any warning on this from the coast?"

"Not a god-damn word."

"What's been done?"

"I've routed the standing patrol in for a confirmed identification. The rest of the Mako flight is up and the Falcons are scrambling now. The *Deering* is alerted and the ground defenses are mobilized."

"Right." Holcomb looked at the screen again, then turned to the comm tech nearest him. "Order the *Deer-*

ing airborne as soon as she's ready. Put the ground defenses on combat status. They are to fire on any approaching force not identified by this office. Report their acknowledgement." He turned back to Hopper. "Captain, you'd better get airborne with your command."

"Aknol, Major." The quiet, spare officer was gone.

"What's the standing patrol's ETA on the unknowns?"

"Fourteen minutes, Major."

"Very good. Get me a priority channel to Niagra." Will Holcomb had to fight back the sickness that threatened to rise in his gut at the sight of those swarms of aircraft closing on the base and people in his charge. If this was a Han attack it dwarfed anything they had mounted on North America in sixty years. But the deepmost root of the sickness was his growing conviction that the approaching host were not Han . . . .

The two Makos cut through the thin desert sky like their deep-sea namesakes through water. Dorothy Chan handled the stick of her ship easily, correcting the slight influences of atmosphere on her course.

Ahead of them the sky was bright with winged metal rushing toward them.

Chan opened her mike. "Badlands this is High Guard. We have the unknowns in sight. High Guard Two, this is One. I'll make the first close pass; go for altitude and cover me."

"Aknol that, One. Take it easy, Dotty."

"Thanks, Tom. I mean to."

The second Mako broke formation and climbed out. The approaching swarm grew steadily before her. Dorothy Chan couldn't remember when she'd last felt quite so alone.

"Badlands, this is High Guard One. Any response

from the incoming ships?"

"Nothing, High Guard."

"Right. Then I won't waste my breath. Hold on, Badlands, ID coming up."

The strange ships were keeping tight formations, six vertical boxes, two high, four low. They were closing on Badlands at barely four hundred kilometers per hour, too slow for an attack, slow enough perhaps to forestall an immediate attack—and to balance out a disparity in abilities between types.

"Badlands, this is High Guard One. I'm going to make my first pass between the high and low formations." She eased the stick forward, fed power to the intake fields. "Going in."

The Mako dropped its nose and fell through the oncoming formation. The swarming aircraft grew large before her, utterly visible—but she didn't want to believe it.

"Badlands, this is High Guard One. Unknown aircraft are ours, repeat ours. Types: Falcon, APC's and heavy transport. Alliance colors, irregulars' markings. Please advise."

A new voice came back to her through her helmet.

"High Guard One, this is Air Leader. Rejoin High Guard Two and fall back towards home. We're coming out to meet you."

"Aknol that, Air Leader. What the hell is going on?"

"We may have to shoot at those people a bit."

"Major, the incoming aircraft still do not reply."

Holcomb swore. Niagra was in as much confusion about the incoming aircraft as he was—and the Southwest SubCouncil was offering no information. No other irregular forces would be coming in from the west, and that prospect worried him more than anything else. He turned to a comm tech.

"Order two reserve companies and a reinforced heavy-weapons section to join the detachments around the Han compound," he said.

"Yes, sir." The order went out.

Holcomb looked back to the screen. Whatever he was going to do next, he had just minutes to do it. He was convinced that the forces approaching Badlands were authentic Southwest troops, and he could make only too good a guess as to what they wanted. It put him in an unenviable position: if the oncoming aircraft did not answer his warning signals soon he could either fire on them and in all likelihood start the Alliance's first civil war—or he could let them land, and most likely lose it.

The comm tech in front of him was still droning out his warnings to the Southwest ships. Holcomb made his decision.

"Missiles," he said into his mike.

"Missiles here, Major."

"Arm a salvo," Holcomb ordered. "Set fuses for five kilometers; fire when the approaching aircraft cross the eight-kilometer mark. Unless ordered otherwise, all subsequent salvoes are to be fired for effect. All *dis* and secondary batteries, same orders. Aknol."

There was a chorus of assent.

"Tie me in to the approach channel," Holcomb said. The commtech switched him on-line. "This is Major Will Holcomb commanding the Alliance Badlands Air Base to the incoming Southwest forces. You are violating the airspace of an Alliance military facility. If you do not alter course I will have no choice but to view your intentions as hostile and open fire. Turn away, *now.*" Not waiting for an acknowledgement, he switched to the tactical channel. "Air Leader, do you copy?"

"Aknol, Badlands."

"Air Leader, if those ships haven't turned away, when

ground batteries open fire you are free to join in the attack, do you copy?"

"Aknol that, Badlands." How could Hopper sound so calm? It must be easier up there, Holcomb thought. Choices always seem much more definite when it's just a matter of not getting killed.

The Southwest aircraft came on. They crossed the twelve-kilometer mark. Holcomb fought the urge to open his microphone, to order the missiles and the *dis* batteries and the planes not to fire, not to start this thing, that would not end before it swallowed them all. They crossed the nine-kilometer mark. Holcomb cursed, reached for the switch.

"Missiles away." the speakers announced. A shower of broken light erupted from the center of the screen and flowed toward the oncoming ships, to erupt in warning fury the barest sliver of glass ahead of them.

"Dis *batteries opening fire."* The thin beams of cerulean energy were invisible on the screen but Holcomb knew what they must look like: great sweeps of radiance cutting back and forth across the paths the attackers must follow.

A new cluster of dots appeared on the screen now, Hopper's defending planes closing with their targets.

"Missiles, ready second salvo. Independent aim, fire for effect." The speaker announced. *"Secondary batteries, fire as the range allows."*

It was too late. Holcomb had himself a war now, whether he wanted it or not. He opened his mike again, to order the ground forces to slant their coverage to favor the Han compound—

"Badlands, Badlands, this is Air Leader. Intruding aircraft are altering course, repeat altering course north."

"Major, the incoming ships are losing height rapidly," a scope operator called.

"Intruders bearing away from the base," Hopper's voice announced.

"Stay with them, Captain!" Holcomb turned to the scope operator. "What's their altitude?"

"Not even three hundred meters—still dropping." The operator sat back. "Off the scope, sir."

"Air leader, this is Holcomb. What the hell are they doing?"

"They've landed sir." Hopper's voice betrayed the first confusion Holcomb had ever heard in it.

"Are they deploying? Is there any activity at all?"

"None, major. They're just sitting there."

"Keep station above them until further orders."

"Aknol, Badlands."

Holcomb turned to the comm tech. "Get me ground tactical."

"Here, Major."

"Captain, deploy all remaining reserve forces in support of the compound garrison. Then send a scout team out to the Southwest position. They are to avoid contact unless fired on. Range all artillery on the Southwest position but do not fire unless fired on or I order it."

"Aknol, Major."

The line went dead. Holcomb looked up at the screen. Badlands lay at the heart of the ranging grid, the Han prison compound just to the north of it. Beyond that, the Southwestern troops sat bottled up in their ships, waiting for he didn't know what. He hated it. But at least it wasn't a battle. Not yet. Things hadn't gone that far; the line was stretched but not broken.

"Ground tactical, Holcomb. Get that scout team moving. I want to know what the hell's going on." He switched off his mike.

"I sure as hell don't know," he muttered.

* * *

"All right," Helden ordered, "Get our people moving. Perimeter and support elements take up station around the APCs. Get the heavy transports away as soon as they off-load."

He switched off his mike and stepped down out of the transport. Behind him his headquarters staff was sliding crates of comm gear and combat data systems down the heavy freight ramp of the ship, while a platoon from the engineers cut the dugout for his bunker with light *dis* beams. Another unit stood by with the inertron-plated armor that would wall and armor the bunker.

All around him the men and women of his command were moving out to establish their positions confronting the federal base. He had laid out their deployment carefully so as to make it abundantly clear to the Badlands defenders that the irregulars were not preparing to move on the air base—but that they would not be moved from their own positions, either. It wasn't how he would have done it. He would rather have attacked immediately and presented the government with a fait accompli, the Han dead and the matter closed. But Teder had overridden him; Teder had wanted this show of force to make it clear that the Southwest would not yield on the fate of the Han, but had ruled out a direct attack until Rogers had been forced to openly defy a direct Council order. The way Cullen Teder had it planned, Rogers would try to—but the odds were that the federal troops would not follow him against the will of their home gang bosses. Then when the Council assumed control of the government as it would have to, it would be Cullen Teder who would have resolved the Han question, and forced the departure of the fractious Rogers, and who was in command of one of the largest organized military forces on the continent.

That was a new angle of Teder's, and one Helden

wasn't happy with. He had gone along with Teder on attacking the Han city: that was what you did with Han, and it had promised to get him out of his dead-end posting to the irregulars. But he had never wanted to become entangled in Council-level political infighting. He had hoped only to do his duty and profit by it in his career. It had never occurred to him that Cullen Teder might want the same.

A comm tech had appeared in the hatchway of the transport. "Commander, Badlands communications is trying to reach us again."

Helden looked up at the man. "Maintain silence as ordered."

"Yes, sir."

"Start pulling your gear. Start transferring to the bunker as soon as the roof's laid in."

"Yes, sir."

The tech hesitated, then turned and reentered the ship to pull the plug on the transceivers squawking for his attention. Another worry for Helden. The troops digging in around him had been eager to move to avenge themselves against any Han they could reach, but how long could that enthusiasm be maintained while they simply sat there and did nothing?

Long enough. It would have to be. Helden would have to make sure of it. He was trapped, as surely as any of those Han in the compound: Teder's patronage and success were all that stood between Helden and the inquiry that would break him.

He almost walked right past his goal.

Mordred had soon lapsed into a steady routine on his long walk inland. Sleep, wake, eat a brief meal from his dwindling stock of staple rations and drink from whatever stream he had collapsed by the day before, and then turn his back on the sea and start walking until fading daylight and his own waning strength forced him to seek a fresh hiding place to collapse in.

He no longer thought in terms of a destination. He had had that beaten out of him early on, when the reality of the vastness of the American continent had been borne in on him, for all that it had looked such a manageable little distance on the map. But the clean simplicity of the map on the screen had given no hint of nature's refusal to reduce itself to pale colored lines against a uniform background. The map gave no *true* indication that a ravine it showed would actually be an intimidating crevasse fully a hundred feet deep that would take over an hour to cross and ruin him for any further travel that day. It had not told him of the *true* nature of travelling cross-country, of the pains in his legs like fire, exacerbated by the uneven terrain, of what the sun could do to skin accustomed to weak city lighting. No map could hint at the despair Mordred had felt when he had deceived himself—more than once—into believing that some chance combination of landmarks was 'close enough' to those he sought to waste a day or two days in pointless searching. No map could describe how a plan would hold up in the real world. And so his plan, his ambitions, his desire for revenge had faded to a dim memory in the face of more current and pragmatic demands on his resources.

That was why he almost missed it. That one mountain to his left had been to his left for the past week, through two other false alarms. That river ahead of him looked no closer than it had yesterday, or the day before that. But the ridgeline was exactly where it should have been, and it was a lot rockier than the others he had wasted his time on. As he drew nearer he could see gaps and fissures cutting deeply into the ridge—and he began to hope again.

The ridge had the aspect of a prostrate camel, with two vertical swellings that rose well above the rest of it, yet still could not be called hills in their own right. Recalling the directions he had so painstakingly memorized, Mordred changed direction toward the northernmost hump.

A crevasse split the base of the hump, driving deep beneath it. Mordred hesitated before it. His previous errors had cost him nothing but time and effort wasted looking for similar fissures where none existed. But if he risked descending into this crevasse, he would be committed. An accident down there, an injury or a rockspill, a foot put wrong or a path followed too far in the wrong direction and he would be lost, trapped, with no hope of rescue or escape. And he could still be wrong; he had erred twice already, and accepted with a humility born of weariness that he could well be wrong a third time. But there was nothing behind him, nothing to go back to —and he couldn't stay where he was. He was low on food, he lacked the equipment and, he was forced to admit, the practical skills to set up any kind of long-term camp, and on top of that the sky was clouding up threateningly. He made his choice. If he had to put himself at peril he would at least do so someplace dry. He eased his way over the lip of the crevasse and began to descend.

This time he was right.

The crevasse was narrow but shallow compared with others he had crossed in his travels. The walls were nearly vertical but there were hand and footholds enough to let him manage.

He reached the bottom. The floor of the crevasse was oddly clean and level, uncluttered by the blown leaves and dust he might have expected there. The walls of the crevasse were broken and uneven around him—except for the perfectly rectangular passage that had been *dis*ed into the rock, its edges still as sharp as the day they had been cut years ago, untouched by erosion. There was no way that entrance could be mistaken for any natural phenomenon.

Mordred moved into the dark passageway. Ten feet down it he came up against the metal plate that took up the whole of the far wall. There was no latching mechanism, no obvious arrangement of controls, but as Mordred touched the plate's four corners once, twice, and a third time in the manner he had memorized a motor began to whine somewhere and the plate swung away. He stepped through into darkness.

With a new sound of engines the plate swung shut behind him and light flooded his surroundings.

The cache had been established in the days of the first Han retreat in America, as part of that people's mass movement to the hidden refuge-cities meant to shelter them from their human pursuers. As the cities were built it swiftly became apparent that the Americans would not give the Han time to recreate their sophisticated life below ground anew. So rather than jettison the vast quantities of resources they would otherwise have had to leave behind, some small part of the Han effort had been diverted into gouging out great hidden caverns into which these materials could be placed, against the day when they would needed in the inevitable Han re-emergence.

From where he stood Mordred could not see the far end of the chamber, nor was the ceiling visible save as the darkness bracketed by the high wall lights.

The room was full. Bales and crates and cartons sectioned off the enormous floor into narrow walkways. Machinery bulked shadowed and incomprehensible around the walls, some of it, some of the machines vast enough that their tops disappeared above the lights. Here were stored tools and weapons and stores enough to maintain a full Han city even if it should lose all other resources.

And it had been used.

Mordred didn't realize it at first. He had walked forward into the maze of stocks and supplies, astonished at the abundance hidden away there. It had been in his mind that to control—or at least occupy—the cache and use its resources to support factions that would in their turn support him in the political maneuverings of the city. That had been back when there was still a city to fight over, of course; now he was there simply because he could think of nowhere else to go. But it slowly dawned on him that someone else had had the same idea at one time. Crates had been opened, parcels broken into, materials scattered about and not replaced as if someone had gone searching in ignorance for something they needed but could not place.

He knelt to examine one of the opened packages: power units, of the sort commonly used in light equipment and hand weapons. He had no way of knowing how long ago the units had been opened; the sealed cavern prevented the accumulation of dust or the corrosion of metals within its walls. Behind the opened package he could see the remains of another that had been entirely emptied and stuffed away between two full ones.

It was as though someone had been breaking into the cache from time to time and pilfering a few units each time—as though they were afraid their loot would be missed or because they simply didn't need anything more. And that was not how any Han from the city would have done it. Any Man-Din who had taken control of such a treasure trove would have put it to use for him at once, and Ho-Tin would have been toppled from his throne long before it was brought down atop him. Yet no one else—

He spun at the sound of the weapon being cocked. His knife was in his belt but he had known better than to go for it. To draw a weapon against an unseen and unknown assailant would have been suicidal under those conditions. He remained poised on one knee, hands spread empty before him, and looked at his opponent.

The man was clad roughly, in clothing that had suffered much from wear and exposure. He weapon he held aimed at Mordred was an old-pattern machine pistol, of a type the cities had not used in years. It looked as used and worn as the man's clothing, but the large-bore muzzle Mordred stared into was clean and intimidating.

And the eyes that studied Mordred over the gun's sights were the dark and lidded eyes of a Han.

The flyer settled quietly into the center of the abandoned gang nexus.

"What is this place?" Lu-An asked.

"An old Pine Barrens Gang-nexus," Ruth answered, powering-down the flyer. "They abandoned it when the sea began to rise during the Peruvian recurrence. This bunch liked where they ended up better and merged with a local gang; they won't be back."

"It doesn't look like very much."

"People built it. They lived here, made it theirs. That makes it something. And it was the best I could find without risking too obvious a search. If you want to hide something properly you don't want to be seen poking at every dark corner."

"That is true enough. And I have no other real options."

"None to mention. Now let's get you unloaded."

Ruth Harris released the flyer's cargo ramp and left the control cabin to begin off-loading food and field gear for Lu'An's seclusion. To her surprise, the city-bred Han woman began to help without even being asked, despite the fact that she had in all likelihood never done any such physical labor before in her life.

The stores they off-loaded were supplies nominally destined for the American research effort at the Prl'lu Antarctic complex. They had been drawn and issued in the conventional manner, and Ruth Harris would log in that they had been duly received. As managing director of the American survey team, once Ruth signed for those supplies they would be effectively untraceable on paper and any shortages would be credited to clerical error at the South Pole end.

They moved the goods into one of the nexus buildings that seemed to be in somewhat better shape than its neighbors. The three large rooms were empty but reasonably clean; the fleeing gang had borne enough affection for their homes to seal them up against their improbable return.

"They won't search this far south for you for at least a month," Ruth said. "They'll think that there's no way anybody on foot could get this far that fast. So you'll have at least that much time, maybe longer. Certainly long enough for this matter to be resolved, one way or the other."

"Yes." Lu-An was staring at the empty room before her, her "home", very possibly, for what might remain of her life.

"Well, then," Ruth said, "I may as well be going. I'm supposed to be halfway over the Atlantic by now."

"But you are, Doctor," Lu-An said. "You certainly can't be here. Why should you be?"

"That's true, too. Well . . . ." Ruth Harris turned for the doorway.

"Doctor Harris." Ruth turned back. "If I am found here, if I am taken, that is the way it will be. You will be safe, still."

"Lu-An," Ruth said, "if you're taken the Alliance will

blow apart at the seams. There won't be any safety, then. . . ."

The projectile hung suspended in the first rings. Hun't'pir looked at it, one hundred tons of stone and iron ore ready to be hurled down upon the unsuspecting world he meant to reconquer. Hun't'pir reached out and activated a communications system.

"Blood of this Blood," he began, "the time is at hand to take back our honor. This world in our care has been stolen from us, by an enemy fierce and cunning and many in number. None of the Blood have ever accepted such a shaming before; we shall not now. For Blood and Breed, we will win."

As his words echoed through the corridors of the base, Hun't'pir touched a second switch. The great ore projectile began to glide along through the rings reaching for the horizon, accelerating smoothly and rapidly until it passed from sight in the distance.

Hun't'pir felt no particular satisfaction as he watched it vanish. The plan was simple enough to admit of no great errors. They had carefully plotted the locations of the indigenous cities of their target and assigned them a strategic priority on the basis of the complexity of the monitored communications filtering in and out of each. They would strike at the most complex first. Then, after the natives had had a chance to reorganize somewhat, they would destroy the next most complex center of communications, and the next, and the next, until finally there were no native structures sophisticated enough to control any sort of coordinated action left. Then it would be safe to revive the remaining stasis-guarded legions of Prl'lu still hidden on the target world, to complete the subjugation of the scattered natives piecemeal and at little cost. It was a simple plan, and the basic aspects of each stage were well within Hun't'pir's capa-

bilities. Therefore its success was a foregone conclusion
and demanded little enthusiasm. Only efficiency.

A telltale before Hun't'pir indicated that the projectile
had left the final ring of the weapon. The second subjugation of mankind was underway.

"You must understand, Marshal, that we have supported you this far only because we had no real choice,"
Carl Banneker said.

Rogers studied the man seated across the rich oaken
desk from him. The offices of Deering Precision Manu-
facturing were an ornate contrast to the functional plant
beneath them, parts of which dated back to the days of
the Liberation. Carl Banneker looked very much more
at home behind the desk than he had down among the
machines.

Yes, the Deerings had supported Rogers; in part because Ruth Harris had demanded it and the Deerings
stood by their own, but also because most of the
Deering-owned industries were heavily dependent on
government defense contracts, and there was no money
to be made from a paralyzed government that held the
pursestrings drawn tight in its frozen grip. So when Rogers had suggested that a recess in Council might be to
everyone's advantage, that strong decisions taken hastily might be strong decisions regretted—and accountable
for—later and that a certain amount of nonconfronta-
tional discussion among the various parties might be a
good idea, the Deerings had gone along. Their Council
representative had quickly seconded Rogers' motion to
recess; other councillors already swayed by the combined Rogers/Deering block had quickly followed suit.

So Rogers now had the free time he desperately
needed. Teder would not be able to ramrod a decision
through the Council while it was in recess, and Rogers
knew he could trust Will Holcomb to keep the lid on the

military situation out at Badlands. Rogers might even be able to use Teder's unilateral show of force to his advantage: most of the other bosses wouldn't be comfortable with such a pushy neighbor.

Only now he didn't know if it mattered.

Dupre and Watson had managed to keep word of Lu-An's escape from Niagra from leaking out, but her disappearance had upset Rogers as surely as though his legs had been swept out from under him.

Why the *hell* had she run? His every action had been based on his certainty that she was honestly no threat to the Alliance (*no, it hadn't,* a niggling thought surfaced, *it had been based on his refusal to believe that she could be such a danger, and that was an altogether different thing*). Didn't she believe he would stand by her (*didn't he know he couldn't, not without pulling down everything his own people had built in the past sixty years?*)?

Admit it, he thought, *she's probably done the one sensible thing she could do. Even if I'd fought Teder off, even if I didn't wreck the god-damned country doing it, life would have been hell for her in Niagra. She would have been the one Han everybody could reach.*

"Your choices haven't changed, Carl," he said. "So how much farther will the Deerings carry the Wyomings behind me?"

"To what?" Banneker demanded. "To the end of this ridiculous crusade of yours to save the Han?"

"To keep the gangs from becoming a race of murderers," Rogers said.

"Is that your choice to make, Marshal?"

"It isn't Teder's."

"The gangs don't seem to agree."

"Then I'll have to change that, won't I?"

"If you can. But will they let you?"

"Will the Deerings let me? That's all I have to know from you."

"I don't know," Banneker said. "It's costing us more every day that you hold the freeze on payment and purchases. It's getting to the point where it won't matter to us whether the Alliance holds together or not; we can't hold off bankruptcy forever."

Rogers had to control the urge to shake his head disgustedly. To hear a Deering moaning about personal hardship was more unsettling than he had thought it would be. If Wilma had chosen to support him, she would have done so, and no complaints. Ruth had done so. But then they were Deerings by blood and Banneker only by marriage, and it seemed to Rogers that all the stories about the Deering women's choice of men were justified.

Like the one Wilma married, he thought, *like me. What the hell have I done since she died, damn it? I played soldier for twenty years, and now in less than six I've almost wrecked everything she worked for.*

And why? Because I won't give up one woman to keep an entire country together? I've already betrayed everything Wilma believed in just keeping the Han alive this long; I've already betrayed Ruth, and she still supports me—

—and maybe that's the point. Maybe there has to be something in your life that you won't betray—

—even if she's betrayed you?

—even if. Or you wind up a nice soft Deering kind of man. And I've been one of those already. The Han won't die.

"And if I back down on this, Carl? Will Deering Precision stave off bankruptcy by selling Teder the guns he wants to kill the Han prisoners? Do you think that's an argument that will sway me?"

"If we're ruined we can't be of any use to you—"

"If you can't help me you're no use to me now!"

The phone on Banneker's desk buzzed. He slapped

the switch down. "I said I wasn't to be disturbed—"

"Marshal Rogers." It was Brock's voice.

"What is it, Captain?"

"Sir, it's Niagra—" Brock sounded even more disoriented than usual.

"Niagra what, Captain?" Rogers said angrily.

"Sir, Niagra is gone. . . ."

CHAPTER SIX

The heart of the city was a bowl of green glass. The Four Towers were gone, vanished as if they had never stood where that enormous cavity had been gouged out of the Earth. In a broad ring immediately around the crater the buildings of the city lay in rubble, not merely toppled but pulverised by some unimaginable impact. Farther out the buildings had actually had time to fall— but all save the massive fragments of wreckage lay *in* towards the center of the calamity, as though whatever destructive force had levelled the city had sought to draw them into its heart.

Rogers stood on the crest of a low hill beyond the ruined city. He felt no rage, no fear, just a total, numbing astonishment at the sheer totality of the devastation.

Small shapes moved in the distance, the hastily mobilized relief and rescue teams sent in from surrounding communities. They flew back and forth around the fringes of the shattered city, collecting injured and directing numbed survivors to the relief centers. They avoided the heart of the city, the band of ruin surrounding the enormous crater; there was no work there for anyone looking to save lives.

"At least there is no radiation, and no fall-out,"

Wolsky said from beside him. "Looking down at that, I would say that was almost a miracle. But we've already cancelled the evacuation of the downwind cities."

Rogers didn't answer him directly. "Dupre, Watson . . . how many others, Heric?"

"We'll have no way of knowing until the search teams are finished, Tony, but right now, based on the survivors already brought out and the area of the city destroyed—fifteen thousand, perhaps twenty."

"Dammit," Rogers said. "Dammit, dammit. How could the Han have had something like this without our knowing about it? How could they get all the way to Niagra without being detected? How?"

"It may not have been the Han, Tony."

"No. The Prl'lu. I know. But I hope to God it isn't those monsters. Because if it is, and they have something like this, then we're beaten before we start."

"That seems to me a particularly useless opinion to hold. . . ."

"Dammit, Wolsky, are you *blind*—" With an effort, Rogers controlled himself. "No. You're right, sorry. Brock, what's happening with communications?"

Rogers' aide stood behind them, at the small comm unit off-loaded from the transport. "Everything's still being handled through the military nets, Marshal. The bypass points for the government channels are making progress, though."

"Good. That isn't vital yet, anyway; we can't use the government channels in any case until the Council's been recalled and a new meeting site selected. What's the word from everyplace else?"

"We still haven't established contact with Boss Loup-Main, sir. In fact, we can't raise Kebec at all."

"Hit too, most likely. After all, it was as obvious a target as Niagra—"

"Marshal Rogers." Brock interrupted them. "There's a new report. Badlands has been hit."

"I can't make any sense out of it, Marshal," Will Holcomb said. Rogers couldn't much past him through the screen, but what he could see was dismaying. Holcomb's office looked like a battle had been fought there. The window behind him was boarded up; what Rogers could see of the walls looked cracked and blackened.

"We had no warning, none. Some of our people claim to have seen a streak of fire dropping straight out of the sky just before the explosion, but they don't know where it came from. We had no strange aircraft on scope; our air patrols saw nothing: whatever it was, it just dropped down out of nowhere."

"What's your status, Major?"

"The Han compound is gone, no survivors—including our garrison. Outside of that, Teder's people caught the worst of it. I've got maybe three hundred of them overflowing my hospital, and that's all. The rest are just gone. I lost six Falcons that were on low patrol over the Han compound and three more that were parked outside their revetments. One Mako, too. I've got perhaps another three hundred wounded from the concussion, and maybe half my above-ground facilities are still functional. The *Deering* is safe. Her hangar was wrecked and she threw her moorings, but the day watch was aboard and they managed to ground her." Holcomb hesitated. "Sir, this is going to sound callous, but I think we got off lightly. I've seen what's left of Helden's positions. *Dis* couldn't have been more thorough."

"I'm amazed that you're here to talk about it at all," Rogers said. "After Niagra. . . ."

"I know," Holcomb said, "I've seen the pictures. It's

wierd, but considering the placement of the crater I almost get the impression that whatever it was was deliberately aimed at Helden's people and not at us."

"Then you got off lucky. What are you doing now?"

"Well, Marshal, I've dispersed my forces as best I could, following the guidelines for nuclear countermeasures. I couldn't move my hospital with all those casualties and I thought it advisable to leave a detail to hold the strip and the *Deering*'s support facilities. Outside of that, the base is largely evacuated except for the command center and myself. They won't catch us the way they caught Helden."

"Good enough, Major. I'll get back to you." Rogers switched off.

So Teder's plans for the Han had come through after all, though certainly in no way he had intended. But that was the least of Rogers' concerns now. Han or Prl'lu, whoever had struck at Niagra and then at Badlands had done so in a manner impossible to trace or counter, and that made them more dangerous than Cullen Teder's speeches could ever be.

And less predictable: Niagra was a sensible first target, by any standard one cared to name, but why *Badlands* next? There were larger, more important military bases; there were certainly more important cities. What made Badlands so special?

The *Deering*, Rogers suddenly realized. It had to be. Nowhere else in the Alliance, nowhere else on Earth could one find that capacity for travel beyond the planet's atmosphere. Now Rogers understood why Badlands had been hit. It was elementary strategy. Whoever controlled the high ground had an incontestable advantage in combat.

And nothing could claim any higher ground than the *Wilma Deering*.

Rogers opened his phone again. "Get me Badlands."

A moment later Will Holcomb was looking out of the screen at him.

"Will, I think I know what's going on here. Is the *Deering* combat-ready?"

"All her systems are operational, her crew's aboard."

"Then get her up. High, Fast. A hundred miles, at least, and hold station. If you see anything approaching this continent above the atmosphere, anything at all, your orders are to attack. Is that understood?"

"Aknol, Marshal. Take station at one hundred miles and attack anything approaching this continent. Sir?"

"What is it?"

"Just what do you think is going on here?"

"Will, whatever hit you people, and destroyed Niagra, didn't come from this world."

It was like living in a bad dream.

These were Han, Mordred realized. But they were like no Han he had ever known. There were thirty-seven of them in this one band, carrying human weapons and wearing clothes either made by hand or stolen long ago. They were taller than city Han, harder—and many of them had eyes as gray as Mordred's own.

The Han who had found him—his name was Tannin, pronounced with slurred quickness Mordred found repellent—had such eyes. He noticed Mordred's stare, and laughed.

"What, city-man, did you think your 'honored' father was the only Han to ever take a human woman? Our fathers had no other. The blessed Man-Din marched them out of their city to fight the humans and then abandoned them in the wilderness when they lost. How many? Hundreds, thousands, maybe more than thousands, we don't know today. Most died, the humans killed them or their own Man-Dins rayed them down to *atone* for their own stupidity in losing. But not all, not my father, not theirs," he said, sweeping an arm behind him to include the other wild Han around them in the cache. "They hid while the humans crushed the cities, and then they ran into the woods, to where the humans were not so many, to where we could take clothes and guns and women and not be found. So they lived, and we live—and now you live. But how long, eh? How long, city-man?"

"I've lived this long," Mordred said. "I found this place."

"And we found you!" Tannin laughed. "We followed you here, city-man, and we thank for such wealth! What else can you give us? Your life maybe? You have good city clothes; I can use them. But what are you worth, city-man? What can you offer to buy your life?"

"Knowledge, perhaps."

"What knowledge?" Tannin said scornfully. "How to live? We know how to live here, city-man. Better than you. You never saw us until we caught you."

"Tell me no lies, wild man," Mordred said. "You never followed me here. I saw the packages broken open outside. You've been looting this cache for months, at least."

Tannin laughed. "Oh, good, city-man! You know how to think! But you don't know how to speak. Never anger a man with a gun when you have none." The grin never slipped as he suddenly lurched forward and struck Mordred across the face with his weapon. Mordred fell back off the crate he had been sitting on, rolled, and came up in a cold rage, his hands ready. But the three wild Han nearest him were ready, too, and their own weapons swung easily to cover him.

"Now what are you worth, city-man?" Tannin asked quietly.

Mordred forced himself to calm down. "As I said, knowledge. Perhaps I can't tell you how to live, but I can tell you where."

"Where?" Tannin asked. "What is wrong with here? Much wealth here."

"And nine parts of it out of ten you cannot use," Mordred said. "You cannot use the heavy machinery; you cannot use the heavy weapons. You are too few, and lack the city-knowledge necessary. But things are different to the north."

"How? There are humans to the north, too many for us."

"No longer. My city was waging war upon the humans. Many are dead. All along this coast the humans are weak, now—and to the north they are gone. Whole towns wait for you, empty, full of wealth you can use. Light tools, materials, weapons. You could do well to journey north, Tannin."

"I could," Tannin said, "and I could do well also to kill you if you lie. But you know how to think, city-man; I think you know that, too." Tannin threw over a packet of condensed rations. "You eat now; sleep, if you're not too scared. I won't waste a man guarding you but all the ways out are watched. If you try to escape, you die." And with that, he stood up and walked off among the stockpiled goods.

At his departure the other Han watching Mordred turned away as well—but the Han outblood put no trust in their indifference. It was one thing to scorn Tannin and his band as illiterate, unthinking scavengers—but it would be something else and folly to consider them stupid, simply because they did not indulge in the decadent city niceties Mordred himself had despised. They were Han, but they had survived for sixty years outside the safety of the concealed cities, vulnerable to the eyes of the humans. They were, he realized, the reality of what he had hoped he could lead the Han to become, honest predators rather than cowering victims. That reality was a good deal grubbier than his dream, but it was real, it worked—and his dreams had never become anything more.

In any event, he did not believe he was not being watched, and there was no place else for him to go in any case. He unwrapped the ration pack and began to eat. . . .

"To hell with your council," Teder said.

The Susquannas' nexus was nothing spectacular as cities went, but it was the nearest site to Niagra where Rogers could find the necessary screen capacity to communicate with the Council. But the capacity to communicate and the willingness to communicate were two different things.

"First you defend the damned Han against their just punishment, then you butcher my people yourself, and you expect me to come sit on your Council like nothing has happened? You're insane, Marshal, insane!"

"What the hell are you babbling about, Teder?" Rogers demanded.

"Get off it, Rogers. You can't tell me your people at Badlands didn't launch an unprovoked attack on my people. I was talking with Helden when it happened; I saw the beginning of the explosion; I saw Helden die."

"Teder, you're sick," Rogers said. "This isn't some petty political squabble. Niagra's been destroyed. The Alliance is under attack—"

"It certainly is, Rogers. But by whom? If Niagra's been destroyed, what kind of position does that leave you in, Marshal? Who controls the only organized power in the Alliance right now?"

"You're mad."

"I didn't wipe out my own city; don't you go making charges of insanity."

"Teder—"

"Save it, Marshal. All I have to say to you is this: both you and your damned Alliance can go to hell. The Southwest doesn't need you; it never did. We'll go our own way from now on."

"The shape you people are in?"

"We've survived before. We'll do it again. But not under you, Rogers. And the rest of you, listening to this, think about it. Think about what this man you've chosen to lead you is capable of."

The screen went dead. Rogers stared at it, numb. Behind him, Wolsky spoke.

"The gangs will never believe him, Tony. He's mad. If you had intended to destroy the Council, then why call for a recess first and scatter the representatives all over the country?"

"Thanks, Heric," Rogers said coldly. "As long as you had to reason out that I wasn't a homicidal tyrant, I'm glad you were so quick about it."

"I didn't mean. . . ."

"I know, I know." He turned to Brock. "Get on the horn to every federal base from Badlands west. Put them on full alert. Inform them that the Southwest SubCouncil has declared its secession from the Alliance and they are now to consider themselves in hostile territory. All forces are to maintain a strictly defensive posture unless ordered otherwise."

"Do you think the Southwestern troops in the Federal garrisons will go along with that?"

"I hope so, Wol—and that's all I can do about it."

Light struck fiercely against the unbreachable hull of the *Deering* as dawn swept over the curve of the horizon.

Peggy Biskani leaned back from her board, wishing she could undo the tight harness that held her to her seat. But she knew better: the *Wilma Deering* had been hanging in free fall ever since they'd established the necessary velocity to keep her in fixed position above her takeoff point. Elsewhere in the ship she would have been safe to drift freely, enjoying the uncanny sensation of zero-gravity—like belting, the way belting should have felt, the way it had been the first time she had been allowed to jump on her own—but on the flight deck she knew better. She grinned briefly at the thought of someone drifting into the ordnance board and providing watchers on the ground with an amazing fireworks display. Around her, Cade the gunner, and Howell the pilot paid close attention to their systems, while Jefferson sat calmly in the captain's chair, overseeing all. In front of her the repeater screens for the ultroscopes that surveyed the space around the ship flicked through their staggered scanning sequences, shifting from pickup to pickup so that no area went unobserved for more than a few seconds.

Behind them one of the manual hatches—favored for reliability—slid open and Jomo Mamboya invested the remaining free space in the control room with his bulk.

"How goes the stargazing, Doctor?" Jefferson asked. The other black man grinned back at him.

"Marvelously," Mamboya said. "You would not believe what an inconvenience an atmosphere truly is, Captain."

"Well, I'm sort of fond of one, myself," Jefferson answered. "Having one around just lets me breathe a little easier. But listen; I know you came along for own reasons, but is there any chance that your people can help us with our patrol duties?"

Mamboya shrugged. "My people are at your disposal

if they are needed, Captain, of course; but I doubt if our facilities will be any use to you unless we are threatened from straight above. Our field of view is somewhat limited, after all. . . ."

"Commander," Kors'in-tu said. "We have located a new center of communications."

"Where?" Hun't'pir asked. He stepped away from his position to let the younger Prl'lu reach the image controls.

"Here, sir, in the lower left portion of the target continent." he touched a switch and a small point of light appeared in the American Southwest before them.

"Its significance?"

"It does not handle a volume of communication greater than that of any other location, Commander— but the greater part by far of all communications in this particular region are routed in and out through it."

"So. Then it would seem crucial, to that area at least."

"I believe so, Commander."

"Very well," Hun't'pir said. "It shall be our next target. Give the launch officer the necessary coordinates."

"As you order, Commander."

Twenty minutes later one hundred tons of stone and ore were hurled down upon Taos.

The wild Han slept.

Tannin gave no sign that he disbelieved Mordred's story about the abandoned human settlements, but neither did he seem to be in any great hurry to get his band moving in that direction. They lay scattered throughout the cache, enjoying the dry, warm shelter it offered.

Mordred rose. At once the Han nearest him was

awake. There was no muzziness, no hesitation; the woman was simply awake and clutching her pistol as she watched him from where she lay.

Mordred scowled at her. "Does one simply soil the floor where they lie here, or has there been a special place set aside for the privilege?"

The woman matched his frown. "I don't know what city-men do today, but over there, far wall." she pointed with the pistol.

Mordred turned and walked off in the direction indicated. Each time he passed a sleeping Han the result was the same: eyes opened and hands reached for weapons. These people's alertness was uncanny; but then they had sixty years of experience to instill it.

The "over there" proved to be a full sanitary facility, as good as anything in the city. Mordred then realized that he had not seen much dirt around these people. Their clothing may have been old and worn, but it was clean, and so were they. These wild Han may have been barbarians but they were disciplined. He wondered if they lived here on a regular basis. Probably not, he decided. The cache was well-hidden but it was also to all intents and purposes indefensible, and a death-trap if the single entrance was barred to anyone within. Most likely they wintered here, and made periodic trips back whenever they needed supplies.

He emerged from the toilet and started back along the wall, trying to orient himself among the bales and machinery. These wild Han had a good arrangement here; so much the worse for Mordred. They would be loathe to give it up to follow him in his campaign against the humans—and there was no way he was liable to compel them. He was capable of nothing that would impress them: their survival skills were doubtless superior to his; his city-bred knowledge was of no value to them. And he knew, from his brief experience of Tannin, that they were probably every bit as capable in terms of fighting skill as he was. What they lacked next to his formal training they more than made up for in real-life experience. Perhaps he could take Tannin; there was still no way to be sure that they would then follow him.

He was thwarted again. In the city he was too human to be tolerated; here, he was too Han.

In anger he struck a fist against the wall—and it dropped away. More precisely, a panel he had not seen was forced inward and dropped from sight, to reveal a single gleaming button set behind it.

For a moment, Mordred hesitated. There was no way to predict what might happen if he pressed that button. The Han who had established this cache years ago would not have wished it to fall into hostile hands; doubtless provision had been made to destroy it if necessary.

But he did not think a destruct control would have been so oddly concealed. A destruct control would more likely have been far more obvious, available to more people than its hider. . . .

He still did not know what the button would do. But then, he thought, there was no real way his own situation could get any worse. He reached out and pressed it firmly.

The back wall of the cache vanished. . . .

Men and material poured into Taos.

The ruined buildings, shattered in the Han attack, had been hastily cleared away with *dis*. Temporary structures dotted the stripped earth in chaotic patterns as the dispossessed gangs of the Southwest answered Teder's call, bringing their people and all the food, tools, and building materials they could salvage in with them. The receiver units from Wolsky's freshwater project were gathered up from the abandoned refugee centers and brought in as well, and water allotment centers were established throughout the city.

But by far the greatest wealth of the Southwest came back with the deserting Federal troops. One entire base had come into the Southwest's hands when the troops stationed there, at Teder's urging, had literally marched the small eastern contingent onto several transports and headed them toward the Atlantic. Other troops were filtering back from other bases still in Federal hands, bringing with them what they could.

Teder laughed as he thought of that. That bastard Rogers had claimed he was allowing it as charity for the dispossessed people of the Southwest, but Teder knew better—he knew it was because that damned old man was afraid to force the matter, afraid to take the chance that the gangs of the East would refuse to turn on their own kind just to ensure his continued authority. Besides, Southwestern wealth had gone into buying a hell of a lot of that material; Teder was just recovering their investment.

It was all so simple, he had come to realize. Rogers' softness toward the Han had been a front all along. He had never given a damn about the Han; he simply had not wanted to give in to Teder, to let the bosses see how thin his control had worn.

And then there had been that Han witch . . . Teder could damn well believe *she'd* had something to do with Rogers' attitude, all right, and now she was dead with the rest of Niagra. Teder wondered if that had been deliberate on Rogers' part, to gull the surviving Council members and rid himself of a dangerous millstone at the same time. That was how *he* would have done it, Teder thought, if he'd had to. . . .

"Boss Teder." Ebben Smith's voice reached him from the back of the shelter. They were still running things from the armored basement complex, would be for months. What little had remained of the executive offices above had had to be *dis*ed away to free those in the shelters after the attack: there wasn't even a foundation left to build on.

"What is it, Major?"

"There's been more trouble, sir. The Dry Ridge and Saguaro Gangs again."

"What damage?"

"Two killed, six wounded."

"Why?"

Ebben shrugged. "Gang thing. There's been bad blood between Dry Ridge and Saguaro for years."

"All right, then split 'em up. Stick Dry Ridge down by Juarez and Chado and put the Saguaro crowd over with the Sioux Bends."

"There's worse feeling between Dry Ridge and Chado than there is between Dry Ridge and Saguaro."

"Well, put them somewhere else, then, dammit. Show some initiative!"

"Yes, sir."

Damn the man anyway, Teder thought, walking back to his desk. What the hell was he supposed to care which gang got along with which? He had a hundred damn gangs to worry about. He switched on his phone.

"Communications, are those calls still going out?"

"Yes, sir."

"Well, keep it up. I know those idiots over at Sand Falls haven't answered yet, and they're sitting on tons of construction sheet. I want them in here."

"We're working on it, sir."

"Well, get it done, then." Teder switched off. This reorganization was not going as readily as he might have hoped. The gangs with more mouths than meals were flocking to the city; the gangs with the actual material wealth that would go far toward correcting this imbalance were holding back, waiting to see just how much of a demand they would face. Well, they would come in, all right; Teder would see to it.

He wasn't going to lose it now. . . .

Peggy Biskani was heartily sick of those screens. She had been staring at them now, watch and watch, for three days. At first the view had delighted her, to the point where she had actually badgered Mamboya for some time on the old-fashioned optical telescope he had mounted in the direct observation chamber to watch them at first hand.

But that was three days ago. In the time since she had come to the sensible conclusion that no matter how long she watched them, they weren't likely to do anything they hadn't been doing when she got there—

Mamboya rushed onto the flight deck, catching his speeding bulk against the back of her chair before momentum carried him into the boards.

"Captain Jefferson, you must come see this."

"What?"

"I must show you."

Jefferson looked at him. Mamboya was not indulging in his usual expansive urgency. He seemed genuinely alarmed.

"All right."

The direct observation chamber was simply an empty room roofed over with clear ultron plating. The bulk of the room was taken up by the elderly telescope Mamboya had installed for his astronomical studies. Mamboya's two assistants had to edge out of the chamber past them before Mamboya and Jefferson could enter.

276

Jefferson moved to the telescope at Mamboya's gesture. "What am I supposed to be seeing?"

"Look."

In freefall it was an easy matter to slide under the nearly-vertical telescope and position himself at the eyepiece.

The stars were brilliant, shining down clearly and unwinking without the distortion of an atmosphere to break up their image.

The projectile was equally as clear, seen edge-on, a tiny, discrete disk in the far distance, even to the powerful telescope.

"What the hell is that?"

"I don't know. But it wasn't there half an hour ago."

"Which means that it's moving, and it's coming this way."

"Rather quickly."

"All right." They made their way back to the flight deck.

"Peggy, give me a vertical scan," Jefferson ordered. "Straight up, your strongest magnification."

Peggy Biskani keyed in the necessary pickups. Even on the powerful ultroscopes, the projectile remained an anonymous disk against the stars.

"How far away is that thing?" Jefferson asked.

"I'll check." Peggy switched over to a pickup at the stern of the ship. Save for the slight flicker of transition, there was no noticeable difference. She then keyed in a second pickup at the bow of the Deering, and superimposed it on the same screen. There was just the least blurring of the projectile disk. Carefully, Peggy adjusted the two pickups until the image was sharp again, one pickup superimposed over the other. After that, a simple triangulating calculation and—

"That thing's a good twelve hundred kilometers out," she said.

"And it's occluding that much of the screen?" Jefferson asked. He reached a decision.

"Cade, warm up your board. Zero that thing when it comes into range."

"It's in range for rockets now, sir."

"Then hit it. Keep hitting it until it isn't there."

"Aknol, Captain." Cade quickly brought the ordnance board to life. "Give me a good angle."

"Right." Howell triggered the *Deering's* attitude jets, swinging the ship so that the weapons pylons aligned on the projectile.

"Good enough," Cade said. "Ready to fire, Captain."

"Open fire."

Missiles leaped from every battery on the ship. There was what seemed to be an eternal wait as the explosives closed on their target. Minutes passed.

Fire burst around the projectile, blossoming on the screen. Then suddenly the slug was through the explosions, still coming on.

"It isn't touched," Peggy said. "What *is* that thing?"

"Something serious," Jefferson said. "Cade, keep hitting it. Don't stop."

"Aknol."

Rockets streamed out again, to burst against the unheeding projectile. They kept exploding. It kept coming.

"Peggy, pass the alarm. General alert, all stations. Cade, *dis* that thing."

"Dis going out, sir."

With no atmosphere to scar in passing, the powerful *dis* beams were invisible in flight. But telltales on Cade's screen marked their course, marked the point where they intersected in the path of the projectile, marked the point where they struck. There was a sudden cloud of radiant blue vapor as the beams scoured matter from the flanks of the projectile—and then it was past them, and still coming, gouged by missile fire, scarred by trenchant *dis,* but still more than ninety tons of ore and lethal kinetic energy.

"I can't track it!" Cade warned. "It's moving faster than I can traverse!"

"Get us out of the way," Jefferson said. Howell's fingers flew over his board, and the *Deering* began to slide, drifting out of the path of its unstoppable opponent.

The projectile seemed to leap forward in the screen—and then it was off the pickups, past them, plunging toward Earth.

"Where the hell did that *thing* come from?" Jefferson asked. "And what are we going to do about it?"

"I don't know," Mamaboya said.

Taos was in chaos.

The influx of refugees to the city had been checked and reversed within minutes of the *Deering's* alarm. For the second time in less than two months Taos was emptying itself in expectation of attack.

"If this is some stunt of Rogers', I'll have his heart out for it," Teder said, staring at the screen full of leaping figures.

"If it's a trick, sir, it's a thorough one," Smith said. "That was an open broadcast, and from what we're picking up on the federal channels every other city between here and the Atlantic is in the same uproar."

"Yeah, but Rogers would jump at a chance to ruin our reorganization—"

"—but I don't think he'd throw his own organization into a panic to do it, sir." Ebben made a point of switching over to a fresh comm channel and asking after sled availability. Teder realized he'd been dismissed. He had to fight down an urge to dress the young officer up and down the shelter.

The defenses of the city had been beyond repair, but

every *dis* unit and long-gun that had come in with the refugees had been commandeered into a new garrison. Now those weapons were manned and armed, their crews at the ready—but with no idea of what they were defending against save that the attack would come from the sky.

One gunner looked up and saw a tiny pinpoint of fire high in the clear desert sky. At his shout, men and women swung their weapons upward—

—and had time for nothing else. At eleven kilometers per second the projectile struck home almost as soon as it could be seen.

It was not a nuclear detonation—but it might as well have been. Ninety tons of iron ore plunging down a gravity well a quarter of a million miles deep hit with a force that could be measured in kilotons. The temporary shelters of the gangs were blown apart like cardhouses. Refugees caught in the air were swept up in the expanding shockwave like dust—the lucky ones died instantly.

There was too much energy in too small a space. Any space would have been too small. A lot of that energy—a hellish lot—was converted to light and heat. The heat turned breathable air to incandescent gas, and the gas began to rise. Air rushed in to fill the vacuum, even as the first fires were beginning among the ruined shelters. Struggling figures were snatched up and drawn helplessly back into the rising column of flame, the inertron belts that were the key to their escape now nails in their coffins, cancelling whatever hope frail human weight might have granted in resisting that lethal suction.

The inertron shielding of the government shelter held, even against that incredible impact. But the shelter moved, thrown violently through earth grown suddenly liquid and then gaseous. Then it was rising, caught in the updraft of the new-born firestorm climbing from the heart of the murdered city. It lurched and tumbled wildly in the savage currents. But it held together. It was still in one piece when it landed, almost half a mile beyond the blast zone.

There was nothing left alive inside.

Rogers had forgotten the true immensity of the Antarctic complex.

After thousands of years of preservation in stasis, the base looked as fresh and modern as it must have the day the last switch was thrown to seal it in.

Rogers, Wolsky and Mamboya were walking down a seemingly endless corridor, its walls line with narrow cylinders of mirror-perfect reflectiveness. Those cylinders were made of nothing material. They were stasis fields, smaller versions of the same system that had protected the base for untold centuries. But these would not be opened—not by humans—each cylinder contained a Prl'lu warrior, identical to the handful of martial nightmares that had all but defeated humanity three years ago.

Ruth Harris was waiting at the end of the corridor when they finally arrived.

"Marshal," she said, "doctors."

"Doctor Harris," Rogers said. "Have you found anything?"

"Something. I don't know if it will help."

"It will have to."

They followed down a shorter cross-corridor, to another room. The walls within were lined with consoles. The center of each console was a flat plate of a dark, glasslike substance, marked off with a fine grid of concentric circles, notated in some unintelligible script.

"Ultroscopes?" Rogers asked.

Ruth shook her head. "Repeater screens of some kind, but not ultronic. Electronic in nature."

"What do they do?"

Ruth sighed. "We think they're some kind of ranging and detections system. But we don't know."

"Why not?"

"They don't work."

"Why not?" Rogers repeated.

"These systems here," she waved at the consoles, "are operational enough. But they're only repeaters. They display information gathered somewhere else. And we think the gathering systems were destroyed when we took the complex. We've traced the connections from these systems to others on the top level of the complex —but there are leads from those up into the open, and whatever they led to is gone."

"So the problem is that you have systems to relay and make sense out of information, but you have no information to make sense of."

"That's it."

"Does anyone have any suggestions?" Rogers asked.

Mamboya had stood silent and scowling through Ruth's speech. "Doctor Harris. In all our own detection systems, the unit has to be aimed at what we with to detect, does it not?"

"With ultroscopes and manual rangefinding systems, yes," Ruth said.

"Then it would not be unreasonable to speculate that these systems required a similar provision."

"It's a fair supposition."

"Ruth, you said these systems are electronic in nature?"

"That's right."

"Did you find any evidence anywhere in the system of provision for conversion to ultronic transmission? Of any sort of conversion?"

"Not in those parts of the system left intact."

"The elements that you have studied," Mamboya asked, "are they capable of transmitting a complete signal?"

"They seem to be."

"Do they put out a signal?"

"The units on the top level do, an electromagnetic pulse. But we have no way of knowing what those impulses might have been converted to."

"Ruth," Rogers said, "if the system is conventional electronics all the way through, then maybe the pulse isn't converted at all. What if it uses a standard radio signal, like an old wireless unit?"

Ruth Harris stared at him. "How can you detect anything by putting out a radio signal?"

"How are we going to tell what else this thing might have used?" Rogers asked. "Ruth, when we hit this place, the top deck was crawling with antennae. Including several big, weird dish-shaped ones, right together. The units these tie into—where are they?"

"Top level, second tier."

"That sounds about right. Could you replicate one of those dish antennae?"

"I won't have to. There are a dozen of them stored here."

"Then run one up."

"We still won't know where we're looking, Tony, even if we get it working. Nobody here reads Prl'lu. No, wait—we could calibrate with over-flights—"

"—or even just eyeball it by following where the dish points. But we have to get it working, first. Can you and your people do it, Ruth?"

"Marshal Rogers, you haven't got anybody who'll give it a better try."

"City-man, you're mad." Tannin faced Mordred over his levelled weapon.

"And you're a fool, Tannin." When the wall of the cache—or the stasis field concealed behind a flimsy shield that had supposedly been the wall—had given way, Mordred had found himself at the top of a long, shallow ramp. By the time his absence had been noted, and by the time the wild Han had worked up the nerve to follow him down the ramp, he had found what he half-expected to find.

Prl'lu. Not as many, perhaps, as were hidden in the fallen Antarctic base, but certainly hundreds of them, perhaps even thousands, hidden away in their individual stasis cylinders. Certainly enough to represent a terrifying power—if Mordred had been fool enough to release them a second time.

He wasn't; Tannin didn't know that, though. But he did know enough to recognize the stylized engravings on the wall, the stark representations of a Prl'lu warrior. Tannin was neither high Man-Din nor even of Man-Din blood, so he had never heard of Prl'lu as Prl'lu—but he recognized the mythical warrior demons of Han legend.

"I think you'll be wanting to go north after all," Mordred said. "This is nothing for you."

"This is nothing for any sane man," Tannin said. "Don't city-men recognize evil when they see it?" He was already nervous, to learn that he and his people had been living on the threshold of such a mystery for so long. The sight of the Prl'lu figures and Mordred's unnatural confidence upset him further.

"Oh, yes, wild man," Mordred said. "We can recognize evil. Better perhaps than you know."

"Then come out of here. Now."

"No. This has value to me, wild man. I have a purpose here."

"Not a good one."

"Not one that need concern you."

"One that does. I would not see such evil loosed near my people."

"Then leave."

"Perhaps I would not see such evil loosed at all."

"How will you stop me?"

"I'll kill you," Tannin said simply. "Now."

"Go ahead," Mordred said. He laughed. "But think first, wild man. I revealed this place. Do you know how?" Tannin didn't answer. "Can you know that killing me would serve your ends? Can you *know* that I could not awaken these demons, even in my death? *Think,* wild man. This is something beyond you."

The weapon wavered.

"I have no quarrel with you, Tannin, or your people. I would let you leave safely, if you wish—and if you leave now. So choose, Tannin. I promise you your lives —or you could ensure your deaths. Choose *now,* wild man."

Tannin took a single step back. Mordred held his look.

The weapon lowered. The wild Han turned to shout up the ramp.

"Ready yourselves!" he called. "We leave at once!" he turned back to Mordred. "Those stories you told, of the humans in the north. Was there truth in them?"

"There was truth, wild man."

"Very well. Perhaps we will go there, then." He turned and started up the ramp, then paused and looked back. "We are content with simple things, city-man. You should learn the same lesson."

Mordred laughed. He felt power again, the strength of command. "Simple things are for simple men, wild man. I am not simple. Now leave."

When Tannin had reached the top of the ramp he turned once and looked back. Then he was gone.

Mordred turned and looked down the length of the stasis columns. Then he walked away from the ramp, into the heart of the Prl'lu complex.

"Has there been any change?" Hun't'pir asked.

"None, Commander. It has been three rotations of the planet and no new nexus of communication has developed on the target continent," Kor'sin-tu said.

"Then either they have collapsed already or they are learning well. I choose to think the latter. We shall resume the bombardment, according to the original scale of priorities. See to it."

"Yes, Commander."

"It works," Rogers said.

"Just don't ask me how," Ruth said. "I don't pretend to understand the principle behind this. The only way I can conceive of this working would be if the wireless pulse, to borrow your phrase, Tony, were actually striking the target ship and bouncing back. And I have no idea how that might work."

"As long as it does, I'm impressed," Rogers told her. "What are we looking at now?"

"If you think you're impressed, listen to this: that's the *Deering.*"

"What? But the Deering is on station, a hundred miles up."

"That's right."

"It isn't even out as far as the first scale on this screen!"

"I said you'd be impressed."

"How far can this thing see?"

"Considering the position of the *Deering,* and assuming the unit will register to the limits of the screen, and it should, then I would say . . . twelve thousand kilometers."

"That's amazing."

"I thought you'd think so."

"Well, at least now we have some chance. We can see them coming, even if we still can't stop them."

"And when we see them?"

"We duck. Evacuate the target area, and—oh, God. . . ."

A blip had appeared on the outermost edge of the screen. Another followed, and another, and a third—Rogers was already on the phone.

"Brock, this is Rogers. It's a new attack, multiple strikes. I want every city that hasn't been evacuated to start, *now*. Notify every population center that they are to consider themselves prime targets."

He didn't wait for Brock's acknowledgement. "How long do we have?"

Ruth Harris was leaning over the screen, trying to make sense of the finer lines of the grid and counting. After perhaps half a minute, she answered.

"I say twelve hours, maybe less."

"Well, that gives us time, at least."

"Time for what?"

"To cut and run, Ruth. After sixty years, we're going back into the forests."

The scene outside Rogers' transport was a grim one. Observer's from the Atlantic seaboard west were reporting a steadily advancing wave of ruin, as projectile after projectile shattered one gang nexus after the next. The Appalachians were burning. The shore of Lake Erie was a steaming bog. A new lake was forming over the ruins of Stilo where the Mississippi was flooding into the fresh crater. Loss of life was lower than it might have been; the evacuations had been largely successful. But sixty years of progress were being methodically eliminated.

"We can't defend against this weapon," Rogers said. "We can't shoot down rocks, and we can't keep a *dis* beam on them long enough to do any good. We don't even know where they're coming from."

Doctor Mamboya spoke up. "I'm afraid we do, Marshal. At least, I believe so. But you won't like it."

"At this point, Doctor, I'll *like* any kind of solid information."

"Very well. Using the Prl'lu tracking system, Doctor Harris and I have managed to extrapolate the trajectory of the projectiles."

"All right—?"

"Marshal Rogers . . . our enemy is striking from the Moon."

"Are you serious?"

"It is the only serious possibility. We know these projectiles are being launched nowhere on this world. We know they are being delivered to a pattern. First the major centers of government on this continent, Niagra and Kebec—and now the lesser cities. I would suspect that our enemy has been selecting his targets by virtue of the volume of monitorable communications each city processes. That would be why they hit Taos out of turn, and Badlands. Teder and Helden both were putting out a considerable volume of transmissions."

"But why limit yourself to the Moon, Doctor?"

"To put it simply, the time element. Neither Badlands nor Taos was a major communications nexus long enough to have been noted and attacked from anywhere else in the solar system in the short time they functioned as such. So that has to be the answer. The Moon."

"All right, then. If we know where we're being attacked from, we can counterattack," Rogers said.

"How, Marshal?"

"That's the one simple question I've heard in the last month. The *Wilma Deering*."

"One ship, Marshal. Against a foe with the power to do—this. I cannot feel any great enthusiasm for such a proposal."

"It isn't a proposal, Doctor. It's the only choice we've got. We fight them on the moon, or they destroy us here on Earth. It's that simple."

Mamboya nodded. "Then it must be done."

"Yes it must." Rogers turned to Brock. "Get me Badlands."

The flyer bearing Ruth Harris back from Antarctica floated to a landed beside the grounded disk of the *Wilma Deering*. An armed crewman escorted her in. Rogers, Mamboya and Jefferson faced her.

Rogers wasted no time. "We're accepting your theory on the origins of the attacks, Ruth. We're going to counter with the Deering, if we can."

"She can get you there, Tony. Whether she'll be any kind of a match for what you find there. . . ."

"Is something we'll know when we arrive." He turned to Captain Jefferson. "How many personnel can the *Deering* carry and support for such a flight?"

"Earth to the moon, at a constant one-gravity's acceleration, for the duration involved . . . I'd say fifty, discounting crew."

"All right. Track down Val Lewis. Tell him to pick forty-seven of his best and get them here, fast."

"I'm afraid that won't work, Marshal," Jefferson said.

"Why the hell not?"

"Because infantry won't do you any good unless you

can get them off the ship. And you'll need vacuum armor for that. And we only have enough armor for twelve, maybe fifteen people outside the crew."

"Fifteen men isn't much."

"Thirty-five more peeing blood and frozen stiff won't do you any good."

"No. All right. Brock, tell Lewis to bring thirteen men —"

"Twelve, Tony."

"No way in hell, Doctor Harris."

"No way in hell not, Marshal. You know as well as I do that those are probably Prl'lu or worse up there. And such as I am, I'm the current expert on Prl'lu and worse in the Alliance."

"She is correct, Marshal. It would be a useful addition. You may have need of proper scientific counsel. And I am entirely too sensible to volunteer for something like this," Mamboya said.

Rogers shook his head. "I don't like this, Ruth."

"Neither do I," she answered. "Aunt Wilma was the brawler in the family. But I don't see any way around it."

"I wish I did. All right, Brock: twelve."

"Commander, the natives have dispatched a ship against us."

Hun't'pir turned to look at his subordinate. "Is this certain?"

"The ship is already beyond the planet's atmosphere," Kor'sin-tu said. "And it is still accelerating."

"Shak'si mir," Hun't'pir swore. "The natives showed no such capacity previously."

"Still, Commander—they are coming."

Hun't'pir swore again; this put the situation in an entirely different light. It was one thing to carry out an assault with an improvised weapons system against a target that could not shoot back. But the Prl'lu commander was under no illusions regarding the combat capabilities of his base. His was an observation and relay facility, not a fighting unit. It had neither the armaments nor the manpower to function as one.

But that did not matter. It would have to. And it would. They were Prl'lu, and the Prl'lu were warriors before all else.

"Ready the base for defense," he said. "I will want personal command of the primary combat system. And maintain the bombardment."

"Sir."

Hun't'pir reached for the controls of the observation chamber and began adjusting them carefully. In seconds he had centered the native ship in front of him, a bright metallic speck rising from his target to challenge him.

Hun't'pir's respect for the natives of his world increased. They meant to give him a fight. They would lose, of course, that could not be questioned; still, the attempt did them credit.

He would honor their memory when they had passed.

"We're making amazing time," Rogers said.

"You'd be surprised," Jefferson answered. "A steady acceleration adds up. It's just as well, too. We're not really set up for it."

That was true. The *Deering* was not laid out for constant-acceleration flight. At a steady one-gravity acceleration the occupants of the ship were effectively lying flat on their backs, the "deck" in reality the aft bulkhead of each cabin.

"We'll have to start decelerating soon," Jefferson said. "That's when I start to worry, Marshal."

"Why then?"

"Because we have to rotate the ship to align the engines for braking thrust. While we're doing that, we won't be able to bring the main weaponry to bear on any target ahead of us."

"There's no way around it?"

"Not unless you want to ram the moon hard enough to ruin your whole morning."

"Then there's no point in worrying about it, is there?"

"No. But I will anyway."

"So will I. But it seemed like the thing to say."

The ship rushed onward.

"Commander, the native ship has completed its braking maneuvers. They are proceeding toward us at a slower pace."

"Very good." Hun't'pir could see the ship clearly now. It was an odd design, primitive and clumsy-looking. Yet it had reached the moon, and Hun't'pir was sure it shared its builders' peculiar lethality."

"Activate the primary weapons system," he ordered.

"Yes, Commander." Targeting brackets flashed into existence in the air before Hun't'pir. He reached to a new corner of his console and dialed them into position on the approaching ship.

Above the base invisible energies stirred into life. Strong magnetic fields began to direct a stream of heavy atomic particles in a tight circle, forcing them into a coherent bean and urging them to higher and higher speeds. . . .

The Wilma Deering descended cautiously toward the dead surface of the Moon. Their destination was plain enough—to reach it they simply followed the steady stream of projectiles being hurled into space at ten minute intervals.

"Marshal, we've located the alien weapon," Jefferson said. "Those rings. They're directing the projectiles somehow."

Rogers studied the enormous accelerator in his own scope. "All right. Before we do anything else, let's see if we can't take it out from here."

"Aknol. Cade, ready on *dis*."

"*Dis* ready."

"Then fire when you're ready."

"Yes sir." Cade reached for the trigger—

—and the *Deering* rang like a gong under some incredible impact that went on and on and on. The ship lurched and bucked under the impact but it didn't quit. Only the inertron plating of the ship stood off the impact—

—and suddenly alarms were shrilling within the ship.

"Pressure loss!" Biskani yelled.

"Seal all sections!" Jefferson ordered. "All cabins, seal and sound off!"

Throughout the ship airtight hatches were slid shut and dogged down. One by one the sections of the ship reported in, until:

"Lewis to flight deck. One of my teams hasn't reported."

"Which team? Where were they berthed?"

"Manelli's. Section Four."

Jefferson turned to Biskani, who was studying the pressure board. She shook her head. A single scarlet telltale glowed in a field of green. "They're gone, Major. Howell, get us out of here before whatever that was comes back."

"Aknol." The Deering started to climb out. Suddenly Biskani yelled.

"Missiles, two, coming up forward!"

"I have them," Cade said. He worked his own board

and rockets stabbed out to cut down the new attack.

"Nice, Cade. Keep climbing."

The Deering lurched again. The howling was back. Howell didn't wait this time. He cut in lateral thrust and the *Deering* slipped down and away from the unfamiliar attack.

Hun't'pir cursed as the particle beam weapon built up a fresh charge. Two clean hits and the native ship was still functioning. That last maneuver had been controlled, nothing random. And those missiles had been a waste.

The native ship had vanished behind a soft ridgeline. Hun't'pir tracked the sights of the beam weapon back and forth, patiently, but it never reappeared.

The *Deering* inched along cautiously behind the shelter of the ridge. More a dune than an honest outcropping, it offered shelter from direct observation but little else. It would give no cover against any serious weapon, and certainly none against the unknown terror that could punch through *dis*-proof inertron plating.

The ship ghosted up to a new formation, an honest outcropping of stone, stark and angular in the harsh lunar sunlight.

"All right," Jefferson said. "Set down in the shadow of that rock."

The *Wilma Deering* eased gently down to the lunar surface, invisible in the total shade.

"We shouldn't stay here," Rogers said.

"I don't want to go any further until I see what kind of shape we're in," Jefferson said. "I know we've lost pressure in at least one section; I want to find out just how bad it is."

"One section is definitely open to vacuum," Peggy Bisakni said. "And we've lost circuits through there as well. Three scope pickups are out; we're blind along our whole port quarter."

"I've got no contact with number three battery," Cade added.

"We need repairs," Jefferson said. "We'll ground here until they're finished. And I want a look at that damaged section; maybe we can figure out what they hit us with."

"All right. Let's get started, then."

"Marshal, come take a look at this."

Rogers eased himself clumsily out of the Deering's pressure-hatch and made his way down the flank of the ship. His headphones crackled and hissed annoyingly: they were limiting themselves to communication by means of their combat suits' emergency beacons, hastily adapted to transmit speech. They had good reason to avoid the more reliable ultronics built into their helmets. Where the massive spike of rock that guarded them from Prl'lu eyes also shielded their radio transmissions, an ultronic broadcast would have been detectable to anyone listening in, regardless of the terrain.

Rogers could see Jefferson now, standing by the powerful worklights set above the damaged section of hull. The Deering's captain wore the same rig as Rogers, an inertron foil battlesuit/insulating overall over an undersuit tight synthetic mesh intended to hold flesh firm against vacuum. The helmets were standard combat helmets, modified to make an airtight seal and accept the life-support leads. But like everyone else, Rogers had discarded his jump-belt. In the feeble one-sixth gravity of the moon, it was the last thing he needed.

"Do you believe this?" Jefferson said as he approached. "Look."

"Holy. . . ."

The inertron plating over that section of the hull was gone. Not punched through, not torn open—simply vanished, as though it had never existed. A neat square of inertron had plainly and inarguably disappeared, leaving behind its mounting frame of alloy—and *that* had had a hole the size of Rogers' chest punched through it. The lips of the hole were bent *outward,* as though whatever had struck there had paused and reversed itself and pulled back out again.

"What the hell could have done that?" Rogers demanded.

"Air," Ruth's voice said in his earphones. "You saw those men we took from that cabin; they were burned to a crisp. Whatever weapon hit us must have turned the air in that cabin to incandescent gas almost instantly. When it blew back out—"

"I wasn't talking about that," Rogers said quietly. "Look at the inertron plating over the damaged area."

"It's been punched through, I know—" Harris began.

"No, it hasn't," Rogers said. "It's gone. The entire panel, not just the plating over the impact point. Look," he said, pointing, "there aren't even any fragments left in the joining slots of the adjacent plates—and they aren't damaged at all."

"Which means?"

"How much are you willing to bet, Captain, that if this ship had been uniformly plated with inertron instead of with sectioned plates, that we would now have no armor at all?"

"That's impossible," Jefferson said.

"Tony, do you know what you're saying?" Ruth asked. That inertron can't exist in a damaged or incomplete state? How could that work?"

"I don't know," Rogers said. "I don't have to know. All I have to do is point and say, 'look, it happened.' " He paused. " 'Look, it happened.' "

"So it has," Ruth said.

"The question," Jefferson said, "is what do we do about it? We can replace the damaged plating from stores, but how do we keep it from happening again?"

"And how do we deal with the Prl'lu if we can't?" Ruth asked.

Rogers had no answer. They were one ship and a handful of people a quarter of a million miles from any possible assistance, facing an enemy of unknown but formidable ability. They had already been detected and savaged by a weapon they had no real defense against. He wasn't sure there was one. . . .

Hun't'pir looked down upon his gathered host, the twelve Prl'lu of the base under his command. The handful of warriors looked pitifully few ranked on the floor of the observation chamber, but the sight of them cheered Hun't'pir as nothing else might have. In the end it had to come to this; when all else had passed it was still the charge of the Prl'lu to do battle for the glory and honor of the Blood—and now they would fulfill that charge.

"*Ahgn'ki Prl'lu,*" he saluted them. "The time is come when you shall affirm your ties to the Blood. Our enemy has reached out to try his strength against us here. He stands against us bravely; twice have we struck him truly and yet he stands to meet us again. We must honor his courage; we shall grant him a warrior's death. You have your assignments. You know which blow you must strike. Now go."

The warriors dispersed from their tight little formation. A moment later, Kors'in-tu stood by his commander's side.

"Have the natives taken any further action since they sought concealment?"

"None, commander."

"We may have injured them. Even unimolecular armor is not proof against the particle weapon. Yet I do not believe we have; that ship was under control when it landed."

"Then it will merely take that much longer to triumph."

"True." Hun't'pir turned back to the moonscape behind him. "Begin the attack."

Jefferson scowled at Rogers in the crowded cabin.

"Our repairs are complete," he said. "But we still haven't got anywhere to go. We can't head back to Earth, not without doing *something* about the projectiles —or we just won't have anything to come back to. But the minute we lift clear of these rocks they're going to hit us again. It's that simple."

"Then it's that simple," Rogers agreed. "We have to let them hit us again. It's the only way we'll have any chance at all to hit back."

"But we could lose."

"We can't win sitting here."

"Do we have any other options?" Ruth asked. "Any at all?"

"I have a squad of good people here, Marshal," Lewis said. "We're willing to try an overland move."

"Against a weapon that can punch through inertron?" Rogers said. "You'd be zeroed the second you stepped into the open."

"You'd never get near the base," Jefferson said.

"We could try—"

"But you could get near the rings," Rogers said. "And if you could do that. . . ."

"Then we could at least stall the bombardment of Earth," Ruth said.

298

"Captain, how far are we from the rings right now?"

"Twelve, maybe fifteen kilometers."

"In this gravity, we could cover that much ground in twenty minutes, maybe less."

"And how many times could they wipe you out in twenty minutes?" Rogers asked.

"Quite a few," Jefferson said. "Unless we give them something else to shoot at."

Hun't'pir watched his "army" roll away across the lunar plain. Five of the score of machines departing from the base were his entire complement of two-warrior scout cars, only lightly armed and armored but his only real fighting vehicles. The rest were the automatic surface construction units Hun't'pir had used to build the rings. They bore no armor, no weapons save their size and mass, but they took up space, and perhaps the humans would waste time destroying them and give the scouts a chance to press home their attack.

Kors'in-tu stood beside him, the only other Prl'lu remaining within the base.

"We can still strike at the natives from here, Commander," he said. "Diffusers and missiles could remove the rock in seconds, and the particle weapon could—"

"—could perhaps fail a third time. And we do not know what they might do in retaliation."

"We know what arms they possess."

"We did not know they could reach this satellite. What else might we not know? We shall make this limited attack first. Let them respond as they will. When we know how they fight we shall know how to defeat them."

"Yes, commander."

Lewis had never felt so alone.

The terrain around him was not the open dust-flats of one of the great lunar *mares,* the broad level plains. The ground he traversed was broken rock and gully; the low promontories on all sides were the foothills of the jagged mountain range behind him.

His belting exprience served him well here. It had taken little time for his squad to adjust to the rhythms of low-gravity movement. If anything, their movement had been restricted somewhat by the one-sixth gravity.

Lewis couldn't see any of his troops: they were too well dispersed and the ground was too uneven. He didn't like being so cut off, but he had agreed with Rogers that it was best to maintain communication blackout against the risk of Prl'lu detection. He would have to trust to their chance to reform while moving toward the rings.

The rock began to thin out as he advanced. Silky lunar dust started to appear in drifts and pockets at the bases of outcroppings. Then he was gliding to cover behind a boulder as the ground cleared and began to slope away down toward the plain below. The rings were a string of mercury beads in the distance.

Lewis opened his mike. "Ready," he said. Seven voices echoed him. He looked around; there was no sign of the squad anywhere along the edge of the rock.

The tactics worked out called for the commando to start for the rings, and the *Deering* to then break cover and draw fire. Lewis could only hope it all went as planned. It was a long walk home otherwise.

"All right . . . go."

Eight figures broke from the concealment of stone in long, fast leaps across the dust.

Leap followed leap—and the rings seemed to draw no closer. There was no sound within his helmet but his own breathing; Lewis had to fight the urge to turn and look for the *Deering.* Whatever happened back there,

there was nothing he could do about it now.

Metal glistened on the plain—new metal, a new column of reflections set at right angles to the rings. Lewis chinned in his mike.

"Armor," he called. "Coming down the line."

"Can we beat them to the rings?" one of his troopers asked.

Lewis tried to gauge the speed of the approaching vehicles, their passage marked by high plumes of the soft dust. "No. Anderson, Baker, Carr. We'll cover for the team. Form on me, kilometer intervals, and dig in. The rest of you keep going. Take out those rings."

He broke rhythm as he landed, bouncing lightly for several yards to kill his momentum. Unslinging his weapon, he *dis*ed a short trench in the plain and jumped in.

The Prl'lu machines were closer now, close enough that he could make out the disparity of their shapes. He locked open the bipod of his weapon and set it to his shoulder.

A long-gun rocket burst brightly against one of the machines. Almost to his surprise, Lewis saw it lurch out of column and glide to a halt. Other shots, Anderson's, Baker's, Carr's, began to impact on and around the column. Lewis saw two more machines erupt and stop in their tracks—and then the column, which had been swinging off at an angle to intercept the troopers still leaping toward the rings, turned back toward the grounded commandos and charged.

Fire sought Lewis' own position now, from a machine off to his right. He felt the sting of his cardiogard disk as *karnak* swept over his trench. He fired a long-gun round back, and followed it with a burst of short-round fire. He didn't even need to bother with elevation in the minimal lunar gravity: trajectory was flat enough to be ignored at almost any range.

The long-gun rocket burst under the tracks of the on-coming machine. It didn't slow. The short-round salvo danced and sparkled about its hull, to no apparent effect. He held off on *dis;* the vehicle was still out of range for his small projector. Perhaps they had refrained from countering with it for the same reason.

But the Prl'lu scout did react. The gunner's counter-battery systems tracked Lewis' fire back; the heavy turret swung to bring its weapons to bear.

Bright clouds of dust and gas laced through with short scarlet bars erupted around the trench. Explosions began to walk in thundering column down on Lewis' position.

He knew better than to trust his feeble little hole for shelter. Directing the multiplex downward Lewis triggered the *dis* projector and began to carve a long, deep tunnel away from his position.

He moved quickly, gliding down the shaft the *dis* carved and then began to angle back toward the surface again, a good fifty meters from his original position.

An armored fighting vehicle was skidding to a halt in front of his first trench, its lighter forward cupola and the heavier weapons turret on the raised deck behind swinging and lowering to bear. Weapons of unfamiliar type hurled bright stabs of light into the trench.

Earth and fire burst upward in response—and new fire erupted from the back of the Prl'lu scout car as two long-gun rockets from Lewis' multiplex slammed into the thinner armor there. The billowing vapor that followed was cut through in strange patterns as Lewis swept *dis* across the back of the scout, cutting into its exposed vitals. After long seconds the hatches still hadn't opened, so Lewis risked ceasing fire and looking around. . . .

The machine was rushing down on him, its great digging blade throwing up a wave of torn soil before it. Lewis jumped, clearing it by a body-length, and came down firing. For all the excavator's fearsome size and appearance, it had little tolerance for close-in rocketfire. There was no rush of escaping cabin air, no gouts of flame; the machine spat metal in vacuum silence and shuddered to a stop.

Lewis looked around. Other machines stood immobile in the distance—but several dust plumes continued in the direction of the rings. Lewis could only hope the rest of his force could reach them first—

—there was a brilliant flash of light at the base of one of the glistening rings. When the explosion had cleared, it was gone.

Lewis leaped toward the distant rings. He was pushing as hard as he could, to make time; he wasn't watching ruined machines; he never saw the cupola of the trackless scout car swivel to train its weapons and shatter his helmet and air bottles, snap his ribs beneath inertron foil, and cast him lifeless to the dust.

Blood sprayed in a mist as fine as the lunar dust. The four human troopers found themselves trapped against the wreckage of the accelerator ring by the remaining Prl'lu machines. The construction units—the bladed graders, the writhing manipulators, the churning borers —fell quickly to human weapons. But the two surviving Prl'lu scout cars did not die so easily. One car was destroyed outright as six long-gun rockets and four *dis* beams sought it out at once; the second was crippled and broken, its atmosphere bleeding away and its crew torn and dying—but even as shrapnel and *dis* had torn at them they had fought their machine, and the commandos had died.

A blur of movement streaked along the line of rings. The great ore projectile leaped from the last ring in column, through the gap where the destroyed ring had stood, and off into space on a harmless course into vacuum.

The ringing of the hull was deafening—and this time it did not stop.

Howell fought the *Deering* forward in a wild careen back and forth over the ring line as blast after blast of the unknown weapon clawed at the ship. Other arms were directed against the ship, missiles and shells; Cade countered the missiles with missiles of his own, and the shells were useless against the inertron plating. But the invisible weapon wasn't. Blast after blast tore at the hull, deafening in their impact. Inertron plates began to fail, vanishing utterly as their integrity was breached. Biskani cursed as circuits and monitors began to fail under the punishment; Howell worked desperately to angle the vulnerable areas of hull away from the attack.

Rogers clung helplessly to his seat, with no action open to him but to watch the men and women under his command struggling to stay alive. On the screen before him the rings swung back and forth across his view.

"The rings!" he shouted. "Cade, take out all the rings you can!" *We can leave that much behind us,* he thought grimly.

The *Deering* lurched onward, explosives and *dis* stabbing down from her lower pylon to topple ring after ring.

The flight deck sang under the impact of a particularly accurate blow. Howell cursed and sideslipped the ship but the weapon followed them this time, and the wearing assault went on and on—

Cade screamed in rage and struck at his board. Mis-

304

siles and rockets streaked blindly for the horizon, *dis* flared ahead of the ship—

—and the cabin was silent. Howell started to swing the *Deering* level—and the noise and destruction was back. Cade cursed and opened every *dis* battery on the ship to wide field. The noise stopped again.

"We can block it!" he shouted. "Whatever it is, *dis* works on it."

"Then keep the projectors going," Rogers ordered. Would this work? Did they have a chance? Might they even win?

Their unseen attacker had plainly noticed the failure of his weapon. Missiles and shells streamed up at the *Deering*. Narrow, impossibly brilliant bars of light lanced out at the ship. Most of the missiles, most of the shells vanished in the *dis;* all but a handful of those remaining burst against the surviving inertron plates. The ones that didn't did further damage, but such comparatively feeble attacks were nearly as good as a full reprieve. The light-bars walked through the *dis,* scoring metal where armor had failed. But any damage they did was more than offset by the infallible guide they offered to their origin point.

"Track their course," Jefferson ordered. "Follow them down. If we can just *see* what we're fighting. . . ."

"Shak'si *mir!*"

The *Deering* flew steadily toward the Prl'lu base, growing in the air before Hun't'pir like some fire-wreathed demon of legend. These humans had surprised him; he had not expected such an immediate, unlikely effort on their part as an infantry attack on the rings. He had had to divert his own assault force to stop them, and now it, too, lay broken on the lunar plain. It was astonishing. The natives of the blue world had engaged

305

an at least equal force of the Blood and achieved mutual destruction . . . and now their ship had found the one defense against the particle weapon that would let them live. The lighter weapons of the base still struck and tore at the ship, but its unimolecular armor held fast.

The door at the far end of the ramp slid open and Kors'in-tu rushed into the observation chamber.

"The native ship is within visual range, Commander,"

Hun't'pir nodded slowly. "We have not done well. We underestimated these humans; they fight with courage, and strength. I fear this base will not stand against them."

"Then it shall fall, Commander. And we shall die." Kors'in-tu showed no fear. He spoke calmly, with acceptance. If there was any emotion in his voice it was sadness, regret at their failure to win back a world.

"We shall die," Hun't'pir agreed. "But we shall not fail."

He reached down to his console, where a gleaming, ebony dome rested in one corner. Slowly, he began to turn it; it rose out of its socket, revealing the threads along its sides. It came free in his hand, to reveal a single large button, deeply recessed, proof against any accidental pressure. He reached down with one strong finger and depressed it, undoing everything Rogers had hoped to achieve on the moon. Methodically, he reattached the cover, and stood back. An instant later the console glowed cherry red and then white, and collapsed in upon itself.

Hun't'pir turned to the younger officer.

"Now let us make our last accounting," he said.

And they left the chamber. . . .

Rogers looked down on the small part of the Prl'lu base that extended above the lunar surface. The ranked launchers and weapons surrounding it were silent now, pounded into submission by the *Deering*'s own fire.

Rogers had refused to order a landing. The Prl'lu base seemed defenseless, but he knew better than to trust to appearances where the alien warrior-demons were involved.

"We'll send down a party first," he decided, "before we risk the ship."

"Why risk it?" Jefferson asked. "We can zero that base from here."

"Because we need that base, and whatever's in it." Rogers swept a hand to take in the boards and panels of the flight deck, liberally speckled with scarlet damage warnings. "Would you trust this ship to get us home in the shape it's in now?"

"Not likely."

"Then we need that base. As intact as possible."

"So you're going to send somebody down there? It could be wall-to-wall Prl'lu in that place, Marshal."

"I know that. That's why I'm going."

"Even worse."

"You can't go down there, Marshal," Howell complained. "You're needed too badly."

"Where?" Rogers asked. "Look what a fine job I've done. I've splintered the country politically, failed to defend it from outside attack. . . . At least I can do this; at least I can still fight." He looked around. They didn't meet his stare. Suddenly he felt his full eighty-five years old again, and more.

Only Ruth Harris met his eyes. "I'm coming too, of course."

"No—of course. You're right, thank you."

Jefferson sighed. "I'll detail a party."

The small repeater screen by the airlock showed

Hun't'pir the figures dropping away from the ship and moving toward the base.

He and Kors'in-tu wore full combat armor, foil and plastic, vacuum undersuits and sealed helmets with a pronounced, overhanging visor ridge to shield the vulnerable face-plates from *dis* from most angles. They bore only basic arms; there was nothing they could hand-carry that would damage the ship outside: they bore straightforward projectile weapons firing caseless, explosive rounds, and would trust to concussion through foil to kill their foes.

Hun't'pir felt the heat, the good heat that the had not felt since he was Kors'in-tu's age, simple readiness and desire to act, to face an enemy directly. He was pleased that the feeling had lost none of its edge in the uncountable years that had passed since he had assumed a garrison command; there were lesser gifts he might have asked for on his dying day.

"They will not stay together," Kors'in-tu said.

"No," Hun't'pir said. "They know better. They will separate and approach the hatch around the superstructure, if they are wise."

"Look, they do separate."

"Good. It is well. They are worth us."

"That is well."

"Ready yourself, brother," Hun't'pir said, and felt pride at the young warrior's pleased expression. "The Blood passes today. But it does not fail. It shall never fail."

"Shak'si'arek," Kors'in-tu saluted him with the ancient invocation.

"Shak'si'arek," Hun't'pir answered. He coded open the inner lock. . . .

"I'll be able to tell once we're inside the structure,"

Ruth said. "If they've stuck to the common pattern of construction I should be able to guide us down there."

The five men and women of Rogers' squad edged along the rounded wall of the hatch superstructure. Another party of equal size repeated their moves on the far side. They had all swung wide to come up to the superstructure from behind, avoiding the direct line of the hatchway and to study the rest of the structure.

They met again on either side of the hatch. Rogers signalled the parties to fan out and back from the structure, in order to avoid each other's line of fire.

The maneuver was never completed.

The hatch blew out in a soundless explosion, and the Prl'lu were among them.

Hun't'pir and Kors'in-tu broke left and right, crossing each other's course and falling on the group opposite. The humans opened fire but the Prl'lu were too fast, too unpredictable. Kors'in-tu fired three times and three humans died. One hurled himself at the Prl'lu and Kors'in-tu clubbed him away to lie writhing in the dust. Then he shouted, once, an animal cry of rage and agony as an unaimed rocket from across the battleground burst against his back and snapped his spine.

Hun't'pir had carromed into a human the instant he turned. He continued his spin, grabbing the man up and whirling him around and hurling him into the next human in line. Rogers and Harris went down in a stunned tangle. Hun't'pir dropped into a firing crouch even as the rockets of the last three humans lanced around him, and fired in quick, economical bursts. One fell, two, thr—

The ground vanished beneath his feet as a beam of *dis* from the *Deering* cut the soil out from beneath him. He flailed briefly above the pit, clawing for balance, to land properly—

—and a full magazine of rockets struck him away from the *dis* crater and threw him to the ground.

Rogers twisted to see Ruth Harris braced over his shoulder, Rogers' pistol in her hand, the slide locked back and the magazine empty. She did not seem aware that the weapon was empty, that she had struck her target. Rogers could see little of her expression through her visor but the prominent whites of her eyes. Her breathing rasped heavily in his headphones.

"All right, Ruth, you got him."

"The hell I did."

Hun't'pir was rising.

One arm hung limp; one leg was plainly crippled. His other hand clutched at the armor over his breast, as though he was holding himself together through main strength. He couldn't attack them. He couldn't even walk. But he stood. Rogers rolled to his feet—

—and Hun't'pir's visor blew out in a cloud of scarlet and white. He dropped limply back to the dust.

Rogers spun. Kors'in-tu looked at him, braced up on one arm, his legs impossibly twisted beneath him, his weapon in his free hand. Before Rogers could move the strength went out of the warrior's limbs and Kors'in-tu fell, and died.

Rogers crossed to the body and took up the weapon. Empty. That one shell had been the last. That was why he was still alive. What had that other Prl'lu been, he wondered. What might he have taught us? And the thought half-formed that he had learned a lesson right then, when the second Prl'lu had killed the first rather than leave him alive for capture.

Rogers looked at Ruth as she straightened, then looked around. Eight humans dead for two Prl'lu; one base taken for all the unguessable damage they had done the gangs. Another victory like that and the Prl'lu might have the planet to themselves.

"Well," Rogers said aloud. "Now what the hell do we do?" He moved to the hatchway, and looked down. The way was clear for a dozen meters, where a plate had sealed off the tunnel against further air leakage.

"Bring the ship in," he ordered. "We'll need to seal off this hatch before we can restore atmosphere in there."

"Are you sure it's clear, Marshal?"

"It's as clear as it's ever going to get, Captain. Bring in the ship."

"Aknol. . . ."

Rogers switched off and turned to look at Earth. The blue-white planet, impossibly small in the distance, smaller than he'd ever thought it could be, looked calm and unscarred floating above the lunar horizon. There was no sign of the havoc wrought by the Prl'lu attack, no sign of the destruction, no sign of the human misery left when fire and devastation had passed. It was as though on the reduced scale at which Rogers saw his world, such things did not matter, were insignificant in such a broad perspective.

But it wasn't insignificant, Rogers thought. *It matters. To me, if to no one else—and I'll change that. I'll make it matter. To the Han, to the Prl'lu, to the whole damned universe that tries to diminish us like that. I'll change it.*

There was a touch on his shoulder. He turned and saw Ruth speaking to him, soundless in his dead earphones. He switched on his phone.

"We should examine the tunnel, Tony," she was saying. "We're going to have a lot of work to do and the sooner we get started the better."

Rogers grinned tiredly.

"Ruth," he said, "you don't know just how big a job this is going to be. . . ."

A world away, in response to Hun't'pir's last command, the first Prl'lu were reviving—

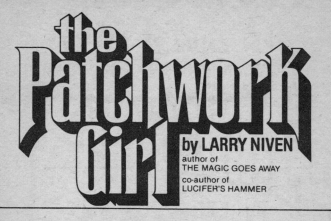

H. Beam Piper

☐ 24890 **Four Day Planet/Lone Star Planet** $2.25

☐ 26192 **Fuzzy Sapiens** 1.95

☐ 48492 **Little Fuzzy** 1.95

☐ 49052 **Lord Kalvan Of Otherwhen** 1.95

☐ 77781 **Space Viking** 1.95

Available wherever paperbacks are sold or use this coupon.

ACE SCIENCE FICTION
P.O. Box 400, Kirkwood, N.Y. 13795

Please send me the titles checked above. I enclose _____.
Include 75¢ for postage and handling if one book is ordered; 50¢ per book for two to five. If six or more are ordered, postage is free. California, Illinois, New York and Tennessee residents please add sales tax.

NAME_____

ADDRESS_____

CITY_____STATE_____ZIP_____